IN HONOR'S NAME

THE BUREAU BOOK SIX

MICHAEL NEWTON

WOLFPACK
PUBLISHING
— EST 2013 —

Copyright © 2018 by Michael Newton
All rights reserved.

Published in the United States by Wolfpack Publishing

Wolfpack Publishing
6032 Wheat Penny Avenue
Las Vegas, NV 89122

wolfpackpublishing.com

Paperback ISBN: 978-1-64119-426-6
Ebook ISBN: 978-1-64119-425-9

To the memory of William Weyland Turner (1927-2015)

DRAMATIS PERSONÆ

Aloysius Gantt: agent of the Federal Bureau of Investigation.
Colby Gantt: his son, agent of the CIA.
Devon Gantt: his son, agent of the FBI.
Declan O'Hara: agent of the FBI.
Nolan O'Hara: his son, an FBI agent.
Fiona O'Hara: Declan's daughter, an attorney.
Gregory Jordan (né Gregorio Giordano): legal counsel for the Giordano crime family.
David Jordan: his son, born 1924, an attorney.
Carlo Giordano: Jordan's brother, a *mafioso*.
Dominic Giordano: his son, also a *mafioso*.
Angelo Giordano: his second son, also a *mafioso*.
Isaac Sawyer: retired agent of the Federal Bureau of Narcotics.
Payton Sawyer: his son, an NYPD officer.
Frederick Douglass Sawyer: Ike's youngest son, a future FBI agent.
Leonid Babin: Soviet intelligence officer, once deported from the United States.

Stefan Babin (aka "Stephen Barnes"): his son, living with sleeper agents in America.

AUTHOR'S NOTE

The Bureau is a work of fiction, but real-life public figures, institutions and events often appear within its pages. Where that occurs, personal conversations and actions are the author's invention, except where drawn directly from reliable nonfiction sources. Timelines of historical events, likewise, may be rearranged, compressed or extended as required for dramatic effect. Anachronistic terms now often deemed offensive—"Negro," "colored," "queer" and the like—are used within these pages as they were applied during the years portrayed. Obsolete geographical names are used as they were normally applied during the years of 1956 to 1964 inclusive.

IN HONOR'S NAME

PROLOGUE

WORD of the bombing reached Reverend Martin Luther King Jr. at 9:15 p.m., as he addressed a meeting of the Montgomery Improvement Association at First Baptist Church. Built in 1866, the Alabama capital's first Negro church, First Baptist wasn't King's church—that was Dexter Avenue Baptist, just over half a mile to the southwest—but it was feared King's church, his first, would be too small to welcome all the MIA's members.

The news was grim. An unseen terrorist had tossed the bomb onto King's porch and strolled away as if he didn't have a worry in the world, and given the Montgomery Police Department's leadership, that may have been the truth. The blast shattered King's porch, front windows, and caved in the front rooms of his home, but while his audience of some 2,000 waited out the interruption, hushed, the news-bearer assured King that his wife and ten-week-old daughter were safe.

King took time to explain the incident as best he could —a tide of moans and wails rising before him—then departed to examine the damage himself. When he arrived at 309 South Jackson Street, King found an angry mob of Negro neighbors, some armed with guns, others with knives, surrounded by a skirmish line of white policemen. After checking on his frightened wife and child inside, he reemerged, hands raised, addressing those who'd gathered in a calm and peaceful voice.

"Don't get panicky," he cautioned. "Don't do anything panicky. Don't get your weapons. If you have weapons, take them home. He who lives by the sword will perish by the sword. Remember that is what Jesus said. We are not advocating violence. We want to love our enemies. I want you to love our enemies. Be good to them. This is what we must live by. We must meet hate with love."

The crowd growled back at King with one voice, like a wounded, cornered animal. It shifted restlessly, some of the armed men eyeing the police.

King kept his hands raised, pressing on. "I did not start this boycott," he reminded them. "I was asked by you to serve as your spokesman. I want it to be known the length and breadth of this land that if I am stopped, this movement will not stop. If I am stopped, our work will not stop. For what we are doing is right. What we are doing is just. And God is with us."

A new tone from the crowd now, several voices crying out, "Amen!" Slowly, by twos and threes, the mob dispersed, returning to their homes, some climbing into cars that had conveyed them to the bombing scene. White cops, fingering weapons, watched them go, a few policemen seeming disappointed that they hadn't had a chance to open fire.

CHAPTER 1

MANHATTAN: MAY 15, 1956

WHO WAS it that once wrote, "No winter lasts forever; no spring skips its turn"? Greg Jordan didn't have a clue, but even though spring had arrived in Gotham, it still felt like winter of the *Cosa Nostra*'s discontent.

Take Frank Costello, for example. He'd been convicted on three federal counts of tax evasion in May 1954, sentenced to five years in prison and fined $30,000. This year, in March, the Supreme Court had quashed Frank's indictment as a product of hearsay evidence, but Justice filed again, and he'd been convicted a second time, nearly two years to the day from the first verdict. Now he was on his way to Atlanta's federal prison.

Joe Adonis had it even worse, convicted of perjury and unable to prove he was born in the States, in January he'd cut a deal for deportation in exchange for a waiver of his prison term. Sailing for Naples, his departure weakened allies Albert Anastasia and Costello as they braced to fight incursions on their turf by Vito Genovese. The only winner in that deal, Greg knew, was Albert A's new underboss, Carlo Gambino, already a millionaire from his black market operations in the last World War, now standing one heartbeat away from mastery of Anastasia's family.

In April, someone had attacked columnist Victor Riesel, a Mob-basher syndicated in 193 newspapers from his home base at the *New York Daily Mirror*. Riesel's latest target was the totally corrupted International Union of Operating Engineers and its mobbed-up president, William De Koning Jr. The assault occurred outside Lindy's, on Broadway, leaving Riesel permanently blinded by sulfuric acid. FBI agents I.D.'d Riesel's assailant as union thug Abraham Telvi, a slugger for *mafioso* Johnny Dioguardi, claiming that he'd earned $500 for blinding Riesel. Dissatisfied, he'd demanded another $45,500 but got a cheap bullet instead, killed in late July on Mulberry Street. Prosecutors indicted Dioguardi anyway, then dropped the charge after a few more witnesses had disappeared.

Changes in the Chicago Outfit had been peaceful for once, Tony Accardo stepping down to serve in an "advisory capacity," succeeded by brash underboss Sam Giancana—born "Gilormo," baptized "Momo Salvatore," nicknamed "Mooney" by his pals. Pittsburgh, likewise, was an anomaly for *Cosa Nostra,* boss Frank Amato ceding power to serve as underboss at sixty-three, switching positions with the former subordinate "Big John" LaRocca, eight years younger than himself.

The Mob had been involved with labor unions, one way or another, since the days of World War One, while Jordan fought the Huns in France. Its latest acquisition was the International Brotherhood of Teamsters, founded in 1903, presently led by former West Coast trucker Dave Back, who'd replaced predecessor Dan Tobin, ending Tobin's near-half-century as president. As crooked as the proverbial corkscrew, Beck was facing Senate hearings on corruption any day, dodging expulsion from the AFL-CIO, and fending off brash up-and-coming rival Jimmy Hoffa. Hoffa, born in Indiana, seasoned in Detroit, was no stranger to *Cosa Nostra* either, and he hoped to edge Beck out as Teamsters' president at the next vote, in 1957.

Meanwhile, Cuba had blossomed for the Syndicate, under the symbiotic leadership of President Batista and Meyer Lansky. Meyer's Havana Rivera had been modeled after Moe Dalitz's original Riviera hotel-casino in Vegas, designed by Alvin Parvin of L.A., who'd finished off the Fabulous Flamingo for Ben Siegel. Financial backers included the Fremont's Ed Levinson and Charles "Babe" Baron, standing in for Chicago's Outfit. Dalitz and his usual partners repaid the compliment by buying Lansky's Hotel Nacional and staffing it with *gringos* they could trust. Florida mobster Norman "Roughhouse" Rothman had the Tropicana in Havana, fronting for the *don* of Tampa, Santo Trafficante Jr.

Everything was running smoothly, so far, in Havana, but with the unruly Castro brothers and their allies spoiling for a fight against Batista, Jordan wondered how long that would last, thankful that brother Carlo Giordano had—so far, at least—resisted the temptation to gamble on the "Pearl of the Antilles" in such troubled times.

———

Bronx Criminal Court: July 20, 1956

"SO, ARE YOU UP FOR THIS?" asked Fiona O'Hara.

"I'm up for anything," Dave Jordan said, ruing his choice of words almost before they left his mouth.

"Not what you'd call a glamour job," Fiona said.

"If I was after glamour, I'd have tried to get a job with Fashion Week."

"*Touché*," she granted, smiling.

They were paired together on a case involving what the press called "fighting gangs," this one a rumble between members of the Comets and the Happy Gents, warring for turf in Morrisania, in the South Bronx. From reading history, Dave knew the neighborhood was named for the pre-Revolutionary Morris family, whose men had signed the Declaration of Independence in 1776, the Articles of Confederation one year later, and the U.S. Constitution in 1787. They'd once owned most of the Bronx plus much of New Jersey, lumped together as the Manor of Morrisania, but you wouldn't know it today, with their former 2,000 acres reduced to less than one-quarter square mile.

No matter. Both the Comets and the Happy Gents wanted as much of it as they could grab and hold against all comers. Enmity between them dated back to 1948, when Comets leader Alfred Washington shot and wounded a Gent. Since then, they'd been skirmishing and "japping" (ambushing) each other wherever possible, battling with knives, broomsticks, baseball bats, chains, car aerials, garrison belts and homemade "zip" guns—or heavier artillery, if they could lay their hands on it. Miraculously, no one had been killed so far, unlike the record trumpeted in headlines for the Politicians in Harlem of two Negro girl gangs in Brooklyn, the Diplomat Queens and the Chaplains.

The latest battleground in Morrisania had been Public School 55 on St. Paul's Place, a short hike from the Comets' clubhouse on Eagle Avenue. Some Gents were playing basketball in the school's gymnasium when Comets surprised them, throwing punches, trading shots with zip guns and an honest-to-God .38 revolver. Once again, their aim was lousy, so the five Comets that Dave and Fee were representing only faced charges of felonious assault, attempted murder, plus the usual disorderly conduct and disturbing the peace.

Both gangs were whites-only cliques, so Dave expected no racial bias from the judge they'd drawn, but there was still the normal prejudice against what were lately being tagged as "juvenile delinquents," frightening their elders to the point that switchblade knives—"The Toy that Kills," according to a 1950 article in *Women's Home Companion*—had been banned in several states, while Congress sought to take proscription nationwide. They hadn't called out for a ban on leather jackets yet, but in the current atmosphere of blaming crime on inanimate objects, Dave wouldn't be surprised if it soon came to that.

Today, he and Fiona had a simple motion to present, seeking a continuance and psychiatric testing for their teenage clients, in hopes of getting the more serious charges reduced at trial. It could go either way. Jordan figured that all five would wind up doing stints in juvie, which would serve them as a training school for bigger, better crimes.

Some life for kids, he thought. *Some life for anyone.*

———

FBI HEADQUARTERS: August 28, 1956

ALOYSIUS GANTT WAS busy at his task of tracking Martin Luther King Jr. as best he could, from burrowing in files on what the Bureau labeled "Racial Matters" to contact with field offices in the South. His partner on the deal, Declan O'Hara, hadn't managed coming up with much so far, but that was fine with Gantt. King was a young preacher, just twenty-seven, only two years in harness at his first real church—Gantt didn't count his daddy's in Atlanta, which had been a favor from the old man—when he'd stepped in shit eight months ago, with the boycott.

Gantt could've been annoyed that Declan wasn't doing his fair share, but truth be told, he liked it better that way since there wasn't much to find on King so far. He'd logged his first arrest under Montgomery's ancient anti-boycott law, ordered to spend 386 days behind bars and cough up a $500 fine. In fact, he'd barely served two weeks before the white folks started getting nervous, and had come out telling journalists, "I'm proud of my crime. It is the crime of joining my people in a nonviolent protest against injustice."

The only other real news from Montgomery was a lawsuit filed two days after a January bomb hit King's house, challenging the city's segregation law on buses. In June, three federal judges deemed the statute unconstitutional and enjoined the state from further enforcement of Jim Crow seating. White men in charge appealed, of course, so *Browder v. Gayle* was en route to the Supreme Court, if and when they got around to it.

More interesting to Gantt were tales of King flirting with members of the CPUSA. That was the kind of thing

Chief Hoover hoped to document—black Reds had always been among his top-ranked bogeymen—but Gantt had precious little for him yet.

And if O'Hara wasn't carrying his weight, why, all the better. Gantt would find a way to let the Chief know when he filed his next report, and maybe take his former law school classmate down a peg or two.

Not that O'Hara seemed to give much of a damn these days.

While Gantt and other G-men kept their eyes on King and company, the Eisenhower White House had displayed no zeal for pushing civil rights. In February, he'd asked Hoover to brief him on "racial tensions and civil rights," an opening that Speed had seized with gusto. On March 1, he'd met with Ike, reporting that "mixed education" and "the specter of racial intermarriages" haunted white southerners, making no secret of which side Hoover himself supported. He'd quoted powerful Senator Eastland, telling a White Citizens' Council rally, "The Anglo-Saxon people have held steadfast to the belief that resistance to tyranny is obedience to God," adding that "acts of violence against members of the white race have been advocated by proponents of integration." Singling out the NAACP and CPUSA as brothers in arms, he'd also condemned Elijah Muhammad's "Muslim cult of Islam"—which, Gantt knew, *opposed* integration—and the obscure Afro-American Congress of Christian Organizations, whose founder allegedly called for retaliation against lynchers.

What about white violence against Negroes? Hoover saw no cause for worry, claiming despite contrary evidence in Mississippi that the Citizen's Councils were promising "a just and legal fight" to save Jim Crow. Its membership, Speed said, "reflects bankers, lawyers, doctors, state legislators and industrialists—in short, some of the leading citizens of the South." The Klan, Hoover averred, was "pretty much defunct"—a blatant lie; Gantt knew it was expanding rapidly—while the Jackson *Clarion Ledger* opined that "a few killings" might be beneficial, as lawmakers considered the abolition of Mississippi's public schools.

Finally, as always, Hoover had capped his report with a flourish of statistics, claiming the number of civil rights cases "handled" by agents had declined by 183 from 1954 to '55. Unmentioned was the fact that zero prosecutions had resulted during either year and that Dixie's Negroes were simply more afraid to contact G-men lately, having seen first-hand that seeking help from Hoover's people got them nowhere.

Anyway, while Hoover tried to fool the president and had his agents stalking Reverend King, another Negro in the South preoccupied his mind. Dr. Theodore Howard, founder of the Regional Council of Negro Leadership, had blasted the Bureau for failing to solve the recent spate of racist murders in his native Mississippi, and Chief Hoover wouldn't take that lying down. In January, Speed had penned an open letter to the doctor and the press at large, branding Howard as "irresponsible" for criticizing G-men when they'd really, truly done their level best. The white press ate it up, as with a headline from Montgomery's *Advertiser*: "Negro Critic Gets Flayed by FBI Boss; Charges Called False." Strutting his stuff, Hoover had vowed, "I do not propose to permit false charges made against this Bureau to go unchallenged."

Black editors—no huge surprise—were slower to adopt the Hoover line. They'd seen his vaunted Bureau persecuting Negro leaders since the First World War, at least, and knew G-men were batting close to zero when it came to solving racist crimes from any quarter of America.

Before he went public, Hoover had ordered dossiers compiled on Dr. Howard and his RCNL, which, in turn, produced a memo that had landed on Gantt's desk only this morning. It announced the creation of a new program called "COINTELPRO"—short for *co*unter*int*elligence *pro*gram—ordering agents to "increase factionalism, cause disruption and win defections" from the CPUSA. Of course, the Bureau had been doing that since 1917, harassing other groups of "radicals" from its creation in 1908, but now the operation was official—and strictly top secret.

As Hoover phrased it, COINTELPRO should "expose, disrupt, misdirect, or otherwise neutralize" groups that the FBI—meaning he—deemed "subversive." While Reds were the anointed targets of the moment, anyone who brushed against them, even in passing, would likewise be fair game. Tactics Speed preferred included infiltration and harassment from outside the CPUSA. Within it, hired *agents provocateur* would sow dissension, play on present feuds and make them worse, slander group leaders with false accusations of embezzlement, and scotch demonstrations by promoting random acts of violence. If Commies wouldn't take the bait, no problem; Bureau spies would carry out the crimes themselves while planting evidence to blame the Party. Likewise, agents should feel free to burglarize, wiretap, and otherwise behave illegally, as long as it worked to the Party's detriment, particularly undercutting mass public opinion.

From without, the Bureau and affiliated law enforcement agencies like NYPD's "BOSS," would mount nonstop surveillance on subversive targets, leaking any dirt the managed to uncover—or to fabricate—as a means to character assassination. False arrests were handy, sapping Party coffers and presenting yet more "proof" that Reds were criminals. Internal Revenue could audit them to hell and back, while G-men whispered to nonprofit donors, cutting off group revenue. Grand juries wasted Party time and money, even if they failed to vote indictments. And the press, of course, would play its part, whether unwittingly, by taking Bureau leaks at face value, reporting them as fact, or winning favor with a small army of "patriotic" columnists.

Gantt didn't know if it was worth the trouble since the Party was already in precipitate decline, informers in some chapters easily outnumbering actual Reds, but Hoover loved intrigue, spying, and blackmail. COINTELPRO might increase appropriations for the Bureau, and if not, at least it kept President Eisenhower happy, poring over files on critics who included Jewish Democratic Party financier Bernard Baruch, ex-First Lady Eleanor Roosevelt, various Puerto Rican nationalist leaders, and Supreme Court Justice William Douglas, who had briefly spared the Rosenbergs from execution during Ike's first year as president.

Enough dirt to please any reader, and that only scratched the surface if said readers were on Hoover's list of chosen friends.

———

BINGHAMTON, New York: October 17, 1956

RIDING in the backseat of a brand-new Cadillac Sixty Special with his dad and younger brother, Papa Carlo in the middle, two *soldatos* up in front, Dominic Giordano watched the miles glide past on Interstate 380. Scranton was a fading image in the Caddy's rearview mirror as they rolled northwest through Lackawanna County, cutting across Northeastern Pennsylvania's Wyoming Valley on their way to Binghamton.

Halfway through a three-hour trip, and Dom was bored as hell. They could've flown from Idlewild to Broome County Airport in one-third the time, but that meant picking up a rental car when they arrived, which raised an issue of security. Travel by rail from Grand Central on the Delaware, Lackawanna and Western Railroad was barely faster than driving—less so, with its stops en route—and would've left them exposed the whole way.

So, it had been the Sixty Special, and Dom hoped the trip paid off.

He hadn't been invited to the *Cosa Nostra*'s May meeting in New York City, though his father let him tag along as muscle, waiting outside with their driver while some thirty-odd made men traipsed in and out. Some of their faces were familiar—heads of the Five Families and their *capi bastone*—but Dom had to ask his driver who the other guys were.

And now, another meet was being held in Binghamton.

Dom knew the basics of local geography and history. Binghamton occupied a bowl-shaped valley where the Susquehanna and Chenango Rivers met. Incorporated in the 1860s, dubbed the "Parlor City" for its stately mansions, twenty years later it ranked as America's second-largest manufacturer of cigars after Tampa.

Immigrants flocked to town for jobs, the factories transformed by Prohibition into making shoes, Bingham's working-class neighborhood nicknamed the "Valley of Opportunity." A local man had patented America's first-time recorder in the early 1900s, sold to factories around the world for keeping track of their employees' hours, and his bright idea had spawned Plant No. 1 of the International Business Machines Corporation, luring General Electric and the Ansco photographic company to Binghamton.

And now, whether the city fathers knew or cared, their city would be hosting a convention of the Mafia.

As far as Dom knew, the meeting's primary purpose was to anoint Carlo Gambino as underboss to Albert Anastasia. Dom had personally met him twice, showing all due respect, although Gambino wasn't much to look at in the flesh: five-foot-seven more or less, around 175 pounds, his hair showing gray at age fifty-four, dark-complexioned with a prominent hooked nose and heart trouble, according to the scuttlebutt. Born in Palermo to a Mafia family, he'd been "made" and did his share of killing before immigrating to the States in 1921, joining his uncle and cousins—the Castellanos—in a family run by Toto. D'Aquila. He'd also married a female first cousin, yet another Castellano, backing the revolutionary side during Gotham's Castellammarese War and made a killing in the 1940s, peddling counterfeit ration stamps. Today, maybe some kind of joke, he listed his occupation as "labor consultant."

Dominic's father described Gambino as a "guy to watch," though Dom wasn't exactly sure if that meant as a friend or a potential enemy. But was there really any difference, in *Cosa Nostra*? All that talk of Honor, but Dom knew a smiling friend might be the first one to step up and cut your throat.

This trip would be a learning journey for himself and brother Angelo. Dom planned to make the most of it while being wined and dined in lavish style over the next two days—all hopefully without an ambush or a lawman to be seen.

———

FBI HEADQUARTERS: November 7, 1956

DECLAN O'HARA KNEW he hadn't done his best work ever with the file on Reverend King so far, but who could blame him, when there were so many other things to focus on around headquarters in this fourth year of the Eisenhower administration? Everywhere he turned, he ran smack into something else demanding his attention right away.

Take the Supreme Court's June ruling in *Cole v. Young*. The case arose from Eisenhower's Executive Order 10450, signed in '53, dismantling Harry Truman's Loyalty Review Board program and replacing it with more general descriptions of "security risks" on the federal payroll, including "any criminal, infamous, dishonest, immoral, or notoriously disgraceful conduct, habitual use of intoxicants to excess, drug addiction, or sexual perversion." When the Food and Drug Administration fired inspector Kendrick Cole for his "close association with individuals reliably reported to be Communists," Cole appealed and the Warren Court ordered his reinstatement, noting that Ike's order failed to clearly define "national security" and citing conflicts with the Veteran's Preference Act, since Cole was a "preference-eligible veteran."

Around the same time, Don Whitehead's *The FBI Story* hit bookstores and became required reading for would-be G-men at the FBI Academy, ensuring Edgar Hoover's cut of the royalties. One early reviewer was pest Larry Fly from the ACLU, blasting the Chief in *Saturday Review* for promoting "suppression by smear" and calling for illegal wiretaps "in the beguiling name of 'security.'" That meant, of course, another fit of pique from Speed, more memos padding Fly's personnel file.

In courts across America, the Smith Act prosecutions rolled along. Gotham publisher Alex Trachtenberg was convicted a second time and sentenced to one year in prison, while John Noto got the same bad news in Buffalo, simply for CPUSA membership, with a five-year term attached. William Sentner and four co-defendants appealed their 1954 St. Louis convictions to the Eighth Circuit Court of Appeals, but that panel was stalling while it awaited instructions from the Supreme Court in D.C.

In April, the Warren Court found that Steve Nelson had been mistried under Pennsylvania's Sedition Act, overturning that statute and remanding the case for a new trial under the federal Smith Act. That same month, the Supremes also reversed lawyer Harriet Sawyer's suspension by the Honolulu Bar Association, but those qualified wins didn't offset losses in other federal appellate courts, affirming various convictions.

In Congress, Joe McCarthy, still a boozy and drug-addled pain in the ass, regained clarity of mind in time to oppose Eisenhower's nomination of William Brennan to the Supreme Court. Brennan's offense: describing McCarthy's investigation of the army as a "witch-hunt" while he—Brennan—was an associate justice of New Jersey's Supreme Court. On October 15, Joe's had been the only Senate vote opposing Brennan's confirmation.

Three weeks later, voters had expressed their pleasure over Eisenhower's work so far by reelecting him to serve a second term as president. The Democrats had nominated Adlai Stevenson again, this time with Estes Kefauver as their man's running mate. Chief Hoover helped the GOP by resurrecting rumors about Stevenson, his intellect and questionable sexuality, flinging more mud atop what Bureau press agents had broadcast four years earlier. It also didn't help that Kefauver was one of only three Dixie senators who'd voted against the Southern Manifesto— formally dubbed the Declaration of Constitutional Principles—opposing the Supreme Court's *Brown* rulings. (The other holdouts had been Tennessee's Al Gore Sr. and Texan Lyndon Johnson.) That decision prompted one Democratic insider to call Kefauver "the most hated man in Congress," and Kefauver's investigation of "indecent publications"—featuring pin-ups of busty model Betty Paige, *Playboy*'s "Miss January 1955—made Kefauver a laughingstock, instead of winning moralists around to vote for him.

Ike, on the other hand, had ended the Korean War, presided over economic growth, handled crises in Europe and the Middle East with what appeared to be deftness, and weathered his first heart attack in 1955, undaunted by predictions that he wouldn't run again. So, it was four more years of Ike and Tricky Dick, triumphing on November 6 with 59 percent of the popular vote, Adlai and Estes trailing Eisenhower by 9.6 million ballots.

A footnote to the Republican landslide was John F. Kennedy of Massachusetts, Papa Joe's eldest surviving son, with three terms in the House, now in the fourth year of a Senate term. He'd considered bidding for the Democratic nomination but recognized a losing proposition when he saw it and wound up making Stevenson's nominating speech at Chicago's International Amphitheatre in August. Knowing that Eisenhower couldn't seek another term in 1960, JFK and Daddy were already courting backers for a run against Dick Nixon down the road.

Declan had no illusions that his vote would make a difference in that campaign, and knowing Edgar Hoover, he supposed the Chief already had his ammunition stockpiled for whichever Democrat secured the nomination. If O'Hara hadn't left the Bureau yet, at sixty-five, he knew he'd have to toe the party line, even if Hoover couldn't follow him into the voting booth.

———

THE LUBYANKA BUILDING: November 10, 1956

MORE CHANGE WAS SWEEPING over Moscow, and Leonid Babin wasn't sure what it would mean to him, except that he—as always—must do everything within his power to outwit potential enemies and hide his tracks from spies.

In faraway New Jersey, Babin's precious bastard, now known to officials in the States as "Stephen Barnes," was ten years old and making good progress in the fifth grade, the last report from his adoptive parents noting that his grades were near straight As, and that he compensated for his reputation as a "brain" by shining as a star of the Minor League division of something Americans called Little League Baseball. His present school, Washington

Elementary, offered no competitive team sports, but Stephen would confront a choice of three sports when he got to middle school, grades six to eight, the bridge he'd have to cross before high school. Babin had no qualms about his son's ability to "cut the mustard," as Americans might say.

In Moscow, late in February First Secretary Nikita Khrushchev had rocked the 20th Communist Party Congress with his so-called "secret speech," formally titled "On the Personality Cult and its Consequences." He'd ripped into Stalin, denouncing the malodorous "Doctors Plot" as a sham "fabricated and set up by Stalin," who had ordered state interrogators to "beat, beat, and beat again" in questioning suspects. In preparation for that case, said Khrushchev, Stalin had warned Minister of State Security Semyon Ignatyev, "If you do not obtain confessions from the doctors we will shorten you by a head." Stalin had also fomented anti-Semitism in Ukraine, allegedly saying, "The good workers at the factory should be given clubs so they can beat the hell out of those Jews." In yet another rage, the Man of Steel had cautioned the Politburo, "You are blind like young kittens. What will happen without me? The country will perish because you do not know how to recognize enemies."

True or false? Babin was privy to some of the dictator's orders and could easily imagine him saying the rest of it, but whether he'd done so or not, Khrushchev's was the new reality in Mother Russia.

And there could be no doubt that she had enemies aplenty—some of them doubtless within.

Two months after Khrushchev's denunciation of Stalin, the Cominform officially dissolved, no longer able to pretend there was a hint of truth behind its motto: "For

Lasting Peace, for People's Democracy!" That must've shocked some Party members, after nine years of broadcasting propaganda to the world, but they had other things to worry them by then.

Vyacheslav Molotov was first to go under the new regime, removed as Foreign Minister, exiled to the diplomatic version of Siberia as ambassador to the Mongolian People's Republic, 6,000 miles from Moscow.

Days later, 100,000 Poles—unhappy with the snail's pace of de-Stalinization in their homeland—first marched, then rioted in Poznań, ransacking Communist Party headquarters and storming the Ministry of Public Security. Konstantin Rokossovsky, Polish Minister of Defense, fought back with troops and armored vehicles, killing at least 100 persons, wounding hundreds more, finally restoring order of a sort. The upshot: in October, liberal Władysław Gomułka was elected First Secretary of the Polish United Workers' Party, initiating what the West hailed as "Gomułka's Thaw" or the "Polish October Revolution."

Babin reckoned that must have pleased the CIA nearly as much as August's ban on the Communist Party in Konrad Adenauer's Federal Republic of Germany. In fact, that was a joke, coming six months after the KGB "accidentally discovered" the CIA's precious Berlin Tunnel. Russia had known about it from the day construction started, betrayed by double agent George Blake of Britain's Secret Intelligence Service, Moscow preserving Blake's cover by claiming workmen found the tunnel "while repairing faulty underground cables."

So much for good news.

Four days after Gomułka's election in Poland, and spurred by that event, the Hungarian Revolution exploded. Seeking similar reforms, 100,000 had marched on parliament in Budapest, repelled and whipped into a frenzy by gunfire from officers of the Hungarian Security Police. All thought of peaceful protest vanished in a muzzle flash, dissidents arming themselves for urban guerrilla warfare. Before day's end, an emergency Central Committee meeting named reformer Imre Nagy as prime minister. On what American's called Halloween, Nagy announced Hungary's exit from the Warsaw Pact.

But it was not so easy to shake free of Moscow, as Budapest swiftly learned. Four days later, a full-scale Red Army invasion began, including infantry, 6,000 tanks, artillery and air strikes. The assault killed more than 2,500 Hungarians against 700 Russian soldiers lost while driving another 200,000 natives into exile. By November 8, pro-Soviet front man János Kádár announced the creation of a new "Revolutionary Worker-Peasant Government," with himself as Prime Minister and General Secretary of the Hungarian Socialist Workers' Party.

Not that Kádár achieved all that alone, by any means. At his elbow stood KGB chief Ivan Serov, kidnapping revolutionary Minister of Defense Pál Maléter during sham peace talks at Tököl, outside Budapest, then deporting Imre Nagy and any other fools in government who chose to speak on his behalf. By November 9 the Hungarian army had ceased all resistance, clearing the way for standard KGB oppression: more than 35,000 Hungarians arrested, 22,000 sentenced to prison, another 13,000 "interned" (as if there were a difference), and at least 229 executed.

Serov, of course, explained it all away. In his version, fascist thugs goaded and financed by the imperialist West were to blame for the October outbreak, whereupon "honest Hungarian people" led by Imre Nagy pled for Warsaw Pact intervention. Sadly, Nagy's regime, in turn, proved ineffective at expelling "Hitlerites," whereupon "patriots" led by János Kádár formed a new government of "honest Hungarian revolutionary workers and peasants" to save the day with Red Army assistance.

And who swallowed that pile of reeking *der'mo*? No one Babin personally knew, but neither were the skeptic's fools enough to call the explanation what it was: an obvious and idiotic lie.

After all, who craved a bloody death or life imprisonment from sheer stupidity?

———

LANGLEY, Virginia: December 3, 1956

COLBY GANTT SURVEYED the property that had been set aside for CIA headquarters, some 3,000 rolling acres, whereupon would stand a "campus," as Director Dulles chose to call it, sprawling over 1.4 million square feet. The builders hadn't broken ground as yet, but Gantt had seen the blueprints drawn by New York architects Harrison & Abramovitz after they'd landed the contract in early July.

As for the real thing, Gantt would have to wait like everybody else and see how it turned out.

This morning he was tired, coffee alone sustaining him after a rowdy, all-night welcome home from wife Eileen, while nine-year-old son Hardy spent the night with his longsuffering grandparents. Feeling rather chafed and sore downstairs, Gantt didn't mind. At least Eileen's enthusiasm nearly laid to rest his fears that she might find a lover on the side during his frequent and protracted absences from home.

Of course, she also had her work at Foggy Bottom to fill up her days, decoding and filing Top Secret messages increased since the first U-2 mission over Russia, back on Independence Day. The "Dragon Lady" had performed to expectations and beyond, leading the Agency into a whole new age of spying—and none too soon, at that.

Wherever Colby looked in a world Atlas, there was trouble brewing, starting close to home in Latin America. In Nicaragua, musician-poet Rigoberto López had shot dictator Anastasio Somoza Garcia in September. Effectively and savagely ruling his nation since 1937—once hailed by FDR as "a son of a bitch, but *our* son of a bitch"—Somoza died eight days later, despite the best efforts of Panamanian surgeons, ceding power to his equally reactionary son, Luis.

But if Nicaraguan friendship with America was temporarily assured, the same couldn't be said of Cuba, in the Caribbean. Three days after Thanksgiving, the Castro brothers and eighty fellow insurgents had sailed from Mexico aboard the yacht *Gramma*, landing in Oriente Province on December 2 and proclaiming that the first day of their Cuban Revolution. Agency analysts weren't sure exactly what to make of it, as yet: would it be wise to back the rebels against Fulgencio Batista's rotten kleptocracy, or was it safer to stick with the devil they already knew? The Castros and their buddy Che Guevara didn't seem to give a damn, already holed up in southeastern Cuba's Sierra Maestra mountains and girding for war.

Europe, of course, was seething after the abortive revolts in Poland and Hungary, not to mention the still unexplained disappearance of British SIS diver Lionel

Crabb, who'd vanished while scouting the Soviet cruiser *Ordzhonikidze* at Portsmouth Royal Dockyard. Reinhard Gehlen fared better in West Germany when his spy network was formally established as that nation's Federal Intelligence Agency, pressing on with business as usual under new masters, but with Gehlen still in charge.

Middle Eastern instability continued, as it had since Israel's foundation eight years earlier. In March, Pakistan had become the world's first Islamic republic, led by President Iskander Mirza. The state's name, Colby knew, was coined by Muslim nationalist Rahmat Ali as an acronym for Pakistan's five Muslim "homelands" in northwestern India: *P*unjab, *A*fghania, *K*ashm*i*r, *S*indh, and Balochi*stan*. Steered by the Muslim League, Pakistan's leaders made no effort to conceal their loathing of Israel.

That worked to Britain's advantage in Egypt, another British colony since 1882, until London and Cairo signed an Evacuation Treaty in 1954. Even so, some troops remained until mid-June of 1956. President Gamal Nasser waited five weeks longer before nationalizing the vital Suez Canal, sparking international condemnation. Three months later, Britain, France and Israel hatched a plot to assault and subjugate Egypt. Israel Defense Forces invaded the Sinai Peninsula on October 29, pushing toward the canal and incidentally murdering 386 Palestinian Arabs at two refugee camps in the Gaza Strip. Britain and France then issued a joint ceasefire ultimatum, ignored by both sides, while London and Paris likewise dismissed a UN General Assembly resolution demanding a withdrawal of all invaders from Egypt. By Thanksgiving, the Suez Crisis had forced gasoline rationing in Britain, and it finally required combined pressure from the U.S. and USSR to compel the aggressors' withdrawal. Even then, Tel Aviv won free passage through the Straits of Tiran, closed to Israeli shipping since 1950, while UN headquarters created a United Nations Emergency Force to keep the uneasy peace along the Egyptian-Israeli border. In London, Prime Minister Anthony Eden resigned under doctors' orders, Canadian Minister of External Affairs Lester Pearson walked off with a Nobel Peace Prize for his negotiating acumen, and President Eisenhower saw his popularity expand at home.

Southeast Asia, on the other hand, remained a region of despair and endless violence. In March, Souvanna Phouma began his second term as Laotian prime minister by entering negotiations with his rival half-brother Prince Souphanouvong, but the talks broke down as Pathet Lao leaders refused to surrender their captive provinces, training reinforcements for their army in North Vietnam. South of the 17th parallel, President Ngô Đình Diệm kept slaughtering Việt Minh adversaries, many of them tortured, then shot "while trying to escape." French troops completed their withdrawal from South Vietnam in April, and July's deadline for unifying elections passed with Diệm refusing to permit a vote shored up by his American sponsors. To the north, Hồ Chí Minh instituted "land reform" and "rent reduction" on a sweeping scale, meeting peasant unrest with an armed force that killed or deported some 6,000 persons. To his credit, Hồ admitted some "excesses" by his troops and restored most of the commandeered land to its original owners. By December, turning his attention southward, Hồ organized a National Liberation Front—aka "Việt Cộng"—with its military arm dubbed the People's Liberation Armed Forces of South Vietnam. The U.S. Army's attaché in Saigon estimated 4,300 Red troops inside "Free Viet Nam," while Diệm posed as a liberator, telling journalists, "We have arrived at a critical point. We must now give meaning to our hard sought liberty"—presumably by killing anyone who disagreed.

At home, Gantt knew George White was still pursuing MIDNIGHT CLIMAX and Project MKULTRA as a kind of private fantasy made flesh, though not without a nod toward his purported duties with the FBN. So far this year, he'd teamed with fellow agent Ira Feldman—posing as an East Coast mobster—to bust seven members of Rinaldo Ferrari's San Francisco heroin ring, then turned around to champion the cause of Robert Enzensperger, a San Jose schoolteacher falsely convicted of transporting marijuana. Such contradictions were the least of White's foibles, still filming and taping orgies at his Frisco party pad, sweating and doing who knew what else in the portable toilet White called his "observation post."

"God save us from the crazies," Colby muttered, even though he recognized no deity. "We've met the enemy and he is us."

———

HARLEM: December 4, 1956

THESE WERE slow days for BOSS and Payton Sawyer in the ghetto, with Malcolm X often out on the road. In February he had led a delegation from Temple No. 7 to Chicago for "Savior's Day," celebrating the alleged birthday of Master Fard Muhammad at Mecca—unless, of course, he'd really drawn his first breath in Afghanistan or New Zealand. August found Malcolm lecturing in Atlanta, reaping new converts on the first Southern Goodwill Tour of the Brotherhood of Islam and riling Klansmen in the process.

Even the Black Hebrew Israelites were relatively quiet for the moment, despite two rival factions jockeying for primacy: the Church of God and Saints of Christ with some 200 "tabernacles" and 37,000 members versus the Harlem-based Commandment Keepers. No matter, BOSS would gladly spy on both, subverting them whenever possible.

Gotham's big news today was an explosion at Bush Terminal in Sunset Park, Brooklyn. Ground zero was the Luckenbach Steamship Company's pier at 35th Street, where a dockworker's oxyacetylene torch had ignited 26,365 pounds of ground-up foam rubber scrap packed in 500 burlap sacks, some of which had ruptured. That blaze, in turn, set off 37,000 pounds of volatile Cordeau Detonant Fuse, shattering glass for a mile around, shaking buildings in Manhattan's Financial Center, thirty-five miles distant. The explosion killed ten people—one of them cut down by shrapnel 1,000 feet from the pier—and wounded another 270, although, almost incredibly, no firefighters were slain, spared when the blast launched its debris far overhead.

NYPD was turning out in force at the disaster site, but Payton had been told to stay away. It wouldn't do for an alleged Black Muslim convert to be mingling with cops in Brooklyn, and he couldn't take the chance. For now, all he could do was watch the smoke still rising skyward, wishing that he didn't feel so damned useless.

———

HARLEM: *December 6, 1956*

FOUR MONTHS NOW, since Ike Sawyer and his children stood beside Talitha's grave, saying farewell forever to his wife, their mother. Sawyer couldn't speak for any of the kids, but he was reasonably certain that the pain of loss and loneliness would never let him go.

It had been cancer, after all, the medics who'd examined her shaking their heads, apologizing with their mealy mouths for how they'd "dropped the ball," like it was all a stupid children's game instead of life and death. They hadn't thought uterine cancer could appear after the change of menopause, so sorry for the slip-up, don't you know. One quack had blathered on about Talitha never showing "common symptoms"—swollen legs or bloody vaginal discharge—as if it were *her* fault for fooling him somehow, casting a shadow on his precious reputation.

Ike wanted to rip into him, but he hadn't yet, although he'd trailed the doctor home one day and made a note of his address. Sometime, maybe.

Talitha rested now at Trinity Church Cemetery, overlooking the Hudson River from upper Riverside Drive, with hundred-year-old oaks and elms guarding the site. He'd been there three times since the graveside ceremony, found no peace, and now was thinking he should scratch it off his list of things to do.

The kids were getting on with life the way they ought to: Payton still with NYPD; Keisha with a four-year-old daughter, Luvenia, swearing the girl would realize her mother's long-abandoned dreams; Fred studying and playing football at UCLA, nearly 3,000 miles from home. Fred phoned sometimes, the others dropping in when they were able, but Ike didn't want to be a frigging albatross around their necks.

These days, he mostly walked or manned a barstool, spending all his time at home just catching up on the news from near and far, through newspapers and on the television that had crowded out his ancient radio.

He knew, for instance, that Congress had passed the Boggs-Daniel Narcotic Control Act, signed by the president back in July, increasing sentences across the board with five years' minimum for selling drugs and ten to forty years for subsequent offenses, no parole, probation, or suspended sentences allowed. Fines ranged from $5,000 to $20,000, and a jury could impose capital punishment in certain cases if the drug offered was heroin.

Would that stop anybody dealing at the prices smack was costing now? Hell, no. But it would boost expenditures for bribes across the board, as prohibition always did.

Most of the other news Ike followed told him Negroes were still suffering and dying everywhere you looked, across America. The South got more attention, as it always did, between the White Citizens' Councils and a brand-new Ku Klux Klan, the North Carolina Knights, led by wall-eyed taxi-driving preacher folks called "Catfish" Cole.

Lynchings? Tuskegee University said none for 1956, but headlines told Ike colored people still kept getting killed, if not always by screaming mobs. Just yesterday, Maybelle Mahone had "sassed" a white farmer in Georgia, so he shot her. Jurors handed down a rare conviction in that case, but then a doctor deemed the murderer insane and let him off the hook.

The biggest name in victims—once again, in Georgia —had been Dr. Thomas Brewer, a crusader for his people's civil rights since sometime in the 1920s, who had managed to survive and reach age sixty-two in February, when white merchant Lucio Flowers shot him seven times at close range, claiming "self-defense." Grand jurors saw no reason to indict him.

Another victim, Mississippi gas pump jockey Clinton Melton, had been gunned down by a redneck customer who claimed Melton had overcharged him. Even though the slayer threatened Melton, then drove home to fetch a shotgun and returned, blasting away in front of witnesses, cops couldn't think of any charge to file.

And why should they, when Emmett Till's lynchers had earned $10,000 selling their confession to *Look* magazine, knowing they'd been acquitted of the murder and couldn't be charged again?

Four months after that story ran, four white men snatched and raped a sixteen-year-old Negro girl in Tylertown. Oddly, for Mississippi, they had been arrested—and confessed their crime, no less—but white jurors acquitted three of the rapists, while the fourth pled guilty to reduced charges and drew a prison term. Ike knew damned well that if the races were reversed, all four offenders would be sitting on death row right now.

Nor was the hatred spawned in Mississippi just a private matter. Governor James Coleman, racist to his core, had founded a State Sovereignty Commission, tasked in the words of its charter "to protect the sovereignty of the state of Mississippi, and her sister states, from encroachment thereon by the Federal Government." That meant propping up Jim Crow by any means, legal or otherwise, while casting the Magnolia State and its oppressive segregation in a favorable light for fools and hypocrites who desperately wanted to believe. State legislators played along, of course, as did the cops, judges, and ragtag vigilantes, while the Sov-Com, as they liked to call it, was bankrolled with $250,000 per year.

If you asked whites below the Mason-Dixon Line, most of them would have blamed the *Brown* decisions on school integration and the "pushy niggers" who believed that a Supreme Court ruling meant something. Most Dixie congressmen, all white, had signed the "Southern Manifesto" back in March, condemning *Brown* as an "abuse of power" by the court. Six months later, Virginia lawmakers had followed Alabama's lead, passing the country's second "pupil placement" law to shore up segregation without any reference to race.

But laws and manifestoes didn't satisfy some local bigots, as August had proved in Tennessee and Texas. Clinton, in the Volunteer State, had exploded first, mobs agitated by two outside rabble-rousers: Jew-hating John Kasper from New York City, of all places, and Asa Carter, out from Birmingham. Both men were tied in with the Klan and Councils, pleased to rant and rave while others followed their instructions, mobbing Negroes on the street, trashing their cars and other property. Kasper spent some time in jail, while Carter took his place behind the megaphone and kept the riots going until Governor Frank Clement sent in troops and tanks to keep an uneasy peace.

In Texas, that same week, mobs rallied to keep twelve black students out of Mansfield High School, armed for war and hanging Negro effigies with signs attached that read, "Stay Away Niggers." Governor Allan Shivers sent six Texas Rangers, minus armored vehicles, and thereby made a mockery of the old saying, "One riot, one Ranger." Briefly pacified, the Mansfield School Board voted to "exhaust all legal remedies to delay integration," presumably continuing for years.

Ike Sawyer was disgusted with it all but still kept reading, staring at the brutal images reflected on his TV screen. He'd also jotted down Lucio Flowers's address in Columbus, Georgia, just in case he ever felt like taking a road trip.

Maybe I'll do that, Sawyer thought. *What have I got to lose?*

FBI MANHATTAN FIELD OFFICE: December 24, 1956

DEVON GANTT HAD PLANNED on working a half-day for Christmas Eve, but he could never tell with the Director's unwritten rule on "voluntary" overtime, passed down through SACs to all the agents working under them. The way it worked, each G-man was expected to stay late, so many days per week, receiving zero extra pay, while Hoover bragged about the money he was saving taxpayers around congressional appropriations time.

Whatever, Devon thought. At least it gave him time to catch up on the news and his leftover paperwork.

NYPD still hunted the unknown "Mad Bomber," winding down his sixteenth year of terrorizing Gotham with no end in sight. Some of the year's devices had been duds, as usual, but one left in a toilet had wounded a septuagenarian Penn Station restroom attendant. Early speculation on the bomber's identity described a skilled mechanic, forty-something, with access to a drill press or lathe, nursing a "deep-seated hatred of the Consolidated Edison Company," although most of his bombs were planted in public venues. The nut job posted letters signed "F. P." from White Plains, but an epic search of drivers' license applications from that city led nowhere. More recently, psychiatrist James Brussel had studied police files, profiling the bomber as "a textbook schizophrenic," fastidious in daily life, tidy, clean-shaven, of Slavic origin. When busted, Dr. Brussel said, he would most likely be wearing a double-breasted suit, its jacket buttoned.

What the hell? That sounded like voodoo to Gantt, but who was he to judge?

From there, his mind strayed to the West, as it so often did these days. Las Vegas celebrated the Hacienda's opening in October, with 256 hotel rooms and a revolving cast of tough guys from Chicago in control. Still farther west, in Hollywood, Columbia Pictures had released *Storm Center,* the first film yet to openly attack McCarthyism. Bette Davis starred as a small-town librarian opposing right-wing book burners. Paul Kelly—once imprisoned at San Quentin for killing a fellow actor in a bar fight—played a judge who tried to teach the local yokels common decency.

Mickey Cohen had emerged from prison in October 1955, resuming his guerrilla war against Jack Dragna while he mixed illegal gambling with running flower shops, a haberdashery, even driving an ice cream van around the ritzy Brentwood district of L.A. from time to time. Mother Nature had whacked Dragna with a heart attack in February, winding up the war for now, and Cohen turned his hand to blackmailing celebrities and politicians with the details of their private lives in bars, casinos and brothels.

Gantt had no sympathy for those whom Mickey victimized since they'd walked into it with eyes wide open, but he still wished he could get a crack at someone from the Syndicate. Before that happened, though, the Bureau's world would have to change, and Devon knew he shared the blame for that.

Hadn't he turned in a report as ordered by the Chief, "proving" the Mob didn't exist?

————

FBI FIELD OFFICE, Birmingham, Alabama: December 29, 1956

IF NOLAN O'HARA thought Florida was strictly segregated, Birmingham took Jim Crow to a whole new level and beyond. Its courts had "separate but equal" Bibles for the swearing in of witnesses. Bus drivers took fares at the front doors of their vehicles, then sent Negroes around to enter from the rear—or watch their ride depart and leave them stranded on the curb. Police Commissioner Eugene "Bull" Connor, nicknamed for the phony plays he used to broadcast as a sports announcer, had a "black squad" on his force to beat and sometimes murder "uppity niggers." No one seemed to know if Connor was himself a Klansman, but he gladly covered for the terrorists whose dynamite had seen their city christened "Bombingham" over the past nine years. Behind most of the blasts at Negro homes and churches, FBI informants named one "Dynamite Bob" Chambliss, who spent his daylight hours tuning cars at Birmingham's municipal garage.

The Cotton State was rife with Klansmen, split among at least three rival factions. Largest was the U.S. Klans, based in Atlanta, where Imperial Wizard Eldon Edwards had hosted the biggest rally since World War Two, drawing 3,000 Kluxers to Stone Mountain. The outfit's Grand Dragon in Alabama, Talladega minister Alvin Horn, had briefly faced a murder charge in 1951, then was released. Elmo Barnard, a gunsmith in Mobile, called his faction the Gulf Coast Ku Klux Klan. Barnard denied any Klan involvement in mayhem, but he'd killed two people himself—a business partner in 1950, then a teenage Negro "burglar" soon afterward—without standing trial.

Still, the Klan that worried Nolan most was based in Birmingham, a spin-off from the North Alabama Citizens' Council, called the Original KKK of the Confederacy. The founder and leader of both groups was Asa Carter—"Ace," to friends—who prided himself on attracting "rednecks," unlike the high-tone members of state senator Sam Engelhardt's Central Alabama Citizens Council. Carter had reaped his first national publicity by inciting race riots at Clinton, Tennessee, but his Alabama troops hadn't been idle prior to that. In February, they'd joined in a riot to keep Negro coed Autherine Lucy out of the state university at Tuscaloosa. Three members—including Bob Chambliss—were jailed there, then quickly released, filing damage claims against the NAACP. Two months later, when singer Nat "King" Cole performed for an all-white audience at Birmingham Municipal Auditorium, three of Ace's goons leapt onstage to assault him, one receiving a broken arm from police for his trouble. In his spare time, Carter served as a radio pundit and disc jockey, slandering Jews and panning rock-and-roll with the slogan "Bebop Promotes Communism."

Nolan expected worse to come from Carter's crowd, but Ace couldn't take credit for all of the state's racial violence. As for Engelhardt's Council being respectable, Nolan recalled a flyer circulated at one of its gatherings in

Montgomery, while Senator James Eastland and Bull Connor graced the stage, calling for mass defiance. Stealing from the Declaration of Independence, that message read:

WHEN IN THE course of human events it becomes necessary to abolish the Negro race, proper methods should be used. Among these are guns, bows and arrows, slingshots and knives. We hold these truths to be self-evident: that all whites are created equal with certain rights; among these are life, liberty and the pursuit of dead niggers. In every stage of the bus boycott, we have been oppressed and degraded because of black slimy, juicy, unbearably stinking niggers. The conduct should not be dwelt upon because behind them they have an ancestral background of Pigmies, headhunters and snot suckers. My friends, it is time we wised up to these black devils. I tell you they are a group of two-legged agitators who persist in walking up and down our streets protruding their black lips. If we don't stop helping these African flesh-eaters, we will soon wake up and find Rev. King in the White House.

LET'S GET ON THE BALL WHITE CITIZENS

NOR HAD the trouble in Montgomery been limited to gutter language. After the preliminary bombing of Reverend King's home in January, the bus boycott had continued, gaining energy. Klansmen had tried again in August, this time for Robert Graetz, a young white minister supportive of the cause, with dynamite that wrecked his house when nobody was home. Mayor William Gayle, immune to rationality, pronounced the bombing "just a publicity stunt to build up interest of the Negroes in their campaign."

Sure thing, O'Hara thought. *And Negroes lynch themselves.*

Nolan knew Edgar Hoover had a team of agents tracking Reverend King, digging for anything that linked him to the CPUSA. So far, they'd come up with a former Red named Stanley Levison, fingered by stoolie brothers Jack and Morris Childs as a "highly important Party operative," forty-four years old, fired as the *Daily Worker*'s editor in Illinois nine years ago. Was Levison still active in the Party? Did it even matter, when he had no hand in starting or continuing the bus boycott?

Meanwhile, back in "Bombingham," the toll of Ku Klux violence continued while Bull Connor saw and heard no evil. Bombers tried to kill another activist, Reverend Fred Shuttlesworth, on Christmas Day—a grim echo for Nolan of the Moore blast, five years earlier. An estimated sixteen sticks of TNT destroyed the house and damaged Bethel Baptist Church next door, one day after Shuttlesworth called upon Birmingham's Negroes to start their own boycott of city buses.

By then, Montgomery's boycott was done, called off on December 20 when city leaders grudgingly accepted the Supreme Court's June ruling in *Browder v. Gayle*. Klansmen, predictably pissed off, hit back by shooting up an integrated bust the week after Christmas, wounding a pregnant woman in both legs.

And still, no federal crimes involved for Nolan to investigate. He kept collecting information, filing memos that went nowhere, hoping for a chance to move against the nightriders, but in the meantime, he still had his wife and son, twelve-year-old Ryan out of school until the New Year holiday was past and keeping Keely on her toes.

Would 1957 see a change in Birmingham, when there'd been no cracks in the city's color bar since 1865?

Nolan could think of no reason to hold his breath, waiting for miracles.

CHAPTER 2

THE SALOON WAS CALLED Judge Crater, named after the Gotham jurist who had climbed into a cab one night in August 1930 and was never seen again, his disappearance still a nagging mystery. Dave Jordan knew, from hints his dad had dropped over the years, that Crater was a close friend of the Syndicate who'd left a wife and three furious mistresses behind when he vanished, most likely killed over some gangland debt or double-cross.

The bar that bore his name stood between First and Second Avenues, most of its clientele being attorneys whom you'd never read about in Henry Luce's *Fortune* magazine. They weren't small-time, exactly, but they didn't serve the city's Big Five law firms or the Top Ten for that matter.

Bottom line: it was *exactly* where you might find two colleagues from Legal Aid.

Tonight, Dave and coworker Fiona O'Hara had a

minor celebration going on, three rounds of whisky shots already downed and yet another on the way.

"No, seriously, David," Fee was saying when a barmaid brought the fourth round to their corner table. "You were *great* in there, today."

"It wasn't hard," he said. "The jury still hasn't forgotten the explosion or the lives it ruined. They were ready for some payback."

"But four hundred *thousand* dollars, counselor! Be happy for the client."

"Oh, I am. Believe me."

That would be a widow, still grieving, whose husband had been killed by flying shrapnel from the blast that tore apart Bush Terminal in December. She—the widow—had been left with three young kids to feed, no job, and tapped-out savings when she came to Legal Aid, asking for help. The Luckenbach Steamship Company had insurance, but the company had tried to lowball her, a measly five grand, and Jordan hadn't wanted them to get away with it.

"You act so casually about it," Fee pressed in on him. "Like it was nothing, but I swear, you had at least four people on the jury crying when you finished your summation."

"Bleeding hearts," Dave said, and downed his shot of Dewar's White Label, chasing it with a sip of beer.

"I wish Sam had been there when you said—"

Dave interrupted her. "I think you mean *Mister* Cronkite. He *is* our boss, right?"

"Okay, be that way." She finished off her drink and set the glass down. "But I still say—"

Dave waited for a second, then Fee raised a hand to her forehead, blinked, and nearly whispered, "Oh, my."

"What?" Suddenly alarmed, he reached across the table without thinking, grasping her free hand. She clutched his fingers tightly as he asked, "Are you okay?"

"I think... Jesus, I guess three shots should be my limit from now on."

Dave was about to flag the waitress down and order coffee, when Fee said, "Could you just take me home, please?"

"Sure."

Dave left enough cash on the table for their tab and tip, then steered her toward the door. Outside, the night was cooler than the atmosphere inside Judge Crater, but Fee seemed a little shaky on her feet, slipping her arm through one of Dave's and hanging on. He was intensely conscious of a firm breast plumped against his bicep.

They were lucky, flagging down a taxi only seconds after exiting the bar. Fee gave the cabbie her address and Dave climbed in beside her. When the taxi reached her four-story apartment block, Dave paid again and walked Fee to the lobby, her arm linked through his.

They climbed two flights of stairs to reach Fee's door, where she stood fumbling with the key just long enough for Dave to help her. Once the door was open, she turned back to face him. Said, "My knight in shining armor. Want to come inside for coffee, or whatever?"

Dave was about to beg off when one of her hands found him and gripped him through his slacks. "Fee, this is—"

"Overdue, I'd say," she interrupted, sounding sober now.

"We shouldn't—"

"Counselor," she stopped him, drawing him across the threshold, captive in her grip. "Objection overruled."

FBI MANHATTAN FIELD OFFICE: June 18, 1957

DEVON GANTT STUDIED the memo in his hand, reading it for the second time. An aide of Albert Anastasia's, Frank "Wacky" Scalice, had been executed by two gunmen yesterday while browsing at a vegetable market in the Bronx. Rumors were flying as to who ordered the hit and why: some said Scalice was selling memberships in *Cosa Nostra* for a fee of fifty grand per head; others opined that he'd screwed up a drug shipment inbound from Sicily. Devon thought it was just as likely this was one more move by Vito Genovese, trying to crown himself the Boss of Bosses nationwide.

War had been brewing since mid-March when Frank Costello was released from prison pending an appeal to the Supreme Court on his tax conviction from last year. Eight weeks after he went free, Costello entered his apartment building on Central Park West and found Genovese soldier Vince Gigante—aka "The Chin"—lying in wait for him. Gigante had called out, "This is for you, Frank!" as he fired his .38, but only creased Costello's scalp instead of dropping him. A doorman recognized him, and The Chin was out on bail, charged with attempted murder, while the rest of Gotham waited for the other shoe to drop.

For most New Yorkers, gangland news was overshadowed by the Mad Bomber's arrest in January, one month after newspapers ran Dr. Brussel's profile and the city offered $26,000 for the terrorist's capture. Con Ed clerks were scouring the firm's "troublesome" workmen's compensation claims, those that included threats against the company, when one noticed a dossier on ex-employee George Metesky, with the company from 1929 to '31, when a boiler backfire scarred his lungs, leading first to pneumonia, then tuberculosis. The company had doled out sick pay for three months, then fired him. Workmen's comp had been denied because Metesky didn't file in time. Hand-printed letters from his file bore various distinctive words repeated in the Mad Bomber's notes: "INJUSTICE," "DASTARDLY DEEDS," and "PERMANENT DISABILITY."

Detectives visited Metesky's Connecticut home, startled by how well he fit the Brussel profile: fifty-three years old, of Slavic ancestry, living with two unmarried sisters, with no social life to speak of. When confronted, he'd confessed immediately and explained the "F. P." signature from many of his letters meant "fair play." He wasn't dressed as Brussel had predicted, but before the cops took him to jail, he'd asked to change clothes first—and came out in a double-breasted suit, the jacket buttoned up.

Metesky's confession directed police to various bombs that hadn't exploded, including a third device stashed at Loew's Theater on Lexington Avenue, site of two prior explosions. He also led investigators to a workshop where they found the tools he'd used to make his bombs. One unfinished device, Metesky said, was earmarked for the New York Coliseum. Metesky faced forty-seven charges, ranging from Sullivan Act violations to attempted murder, but Judge Samuel Leibowitz sent him to Bellevue Hospital for evaluation, where psychiatrists deemed him a paranoid schizophrenic, "hopeless and incurable both mentally and physically." Leibowitz ruled him insane and packed him off to Matteawan Hospital for the Criminally Insane, where orderlies who'd carried him inside expected him to die from his TB at any moment. Despite that, he had battled back to something like full health, described by staffers as a model prisoner.

The next biggest crime news, also from Connecticut, had come in April when fugitive bandit Francis Kowalski shot and killed Bureau agent Richard Horan in Suffield. Cornered in the basement of his sister's home, Kowalski shot himself and spared the government a costly trial.

The only rumble from out west, so far, was the announcement of another carpet joint's debut on the Las Vegas Strip. The Tropicana opened with 600 hotel rooms, leased by builder Ben Jaffe of the Fontainebleau Miami Beach to mobster Dandy Phil Kastel. The state's Gaming Control Board smelled a rat in May when Frank Costello had his brush with death in Gotham, and a note found in his pocket read: "Gross casino wins as of 4-26-57: $651,284. Casino wins less markers $434,595.00 Slot wins $62,844. Paid to Mike, Jake, L., and H." Costello refused to explain, spending two weeks in jail for contempt, by which time lawmen knew the figures tallied perfectly with income from the Tropicana. As for named recipients of cash, Nevada gumshoes now suspected Trop executive director Louis Lederer and cashier Michael Tanico, both of whom quickly resigned. "H" might've been John Houssels, yet another of the Tropicana's managers, and few doubted that "Jake" was Meyer Lansky's brother.

If that wasn't enough, a trusted FBI informer said that John Rosselli was a fixture at the Trop, throwing his weight around as if he owned the place.

No such thing as a national syndicate? Gantt mused. *Not much. And Chief Hoover can kiss my ass.*

HARLEM: September 5, 1957

IKE SAWYER COULDN'T HELP it. Sometimes, when he read or watched the news, reports of drug smugglers reached out and grabbed him, even though he had resolved to let it go.

Take Joe Valachi, for example. Back in 1954, he'd been convicted with four other Genovese family members for smuggling heroin from Italy and France into the States over a five-year period from 1949 to '52. A sixth conspirator, Gene Gianini, had been Ike's informer, sniffed out by the Mafia and murdered for betraying them before other conspirators faced trial. In March, the Second Circuit Court of Appeals reviewed the survivors' complaints, affirming four of the convictions but reversing Valachi's on grounds that the statute of limitations had expired on his last known "overt acts" as part of the drug ring.

Bullshit, Ike thought, but found it didn't bother him the way it would have, prior to his retirement from the FBN.

These days, he fretted more about the torment suffered by his people from discrimination and the violence that kept Jim Crow in place. And as it turned out, there *was* something Sawyer could do about that, even if the world at large would never recognize his helping hand.

In February, nearly one year to the day after he'd murdered Dr. Thomas Brewer in Columbus, Georgia, triggerman Lucio Flowers had run out of time. Local police said it "appeared" some unknown caller lured Flowers to the town's Old Dixie Theater—a cinema for Negroes only —and his corpse was found there afterward, shot through the head. An autopsy suggested suicide, although no gun was found; now local rumors claimed some white bigwig behind the Brewer slaying had decided Flowers knew too much and couldn't keep his mouth shut.

Wrong and wrong again, Ike thought, remembering his round trip of nearly 2,000 miles, passed off as a "vacation" to his kids, driving so there would be no records of a train trip, gassing up at stations run by Negroes once he'd crossed the Mason-Dixon Line, not even staying overnight once he was done.

The missing gun? Right where he always kept it when at home, tucked underneath his pillow, just in case.

It was a small thing, but Ike felt better for having done it—not his first murder in cracker land, although the others had been long ago and even farther from his Harlem home.

Elsewhere across the South, Negroes had nothing much to cheer. They'd won the Alabama bus boycott, of course, but victory was followed by another rash of racist bombings and at least one murder Sawyer knew about. In Tennessee, Clinton High School was finally desegregated, more or less, its first black graduate passed through in May.

That wouldn't be the case in Little Rock, where raging mobs had blocked nine Negro students from entering Central High under a court order, and when Governor Orval Faubus called out the National Guard, it was to keep the school white. For the first time, President Eisenhower had been forced to act, federalizing the Guard, then sending in the U.S. Army's 101st Airborne Division under Major General Edwin Walker—after all its Negro soldiers were relieved of duty for the duration of the crisis.

By that time, five days after Governor Faubus first mobilized his troops, Congress had passed the first Civil

Rights Act since 1875. That one had been declared unconstitutional by the Supreme Court eight years later, and Ike wasn't altogether sure this one would stick, either, after time wrought its inevitable changes on the Warren Court. Concerned primarily with suffrage, not integration, the new law had managed to survive a Senate filibuster led by Strom Thurmond, but Jim Eastland tried his best to emasculate the bill through his Judiciary Committee. The final, watered-down version established a six-member Civil Rights Commission to "gather information" on racist denials of suffrage, passing results on to a new Assistant Attorney General for Civil Rights at Justice. Henceforth, obstruction of Negro suffrage might carry penalties of six months in jail and a $1,000 fine, assuming G-men bothered to investigate, and U.S. attorneys chose to prosecute. Another clause said "any citizen" age twenty-one or older, literate in English and without a criminal conviction on the record, should be eligible for jury duty in a federal court.

There was nothing in the law to punish bombings like the Nashville blast that shattered newly integrated Hattie Cotton Elementary School, bigots infuriated by the admission of a single Negro to "pollute" the student body of 388 white kids. Now, it appeared none of them would receive an education till the damage was repaired.

Meanwhile, Negro students at colleges in Baltimore and Durham, North Carolina, had answered calls from the Congress of Racial Equality, seeking volunteers for "sit-ins" at selected whites-only cafés and drugstore lunch counters. Read's Department Stores, based in Connecticut, had quickly acquiesced, announcing full desegregation of facilities in all its stores. Durham was tougher, having protesters arrested for trespassing and penalized in court.

Still, most Negroes could get along without a hot dog or an ice cream sundae, even if it galled them to be turned away. Survival was another matter altogether, and the southern death toll kept mounting.

In February, Willie Joe Sanford disappeared from home and work in Hawkinsville, Georgia. When found on March 1, bound and submerged in nearby Limestone Creek, his skull was fractured, torso scarred by numerous stab wounds. Police were "at a loss" to solve the twenty-four-year-old's murder.

In April, prominent black doctor George Washington Singleton suffered fatal burns from a fire at his office in Columbia, South Carolina. The circumstances were mysterious: the blaze broke out at 1:30 a.m., police initially reporting Dr. Singleton was clubbed unconscious by persons unknown before they doused the place with gasoline and struck a match. Singleton had been involved in efforts to desegregate a school in Shelby—135 miles northwest of Columbia, in North Carolina—but official spokesmen saw no link between that controversy and his death. He *was* fighting an imminent eviction from his office by a white landlord, but that was mere "coincidence."

Seven weeks precisely after Dr. Singleton's incineration, Negro U.S. Air Force Airman Charles Brown had been shot and killed in Yazoo City, Mississippi. Slayer Raiford Walton, fifty, openly admitted that he'd executed Brown—one of his former farmhands—when he caught Brown "visiting" his sister at her home, invited there for dinner and whatever. FBI agents investigated that case, learning that Walton had served time for killing his daughter's late husband, subsequently shooting Brown for being "too friendly" with the widow. G-men passed on their findings to Yazoo County authorities, and there the case had died.

Thinking about it, Sawyer wondered if he ought to plan another road trip in the months ahead.

———

Communist spies were making headlines once again, after a four-year lapse, Declan O'Hara pleased to know it was a real one this time, rather than a limp red herring tossed out by congressional witch-hunters. Even so, the papers and TV had nearly all the facts wrong, courtesy of Edgar Hoover's finely oiled publicity machine.

For starters, they were wrong about the agent's name, calling him Rudolf Abel when his Russian émigré parents named him Vilyam Fisher at his birth in Britain, in July 1903. His father was of German derivation, once a college friend of Lenin, and his mother, Russian. Fisher grew up fluent in five languages, including Polish and Yiddish. His family went home in 1921, Vilyam employed as a translator for the Cominform, then drifting into Soviet intelligence with World War Two. He weathered Stalin's purges of the Thirties, even though his older brother was a Trotskyite, and infiltrated the United States in 1948, under the alias "Andrew Kayotis." There, he'd teamed with other spies sniffing around Los Alamos, nearly betrayed when G-men nabbed the Rosenbergs, working for KGB Lieutenant Reino

Häyhänen until his boss defected to the enemy in May of this year.

Thanks to Häyhänen, G-men had cracked the "Hollow Nickel Case" in Gotham, wherein Russian agents passed their microfilm from hand to hand in hollowed-out nickels that could've passed for the real thing—almost. Agents had been chasing that lead since June of 1953 when a newsboy dropped one of the coins and it popped open at his feet. Still, it was nearly four years to the day before they busted Fisher on June 21 of this year, after Reino Häyhänen had flown the coop and started squealing to the feds. By then, Fisher was traveling as Abel, a name borrowed from a dead comrade. Held initially as an illegal alien, Fisher was charged with spying after G-men searched his digs and hauled off boxes filled with cloak-and-dagger gear. He was awaiting trial now, facing half a century in prison, and his bust was the first hint his Moscow masters had of Häyhänen's defection to the West.

While "Abel" hogged front pages, Illinois Governor William Stratton treated longtime convict Roger Touhy to a measure of mercy, knocking twenty-seven years off Touhy's ninety-nine-year kidnapping sentence and trimming his 199-year sentence for escape to three years. That would've brought relief to some, but it meant Touhy had another twenty-eight months left to serve before he was paroled—all based upon a Bureau frame-up for a snatch that never happened in real life.

Declan had been a witness to that tragic farce, when he'd worked under Melvin Purvis in Chicago, back in 1933. And he'd been sickened just last night when Purvis turned up on TV as a contestant on the CBS game show, *To Tell the Truth*.

When had he ever, in the years he'd served the

Bureau, chasing "public enemies"? If pressed, O'Hara couldn't think of one instance.

Speaking of justice, it appeared the Smith Act trials were coming to an end at last. Since 1949, nationwide, 144 CPUSA members had been indicted, with more than 100 convicted, hit with sentences up to six years in prison, plus fines maxed out at $10,000 apiece. Irving Potash had been doubly unlucky, deported to Czechoslovakia in 1955, returning two years later and landing in jail as the Party's National Labor Secretary.

But now, at last, the Supreme Court had cut short the madness, six years after Justice William Douglas voiced his hope for future "calmer times." The court had changed dramatically since 1951, with Earl Warren replacing Fred Vinson in 1954, John Harlan II succeeding Robert Jackson in '55, William Brennan and Charles Whittaker replacing Sherman Minton and Stanley Reed in March of this year. All were liberals, as witnessed by the *Brown* decisions and *Hernandez v. Texas*, expanding civil rights for Mexican-Americans. Granted, they'd stopped short of dismissing a Red world conspiracy in last year's *Communist Party of the United States v. Subversive Activities Control Board,* but Warren, Hugo Black and William Douglas had dissented from the majority verdict supporting registration of CPUSA members as foreign agents.

The axe fell for Smith Act enthusiasts on June 17, described in right-wing editorials as "Red Monday." That afternoon, the court rendered decisions on four cases lumped together from appeals filed during 1956. *Yates v. the United States* decreed First Amendment protection for radical and reactionary speech unless it posed a "clear and present danger" of some overt criminal activity. *Watkins v. the United States* declared that Congress did not hold the unlimited power to bare a citizen's private affairs. *Schneiderman v. the United States* restored the citizenship of a naturalized American who "subscribed to the principles of Socialism" but decried violence, insisting that the Party's goals could be achieved by democratic processes. *Sweezy v. New Hampshire* found that the Granite State's attorney general had exceeded his authority and violated academic freedom while investigating alleged "subversive" college professors.

Smith Act defendants nationwide were freed at last by those decisions, while an apoplectic Edgar Hoover called Red Monday "the greatest victory the Communist Party in America ever received." At the White House, Ike ducked questions from reporters, then sent Earl Warren a letter of conciliation after press leaks claimed the president was "mad as hell." Left-wing journalist Isidor Stone told readers of his weekly newsletter that Red Monday "will go down in the history books as the day on which the Supreme Court irreparably crippled the witch hunt."

Shudders from that liberal landslide continued. Come August, the Tenth Circuit Court of Appeals struck down convictions of seven Denver Reds in the case of *Bary et al. v. United States*, Judges Sam Bratton, David Lewis and Orie Phillips rejecting the government's contention that "every member of the Communist Party is an agent to execute the Communist program," even if they only spoke in general support of socialism without personally advocating or committing acts of violence. Three months later, Third Circuit Judges Herbert Goodrich, William Hastie and Austin Staley directed acquittals of nine Philadelphia CPUSA members.

A footnote to the long, bizarre sideshow came when tax auditors learned that Alex Bittelman—released from prison in May—had received Social Security checks during his three years behind bars. Furious congressmen quickly amended the Internal Revenue Code, denying future benefits to employees of any group deemed communistic under the Internal Security Act of 1950.

Joe McCarthy didn't live to see or rail against Red Monday, having died on May 2 at Bethesda Naval Hospital. Doctors listed the cause of death as "Hepatitis, acute, cause unknown"—in Declan's view, likely resulting from McCarthy's hush-hush heroin habit. In a special election, held to name his successor, voters chose Democrat William Proxmire, a state assemblyman who'd called Tail-Gunner Joe "a disgrace to Wisconsin, to the Senate, and to America."

McCarthy's last victim in government, John Service, enjoyed a victory from the Supreme Court on Red Monday, a unanimous panel ruling that Dean Acheson's decision to dismiss him "violated regulations of the Department of State which were binding on the Secretary." Since a Loyalty Review Board failed to link Service with any group on the Attorney General's list, firing him was illegal. That brought him back to State, in its transportation division, but subtly excluded from future promotions.

Win some, lose some, O'Hara thought. *And hope that you're still standing in the end.*

———

THE LUBYANKA BUILDING, Moscow: October 5, 1957

ALL OF MOSCOW was elated by the news from outer space,

and Leonid Babin was no exception. *Sputnik 1*, the Earth's first artificial satellite, had been launched yesterday from Tyuratam in the Kazakh SSR, and Chairman Khrushchev had declared Russian superiority over America in the "space race," if only momentarily.

Granted, *Sputnik* was less than two feet in diameter, a polished metal sphere with four external radio transmitters, powered by batteries with a three-week lifespan, but it was *up there*, emitting pulses audible even to amateur radio builders, its elliptical orbit carrying the orb over most of the planet's inhabited landmasses once every four days.

At that, Khrushchev had fought to keep his job until *Sputnik* was sent aloft. In June, Presidium members of a pro-Stalinist Anti-Party Group—led by Georgy Malenkov, Vyacheslav Molotov and Lazar Kaganovich—tried to depose Khrushchev as First Secretary, but a vote of seven to four deferred that decision to the full Central Committee, meeting eleven days later. That body, in turn, had affirmed Khrushchev's position while dropping Malenkov, Molotov and Kaganovich from its Secretariat.

The KGB, meanwhile, was still recovering from Reino Häyhänen's defection to the West and the capture of Vilyam Fisher. East Germany's Stasi had fared little better, with Ernst Wollweber's resignation as Minister of State Security, replaced by Erich Mielke, although Moscow cherished hopes for Markus Wolf, now chief of Stasi's foreign intelligence service, the Main Reconnaissance Administration. Wolf's chief goal: infiltration of West German politics and business circles, boring from within, striving to foul Chancellor Konrad Adenaur's nest.

Aftershocks from the Hungarian rebellion still rippled throughout the Eastern Bloc, as Moscow sought to put a brave face on the situation. In January, Soviet diplomats met representatives of Bulgaria, Hungary and Romania in Budapest, "unanimously concluding" that brave workers had welcomed Russian troops "to eliminate the socialist achievements of the Hungarian people." Oddly, given that finding, workers' councils had sponsored strikes and other forms of resistance through summer, disrupting the Hungarian economy. KGB agents purged the Hungarian army and supervised political indoctrination within units that survived. UN Secretary-General Dag Hammarskjöld called for an investigation of events in occupied Hungary, but none was forthcoming, as both Hungarian and Romanian authorities barred inspectors from their territory. The Red Cross supervised refugee camps in Austria, but Khrushchev rebuffed American aid offers, saying, "Support by the United States is rather in the nature of the support that a rope gives to a hanged man."

Babin, for his part, was more concerned with matters in New Jersey, where his son—now eleven years old—was busily impressing teachers and athletic coaches in the sixth grade of his middle school. Time seemed to crawl between reports from the United States, but Babin still remembered how the weeks and months flew past for children as they grew, learned, and in Stefan's case, prepared themselves to realize a destiny ordained before he was conceived.

He only had to stay the course and do his part, directed and nurtured by his adoptive parents. Babin's task was to survive, if possible, until his master plan for vengeance started bearing fruit.

And if he couldn't manage that, at least he'd die a reasonably happy man, knowing his human weapon was proceeding on its course, pledged to create chaos within the FBI.

———

NOLAN O'HARA SAW nothing but violence ahead for Alabama and the other Deep South states as he perused the Bureau's latest files. Not that he had an opportunity to act on any of the recent crimes, mind you. The occasional investigation was the end of it, reports typed up in triplicate and neatly filed away.

Montgomery's bombers were out in force, six blasts scarring Negro churches and two preachers' homes, all on one January night. The city's fathers gave up their beloved Jim Crow buses, but tightened the screws on segregation elsewhere, passing a new ordinance forbidding whites and Negroes "to play together, or, in company with each other" at any known sport, swimming venue, or gambling pursuits.

That didn't pacify the local Klan, whose members heard rumors of a Negro truck driver "offending white women" around the capital. Clueless as to the fiend's identity, they ambushed Willie Edwards Jr., drove him to the Tyler Goodwin Bridge outside of town, and made him jump 125 feet to his death in the Alabama River. Before fishermen found his corpse in April, two Klansmen were charged with January's bombings and confessed—which, naturally, didn't stop white jurors from acquitting them in May, while the courtroom burst into cheers.

Terrorists in Birmingham and Bessemer—rough

factory towns sixteen miles apart in Jefferson County, dubbed the "Magic City" and "Marvel City respectively" by someone with a twisted sense of humor—did their best to keep up with their brothers in the capital. Starting in April, dynamite rocked eight homes and one church in "Bombingham," another church and home in Bessemer. When Fred Shuttlesworth, his wife and a minister friend tried to enroll their kids at a white school in early September, Klansmen mobbed them, beating them with chains and brass knuckles, stabbing Mrs. Shuttlesworth in the hip, while cops and Ace Carter stood watching.

Carter's Klan wasn't the only one at work inside the Cotton State, of course. Self-ordained minister Alvin Horn, age forty-five, was "grand dragon" of the Georgia-based U.S. Klans until June when he impregnated a fifteen-year-old girl and had to marry her. Imperial Wizard Eldon Edwards fired Horn—while denouncing critical publicity as "unfair, unjust and untrue"—replacing him with Robert Shelton of Tuscaloosa, a salesman for B. F. Goodrich.

Down in Mobile, rival Klan leader, Elmo Barnard ran for mayor in the city's biennial election, opposing Catholic moderate Joseph Langan. One of Barnard's nightshirt knights, Cluis Dykes, sought a seat on the city commission, asking white voters to ensure that "the Negro will be kept in his place." The Gulf Coast Klan printed flyers reading "WHITE SUPREMACY NOW & FOREVER," with campaign buttons depicting two black corpses hanging. Thankfully, the local Non-Partisan Voters League weighed in for Langan, but Barnard still claimed 2,000 votes, while Dykes received 1,000.

Another Klan founded this year, headquartered far away in Waco, Texas, seemed to be a one-man operation run from home by Horace Miller, a disabled veteran of World War One, who called his "group" the Aryan Knights and mailed its *Aryan Views* newsletter far and wide, some copies turning up in Austria and South America.

More troubling to O'Hara was the Dixie Klans, a spin-off from the Edwards group, founded in Chattanooga, Tennessee, by brothers Jack and Harry Brown. They talked tough, stockpiled guns, and were rumored to have a fondness for explosives like the charge that caused $71,000 damage to Nashville's Hattie Cotton Elementary.

So far this year, despite the frequent bombings around Alabama, Nolan only knew of one murder besides the Willie Edwards lynching that might qualify for federal intervention as a civil rights case. Only yesterday, two white men had removed Negro teenager Rogers Hamilton from his home in Lowndes County, then shot him dead and dumped him on the road nearby, for his mother to find. Local gossips claimed the victim had been warned to stay away from Negro girls in Hayneville, which made no sense to Nolan in the racist scheme of things, but who could look inside such twisted minds?

In any case, he didn't have a handle on that murder for the Bureau yet, and agents under pressure from head-quarters were intent on shadowing the newest civil rights group on the scene, the Southern Christian Leadership Conference. Founded in January, by sixty Negro ministers convened at Georgia's Ebenezer Baptist Church, the SCLC's leadership included Martin Luther King Jr., long-time activist and not-so-closet homosexual Bayard Rustin, and widely traveled NAACP organizer Ella Baker. Those were bad enough in Edgar Hoover's view, but Stanley Levison was also part of the administrative team, along with Charles Kenzie Steele, leader of Tallahassee's bus boycott in 1956, and Birmingham's Fred Shuttlesworth. Put them all together, preaching Gandhism to Negroes nationwide, and Hoover saw the Red Menace at work.

The local Bureau had no time for Edward Aaron, a simple-minded handyman his friends called "Judge," who'd been kidnapped by six of Asa Carter's Klansmen one week prior to the Shuttlesworth attack. They planned to "send a message" and required a candidate for "captain" in order to engage in bloodletting to prove that he was fit to lead. Grabbing Aaron at random, they'd conveyed him to a dirt-floor shack that served them as a clubhouse, beating and interrogating him about his nonexistent views of civil rights. When they got tired, "Exalted Cyclops" Joe Pritchett watched rookie Bart Floyd castrate Aaron with a razor blade, then douse the wound with turpentine to make him scream a little more. They'd left him lurching down the highway, blood-drenched, till a motorist took pity, driving him to Hillman Hospital, where doctors saved his life.

The guilty parties were no strangers to police in Birmingham. Two of them—Floyd and Jesse Mabry—were among the gang that beat up Nat "King" Cole in 1956. Others were involved in the September mob attack upon Fred Shuttlesworth, his wife and children. Before Nolan had a chance to get involved, state police tracked down Pritchett, Mabry and Floyd, plus their accomplices: James Griffin, Grover McCullough and William Miller. An investigator warned them that if Edward Aaron proved to be a "good nigger" he'd throw the book at them, and so he did. The charge was mayhem; Griffin and Miller turned state's evidence against the rest, and all received twenty-year terms at Kilby Prison.

Bad publicity from Aaron's case wasn't Ace Carter's

only problem, either. He and brother James were jailed for brawling with police who came to arrest Aaron's mutilators, then, days later, Ace shot two Klansmen who'd objected to his handling of the order's treasury. They lived, reducing Carter's charges to attempted murder, but the D.A. let it drop without a trial.

Nothing new under the southern sun, O'Hara thought and wondered if that trend would ever change.

———

HARLEM: November 9, 1957

PAYTON SAWYER HAD BEEN WORKING overtime for BOSS, spying on Malcolm X and company since April, when Johnson X Hinton and two other Muslims from Temple No. 7 saw a pair of NYPD cops beating a black man, Roscoe Poe, on a street corner. They'd moved in, shouting, "You're not in Alabama, this is New York!" Whereupon the cops attacked Hinton in turn, inflicting a concussion and subdural hemorrhaging before they dragged all four men to the 123rd Street station.

Malcolm, notified of the event by witnesses, went to the precinct house, demanding to see Hinton. Cops on duty first denied arresting any Muslims, then relented as the seething crowd outside surpassed 500. They allowed Malcolm to speak with Hinton, then summoned an ambulance that carried him to Harlem Hospital. A doctor treated him, and by the time Hinton returned to jail, the mob outside had swelled to 4,000, with Payton Sawyer in their midst. The cops inside, besieged, were on the verge of calling reinforcements until Malcolm stepped outside and gave a silent hand signal. All members of the Nation present instantly departed, Payton trailing them, and the remainder of the crowd dispersed in turn.

Next morning, a department spokesman advised the *New York Amsterdam News*, a Negro newspaper, "No one man should have that much power." Word came down to Sawyer from Inspector Patrick Flannery to double down on Malcolm and the Temple: "Get me something, anything, and do it soon."

The problem: since the Hinton episode, Malcolm was all over the map. The *Los Angeles Herald Dispatch* ran a feature headlined "Young Moslem Leader Explains The Doctrine of Mohammedanism," and the *Amsterdam News* handed Malcolm a weekly column called "God's Angry Man." September found him serving as interim minister at Detroit's Temple No. 1, then he was back in Gotham, helping Johnson Hinton file a $1 million lawsuit against the cops who'd beaten him. An all-white jury trimmed the award down to $70,000, still the city's largest brutality payout to date.

But so far, Payton still had nothing that would help his bosses lock Malcolm away. And lately, he was wondering if that should trouble him or make him glad.

———

APALACHIN, New York: November 14, 1957

"You been up here before, Pop?"

"Yeah, a couple times," said Carlo Giordano.

"Hell, there's nothin' to it," Angelo chimed in.

"Hey, keep your voice down," Carlo warned his younger son. "Show some respect, for *Cristo*'s sake."

"Okay. Sorry."

Dominic knew what his brother meant about the town, less than 300 people living in it, planted some 200 miles northwest of Manhattan in Tioga County. It was the kind of place where half-assed cops rolled up the sidewalks at sundown. They even said the town's name funny: "apple-*lay*-kin," nothing like the chain of mountains running down from Canada into Virginia.

They were standing on the property of Giuseppe Barbara—or "Joe the Barber" to his *Cosa Nostra* friends— the biggest man in Apalachin since old-time Secretary of the Navy Ben Tracy had kicked the bucket, back in 1915.

Dominic was no historian, but he knew Barbara had some from Sicily, Castellammare del Golfo, at the start of Prohibition, working as a trigger for the Buffalino family, suspected of the cops of half a dozen murders while he climbed the ladder of command. He'd bought the acreage they stood on now in 1944, plus a Canada Dry bottling plant, and cornered the Binghamton market for beer and sodas. When he wanted a pistol permit, the police chief of Endicott—eight miles distant, with a population eighty times larger than Apalachin's—made it happen.

Everybody knew that Joe the Barber was connected. In October 1956 state troopers nabbed Carmine Galante, underboss of the Bonanno family, leaving Barbara's place and held him on "suspicion." Pretty quick, a group of Jersey cops turned up and offered bribes to get Galante out of jail. Instead, they were indicted, and Carmine spent thirty days inside. Since then, a detail of state troopers led by Sergeant Edgar Croswell kept an eye on Barbara whenever they had time.

It seemed to Dominic that meeting here was dumb, under the circumstances, but he couldn't say that to the guy who'd called the sit-down in the first place: Vito Genovese. He wanted to be Boss of Bosses, even though the title had been laid to rest in 1931, but with a guy like *Don* Vito, you always had to keep your lip buttoned and watch your back. He'd made a move on Frank Costello back in May and muffed it, even though Costello had supposedly retired, and then some shooters took out Albert Anastasia in October—as the story came to Dominic, without advance approval from the Mafia's *Commissioner*.

Today's meeting, more than a hundred *Mafiosi* gathered for a barbecue and booze, was meant to hash things out, let Vito plead his case for whacking Anastasia as an act of self-defense, and claim the throne he'd lusted after all his life. So far, Dom had seen guys he knew and others he had only heard about from Gotham's powerful Five Families, Buffalo and Rochester, New Jersey and New England, Philadelphia, Pittsburgh, Chicago, Cleveland, Tampa, Dallas, even Denver and Los Angeles. With all that power gathered in one place, so many ancient rivalries and grudges more or less submerged since Lucky Luciano's time, Dom wondered if a shooting match might start right there.

For now, though, they were all lounging inside The Barber's house or wandering around his spacious grounds, shooting the shit in whispered tones and waiting for the chef to start serving their lunch of two-inch steaks and lobsters fresh from Maine or someplace. All of it smelled great. Dom's mouth was watering when, out of nowhere, one of Barbara's gorillas came running along the driveway toward the house and patio, shouting, "It's cops! The fuckin' cops is here!"

You would've thought a bomb had gone off in the midst of all the delegates. Some of them started for their cars where drivers waited, keeping to themselves, apparently thinking they could cruise *past* the fuzz outside with no one stopping them.

Stupid.

Dom knew exactly what he had to do, grabbing his father's arm with one hand, brother Ange's with the other, hissing at them, "Come with me!"

His old man hesitated. "Dom—"

"Just listen, will ya? There are cops outside the gates. They're gonna stop cars goin' out and check I.D.s, at least. More likely, they'll be haulin' people in and grillin' 'em. You wanna go through that and have it get back to the city papers?"

"What's *your* plan?" his father asked.

"Get outa here on foot, into the woods. We'll make it to the highway we came in on, past the law, and hoof it to another town close by."

"Another town?" Angelo challenged him. "That's *miles*."

"You'd rather sit in jail? Have our *padre* get booked with the fuckin' reporters everywhere?"

"Supposin' we get lost, Dom? We could *starve* out there."

"Starvin' takes days," Dominic answered back. "You want to, grab one a them steaks and eat it on the run. The main thing is, we gotta go right fuckin' now!"

And so they did, father and sons plunging into the forest that surrounded Barbara's estate and running for their lives.

———

ALOYSIUS GANTT SUPPOSED he should've been expecting it, his hard work for Chief Hoover on a monograph "disproving" the existence of a National Crime Syndicate first buried in a file somewhere, and now shot down in flames.

Across the country, coast to coast, reporters and your standard lying politicians feigned amazement at the Apalachin gathering, with fifty-eight Italian mobsters held for questioning, some pundits speculating that an equal number had escaped during the chaos. Some wrung their hands and bleated, "How could we have known?" despite the crushing weight of evidence compiled since 1920. Others ducked and dodged questions, hoping none of the shit would stick to them after it hit the fan.

And Edgar J. Hoover, after three decades of claiming gangsters were a strictly local problem, never truly organized, now claimed he'd known it all along. Hell yes, wasn't he the one man in America on top of everything?

Of course, that meant the Bureau had to play catch-up and make it snappy. Overnight, almost before the ink on fingerprints from Apalachin had a chance to dry, Speed had resuscitated the "Top Hoodlum Program," launched provisionally by Manhattan's field office in 1953, building upon the "CAPGA" files Tom Clark, as the Attorney General, had ordered closed in '46. Under the not-so-new program, each field office from coast to coast was ordered to compile a list of ten mobsters active within its jurisdiction—and that meant *exactly* ten; no more, no less.

A blind man could've seen the problem at a glance,

but Edgar Hoover was a man who placed appearances above substance, the task of looking busy, seeming knowledgeable, honed to an art form. The rub: cities like Gotham and Chicago, Cleveland and Miami, even San Francisco and Los Angeles, had gangsters by the hundreds, big and small. But agents in Juneau, Alaska, or in Butte, Montana—the Bureau's "Siberia," reserved for agents exiled in disgrace—might only manage to dig up a single smalltime pimp or bookie for their pains, which left them scrounging for the rest from files on petty thieves or transient stickup men, if they weren't fabricated from thin air.

Chicago was a perfect case in point. It's "Top Ten Hoodlums," in the order listed, were Sam Giancana, Anthony Accardo, South Side gambling boss Ralph Pierce, Gus Alex from the Loop, political fixer Murray Humphreys, West Side enforcer Fiore Buccieri, North Siders Ross Prio and Lennie Patrick, Marshal Caifano fronting for the Outfit in Nevada, and far South Side gambling kingpin Frank La Porte. That was the list, ten guys picked out of hundreds, maybe thousands, from a network dating back nearly four decades.

But the worst of it, adding insult to injury, came from the Chief himself. After Gantt and his son had wasted weeks fudging the truth, trying to prove the Mafia didn't exist, now Hoover had commissioned yet another monograph, to prove it *did* and that the FBI had been on top of it from the beginning of his tenure as Director.

Gantt wouldn't be writing *that* report, of course. The honor went to William Sullivan, who hadn't joined the Bureau until August 1941 and bounced around various field postings till Hoover called him back to headquarters in '44. Today, he labored in the Research Section of Crime

Records, ghostwriting a book for Hoover on the perils of communism until the new project fell in his lap.

How would he handle it?

This time, unlike Gantt's mockery of history, cranked out in 1953, the evidence was copious and readily available. Sullivan might be pressed for time, but he would do as he was ordered: write the goddamned thing and help his boss emerge from Apalachin's fallout smelling like a rose.

————

LANGLEY, Virginia: December 4, 1957

COLBY GANTT WAS BRIEFLY HOME AGAIN, WORKING at Foggy Bottom in D.C., where wife Eileen could keep an eye on him and he could spend time in the evening with ten-year-old son Hardy, presently a fifth-grader and struggling with arithmetic.

This afternoon he'd stolen time for a side trip into Fairfax County, where construction workers had been clearing land since mid-October for the Agency's new headquarters. He guessed they'd get it done eventually, but he couldn't picture it right now, the heaps of dirt and bulldozers growling away, two giant excavators gouging out the future basement levels like a pair of yellow dinosaurs grazing.

Gantt was impatient for the new facility to open, even more so for another posting to the field—and that meant damned near anywhere on Earth these days. In the Caribbean, Francois Duvalier—a black tyrant commonly known as "Papa Doc"—had been elected in September to a one-time-only six-year term as president of Haiti, but insiders whispered that he had no plans for stepping down in 1963. Instead, he'd organized a personal Gestapo, the *Tonton Macoute*, named for an island bogeyman whose moniker translated into "Uncle Gunnysack," the tool he used to kidnap bratty kids before consuming them alive. Duvalier's *Tonton Macoute* was even worse, already killing off his critics by the hundreds with no end in sight.

Fulgencio Batista could've used a force like that in Cuba, coping with the Castro brothers and their 26th July Movement based in Oriente Province, while a younger group, the anticommunist Student Revolutionary Directorate, raised hell in Havana, storming the presidential palace on March 13, in a failed attempt to depose Batista. Government troops killed SRD leader José Echeverría at Havana's main radio station while survivors withdrew and regrouped in the Escambray Mountains of Las Villas Province, calling themselves the 13 March Movement. In June, Washington recalled Ambassador Arthur Gardner and placed an embargo on Batista's government, but mobsters and United Fruit were still supporting him, even after he'd commandeered the island's oil refineries.

In Britain, a riddle from last year might have been solved when two fishermen hauled a man's corpse out of Chichester Harbor in June. The floater was missing its head and both hands, but otherwise its size and diving gear appeared to match those of Royal Navy frogman Lionel Crabb, missing for fourteen months since he'd gone spying of the Soviet cruiser *Ordzhonikidze* at Portsmouth. Neither Crabb's ex-wife nor girlfriend could identify the corpse, while old friend Sydney Knowles insisted that the stiff lacked two prominent scars Crabb bore on his left leg. A pathologist disputed that, confirming both scars where they ought to be, and while experts saw "nothing sinister" about the missing head or hands, theories abounded: Crabb was killed by troops aboard the *Ordzhonikidze* or was captured, dying under torture; he was brainwashed and enlisted as a double agent, or the SIS had meant for him to infiltrate the Russian navy's Black Sea Fleet, where he remained alive today. Officially, death was attributed to misadventure from a problem with his scuba tank.

Miles overhead, in outer space, the launch of *Sputnik 1* had rocked America, but now the CIA and Air Force were on track to overtake the Reds. Beginning two months after *Sputnik* soared aloft, a collaborative effort had begun on the CORONA project, planning a launch for the first U.S. photoreconnaissance satellite sometime in early 1959. Until that paid off, U-2 spying flights would have to do.

The Middle East had calmed a bit since the Suez Crisis, encouraged by the announcement of the Eisenhower Doctrine in early January. As the president told Congress and the world at large, any Middle Eastern nation could request American economic or military aid if it was being threatened by armed aggression, all part of U.S. dedication "to secure and protect the territorial integrity and political independence of such nations, requesting such aid against overt armed aggression from any nation controlled by international communism."

And if the people of said nations voted in a leader deemed too liberal—well, they could count on seeing U.S. troops as well, to topple the regime they'd voted for, as in Iran and Guatemala.

Support from Washington would always be a two-edged sword.

Southeast Asia proved that point in spades. In

February the CIA's Programs Evaluation Office began supplying "training materials" to the French Military Mission in Laos, passed on to the Royal Lao Army. At the same time, Washington started paying the RLA's salaries, while funneling arms to friendly—anticommunist—Hmong guerrillas.

A month before that program started, Moscow proposed a permanent division of Vietnam into North and South, à la Korea, with both nations admitted separately to the United Nations. Washington scotched that, denying recognition to any government led by Hồ Chí Minh. President Diệm visited the White House in May and left with Eisenhower calling him Asia's "miracle man," further declaring, "The cost of defending freedom, of defending America, must be paid in many forms and in many places. Military, as well as economic help, is currently needed in Vietnam." Meanwhile, an article in *Foreign Affairs* found that "South Viet Nam is today a quasi-police state characterized by arbitrary arrests and imprisonment, strict censorship of the press and the absence of effective political opposition." Against that non-democracy, Việt Minh guerrillas had mounted a campaign of bombings and murders in early October, claiming the lives of 400 officials so far. Observers from the International Control Commission, formed in 1954 to oversee implementation of that year's Geneva Accords, reported that fair elections were presently impossible on either side of the 17th parallel.

Nor, Gantt knew, would they ever be. Any idealist who thought America was seriously interested in "democracy" for Vietnam or any other part of Southeast Asia had to be a hopeless idiot.

———

THIS CHRISTMAS, Greg Jordan was thankful that his brother and two nephews had escaped the Apalachin dragnet, and that the upheavals of the *Cosa Nostra* in Gotham had so far spared his family. If Carlo had been more impetuous, they could have been sucked into Vito Genovese's power play against his rivals—nearly killing Frank Costello and assassinating Albert Anastasia, with aid from Carlo Gambino and Meyer Lansky, who resented Anastasia's horning in on Cuba.

Joining in that feud on either side would have been madness, coming at a time when *Cosa Nostra* was in flux and under fire from enemies outside the brotherhood, taking new risks that might destroy the whole Honored Society.

And even so, Greg had gone back to carrying a pistol when he left home, even though his driver doubled as a bodyguard.

Two weeks before *Don* Anastasia sat down for his last shave in the barbershop at the Park Sheraton Hotel, Joe Bonanno had joined the Maggadino brothers from Buffalo and Papa John Priziola, trailing various subordinates, for a five-day meeting with Sicilian Mafia leaders at Palermo's Grand Hotel des Palmes for a kind of "heroin summit," arranging details of new delivery routes and schedules. Charlie Luciano had joined in, speaking more or less for *Don* Calò Vizzini's family based in Villalba. Jordan's brother Carlo was invited to attend, but offered vague excuses, honoring his promise to refrain from dealing drugs.

Jordan wondered if nephew Dominic would hew the same line when he rose to lead the family someday.

Meanwhile, the Syndicate's action in Cuba was still going like a house afire, despite the threat of revolutions from both left and right. Lansky's Havana Riviera opened on December 10, with Ginger Rogers starring at the hotel's Copa Cabaret. (For all her fame in films, dancing with Fred Astaire, Meyer opined that Rogers "can wiggle her ass but she can't sing a goddamn note.") Other celebrities on hand included William Holden, Nat "King" Cole, Steve Allen and Ava Gardner—who allegedly killed time by dragging bellhops into bed. Reporters on the scene noted that while "the bar was tended by local bartenders, the casino was managed by gentlemen from Las Vegas."

In Washington, a new gang-busting Senate committee was giving crooked unions the fits. Led by John McClellan of Arkansas, with Robert Kennedy serving as gung-ho general counsel, the Senate Select Committee on Improper Activities in Labor and Management was formed at January's end, committed to unmasking racketeers wherever they had burrowed into unions meant to help American workers. The panel started out with the International Brotherhood of Teamsters, organized in 1903 and led since then by only three presidents: Cornelius Shea, Dan Tobin, and Dave Beck. Each proved more corrupt than the last, repeatedly indicted but never convicted so far. A new contender for the throne, James Riddle Hoffa, had a record of arrests dating from 1937, but as usual, he hadn't been convicted yet.

The charge that set McClellan's committee sniffing after the IBT involved a 1955 meeting between Hoffa and mobster Johnny Dio, creating fifteen nonexistent "paper" locals to inflate Hoffa's delegate count at the next convention. In February, the committee played tapes of that meeting for a national TV audience, and March saw Hoffa arrested for trying to bribe committee investigator John Cheasty, offering him $18,000 to deliver various classified documents. Miami lawyer Hyman Fischbach also faced indictment as the go-between.

Less than a week later, Dave Beck emerged from hiding, confessed receiving a $300,000 "loan" from the Teamsters he'd never repaid, then was suspended from the AFL-CIO and slapped with tax-evasion charges. In May, the AFL-CIO charged Beck and IBT Vice President Frank Brewster with embezzling union funds. The parent group also accused Minneapolis Vice President Sydney Brennan of taking bribes from management and blamed the IBT's remaining leaders for failing to take out the trash. Beck denied chartering Hoffa's paper locals, but that didn't stop the AFL-CIO's Ethical Practices Committee from citing widespread violations of corrupt leadership, naming Hoffa in particular, finally expelling the whole union one week shy of Halloween.

In the meantime, Beck and Hoffa had their hands full with indictments, trials, and jockeying for power in the IBT. The Hoffa-Fischbach trial was set for May, pushed back till June, then saw the pair acquitted in July. G-men moved in with John Cheasty's family, despite Chief Hoover's 1950 testimony to the Kefauver Committee that his bureau was "not empowered to perform guard duties" for federal witnesses.

While that went on, Hoffa testified before a federal grand jury about wiretaps he allegedly planted on Teamsters HQ in Detroit, resulting in a perjury indictment of himself and hired eavesdropper Bernard Spindel. At trial in November, testimony claimed that Johnny Dio helped arrange the Motown taps, at the behest of Hoffa and Teamsters rising star-turned-codefendant Bert Brennan. Jurors deadlocked five days prior to Christmas, and U.S. Attorney Paul Williams announced a retrial set for January.

As to paper locals, Senator McClellan sprang Johnny Dio from prison long enough to testify before the Senate, but he stonewalled, as did top leaders of New York City Local 284 in August. Hoffa answered a subpoena to appear in Washington, grilled with unmasked animosity by Bobby Kennedy and claimed he "couldn't remember" his meetings with Dio. McClellan tried to cure that amnesia, listing forty-eight conflicts on interest on Hoffa's part, mostly "questionable" spending that included the purchase of mobster Paul Ricca's home by Detroit Locals 299 and 337. Jimmy blamed a pair of Gotham rivals, Tom Hickey and Martin Lacey, for creating paper locals in a bid to frame Hoffa.

It wasn't all one-way, of course. In mid-September, thirteen Teamster members from New York filed suit to stall the union's next presidential election, claiming Hoffa had hand-picked 80 percent of the convention delegates. Federal judge Fred Letts ordered the union to show cause before September 27 why the meeting in Miami Beach—scheduled to open three days later—shouldn't be postponed. No answer was forthcoming by the deadline, so Letts issued an injunction and the IBT appealed. DC's Circuit Court of Appeals revoked that order one day later, while Senator McClellan broadcast thirty-four new charges against Jimmy Hoffa. McClellan also sent Dave

Beck a telegram, claiming that some convention delegates were picked illegally.

When the convention opened on September 30, four candidates besides Hoffa sought to replace Dave Beck as president. In Washington, Earl Warren found no reason to prolong the Letts injunction, which passed into history. Dave Beck announced "early retirement," and Hoffa swept to triumph with 1,208 votes from the convention's 1,700 delegates. A day later, by a vote of 1,105 to 133, attendees replaced Gotham Vice President "Honest Tom" Hickey with Hoffa ally John O'Rourke. In Washington, the day after that final vote, a hotel maid allegedly burned Teamster records subpoenaed by the McClellan Committee, then dropped dead from a heart attack. Hoffa offered to send Bobby Kennedy the ashes from his trashcan "for investigation."

It was all too much, too fast. Judge Letts issued a restraining order, barring Hoffa and company from assuming their new offices, and Dave Beck promised to stay on until the matter was resolved. The AFL-CIO suspended Hoffa and two of his recently elected allies from the parent union, then expelled the whole union on Christmas Eve. Twenty Teamsters leaders from across the country told McClellan that their financial and election records were unavailable. Six days shy of Thanksgiving, Seattle jurors convicted Dave Beck Jr. on two counts of grand larceny; his father's embezzlement trial began ten days later, ending with conviction and a prison term, deferred while he awaited yet another trial on tax-evasion charges. One day prior to Beck Sr.'s conviction in Seattle, Gotham jurors convicted Johnny Dio and Teamsters official John McNamara of extortion, with sentencing scheduled for January.

The upshot of all that: the AFL-CIO lost its most powerful member union, while Hoffa took charge, awaiting the inevitable future trials. *Mafiosi* clung to their Teamsters positions, and some Americans blamed Bobby Kennedy for browbeating union leaders, calling him insolent, overbearing, even vicious. Papa Joe deplored his son's actions but, for once, couldn't bring Bobby under control. While he fought to salvage son John's presidential hopes for 1960, the McClellan Committee moved on to probe other unions and corporations.

And as for *Cosa Nostra*, it endured.

CHAPTER 3

York Theatre, First Avenue, Manhattan: May 17, 1958

"Some wise guy, this one," Dominic Giordano groused. "Guy's not even Italian."

"You sure about that?" asked his date, Aurora Russo.

"Sure I'm sure," Dom answered. "Take my word for it."

The film onscreen, *I Mobster,* was supposed to chart the rise and fall of gang lord Joe Sante, but the star was Steve Cochran, a logger's son from California who'd mostly grown up in Wyoming. He'd broken into movies back in 1945, often playing a gangster, but he was white bread all the way.

And hell yes, Dom had learned that skimming over movie magazines. Why not?

"Well, he's convincing me," Aurora said, snuggling a little closer, so her breast nuzzled against Dom's arm. He idly wondered whether she was conscious of the Smith & Wesson Model 28 wedged in a shoulder holster, under-

neath that same left arm, and guessed she must be, probably enjoying it.

Aurora was a doll and a great lay, at twenty-two a
dozen years younger than Dominic. She was a barber's
daughter and he liked her fine but didn't count her as his
only girl by any means, although his parents had been
riding him the last couple of years, wondering when he
planned to "settle down" and start a family. Grandkids
were damned near all his mom could talk about these
days, and Dom was getting sick of it, but he just smiled
and nodded over dinner once a week, while brother
Angelo winked at him from across the table.

I Mobster was the same old thing he'd seen before,
time and again while he was growing up, its only real
bright spot a cameo appearance by striptease artist Lili St.
Cyr, playing herself. Dom had preferred the first feature:
Machine Gun Kelly, with a new guy named Charles
Bronson in the title role. His onscreen wife bossed him
around too much, which Dom had heard was true of Kelly
in real life, but otherwise, predictably, the movie barely
came within a country mile of truth. The dumbest part
was casting bug-eyed comic Morey Amsterdam as Kelly's
mythical sidekick, "Michael Fandango," who gets pissed
because he's lost an arm in one of their stickups and
fingers Kelly for the law. The funny bit was where Kelly
gunned down a bunch of gangsters playing poker—total
bullshit since in life he'd never shot a soul.

Real mobsters, on the other hand, were having a hard
time this year. Hitman and occasional bank robber Elmer
"Trigger" Burke had fried at Sing Sing, back in January, for
killing a bartender, but he'd gone out smiling, waving at
assembled witnesses. Joe Barbara had suffered great
humiliation after the fiasco at his Apalachin homestead,

stripped of his pistol permit, facing closure of his bottling plant and an IRS tax audit. To his credit, Joe the Barber *had* cautioned Stefano Magaddino against two meets at his house within a twelve-month period, given his hassles from the state police, but Magaddino wouldn't listen, and now Vito Genovese was blaming him. Somebody'd tossed a hand grenade at Maggadino's home in Buffalo, but it turned out to be a dud.

Even across the water, *Mafiosi* were at war with one another. Being copycats, they'd borrowed av American idea, creating for the first time a *commissione* to settle problems, naming Salvatore Greco from Ciaculli "first among equals" to keep the other *dons* in line. So far, it wasn't working out too well: gunmen had ambushed Dr. Michele Navarra, a physician who doubled as boss of the Mafia's Corelonese family, killing another doctor—and non-*mafioso*—in the same machinegun fusillade.

At least Dom, with his dad and brother, had escaped the Apalachin raid without logging arrests, and that felt pretty goddamned good.

Speaking of feeling good...

He reached over with his right hand, undid a button on Aurora's blouse, and slipped his hand inside.

"What do you think you're doing?" she asked.

"This," Dom said, and eased his fingers underneath her lacy next-to-nothing bra, smiling as she began to moan softly and wriggled closer to him in the dark.

———

MANHATTAN: *July 4, 1958*

INDEPENDENCE DAY: a rare day off from "voluntary" Bureau overtime for grilling steaks and hot dogs, with Camille the next best thing to happy, Wyman—now eleven—playing football with his school buddies at a park nearby, and *still,* all Devon Gantt could really think about was work.

Since Edgar Hoover now believed there just might be a Syndicate, Devon could chase some of his usual research without having to hide it as if he were stealing paperclips and pencils from the office. In Washington, Bill Sullivan had finished off his monograph replete with details on the Mafia, but Gantt had yet to see a copy if it ever turned up in New York. Meanwhile, Gotham was full of gangsters, well known to whoever owned a TV set, a radio, or opened up a newspaper, but Devon still enjoyed hearing about the made men and their aides out west.

Two stories had enticed him recently, one coming to him only yesterday, in Thursday's *New York Post.* A new Stardust hotel-casino had opened on the Vegas Strip two days ago, boasting 1,000 rooms, designed for suckers who wouldn't fit in with higher-class players and "whales" across the street, at Cleveland's Desert Inn. No problem, though: Moe Dalitz and his partners owned both joints and, in the process, neatly tied together certain dangling threads of history.

The Stardust had replaced the Royal Nevada, going strong since April 1955. Before its formal opening, the Dalitz mob had thrown a special party for "atomic soldiers"—that is, GIs who had been exposed to radiation at the Silver State's nuclear test site, 100-odd miles north of town. If any of them started glowing in the dark, Gantt guessed that Moe and company could trim their neon bill.

The Stardust had been "Admiral" Tony Cornero's brainchild, but the old bootlegger had run out of cash in

July of '55, wandered across the street to the DI, and dropped dead at a crap table with Dalitz watching him, after a waitress told him there'd be no more drinking on the cuff. The joint had passed from Tony's lifeless hands to Jake the Barber Factor, tool of Al Capone in framing Roger Touhy for a mythical kidnapping two decades back. Factor, in turn, had "leased" it to the Cleveland mob, and dropped in when he felt like it to see nude dancers from the Lido de Paris or paddle in the joint's Big Dipper swimming pool.

From Gantt's old L.A. haunts, there'd been more news of Mickey Cohen. Freed from prison in October 1955, Mickey had "gone legit," supposedly. In fact, aside from fronting various legit establishments, he also did a lively trade in blackmailing celebrities with secrets he'd collected over twenty years in La-La Land. Pay up and keep it coming, or the ex-King of Los Angeles would bare your secrets in the tabloid press.

Most recently, the dirt he mined involved movie bombshell Lana Turner and her late, abusive lover, Johnny Stompanato Jr. Stompanato was—*had been*—a Scotsman, ex-marine, and underworld fringe player, tight with Cohen off and on. In early April, Turner's fourteen-year-old daughter, Cheryl Crane, allegedly stabbed Johnny to prevent his latest vicious beating of her mom. L.A.'s coroner called it justifiable—Cohen had testified at the inquest, claiming that *he* had briefly been a suspect in the homicide—but Stompanato's family still sued Lana for $750,000, settling for twenty grand.

Then more bad news for Lana, star of last year's *Peyton Place,* who'd earned an Oscar nomination as Best Actress but lost out to Joanne Woodward: Mickey got his grubby hands on love letters she'd sent to Stompanato during their tempestuous romance. Word had it that Turner had anted up five figures for the steamy missives, but he'd turned around and sold them to a tabloid anyway.

All class that Mickey Devon thought. *But now, at least, the Bureau can admit that he's a mobster.*

———

FBI HEADQUARTERS: July 20, 1958

ALOYSIUS GANTT HAD FINALLY OBTAINED a copy of Bill Sullivan's Mafia monograph, delivered to the Chief via Assistant Director Alan Belmont on July 9. Sullivan's title was succinct—"Mafia"—and Gantt was relieved he'd spelled it properly, unlike Belmont, when he'd described the group as mythical in 1953.

The document, crediting Edgar Hoover as its author, spanned 117 pages of text, listing 131 reference notes, plus helpful maps: one of the modern Mafia's birthplace in Sicily; another of known gatherings in the U.S. since 1929 (a typo: Cleveland's meeting was exposed in 1928); and a third pinpointing headquarters of the *mafiosi* busted at Apalachin last November. It neatly tied the Old World of the 1860s up to present-day America, including modern transatlantic links between Mafia families.

The document was clearly stamped "FOR OFFICIAL USE ONLY," but something had gone wrong in that regard. Upon receiving his copy, Hoover didn't bother reading it, sending a note to Sullivan that said, "The point has been missed. It is not now necessary to read the monograph to know that the Mafia exists in the United States." Proud of his unacknowledged work, Sullivan sent twenty-five copies off to DOJ bigwigs while Speed and Tolson were at lunch. Returning, Edgar started thumbing through the monograph and scrawled "Baloney!" on the title page—then learned of Sullivan's hasty distribution effort.

So the word came down: retrieve all copies by day's end.

Poor Sullivan, Gantt thought. Bill might've been shipped off to Butte or Juneau, but he'd also recently ghostwritten Edgar Hoover's study of the CPUSA —*Masters of Deceit: The Story of Communism in America and How to Fight It*—published in April by Henry Holt & Company. Gantt knew it would join Whitehead's *FBI Story* as required reading at the Quantico academy, and he could only wonder how Sullivan found the time, on top of his involvement with the COINTELPRO operation. Sullivan wouldn't discuss it, nor would he admit that Party ranks had shriveled to a mere 5,000, down from 80,000 during World War Two, with one-third of its current members being paid Bureau informers.

Tangled webs, and lately Gantt imagined that if any true subversives were ensnared, it had to be by accident.

———

HARLEM: August 1, 1958

THINGS WERE POPPING in the Gotham ghetto and beyond, for BOSS and Payton Sawyer. In January, Malcolm X had telephoned his marriage proposal to Berry Sanders from a Detroit gas station. She'd agreed, and a justice of the peace married them two days later, in Lansing. Back in

New York after a five-day honeymoon, they'd settled in three rooms of a two-family apartment in East Elmhurst, Queens.

NYPD's 115th Precinct ruled the roost out there, but Payton had his orders: keep close tabs on Malcolm while he was in Gotham and do anything possible to keep track of him when he was on the road.

The same day Malcolm and his bride returned, a journalist had asked him what he thought about the Prayer Pilgrimage for Freedom in D.C., a three-hour demonstration drawing 25,000 persons to the Lincoln Memorial, staged on the *Brown* decision's third anniversary. Martin Luther King Jr. had been that outing's star, delivering his now famous "Give Us the Ballot" speech. Malcolm, in his reply, was unimpressed, asking why Negroes should become excited by a protest "run by whites in front of a statue of a president who has been dead for a hundred years and who didn't like us when he was alive."

That much was true. From studying his people's history in school, Payton knew Honest Abe had been a Union man, not a committed abolitionist. In 1862 he wrote to Horace Greeley, saying, "If I could save the Union without freeing any slave I would do it, and if I could save it by freeing all the slaves I would do it, and if I could save it by freeing some and leaving others alone I would also do that." In fact, his great Emancipation Proclamation, issued five months later, freed only those slaves in regions still controlled by the Confederacy; those in the Border South and Washington itself, he'd left in chains.

Payton stayed home in May, when Malcolm visited Chicago for the funeral of Elijah Muhammad's mother and spent his time filing reports on New York's first Puerto Rican Day Parade, staged on April 13. That gave Puerto

Ricans a six-month jump on the older Hispanic Day Parade, traditionally held in mid-October. Payton had been on alert for any nationalist outbreak during the procession, but the closest thing he'd found were cheaply printed flyers from the Puerto Rican Nationalist Party, led after a fashion by Pedro Albizu Campos in San Juan. Imprisoned from 1954 to '59 after the raid on Congress by four of his followers, he acted now as if he'd lost his mind, claiming authorities at La Princesa prison had bombarded him with "colored rays" that no one else could see.

Payton didn't doubt that he'd been tortured by his jailers, but the sci-fi aspect of it *did* sound crazy, all the more when Albizu tried to protect himself with wet towels wrapped around his head, prompting other cons to nickname him "King of the Towels."

By August, with wife Betty—now surnamed Shabazz—expecting their first child in November, Malcolm had been back in Harlem, speaking at a street rally on Seventh Avenue, a long block east of the Apollo Theater. Payton was in the crowd, hanging on every word, with no doubt whatsoever as to why America's white leaders deemed Malcolm, a devil in the flesh.

————

LITTLE ITALY, *Manhattan: August 13, 1958*

ANOTHER YEAR, more hassles for *Cosa Nostra* from lawmen and members of its not-so-brotherly society. Greg Jordan tried to keep his family out of it, but that was growing harder every day.

It started off a short week after New Year's Day, when

Gotham jurors convicted Johnny Dio of extortion and conspiracy, adding another fifteen years minimum onto his outstanding time. Things went better for Vincent Gigante in May: acquitted of wounding Frank Costello at trial, he'd thanked Frank in court for refusing to name him, then kissed and made up over dinner at Costello's place on Central Park West.

Teamsters weren't having it so easy. Troublesome Judge Letts, in Washington, permitted Jimmy Hoffa to take office as the union's president but named three hostile lawyers to a board of monitors to draft bylaws and keep the Teamsters' business straight for one year, minimum. The union got more bad press when it paid $163,000 for Dave Beck's Florida home, then allowed him to stay on rent-free. That didn't last long, though, as Beck received a three-to-fifteen year sentence for embezzlement in February. From Washington, McClellan's Senate panel called the IBT a "hoodlum empire" run by Hoffa for the benefit of thugs. June brought a brief respite for Jimmy, as Gotham jurors acquitted him and his two co-defendants of wiretapping, but Judge Thomas Murphy announced an impending probe of jury tampering. Meanwhile, in New Jersey, Local 560 founder John Conlin dropped dead, replaced by Tony Provenzano, a *caporegime* with the Genovese family.

As for *Don* Vito, he testified before McClellan's panel in the midst of Hoffa's Gotham trial, pleading the Fifth 150 times, then found himself and sixteen other members of his family indicted one month later, charged with conspiracy to import and sell heroin. The government's star witness was a small-time Puerto Rican dealer, Nelson Cantellops, who claimed that Genovese sat down with him in person to plot strategy.

Bullshit, Greg thought. But if jurors believed it...

From the Teamsters, John McClellan's hunters switched to the United Auto Workers, but the found no mob connections since the Reuther brothers hated gangsters who had tried to murder both of them. After the hoopla over Jimmy Hoffa and his contacts, Congress yearned for legislation it could pass, but what they got was the Kennedy-Ives Bill, aka the Labor Reform Bill. Named in part for JFK, not Bobby, the proposed law would've covered thirty areas of union business including finances and record keeping, democratic rules and organizational structures. The Senate passed it by a vote of 88-to-1, then Eisenhower's disapproval killed it in the House. Stung by defeat, Jack Kennedy pointed his finger at the Teamsters' president and a longtime Sears "labor consultant" when he complained, "Only the Jimmy Hoffas and the Nathan Sheffermans can find satisfaction in the failure of this Congress to pass the Labor Reform Bill. Honest union members, informed businessmen, responsible labor leaders, law enforcement officers, and the general public—all of these will suffer as the result of this bill's death in the House of Representatives."

So what if that was mostly sour grapes? It got more press for old Joe Kennedy's eldest surviving son, and anyone who didn't realize that he'd be running for the White House two years down the road was terminally out of touch.

———

FBI BIRMINGHAM FIELD OFFICE: October 15, 1958

RACIAL MATTERS, as the Bureau called them, had been heating up in Alabama and the South at large, but Nolan O'Hara's efforts to get something beyond simple information on the region's Klan types still weren't paying off.

His best hope, during June, had come from rival Ku Klux leaders squabbling among themselves. Racist bombings echoed across Dixie, still with Birmingham at ground zero. Negro residents of Fountain Heights had caught three Klansmen in the act and roughed them up before police arrived, but guilty pleas in court saw them released on meaningless probation. Only April rain had stopped a massive bomb from taking down the Temple Beth-El synagogue, and then Bill Morris, founding father of the Federated Knights in 1949, approached Bull Connor, blaming Georgia nut-job Jesse Stoner—self-proclaimed "arch leader" of the Christian Knights—as Dixie's most prolific racist bomber. He'd not only tried to hit Temple Beth-El, but Morris also blamed Stoner for countless other blasts since the late Forties, several of them claimed by callers from a "Confederate Underground."

Connor had a brainstorm, huddling with Bureau SAC Clarence Kelly to set a trap for Stoner. Two of Connor's plainclothesmen posed as "steelworkers" and invited Stoner to blow up the Bethel Baptist Church on contract. Stoner agreed, and while the lawmen mounted stakeouts, someone bombed the church as planned, slipping away before the net could close. Disgusted, Edgar Hoover fired a memo to the field, instructing Kelly to limit contact with Connor, based on Bull's rank reputation and shady connections. Stoner, still a Klansman, had moved on to found the National States Rights Party six weeks after the Bethel blast, with jailbird John Kasper attending its first meeting.

Ace Carter quit the Klan—well, theoretically, at least —to campaign for lieutenant governor in May's Democratic primary, but he ran last in a field of five contenders, albeit with 35,501 votes. The year's big winner was governor-elect John Patterson, parlaying sympathy for his attorney general father's murder in 1954 (son John replaced him in the empty office), his cleanup of mobsters around Phenix City (his father's presumed murderers), and his exile of NAACP organizers from the Cotton State over their failure to register as agents of a "foreign" movement. An eleventh-hour campaign mailing put him over the top: a letter signed by Patterson, typed on attorney general's stationery, inviting Klansmen to support him as a "mutual friend" of Grand Dragon Robert Shelton.

The *Montgomery Advertiser* got a copy of that letter, running it on page one with a scathing editorial, but all in vain. Voters swallowed the lie that Patterson didn't know Shelton and had no ties to the Klan. "When you're running for governor and somebody wants to support you," Patterson said, "as long as you're free and twenty-one, you don't run anyone off."

Of course, he forgot to add "white."

In fact, voters were more impressed by Patterson's vow that "if a school is ordered to be integrated, it will be closed down." His closest rival, Circuit Judge George Wallace out of Barbour County, tried to court black ballots and lampooned his rival for soliciting the Klan's support, but Patterson annihilated him in June's runoff election, banking 315,353 votes to Wallace's 250,451. Afterward, Wallace promised intimates, "No sonofabitch will ever out-nigger me again."

Two months after the National States Rights Party was born, five of its members faced charges of bombing

Atlanta's Hebrew Benevolent Congregation, the oldest synagogue in a city "too busy to hate." James Venable, lead counsel for the U.S. Klans, stepped up to plead their case, beginning with George Bright, a ratty character who'd knocked around the fascist fringe since 1946. The FBI furnished informants to the prosecutor's office, while Venable called "character witnesses" from the Klan, including Imperial Wizard Edwards, plus an alibi provided by a lunatic asylum inmate testifying in a moment of "temporary lucidity." Jurors deadlocked at Bright's first trial, acquitted him the second time around, and all charges against his four accomplices were dropped.

The bombing had turned into the South's worst PR nightmare, eclipsing Jim Crow's daily abuses and mayhem against blacks with a virulent strain of anti-Semitism on the rise. Atlanta's temple was the year's fifth synagogue attack, followed two days later by another blast in Illinois. That seemed to be an aberration, with Dixie contributing most of the damage, so police had organized a Southern Conference on Bombing based in Jacksonville, designed to be a clearinghouse for information, hopefully producing some convictions at long last. FBI headquarters predictably refused to help, but the SCB *did* acquire an ex-G-man as chief investigator. At its premier meeting, he'd read off a list of the South's most notorious anti-Semites, including Bill Hendrix, John Kasper and Jesse Stoner, then raised a ruckus by naming Bull Connor, one of the police officials sitting in his audience. That brought a hasty, undeserved apology to Bull, and their matters were stalled, with no arrests so far and nothing to suggest when they'd occur.

Nolan suspected he might have more luck arresting

murderous police, but Edgar Hoover was gun-shy. In 1943, Sheriff Claude Screws of Baker County, Georgia, with two of his slack-jawed subordinates, fatally beat a Negro prisoner in full view of multiple witnesses. Amazingly, jurors convicted all three of violating their victim's civil rights, but the Supreme Court overturned those verdicts just before V-E Day. The court acknowledged "a shocking and revolting episode in law enforcement," but held that Screws and his cohorts hadn't "willfully" deprived their prisoner of civil rights. They were just three more inbred rednecks to whom badges were a hunting license. While liable for murder charges—never filed, of course—they hadn't violated any federal law.

Hoover, perhaps relieved, had not pursued another case against brutal police for thirteen years and counting, now.

To Nolan, that meant he would never lay his hands on the Mississippi cops who'd gunned down George Love in January, "resisting arrest" for a crime it was later proven he didn't commit. Nor the Georgia "peace officers" who'd beaten James Brazier to death in April, a virtual replay of the Screws case, followed by their murder of victim Willie Countryman a month later. Nor another Georgia cop who'd gunned down Ernest Hunter at the Camden County jail, after Hunter "interfered" with his wife's arrest on petty traffic charges.

It disgusted Nolan that he couldn't lock those killers up, but in the absence of support from either SAC Kelly or Chief Hoover, the best that he could do was keep collecting evidence and bide his time.

One day, he thought. *Maybe one day...*

———

PORT-AU-PRINCE, Haiti: October 15, 1958

COLBY GANTT STOOD on a pier overlooking the Gulf of Gonâve, Haiti's preeminent natural harbor and lifeline to the outside world since Arawak tribesmen foolishly welcomed the Spaniards in 1492. His presence in the capital was strictly off the record, and he had avoided contact with the U.S. embassy, mindful of recent upheavals against Papa Doc Duvalier and longstanding hatred of Americans, spawned by military occupation of Haiti from 1915 to '34.

No sooner had the Yankees left, than Haiti lapsed into a period of intermittent warfare with its neighbor on the bitterly divided island, the Dominican Republic—also occupied by U.S. troops from 1916 until '24. Dictator Rafael Trujillo lusted after Haitian land and had been known to send his troops across the border on a whim, as with the gruesome "parsley massacre," killing as many as 12,000 hapless Haitian farmers.

Colby's presence in Haiti was simply to confirm the failure of June's bungled *coup d'état* against Duvalier, led by three crackpot ex-sheriff's deputies from Florida and Buffalo, New York, backed up by half a dozen mercenaries —all of whom were now stone dead. Gantt would confirm Duvalier's triumph but didn't want to hang around much longer on an island where 80 percent of the people sweltered in abject poverty and Papa Doc's *Tonton Macoute* killed Haitians faster than Trujillo ever dreamed of.

From where he stood, Gantt couldn't literally see Cuba, lying 200 miles northwesterly, across the Windward Passage, but it still felt almost close enough for him to touch. On that embattled isle, the Castros and an estimated 200 guerrillas were outnumbered 190-to-1, but they kept winning engagements, like the Battle of La Plata in July and beamed their message to the world over a pirate "Radio Rebel" station. Batista had launched *La Ofensiva* in August, killing seventy insurgents, but the rest escaped to fight again after General Eulogio Cantillo foolishly granted a ceasefire.

Americans involved with the guerrillas presently included mobster Norman "Roughhouse" Rothman, who'd stolen $13.5 million in bonds, cash and jewelry from a Canadian bank, splitting the take with Montreal's Cotroni Mafia family, planning to aid Castro's rebels by flooding Havana with counterfeit pesos to upset the Cuban economy. Just yesterday, he'd also stolen 300-odd weapons from an Ohio National Guard armory, earmarked for the 26th July Movement, but feds were hot on his trail, adding mobsters Joe Merola (once Batista's personal pilot) and Edward Browder Jr. (no relation to CPUSA leader Earl Browder) to their WANTED list.

That meddling wouldn't please the Syndicate, of course, but its Havana representatives were standing back, watching the game play out, as long as none of their investments in Havana were affected. On the other hand, Moe Dalitz and his Cleveland partners had grown nervous in April, quietly persuading Nevada authorities to ban Vegas gamblers from owning Cuban casinos. Five months later, they sold the Hotel Nacional to Mike McLaney, a golf and tennis pro with strong ties to the Mob. Cleveland reaped a windfall, and if things went sour in Havana, it was McLaney's problem.

Stateside, there was nothing cooking at the moment to hold Colby's interest. Blueprints had been approved in March for the Agency's new H-shaped headquarters in

Langley, but completion was still months away. Project MKULTRA kept churning along, most recently including human experimentation by the Agency-sponsored Department of Social Relations, using a range of subjects including teenage freshman prodigy Theodore John Kaczynski. Colby was intent on staying out of it, letting George White and his collaborators take risks.

Southeast Asia, on the other hand, commanded Gantt's attention. In Laos, by June, thirty-seven companies of Red combatants started training in the Mekong Delta. Brigadier General John Heintges revamped the Agency's Programs Evaluation Office, replacing French "advisors" with 149 U.S. Green Berets and 103 Filipino veterans, technically employed by a new CIA front, the Eastern Construction Company, based in Vientiane.

Vietnam remained chaotic, President Diệm suppressing hostile newspapers and the small Free Democratic Party, appointing army officers to rule thirty-six provinces, blaming Reds for "sabotage" of the Geneva Accords that Diệm had himself rendered moot. The Việt Cộng murdered at least 193 civilian leaders, kidnapping 236 more in their "just struggle for the people," and Colby knew both estimates were conservative.

Meanwhile, the CIA was backing a revolt against Indonesia President Sukarno, an advocate since 1955 of uniting developing Asian and African countries into a "non-aligned movement" countering both the U.S. and the USSR. The Agency's vehicle was *Piagam Perjuangan Semesta* ("Universal Struggle Charter"), Permesta for short. Organized in March 1957 under Lieutenant Herman Ventje Sumual and Alexander Evert Kawilarang, ex-Indonesian military attaché to the United States, Permesta's CIA connection was revealed in May when Sukarno's troops shot down and captured Agency contract pilot Allen Pope on Ambon Island.

Gantt knew Pope's résumé: a former Air Force pilot, he'd resigned in March 1954 to join the Agency's Civil Air Transport front, airlifting supplies to the doomed French garrison at Điện Biên Phủ, remaining with CAT till August and the end of the First Indochina War. Next, he'd flown civilian charter flights from Taiwan, then Saigon, until CAT recalled him in April 1958, outfitting him with a B-26 Invader as part of Permesta's *Angkatan Udara Revolusioner* ("Revolutionary Air Force," or AUREV). He'd led bombing raids against Sukarno troop emplacements on Ambon, Morotai, and Sulawesi, also sinking three foreign merchant ships at the Port of Donggala. When he'd returned for another strike on Ambon, Sukarno's commanders scrambled their only fighter plane—a P-51 Mustang—and finally brought him down. In custody, he stood accused of making war against the Indonesian government and killing numerous civilians in an accidental strike on Ambon's largest marketplace.

Six weeks after Pope's capture, Indonesian Army troops seized the Permesta capital—Manado, in North Sulawesi Province—and that ended the revolt, at least for now. Pope still awaited trial, the CIA was publicly embarrassed once again, and Colby thanked his lucky stars that he wasn't involved.

But next time, who could say?

———

Brooklyn Criminal Court: November 22, 1958

AMERICA WAS GOING apeshit crazy over juvenile delinquents, caught in a bizarre love/hate relationship with its
uneasy children. From his front-row seat, considering his
family, Dave Jordan had to wonder how he might have
turned out if he'd been born fifteen years later and had
never gone to war in Europe, growing up on Little Italy's
mean streets.

Two poster children for the current craze were
Charles Starkweather and his girlfriend, Caril Ann
Fugate, of Lincoln, Nebraska. Charles had killed a gas
station attendant in November of last year, then the young
lovers—he nineteen, she fifteen—had embarked upon a
murder spree spanning Nebraska and Wyoming. Starting
with Caril's mother, stepfather, and two-year-old sister,
they'd shot and stabbed eleven victims prior to being
captured. Starkweather was sitting on death row today, his
testimony all it took to send Fugate away for life, despite
her claims that she'd been brainwashed and coerced.

Hollywood had quickly climbed aboard the bandwagon. So far this year alone, it had produced low-budget
features titled *Young and Wild*, *The Party Crashers*, *The Cool
and the Crazy*, *Dragstrip Riot*, and *Stakeout on Dope Street*.
Even the Brits were involved, with *Violent Playground* set in
Liverpool's crime-ridden housing estates.

The stark reality, as Jordan had discovered, was a far
cry from the stage sets of Los Angeles or far-off Pinewood
Studios. Gotham had only logged four juvey homicides so
far this year, out of 345 total slayings, but the crimes of
"savage youth" hogged headlines out of all proportion to
their numbers. From Washington, Edgar Hoover
contributed an article titled "Punish the Parent?" for *The
Rotarian*, warning that negligent parents had produced "a
rapidly increasing army" of criminal teens.

Aside from being reasonably certain Hoover hadn't penned the article himself, Dave knew that view was over-simplified, convinced that fining or arresting inner-city parents would no more stem the present violence than would August's Switchblade Knife Act, banning interstate shipments of "criminal" cutlery.

Today, he was in court alone, handling a pretrial motion for members of the Jonquils gang, accused of stabbing two teenagers, killing one of them, during a rumble with a rival clique called the Corsair Lords three days ago. They were incarcerated without bail so far, and while Dave knew he couldn't change that, he was going through the motions on behalf of Legal Aid.

Fiona O'Hara was in a separate courtroom, on a similar case, representing two members of the Ditmas Dukes for slaying navy veteran Louis Cuomo in a January brawl with rivals from the Gremlins gang. He hoped she would have better luck than he expected, though he doubted it.

David's first night with Fee, now eighteen months behind him, had been unexpected and a kind of revelation. With her clothes off, she was every bit what he'd expected, save for taking in his scars and still embracing him instead of pushing him away, revulsion in her eyes. Since then, they'd been together at her place or his whenever time allowed, trying to make up for lost time but taking extra care—condoms for him, a diaphragm for her —against costly mistakes. Neither of them had used the "L" word yet, nor shared the news with either of their families, but Dave thought that they might be drifting cautiously in that direction.

First, of course, he'd have to tell Fee more about *his* family, and it seemed fairly certain—sixty-forty, anyway—

that news would send a G-man's daughter heading for the hills.

And maybe, in his darker moments, that was what Dave hoped for, after all.

Too late for me, he thought, but he might still save Fee.

———

HARLEM: November 25, 1958

THANKSGIVING dinner with his daughter and her family didn't remind Ike Sawyer much of old-time holidays. He still thought of Talitha busy cooking, with their three surviving children underfoot and sometimes squabbling, but his sons were both tied up this year.

Payton was snooping overtime for BOSS on this holiday the Muslims shunned because their scripture banned their imitating unbelievers and they planned alternative activities. Fred was at UCLA studying, the football season having ended three days ago with a 15-15 tie against USC's Trojans at L.A.'s Memorial Coliseum. According to yearly grudge match rules, that meant last year's winner—the Bruins—hung on to the coveted Victory Bell award for another full year.

As for the family he still had left in town, Ike's son-in-law had bailed before dinner was served, another call from work. "It's triple time, ya know," he'd said. "What can I do?" That left Ike with daughter Keisha and *her* daughter, eight-month-old Luvenia, who still reminded Ike of Aunt Jemima, shrunken down and swaddled in a diaper.

He went through the charade of listening while Keisha maundered on about her problems—same things that she spilled in weekly phone calls—and replied as he supposed a loving father should. Ike *did* love her, of course, but there were times he wanted to remind her that she'd made her saggy bed and now she'd have to lie in it or give her often-absent mate the boot.

Sawyer had long since learned to think of other things while keeping up a civil conversation, and he did so now, his thoughts straying to Dixie and his people's bondage there. It was another lynch-free year, according to Tuskegee University, and he supposed they wouldn't count Ed Smith of State Line, Mississippi, gunned down in his front yard with his wife watching, by solitary redneck L. D. Clark. Grand jurors saw no reason to indict Clark, even when he bragged about the murder far and wide.

Another name for Sawyer's growing list, in case his feet got restless someday soon.

He'd had a good laugh at the Klan in January, "Catfish" Cole's North Carolina Knights tangling with Lumbee Indians in Robeson County. Lumbees were already segregated by a three-way system, keeping them away from whites *and* Negroes, but Catfish still longed to "scare 'em up," particularly after Robert Williams and his Black Armed Guard had chased Cole's ass out of Monroe during October 1957. Three months later, when he led a rally at Hayes Pond, near Maxton, fifty Klansmen showed, outnumbered ten-to-one by hostiles packing guns. They'd lost their banner, unlit cross, their sound equipment and some robes discarded as they fled, leaving one passed-out drunk behind to be arrested, while the county charged Cole with inciting a riot.

Good times, but most of what was happening in race relations didn't make Ike smile. He admired the summer's sit-in demonstrators who'd desegregated drugstore lunch counters in Wichita and Oklahoma City, but in Little Rock, white voters opted to dispense with public schools rather than integrate, already planning on a "lost year" for their kids of high school age.

Clinton High in Tennessee was integrated after riots two years back, but on a Sunday morning in October bombers caused $300,000 damage to the school. A month later—just yesterday, in fact—the Supreme Court had approved Alabama's racist pupil placement law, pulling whatever feeble teeth the *Brown* decision ever had.

Worse news, if that were possible, had come from Ike's home turf in Harlem, in the third week of September. Martin Luther King Jr. was signing his first book, *Stride Toward Freedom*, at Blumstein's Department Store on West 125th Street, when a mentally unbalanced Negro woman stabbed him with an eight-inch letter opener, grazing the minister's aorta. King had lived through surgery, issued a statement two days later praising "the redemptive power of nonviolence," and emerged from Harlem Hospital to greet 500 cheering fans two weeks after his brush with death.

But it was so damned *close*.

"Dad, are you listening?" asked Keisha, with that whiny tone he'd started to despise.

"All years, darlin'."

"As I was *saying*, Eulis has to work so much these days—"

Ike nodded, tuned her out again, and wished he were at home, alone, where he could pour himself a good, stiff drink.

SERPUKHOV, *Moscow Oblast: December 26, 1958*

LEONID BABIN FED the latest coded letter from New Jersey into his log fire and watched it blacken to a curl of ash. His son, Stefan, now looking forward to his thirteenth birthday three months hence, was well established at his Trenton middle school, in seventh grade, and while he'd broken his left radius while playing football, he would shed the plaster cast soon, with a full recovery expected.

A minor setback, nothing that should bar him from the FBI when he was old enough to join.

In Moscow, changes fell as usual. Khrushchev now had effective control of the Soviet government, having replaced Nikolai Bulganin as premier in March, while remaining the Party's First Secretary. Ivan Serov had survived as the KGB's chairman until early December, removed after Khrushchev decreed that Western visitors to Moscow "shouldn't see so many policemen around the place." Serov shifted sideways to command the Red Army's Main Intelligence Directorate, replaced at Lubyanka headquarters on Christmas Day by Alexander Shelepin, longtime member of the Party's Central Committee and a protégé of Stalin who'd survived the purges following his mentor's death. Khrushchev picked him in equal parts because he was a state security outsider, graced with higher education and an intellectual approach to tyranny. According to the Moscow rumor mill, he planned to staff the KGB with new blood from the Communist Youth League and Russian universities.

Meaning that Babin, as a "dinosaur" of sorts, would have to keep his guard up day and night.

Meanwhile, the KGB had ample problems to distract it

from his own secret designs. The European Common Market, organized in January, was another capitalist scheme to limit Soviet expansion into Western Europe. Hungary kept grumbling after its revolt two years ago, while European Communists abandoned their respective parties by the thousands in protest. In June, prisoners Imre Nagy, Miklós Gimes and Pál Maléter were returned to Budapest for secret trials, then shot and dumped in unmarked graves.

In China, Chairman Mao launched his "Great Leap Forward" in May, collectivizing agriculture in a way that spawned more deaths than Stalin's "dekulakization" drive of 1929-32. Mao paired that effort with a "Hundred Flowers Campaign," inviting critics of his government to speak freely, at least until they were arrested when a grim "Anti-Rightist Campaign" took its place. By August, he had sparked another Taiwan Straits crisis, shelling KMT strongholds on Kinmen and Matsu islands. Once again, America was outraged—all except for Mississippi's governor, apparently. When a reporter asked that moron what he thought of Kinmen and Matsu, he had replied, "I think we could find a position for them on the Fish and Game Commission."

August also brought riots to Grozny, capital of Chechen-Ingush ASSR, 1,850 miles southeast of Moscow. The trouble started when an Ingush killed a Russian sailor for pawing his fiancée. Ethnic rivalry was an old story in the region, quickly escalating from that trigger incident to stone-throwing and beatings at the sailor's funeral, one aged Ingush victim slain while the police stood idly by. After five days, an uneasy peace prevailed, but the outbreak embarrassed Moscow at a time when

TASS was broadcasting reports of race riots in the United States.

And still, the trouble wouldn't end. On November 10, Premier Khrushchev made a speech demanding that his country's former allies vacate West Berlin—a small but suppurating sore surrounded by East German soil and troops, constantly targeted by agents of the KGB and Stasi. In Washington, President Eisenhower spurned the ultimatum but agreed to a foreign minister's conference in Geneva to settle the matter, convening in May.

Assuming no one hit "the button" first and turned the world into a graveyard of irradiated ash. Such things were out of Babin's hands—"above his pay grade," as Americans might say—but it still worried him, after he'd come so far, at such a cost, in his pursuit of sweet revenge for ancient wrongs.

―――――

FBI HEADQUARTERS: December 31, 1958

DECLAN O'HARA'S wife expected him at home by six o'clock, no later, for a New Year's Eve party one of their neighbors had been planning since Thanksgiving. He intended to be home on time this year and feigning bonhomie until the alcohol kicked in, imparting genuine good cheer.

Last June's "Red Monday" had essentially disarmed the Smith Act, but various cases still waited to be resolved in 1958. In January, the Ninth Circuit Court of Appeals reversed Judge Wiig's conviction of the "Hawaii Seven," then stalled until November before disposing of Harriet Sawyer's disciplinary action from the Bar Association, ruling that it "would be hard to find a more frivolous charge."

Between those two rulings, in February, North Carolina CPUSA leader Junius Scales was convicted a second time—the last Red in America to draw a prison term, not for espousing Party rhetoric, but for instructing his disciples in karate, deemed an "overt act" of violence against the U.S. government. The Fourth Circuit reviewed that case, as it had done in 1955, but this time, in October, it affirmed the verdict.

April's upset for the government came from the Eighth Circuit in April, reversing the convictions of five St. Louis defendants. Philadelphia's prosecutor beat appellate judges to the punch in May, dismissing indictments of five convicted Reds. One week later, in Cleveland, the Sixth Circuit liberated six imprisoned Reds. In August, the Second Circuit reversed Alex Trachtenberg's second conviction for publishing radical screeds. John Noto was the year's other big loser, his New York conviction upheld by the Second Circuit in December, the panel ruling, "Clearly this is not a prosecution of membership per se but of membership with knowledge and criminal intent."

Some win, some lose, O'Hara thought. As for himself, right now he simply wanted to get drunk.

CHAPTER 4

Four years since April 15 had become national Tax Day, shifted two months forward from the Ides of March where it had stood since 1918, but it still sneaked up on Devon Gantt and left him burning the midnight oil to finish his return in time. One more damned thing to fret about while he was Mob-watching under the Bureau's new Top Hoodlum Program.

One gangster who couldn't shy away from trouble if his life depended on it, Mickey Cohen, had turned up in Vegas recently, accompanied by Dallas lawyer Melvin Belli when he registered as a convicted felon with Clark County's sheriff. Gantt's brother, Colby, had provided him with CIA memos connecting Belli to Victor Velasquez, a Mexican attorney, once a fascist spokesman during World War Two, now chairman of the International Academy of Trial Lawyers. He'd also be defending Cohen in L.A. soon, on a charge of assaulting Federal Bureau of Narcotics agent Howard Chappell.

Back on Belli's Dallas turf—where he liked to say, "My fee alone is punishment enough for any crime"—a thug named Russell David Matthews, lifelong friend of Dallas County Sheriff Bill Decker, had been working at Havana's Hotel Deauville when the Castro revolution sent Fulgencio Batista packing at New Year's, and informers told the Bureau he was working with a Dallas small-timer, Jack Ruby, to get Tampa *mafioso* Santo Trafficante Jr. out of prison on the island. An FBN memo on Matthews claimed he'd been tight with Ruby's girlfriend, stripper "Candy Barr," when she caught fifteen years for peddling grass and Matthews did a couple for cocaine possession.

Funny how those Texans figured weed was so much worse than coke. Devon could never work that out, but at the moment he had more important things to do—like Mob-watching and serving up his pound of flesh to Uncle Sam before midnight tomorrow.

———

Nation of Islam Temple No. 7, Harlem: September 9, 1959

Malcolm X—or Malik el-Shabazz, as he preferred these days—commanded silence from his audience without saying a word, his raised hand from the podium enough to silence everyone. He scanned the crowd before him through his horn-rimmed glasses, eyes alighting for a moment on the upturned face of Payton Sawyer, known within the NOI as Philip X Samson. When the minister began to speak, he didn't seem to need his microphone.

"I have a letter here, brothers and sisters," he began, "sent from a Georgia cracker by the name of J. B. Stoner, calls himself 'Arch Leader' of the *Christian* Party and 'Imperial Wizard' of the Ku Klux *Christian* Knights. You know this boy's confused before you ever read a word since he's writing from Louisville and listing an Atlanta address."

That brought laughter from the audience, but Payton reckoned they wouldn't be laughing long. He'd seen a copy of the letter back in August, at the BOSS office, soon after it arrived.

"You'll never guess who 'Wizard' Stoner sent his letter to," Malcolm pressed on. "Of course, he marked it 'CONFI-DENTIAL AND TOP SECRET,' but you know, we have our ways."

More laughter now, but with a nervous edge to it.

"Old J. B. wrote this to 'the Honorable Stephen Kennedy,'" Malcolm revealed. "I wouldn't call him *honorable*, but he is commissioner of the New York City Police Department."

Laughter turning into growls.

"What does he say, here? Let me see." Malcolm flourished the paper in his hand, though Payton had no doubt he'd memorized it before stepping up on stage. "It opens with 'Dear Fellow Whiteman,' and its subject is Black Muslims. You and me, in other words."

Dead silence now, but thrumming with tension.

"What does he want from the commissioner? Well, let me tell you. 'I have a report from one of your Klansmen on the New York police force—"

Snarls interrupted him, but Malcolm didn't hesitate. "Oh, what? Does that *surprise* you? This Klan cop tells Wizard Stoner 'that the nigger Muslims are in rebellion against White law and order. He reports that those blacks have no respect for you honest White Christian policemen. Therefore, I'm offering you the support of the Christian Knights'."

"Oh no, he didn't!" someone in the audience called out.

"Oh yes, he did," Malcolm assured them. "All he wants from the NYPD is some basic hardware: 'I will expect you to supply my Klansmen with police pistols, so they won't have to carry their own. They will also require machine guns, riot guns, tear gas and big clubs. They will especially want some big sticks with iron inside the wood so they can crack hard nigger skulls."

The crowd was het up now, as Payton's old man might've said. Malcolm saw that and kept on going, stoking it. "The Wizard writes, 'You and I must join forces to stop the black Muslims now, or they will soon drive every White person out of New York City. The largest city in the world will then be an all nigger city of black supremacy where White people will not be allowed to live.' Remember, *he* said that, not *me*."

"Devils!" another man shouted.

"You ain't heard nothin' yet," said Malcolm, slipping into street talk for a moment. "This here *Wizard* is a Georgia *lawyer* if you can believe it. 'I insist on doing everything according to law,' he says."

Payton braced himself, fighting an urge to glance around him as Malcolm reached the part that worried him most. "This *Wizard* says, 'I think we need to put that evil *genius* Elijah Muhammad out of business in a legal way and not use the criminal methods that the communist FBI is using against him. I hear that the FBI is hiring nigger pimps to join up with the Muslims so they can spy on them. They also start arguments in meetings so as to *disrupt* them. They also try to turn niggers away from Islam by accusing Muhammad and other Muslim officials of stealing money because the FBI knows most niggers will believe these kind of false charges without any proof.'"

Some members of the audience were on their feet now, furious, some calling out, "No! No!"

"*Yes*, my brothers and sisters," Malcolm replied. "This sad old bigot is *exactly* right about the FBI and NYPD, too. They'll stop at *nothing* to destroy us, turning one against another. I've warned you before about these traitors and stool pigeons who will sell you out like Judas for a handful of small change. Be *vigilant* today."

The crowd was rumbling, but now a grin cracked Malcolm's face. "Before he signs off, Stoner warns the commissioner, 'In case you decided to keep our plans secret, remember that the secret might leak out.' And here I stand. Surprise! It's leaking, Mr. Georgia Lawyer, Mr. Honorable White Commissioner. You don't have any secrets from us anymore. We're on alert and ready for you, anytime you want to make your move!"

Applause broke out, together with some cheering. Payton smiled to beat the band, applauding, while he wondered how soon he could slip away and phone Inspector Flannery.

———

Foggy Bottom, Washington, D.C.: September 14, 1959

COLBY GANTT FIGURED the CIA's E Street headquarters had to be living on borrowed time. Construction at the Langley site had started up in May, after a fashion, and the president himself was set to lay the cornerstone and time capsule when they officially broke ground in November. A reporter had asked Allen Dulles what was in the box, and laughed obligingly when Dulles answered, "It's a secret."

Colby didn't know if he'd be stateside for the new plant's opening, the way the world was shaping up—or ripping at the seams. He wanted to be everywhere at once, fighting the fires, but hadn't worked out how to manage that.

In the Caribbean, Haiti's Papa Doc Duvalier had survived a May heart attack, but with evident neurological damage making him more unstable than ever. He'd locked up ex-*Tonton Macoute* chief Clément Barbot for questioning Duvalier's sanity, then survived a June air raid on his presidential palace by foreign mercenaries when the bombs didn't explode. In August, French Algerian émigré Henri d' Anton led a band of Haitian exiles and Cuban guerrillas against Papa Doc, but Duvalier's troops wiped them out in ten days.

The same couldn't be said in Cuba, where rebels led by the Castros and Che Guevara bested President Batista's troops at Santa Clara on New Year's Eve, then entered Havana the next day, prompting Batista's flight to the Dominican Republic. Meyer Lansky fled to the Bahamas and began negotiations for a new gambling empire. Fidel held his first press conference in the Havana Riviera's Copa Room, briefly closing the Mob-run casinos, jailing Santo Trafficante Jr. and Mike McLaney—who'd lost $7 million on the Hotel Nacional. In March, FBI agents captured fugitive Ed Browder in Miami, relieving him of a pistol and the phone number of lawyer Morris Ernst, a co-founder of the ACLU, confidante of Edgar Hoover, and partner of Frank Costello's attorney.

Browder admitted raising funds for Castro's guerrillas, while a federal grand jury indicted Roughhouse Rothman for smuggling stolen arms to Cuba for the other side. Still tight with Batista, before his arrest and indictment Rothman got the ex-*president* settled in a Miami Beach hotel he—Rothman—managed, the Biltmore Terrace. Back in '52, he'd run Havana's San Souci Casino with Trafficante, and four years later he'd been charged with illegally shipping slot machines to Cuba. Rothman walked on that, but his slots got the ax. Now, in addition to the stolen arms case, Browder stood accused of purchasing Italian weapons with a million-dollar slush fund established by Batista, Rafael Trujillo, Nicaragua's Luis Somoza, and temporarily exiled Argentinian president Juan Perón.

At the same time, Colby knew from secret government reports, Chicago-Dallas mobster Jack Ruby was bargaining to get *Don* Trafficante and former Tropicana manager Lewis McWillie out of prison, fronting for a U.S. firm on a Scandinavian arms deal, and finagling sale of some decrepit Jeeps to the Cuban Air Force. Fidel took a fling at capitalism in March, reopening Havana's casinos under new Minister of Games of Chance Frank Sturgis (né Fiorini)—a veteran of three U.S. military branches before he'd defected to the 26th July Movement in 1957, helping execute seventy-one Batista loyalists on San Juan Hill in January '59, amiably sharing mistress Marita Lorenz with Fidel—but wealthy tourists stayed away in droves and the joints closed again in early June, around the same time Sturgis offered his services to the CIA in Miami, bringing Marita along for the ride.

Plans were already afoot to oust Fidel, the first unofficial effort led by American Paul Hughes and sixty-five fellow mercenaries in late June, but Castro's National

Revolutionary Police Force bagged then all within two weeks. More promising, in Gantt's view, was a million-dollar bounty on "The Beard," offered to all comers by Lansky and Trafficante, hoping to recoup their losses with a counterrevolution. Meanwhile, NSA "Project SHAM-ROCK" was busily tapping all cable traffic between Cuba and the States, looking for places where the Agency could drive a lethal wedge.

In the heady post-takeover days, Castro had planned an invasion of Panama in April, shipping eighty-five guerrillas from Batabanó aboard the *Mayari Cuba*. An American merc led the force of two Panamanians and eighty-two Cubans; all quickly captured while the newspaper *La Estrella de Panama* detailed their clumsy failure. Some anonymous scribe under Fidel's wing blamed the effort on a "crisis in the Caribbean" sparked by right-wing tyrants like Somoza and Trujillo, but one of those involved was Joe Merola, an associate of Roughhouse Rothman and Pittsburgh *mafiosi* Gabriel and Sam Mannarino. As soon as the invasion flopped, Merola turned to counterfeiting Cuban pesos in a bid to undermine Castro's economy, encouraged by the CIA.

In war-torn Southeast Asia, U.S. Special Forces soldiers were "advising" the Royal Laotian Army, along with Hmong and Tao tribesmen, via "Operation Hotfoot." Since Laos was ostensibly a neutral land, the Green Berets commanded by Lieutenant Colonel Arthur "Bull" Simons wore generic uniforms. Supplies arrived from Air America, living up to its motto of "Anything, Anywhere, Anytime, Professionally." Against them stood 1,500 Pathet Lao troops, supplied by Group 559 from the People's Army of Vietnam, creators of the extensive Hồ Chí Minh trail spanning parts of four nations.

In Vietnam proper, Hô had declared a "People's War" to reunite his bisected homeland, overseen by Hanoi's Central Office of South Vietnam. By July, 4,000 Việt Minh guerrillas had infiltrated South Vietnam, claiming their first American casualties: "advisors" Major Dale Buis and Sergeant Chester Ovnand, slain at Biên Hòa. So far, the CIA had few contacts among the Việt Cộng, but President Diệm had closed two more critical newspapers and seemed to think the war was going well. Colby wasn't convinced of that, considering the murders of 1,200 village chiefs by Việt Cộng so far this year.

At home, sadistic hypocrite and double agent George White had taken time off from Operation MKULTRA to regale a Senate subcommittee with the perils of marijuana. Colby couldn't help smiling at that, imagining how the self-righteous pols would have responded if they'd known about White's wild experiments with LSD and kinky sex on camera.

With any luck, they'd never have a fucking clue.

———

LITTLE ITALY, Manhattan: September 26, 1959

THE GIORDANO BROTHERS, Dominic and Angelo, sat huddled in a corner booth of Biondi's Social Club on Mulberry Street. Facing each other across a narrow table marked by water rings and cigarette burns, they were far enough apart to demonstrate that both of them were "straight," but leaning forward to converse in muted tones.

"I'm tellin' ya," said Angelo, "they're killin' off the upper-level guys."

"Yeah?" Dom answered back. "So who in the fuck is *they*?"

"If I knew that..." Ange let it trail away, unfinished.

"You'd do what? Fight back against somebody who hasn't made a move on us?"

"Hey, by the time they make a move, it's too damned late."

"Okay, what have you got?"

"First there was Longie, now it's Little Augie."

Dom was nodding. "Seven months apart, though, and the first guy wasn't even one of our *amici*."

"Don't mean nothin' if we figure out who's doin' it."

Longie was—*had* been—one of the big Jews in the Syndicate, known by the nickname he'd acquired as a teenager when he topped six feet in height. Back in Prohibition, newspapers called him "the Al Capone of New Jersey," partnered with Willie Moretti until shooters executed Willie back in 1951. At the tag end of February, Zwillman's wife had found him hanging in their basement with an electrical cord around his neck. The cops called it a suicide, brought on by recent chest pains, an impending tax audit, and a subpoena from the goddamned McClellan Committee.

Okay, far as it went—but why had there been bruises on his wrists, like they were tied behind his back while someone strangled him, then strung him up to make it *look* like a suicide? That wasn't an accident, and Dom knew damned well that you couldn't bruise a corpse like that after the heart stopped pumping blood.

"And now, last night, it's Little Augie. Nobody can claim he did it to hisself."

Dom had to nod at that. Tony Carfano, better known as Little Augie Pisano, had been shot last night with Janice

Drake, a former Miss New Jersey and the wife of some comedian, who'd been called in to testify about the hits on Albert Anastasia and Nat Nelson, a big wheel in Gotham's garment industry. Carfano, a *caporegime* in the Costello family, had been out to dinner in Midtown the night he died, with Genovese family *capo* "Tony Bender" Strollo. After that, he'd hooked up with the Drake babe some-where—thirty-odd years younger than Carfano—and they'd hung out for a while. Reports differed on whether Augie had been driving her back home to Queens or they were heading off to a Miami flight out of La Guardia. Whatever, they'd been found together, both shot from behind slumped in the front seat of Carfano's Cadillac, parked on a residential street in Jackson Heights. Cops said one shooter, maybe two had done the deed from the backseat.

"So, I'll ask ya again," Dom said. "Who done all this?"

"I'm guessing it was *Don* Vito," Ange said, referring to that fucker Genovese who'd put the hit on Anastasia after Vince Gigante bungled an attempt on Frank Costello five months earlier.

"I grant you, Augie disrespected Vito after all that mess a couple years ago, and he's been wanting to take over Longie's territory in New Jersey. But to start another war when he's already facing that narcotics beef—"

"Or maybe it was Meyer, eh? He ain't been happy, Augie movin' in on his Florida turf, and if he heard those rumors Longie was about to rat and save himself..."

"No 'if' about it," Dom replied. "*We* heard that talk, so Meyer must've. And he's snugglin' up to Genovese lately, all cozy-like."

"You see? What are we gonna do about it, Dom?"

"Nothin', that's what. I'll talk to Pop about it in the

morning, but you keep your lips zipped, *fratellino*. If we ain't in line for any shit on this, don't blab and bring it down on us."

"And if we are?"

Dom quaffed his beer and answered back, "The old man will know what to do."

———

THE LUBYANKA BUILDING: September 27, 1959

LEONID BABIN WOULD NEVER HAVE GUESSED that Premier Khrushchev might precipitate a thaw of sorts in the Cold War, but now he wondered if he'd been mistaken. Three years earlier, addressing Western ambassadors at the Polish embassy in Moscow, Khrushchev had informed them, "We will bury you!" Then came last year's second Berlin crisis, but now Babin wondered if the course of history was slowly changing.

During May, the Geneva Conference of Foreign Ministers convened in search of a solution for Berlin, but nothing much had been accomplished by the time that meeting was adjourned in early August. Meanwhile, in July, Moscow and Washington had carried out a cultural exchange program of sorts, each erecting a model home on the other's soil, displaying the relative state of abundance produced under socialism and capitalism. On July 24, at the American National Exhibition in Sokolniki Park, Khrushchev and Vice President Nixon had faced off in the now famous "kitchen debate," sparring over the respective triumphs of their homelands. Television cameras caught it all, down to the last vigorous handshake, meant to air simultaneously in both nations, but America's three major networks jumped the gun by two days, prompting Khrushchev to accuse the *amerikantsy* of willful deception.

Finally, early this month, the UN had created a Ten-Nation Committee on Disarmament including diplomats from the U.S. and USSR, Britain, Canada, France, Bulgaria, Czechoslovakia, Poland, and Romania. That was on Khrushchev's mind, of course, as he embarked on an extended visit to America six days later. Khrushchev had landed in Washington, amid much pomp and circumstance, then flew off to Los Angeles, raging over anti-communist remarks from the head of Twentieth Century Fox and his exclusion from Disneyland for "security concerns." From there, it was back east to Camp David for two days of meetings with President Eisenhower, closing with a joint communiqué claiming both leaders "agreed that these discussions have been useful in clarifying each other's position on a number of subjects," and that they hoped "their exchanges of views will contribute to a better understanding of the motives and position of each, and thus to the achievement of a just and lasting peace."

Perhaps, but Babin wouldn't bet his dacha on it. At the moment, he was more concerned with reports of Stefan in New Jersey, broken arm all healed and fully functional, as he proceeded through eighth grade. By now, he would have learned and understood his mission in America—no small thing for a thirteen-year-old boy—and had apparently accepted it.

The boy's teen years still lay ahead of him, assuming Babin, just turned seventy, survived that long, but he was not in a position to reach out and micromanage details of events occurring more than 7,000 miles away, in the United States.

Be patient, Babin thought. *Be patient and hang on.*

———

BROOKLYN CRIMINAL COURT: September 30, 1959

ANOTHER DAY, another juvenile arraignment on murder charges. This time, David Jordan and Fiona O'Hara were teamed to defend three members of the Bishops, an all-Negro gang from the Bedford-Stuyvesant ghetto, occupied since 1936 by residents seeking a break from overcrowded Harlem. What they'd found, instead, were more gangs, more crime, and the same white cops they'd come to loathe.

The case at hand was Gotham's eleventh gang-related killing for the year so far, but hardly the most infamous. That would've been the August stabbing of two youths with no known gang affiliations by a Puerto Rican clique, the Vampires, who mistook them for Irish punks from the rival Norsemen. Two Vampires, nicknamed "Cape Man" and "Umbrella Man"—the latter for his choice of weapon —killed both innocents at an unnamed Hell's Kitchen park and now were likely on their way to death row at Sing Sing.

Jordan and Fee's case had been in the making since July, when a group of Bishops traveled five miles from Bed-Stuy down to Flatbush, searching for the white kid from Erasmus Hall High School who'd called one member of their gang a "black nigger." Instead, they'd picked a fight with other Negroes and eight of the Bishops went to jail for packing a zip gun, knives, and four Molotov cocktails.

That snafu must've pissed off the Bishops. Last night, when victim Roosevelt Bennett allegedly rolled up on some of them and made a homosexual suggestion, they had beaten him and left him bleeding out from switchblade wounds. That didn't measure up to the Hell's Kitchen double slaying, but Dave hoped like hell he wouldn't have to drag the dead boy's name through too much shit to win his clients lighter sentences.

Outside of court, he had been spending more time with Fiona, which was *very* good, and still surprising when he realized that she could stand the sight of him, much less bear touching him and all the rest of it. It felt like heaven to him when they were together; then his mind would start reminding Dave that all good things come to an end, and quicker for the very best of times.

"A penny for them," Fee whispered, meaning for Jordan's thoughts.

"You wouldn't get your money's worth," he said, a split second before the bailiff shouted to the court at large, "All rise!"

———

FBI Headquarters: October 23, 1959

CHIEF HOOVER HAD a new bee in his bonnet, and this time the culprit was TV, specifically the ABC network. He had been fuming since April, when Westinghouse Desilu Playhouse aired a two-part drama on the old Capone gang, starring longtime Hollywood star Robert Stack as former Prohibition agent Eliot Ness.

Where to begin with why Speed hated it so passionately? Aloysius Gantt could count the ways.

First, there was Ness himself, a headline hog on par with Hoover who'd been living off an unearned reputation as "the man who got Capone" since 1931, most recently from *The Untouchables,* an alleged nonfiction bestseller, coauthored with newsman Oscar Fraley. Granted, Ness had gone to his reward after a heart attack in May of '57, but then Desilu had come along and started making gold out of his memory.

The Desilu, of course, was short for *Desi* Arnaz and wife *Lu*cille Ball, celebrities whom Speed still viewed as Reds who got away despite the best efforts of HUAC. ABC picked up the pilot for their Ness series, and *The Untouchables* had aired its first episode in October. One week later, in "Ma Barker and Her Boys," Ness got the credit for annihilating the bank-robbing Barker gang in Florida—a case Ness had no part in since he'd been an alcohol tax agent in the "moonshine mountains" of Ohio and Kentucky when it all went down.

Predictably, Hoover saw red over that farce, and in more ways than one. He couldn't sue, but nothin on God's Earth would stop him talking to the press, claiming the Bureau's rightful due and slinging mud at Desilu in the process.

Another offering from Hollywood—*The FBI Story*, from Whitehead's book of the same title, might placate him a bit, but Gantt knew Speed never forgot a slight, much less forgiving one.

Gantt and his wife had seen *The FBI Story* on its opening

night in Washington, and while he liked James Stewart as fictional agent Chip Hardesty, married to comely Vera Myles, most of the film was slanted pseudohistory, some of it wholly fictional. Gantt nearly laughed aloud at the scene where Hardesty busted a truckload of hooded Klansmen for raiding a newspaper office and shook his head at writer Richard Breen's perpetuation of the lie that G-men never carried guns till 1934. After their arsenal was legalized, Baby Face Nelson killed Chip's partner, Larry Crandall (standing in for Carter Baum), and then the "public enemies" began to fall like dominoes. "One of the last to go," as narrated by Stewart, was Machine Gun Kelly, shouting those now famous words he'd never said: "Don't shoot, G-men!"

Ridiculous, Gantt thought. You only had to open Whitehead's book—itself more Bureau propaganda than pure history—to know that Kelly was arrested months *before* the deaths of John Dillinger, Nelson, and Pretty Boy Floyd.

From the 1930s, the movie carried viewers through World War II, Nazi spies and the Special Intelligence Service—Stewart chasing Axis agents through the jungle —then back to New York, where postwar inflation turned a Russian spy's hollowed-out nickel into the "fifty-cent clue." The movie ended with Stewart addressing fellow agents, leaving headquarters to meet his family, including a grandchild wearing an old hat that played "Yankee Doodle." As they drove into the sunset, Stewart said, "I guess I'll never understand how one little family can collect so much junk."

That summed it up for Gantt, and while the movie had been entertaining, most of it remained well outside shouting distance from objective fact. And with each passing year, he recognized, more flattering mythology was heaped on top of old, trying to bury the truth.

―――――

HARLEM: November 29, 1959

SOME MORNINGS, when he woke from fitful sleep, Ike Sawyer could've sworn he saw his life flashing before his eyes: the Bureau of Investigation, then the FBN, losing his first son as a toddler, and his wife three years ago.

He still had three children, of course. Payton was pushing thirty now, and coming up on nine years with NYPD. Keisha was twenty-six and seriously doubting husband Eulis's fidelity, though so far she'd done nothing but complain about it to her old man when they had some private time together. Fred, the football star, would soon be twenty-one and graduating from UCLA next spring unless he hung around to try graduate school. There'd be no scholarship for that unless he lucked into an academic prize Ike hadn't heard of yet, but Fred was gambling on an offer from the pros, maybe the L.A. Rams to keep him near the beaches between games,

Ike, for his part, spent most of his time in Dixie, albeit vicariously, through TV and newspaper reports of the accelerating civil rights movement and brutal white resistance.

As usual, the worst crimes were reported out of darkest Mississippi, starting with the year's only acknowledged lynching. Accused of raping a pregnant white woman whose car had broken down, Mack Charles Parker denied it, and rumors circulating around Poplarville suggested a possible Groveland-style frame-up. Police had no conclusive evidence, but that couldn't dissuade the mob that took Parker from jail, three days before his scheduled trial, beating and shooting him before they dumped his weighted corpse into the Pearl River. FBI agents identified eight lynchers, including an ex-sheriff's deputy and a self-ordained preacher, but Judge Sebe Dale Sr.—a White Citizens' Council member —blocked indictments by telling grand jurors to "have the backbone to stand against any tyranny," adding, "You are now engaged in battle for our laws and courts, for the preservation of our freedom and our way of life."

Two weeks later, in Clarksdale, white terrorists attacked the home of septuagenarian Jonas Causey, wounding his wife before Causey repelled them with gunfire, injuring two assailants. Police turned out that time, all right—to riddle Causey with bullets for fending off demented thugs in self-defense.

In mid-August, at Centreville, unknown gunmen killed "uppity" black businessman Sam O'Quinn, a fifty-something father of eleven, only days after he joined the NAACP.

October was the worst month yet for the Magnolia State. On the twelfth, back at Clarksdale, a motorist found Booker Mixon's naked corpse beside a rural road, torn up so badly that police guessed he'd been dragged behind a car. Two weeks later, Neshoba County police officer Lawrence Rainey shot Luther Jackson in cold blood for sitting in a parked car, chatting with his girlfriend on a street in Philadelphia. Last up, at month's end, fifteen-year-old William Prather was slain by eight white punks in Corinth. Prosecutors called it a "Halloween prank," inditing one of the eight for manslaughter and soft-pedaling the case.

North Carolina had contributed one murder to the butcher's bill: farmer Roger Williams shot one of his field hands in the back, then passed it off as "horseplay," claiming victim William Person was "one of my best friends." Oddly, Williams pled guilty to manslaughter, receiving a prison sentence—which Judge William Bickett then suspended, as long as Williams promised to "remain of good behavior and law-abiding."

More names went into Ike's notebook.

In Little Rock, on Labor Day, bombs rocked the mayor's and school board's offices, together with a car belonging to the city's fire chief. Since the targets were white, Little Rock's Chamber of Commerce had offered a $25,000 reward, and G-men entered the case when state attorney general Bruce Bennett blamed the incidents on communists. While that charade went on, local cops learned the bombings were planned at a Klan meeting by roofing contractor E. A. Lauderdale—leader of the "respectable" Capital Citizens' Council—and carried out by "a confidential squad": carpenter Samuel Beavers, used-car salesman John Coggins, with truckers Jesse Perry and J. D. Sims. Sims pled guilty and turned state's evidence against his master and three cohorts, all sentenced to prison and fined $500 each, remaining free while it was on appeal.

Ike jotted down the latest names and asked himself, *Where will I find the time?*

———

Birmingham FBI Field Office: November 24, 1959

NOLAN O'HARA COULD'VE TOLD his SAC or anyone at Bureau headquarters that things were getting worse, not better, in the South. They likely wouldn't hear him, though, preoccupied as they all were with tracking Martin Luther King. Nolan had been relieved in February, when King and his wife departed for a month-long trip to India, home of the late Mahatma Gandhi, getting them away from Alabama for a while.

That didn't help another Negro minister, Charles Billups—a Medal of Honor winner and pastor of Birmingham's New Pilgrim Baptist Church—who'd been kidnapped by Klansmen in April, whipped with chains before they branded "KKK" on his stomach. Governor Patterson was too busy to investigate, tied up expelling sit-in demonstrators from the state university and defending his state's rancid record of voting discrimination. On the side, from what Nolan had heard, Patterson also had his hands full with the CIA's schemes, loaning out Alabama Air National Guardsmen to train pilots for an Agency bid to depose Fidel Castro.

Sixteen miles to the southwest, in Bessemer, Negro suffrage activist Asbury Howard had been convicted in January of violating 'Bama's law against publishing "intemperate matter tending to provoke a breach of the peace or any matter prejudicial to good morals." The item in question: a cartoon from the *Kansas City Call,* a Negro paper, showing a black man in handcuffs, dangling a tag that said, "You can't enter here. You can't ride here. You can't work here. You can't play here. You can't study here. You can't eat here. You can't drink here. You can't walk here. You can't worship here." Its caption read "These

Hands Can Still Pray," but Asbury added another—"Vote Today for a Better Tomorrow"—when he hired a poster-maker to enlarge it. A white customer saw the work in progress, asked who'd ordered it, and passed that information on to Bessemer's police. Howard soon had handcuffs of his own, as did the printer whom he'd hired.

At trial, the prosecutor told Howard's judge, "It is my opinion that showing a man in chains is prejudicial to good order." The judge agreed, fined Howard and gave him six months on a prison road gang. Leaving court to file his appeal, Howard was mobbed and badly beaten by a gang of forty white men. Fifteen cops stood idly by, then busted Howard's son for trying to defend his father.

Prejudicial to good order? Nolan thought. *You all can kiss my ass.*

Closer to home, Carl and Alexina Baldwin were fighting to integrate Birmingham's Terminal Station. Bull Connor's cops had jailed them for entering the depot's white waiting room in 1956, prompting a 1957 lawsuit which Alabama-born federal judge Seybourn Lynne had dismissed. The Baldwins appealed, and it came back to Lynne only yesterday, tossed out a second time.

Next door, Mississippi simmered under its dark cloud of murder and hatred. Negro physician Gilbert Mason Sr. led a "wade-in" at Biloxi's beach in May, threatened with arrest if protesters returned, on the grounds that "only the public can use the beach." In June, Dr. Felix Dunn asked the Harrison County Board of Supervisors, "What laws, if any, prohibit the use of the beach facilities by Negro citizens?" The board replied that white property owners controlled the beach and ocean stretching out 500 yards from shore. An October petition demanded "unrestrained use of the beach, and when officials countered with the offer of a segregated stretch of sand, Mason insisted on access to "every damn inch of it." Backstage, the State Sovereignty Commission helped out, pressuring employers to fire petition signers, while Harrison County's sheriff stalked Dunn and Mason, reporting their every move.

From his school days, Nolan recalled the words of Thomas Jefferson: "I tremble for my country when I reflect that God is just." Of course, America's third president and author of its Declaration of Independence had owned slaves till the day he died, leaving his widow to sell them and pay off her late husband's debts. In life, Jefferson had also fathered several children with slave concubine Sally Hemmings, freeing two of their sons in his will.

Nothing new under the sun, he thought. *And isn't that a goddamned shame.*

———

FBI HEADQUARTERS: December 17, 1959

MARK TWAIN ONCE WROTE, "Truth is stranger than fiction, but it is because Fiction is obliged to stick to possibilities; Truth isn't." Scanning a page-three story in the *Post* before he started wading through his daily paperwork, Declan O'Hara could agree with that, in spades.

In mid-November, Roger Touhy had finally been released from prison after serving more than a quarter-century for a kidnapping that never happened, plus a prison break that did. The judge who'd set him free at last blamed perjury and prosecutorial misconduct for Touhy's wrongful conviction, stage managed by Melvin Purvis. Not that it mattered much. Last night, while lounging on his sister's porch in Chicago, Touhy and ex-detective Walter Miller had been struck with drive-by shotgun fire. Miller was likely to survive, but Touhy died soon after reaching St. Anne's Hospital, telling the cops, "I've been expecting it. The bastards never forget."

Another casualty from bygone days was Bartley Crum, hounded by G-men for a dozen years because he dared to represent members of the "Hollywood Ten" and others called before HUAC. It ultimately proved too much for him, and Crum had killed himself with secobarbital and whisky on December 9. Belatedly, ex-President Truman had called HUAC "the most un-American thing in the country today."

And speaking of un-American things, the Attorney General's list of subversive organizations had ballooned to include seventy-three groups, some of them disbanded in the 1930s and '40s. The Abraham Lincoln Brigade had gone belly-up in 1938, and the Knights of the White Camellia one year later. The Silver Shirt Legion, defunct since 1941, had been omitted from 1948's list, but now made a comeback, as if it still existed. Justice finally listed the Ku Klux Klan, named as if it were a single unit, ignoring more than a dozen factions thriving in Dixie today.

Longtime McCarthy target John Service had regained his security clearance, but Undersecretary of State for Administration Loy Henderson termed his involvement in the *Amerasia* case "reprehensible," effectively cutting him off from advancement. Rather than risk confirmation problems in the Senate, State sent Service off to head its consulate in Liverpool, "but without the associated title or pay grade."

Screwed again.

In the Senate, Estes Kefauver announced he wouldn't mount another presidential race, thereby initiating his slow fade from public consciousness. The McClellan Committee began investigating the Mafia in February, then switched gears in September for six days of hearings on the United Auto Workers. Finding no malfeasance there, the embarrassed panel dissolved, counsel Robert Kennedy resigning to lead his brother Jack's White House campaign.

With crime in mind, O'Hara scanned the Bureau's growing file on Jack Ruby, né Rubenstein. Spurned by the Kefauver Committee back in 1950, Ruby had approached the Bureau in March, offering to serve as a criminal informant. Initial interviews revealed nothing worthwhile, but Jack had spent $500 on miniature recording equipment as if he planned to go ahead regardless. May found Ruby in Cuba, passing coded notes to gambler Lewis McWillie in prison but failing to record their chitchat. By July, Dallas SAC Curtis Lynum had recommended cutting Ruby loose, but Jack remained on the paid squealer list until early November, delivering squat.

Declan wondered what that was all about but finally dismissed it. Lying down with dogs encouraged fleabites, and he hoped the FBI had seen the last of Ruby for a good, long time.

————

Little Italy, Manhattan: December 19, 1959

THE GOVERNMENT WAS CRACKING DOWN, and the best Greg

Jordan could do for his family was watch and wait, keeping his fingers crossed that they'd be overlooked, passed by. His brother Carlo and Greg's nephews had escaped from Apalachin last November, unidentified in the confusion, but he didn't know how far dumb luck would carry them.

In April, jurors had convicted Vito Genovese and fifteen underlings of conspiracy to import heroin, despite suspicions that key witness Nelson Cantellops had lied his ass off under oath. Defendant Salvatore Santoro drew the harshest sentence—twenty years—while Vito got fifteen and the others were locked up for shorter terms. Greg knew what most observers didn't: Vito's downfall had been orchestrated by Meyer Lansky, Frank Costello, Charlie Luciano, Carlo Gambino, and Vito's own *caporegime,* Tony Strollo.

A month later, two weeks before a heart attack killed Joe Barbara; twenty-three Apalachin delegates were indicted on charges of perjury and conspiracy to obstruct justice. Their trial began in late October, ending with twenty convicted yesterday, drawing prison terms ranging from three to five years, with thirteen fined $10,000 each.

That case was on appeal, while the McClellan Committee kept unearthing new Teamsters scandals. Anthony Provenzano refused to answer any questions in July, concerning bribery of Hudson County Assistant D.A. Michael Communale, but Communale admitted taking $14,000 as a "retainer," losing his job, and a Jersey grand jury indicted Tony Pro. In September, the IBT's Board of Monitors urged Hoffa to fire Provenzano, along with local union bosses Joey Glimco in Chicago and Harold Gross in Miami. Jimmy refused, and Provenzano won reelection as Local 560's leader by a 20-to-1 margin.

The year's other big news had been the Cuban revolution and a budding plot to overturn it, while Meyer Lansky looked to the Bahamas as a future gambling haven and considered building carpet joints in Britain if the gaming laws could be finessed.

Jordan was doing everything he could to keep the Giordano family away from those potential minefields, but it would be Carlo's call when all was said and done. Greg only hoped greed and ambition wouldn't land them all in prison. He was sixty-three, his brother five years older, and he doubted whether either one of them would come out of the joint alive.

CHAPTER 5

Aloysius Gantt had to play early bird around the office these days, never mind that he was staring down the barrel of his sixty-fourth birthday. Clyde Tolson, who had only planned to stick around a year or so when he'd joined up in 1928, was still hanging around as No. 2, the closest friend that Edgar Hoover had—and likely more than friends in Gantt's opinion. Coming up behind Clyde now were the upstarts: William Sullivan and Deke Deloach, signed up in 1941 and '42, respectively.

One way to get around them, Gantt hoped, was to find the next new menace coming down the pike. It should be something radical and ominous enough to stir up the Director's knee-jerk anticommunism, vulnerable to the Bureau's extralegal methods polished to an art form over half a century.

The "New Left" seemed to fit Gantt's need precisely.

Christened in an open letter to young would-be radicals from sociologist Charles Wright Mills, the movement —if it ever got that far—despised what it called "The Establishment," although its mostly white members were generally kids of the middle class or wealthy parents, rebelling against government and family in equal parts. This year, more than one-third of all the U.S. population was below age eighteen, and how was *that* for a potential "army" of the future, bent on tearing down all that their forebears had created in the name of "peace" and "love"?

Of course, a new crusade required a target, and Gantt had one standing by.

The leftist Student League for Industrial Democracy had been around since 1935, infesting campuses nationwide since '47, when Frank Wallick planted its flag at Ohio's Antioch College. That year it had branched out to Harvard, Cornell, and a host of other campuses. McCarthyism slowed things down a bit but also gave the SLID an aura of dangerous allure. By 1960, headquarters was situated in Ann Arbor, at the University of Michigan, and it was there, symbolically on New Year's Day, that the group adopted a new name: Students for a Democratic Society.

That said it all, casting the new outfit as Chief Hoover's worst nightmare. Its new leader was professional student Robert Alan Haber, still chasing a simple bachelor's degree after six years and counting, but with solid "Old Left" credentials. His father, an economist, had been a professor and dean at Ann Arbor, as well as a noisy New Deal supporter in the 1930s, no enemy of Reds by any means.

It was perfect, Gantt thought. He simply had to wrap the package, decorate it with a crimson bow—some kind of protest demonstration would be nice—and place it with all due respect on Edgar Hoover's desk. The Chief would run with it from there, while Gantt made goddamned sure he got full credit for the plan.

Let Clyde and Deke top that, he thought, and smiled.

———

FBI HEADQUARTERS: *May 15, 1960*

"I UNDERSTAND THAT SIR," Declan O'Hara said, clenching his telephone receiver, trying not to let his mounting anger get the better of him. "But you understand we still need *proof* it was a bomb. If some of our technicians could review the evidence—"

The caller's voice droned on in Declan's ear until he'd had enough. He interrupted, none too gently, "You *do* understand, I take it, that the Bureau has authority to intervene under the Federal Aviation Act of 1958. Yes, sir. And I *am* sending our technicians to assist your people in examining the wreckage. No, sir, they'll be there later today. We need to get this moving, right? That's right. And thanks *so much* for your cooperation."

Cradling the receiver, Declan muttered, "Asshole," then relaxed and smiled.

There'd been no federal laws on aircraft sabotage in 1955 when Jack Graham had bombed United Airlines Flight 629 to kill his mother and collect her life insurance. Even then, Congress had dragged its feet, passing a law in August 1958 that created the Federal Aviation Agency, tasked with regulating all aspects of civil aviation. Under its auspices, the Civil Aeronautics Board—created as a bureaucratic pygmy back in 1939, later moved into spacious new headquarters on Dupont Circle—was the FAA's arm for looking into crashes, trying to determine whether they'd been accidental or deliberate.

And in the process, like all bureaus everywhere, the CAB didn't always play well with others.

Now, the FBI would be joining the investigation of National Airlines Flight 2511, lost in January when it had exploded in midair, en route from New York City to Miami. Thirty-four persons were killed when the Douglas DC-6 became a tumbling fireball, notably including retired U.S. Navy Vice Admiral Edward McDonnell, a Medal of Honor winner and veteran of both World Wars. Officials from the president on down demanded answers, and they wanted them right fucking now.

From what O'Hara knew so far, the flight could've been cursed. The scheduled Boeing 707 turned up with a cracked cockpit windshield, so National split its 105 scheduled passengers between two reserve propliner aircraft. Seventy-six reached Florida safely, aboard a Lockheed L-188 Electra, while the other twenty-nine, plus five crewmembers, boarded a Douglas DC-6B and died aloft over North Carolina at 2:33 a.m. Corpses and wreckage covered some twenty acres of farmland, marsh, and pine forests, with one body found along the Cape Fear River, sixteen miles from the primary crash site.

CAB investigators recovered most of the wreckage, except for a jagged triangular piece still missing from above and forward of the right wing, tagged as the epicenter of the explosion. Toss in the twice-autopsied corpse of Gotham lawyer Julian Frank—the Cape Fear body—bearing wounds a coroner deemed inconsistent with those found on "normal" air crash victims, plus unsettling rumors of embezzlement back home, and you were left with a bona fide riddle.

Why, for instance, was residue including sodium carbonate, sodium nitrate, and mixtures of sodium-sulfur compounds found in the plane's starboard air vents and elsewhere? Why were some of the dead found wearing life jackets? Why was Frank's body riddled with fragments of wire, brass, and weird miscellany including a onetime hat ornament? Why did four of his severed fingers go down with the plane, when he'd been ejected miles away? And why did pathologists note multiple blackened patches on his corpse, closely resembling point-blank gunshot residue?

O'Hara didn't have a clue, but if the Bureau could determine what happened and why it would reap accolades for Edgar Hoover and his G-men. CAB techs were leaning toward a dynamite explosion, but they hadn't ruled out metal fatigue, a defective propeller blade, lightning, combustion of fuel vapor, or even some unspecified "foreign object" striking the plane and piercing its cabin.

In short, they didn't know squat, and if the Bureau could crack it, *voila*, priceless headlines.

Amidst that ongoing investigation and so many others, came the February news of Melvin Purvis dying at his home in South Carolina, shot in the head with the pistol fellow G-men gave him as a retirement gift in 1935. First responders called it suicide, but someone higher up switched that to accidental death, suffered while trying to extract a jammed tracer round from the Colt .45.

Was that even possible? Declan didn't know and didn't care. He'd chalk it up to karma from the bad old days.

HUAC was also on the skids, it seemed, though far from dead. When Francis Walters brought its roadshow to

San Francisco in May, hundreds of students from UC Berkeley, Stanford, and other nearby colleges turned out to demonstrate at City Hall, prompting police to blast them with fire hoses, club the ones still standing, and drag them down the marble steps. The committee produced a film of the event, titled *Operation Abolition,* while the ACLU weighed in with another, *Operation Correction*, listing the first film's falsehoods.

Chief Hoover still loved HUAC—no shock there—and in March he'd launched a COINTELPRO spin-off labeled COMINFIL, for "*com*munist *infil*tration." To rate a dossier, groups merely had to be "in contact" with some other outfit named on the Attorney General's Subversive List. First up for augmented investigation: the NAACP and the Southern Christian Leadership Conference.

In his spare time, Hoover kept a close eye on the Kennedys, aware that Jack would run for president this year, while brother Bobby craved a new director for the FBI after their run-ins during the McClellan hearings. Luckily, Hoover had a file on JFK's wartime affair with Inga Arvad, a Danish citizen who'd been among Hitler's special guests at the 1936 Summer Olympics before she'd moved on to write screenplays for Metro-Goldwyn-Mayer and marry cowboy actor Tim McCoy, typically cast as a frontier lawman in films like *Arizona Gang Busters* and *Ghost Town Law*.

Better still, Jack had eloped with Palm Beach socialite Durie Malcolm after a booze party in 1947, saying, "I do" before a justice of the peace. Papa Joe had quashed that sometime before Jack married again, in September 1953, to Wall Street heiress Jacqueline Bouvier. Since good Catholics couldn't divorce, Joe Sr. had persuaded Boston's Cardinal Richard Cushing to grant an annulment, declaring the childless marriage "invalid." Lawyer friend Clark Clifford leaned on Malcolm, procuring an affidavit denying the marriage and claiming she wouldn't marry JFK "for all the tea in China." When word of the union surfaced in '57, journalist Ben Bradlee—once a Harvard classmate of Jack's, now a Washington neighbor—worked overtime to debunk the "rumors."

Now, Edgar Hoover had it all on file, safe under lock and key. If Kennedy should be elected in November, Declan had a hunch that the Director would be left in charge of his domain.

———

BROOKLYN CRIMINAL COURT: *September 25, 1960*

DAVE JORDAN HAD GROWN TIRED of teenage murder cases, but he couldn't seem to shake them. Today's arraignment would inevitably lead to a trial for his five clients, members of the Marcy Chaplains gang. Two days ago, they had "allegedly" attacked a member of the rival Buccaneers at Marcy Playground—from which the Chaplains took their name—and bludgeoned him to death with baseball bats.

More than the crime itself, which struck Jordan as more or less routine, Dave missed going to court with Fee O'Hara. She was tied up with another gang-related murder from Williamsburg, trial just beginning for a member of the Young Lords who had knifed one of the hostile Young Burners, "peewee" branch of the older and more ferocious Hellburners.

How did they come up with these names? Was

anything behind it, other than an urge to shock and mortify so-called polite society?

When not defending juvey criminals, Dave and Fiona —more or less officially his lover now, and who on Earth could ever have predicted *that*?—kept busy with the daily legal work surrounding broken families and chronic unemployment, truancy and rent abatement. Gotham presently hosted 129,000 SRO units—single-room occupancy blocks housing lone adults or couples, while extended-stay residency hotels gave shelter to hard-up families. The SRO units typically lacked private kitchen or bathroom facilities but left occupants vulnerable to predatory landlords and absentee owners. Rent control, first managed by the feds, then passed to state authorities in 1950, affected some 2.1 million Gotham apartments, but could be stripped away if tenants breached their legal qualifications. Landlords helped that process along by shirking repairs, ignoring pest control, and terminating heat during the city's frigid winters.

Always something, and despite his daily helping of frustration, Jordan liked the feeling that he might be helping somebody, somehow, through Legal Aid. As for having Fiona in his life...well, what could be better than that?

But did he count on that lasting long-term? No frig-ging way.

———

THE LUBYANKA BUILDING: October 10, 1960

JUST WHEN LEONID BABIN thought the USSR might have

reached some measure of accommodation with the West, delaying open confrontation while his bastard son Stefan grew tall and strong with his adoptive parents in America, another problem reared its ugly head.

Initial cautious optimism after Premier Khrushchev's visit to the States last year had spawned a Ten-Nation Committee on Disarmament in March, convened in Geneva, but the effort started to disintegrate in May, when a Soviet S-75 Dvina ground-to-air missile brought down a U-2 spy plane over Aramil, in Sverdlovsk Oblast. Washington denied any knowledge of high-altitude espionage, whereupon the Warsaw Pact's delegates left Switzerland, and by June there was no more Ten Nation Committee.

Perhaps coincidentally, June had also witnessed a rift between Moscow and China's Mao Zedong, brewing since April when a Chinese Communist newspaper accused Khrushchev's regime of "revisionism." Mao favored Stalinesque belligerence toward capitalist nations and eschewed Khrushchev's approach to peaceful coexistence with the West. Khrushchev replied by calling Mao "a nationalist, an adventurist, and a deviationist," facetiously adding, "If we could promise the people nothing except revolution, they would scratch their heads and say, 'Isn't it better to have good goulash?' " By July, Moscow had recalled thousands of Soviet advisors from China, terminating economic and military aid.

Adding insult to injury this month, while Beijing celebrated the tenth anniversary of the People's Republic, Khrushchev sent KGB agent and TASS correspondent Aleksandr Alekseyev to Havana, lavishing the Castro brothers and Che Guevara with vows of Soviet friendship in the face of harsh American hostility.

Today, all that seemed worlds away from Babin—

3,600 miles from Beijing, nearly 6,000 miles from Cuba—and his private focus still remained on Trenton, New Jersey's capital and home of his fourteen-year-old avatar, one year away from high school now, training and studying each day to take his place within the FBI that Babin hated above all else, hoping to bring it down.

If Babin could survive to see that, he would be a lucky man indeed.

If not, at least he'd know that he had done his level best.

———

Birmingham, Alabama: October 14, 1960

"Are these people insane?" Keely O'Hara asked her husband, Nolan. "I mean, seriously?"

It was Friday night, Nolan and Keely eating pot roast with their daughter Erin, now thirteen years old. Their son, Ryan, four years older, had gone off with friends to watch an intramural football game at Woodlawn High School, where he was on track to graduate in June.

"Yes, Mom," Erin chimed in. "They're *seriously* crazy. All they talk about is 'nigger' this and 'nigger' that."

"We don't use that word in this house," Nolan reminded her. "And *never* tell your friends what we discuss here, right? Under no circumstances known to man."

"Or woman," Keely added.

Erin nodded, not quite blushing, but Nolan knew what she meant and couldn't argue with the view that many whites in Birmingham seemed to be clinically insane, at least where racial matters were concerned.

Of course, he could say that about the South at large, from memos that had crossed his desk so far this year.

At February's end, leaders of several Klan factions packed Atlanta's Henry Grady Hotel to form a "National Grand Council." In May, a second Klan convention in Atlanta had officially united nine former competitors from eight southern states. Left out of that mix was a Louisiana upstart Klan, the fast-growing Original Knights, and Robert Shelton's Alabama Knights, formed when Governor Patterson's good friend squabbled with Wizard Eldon Edwards, got his walking papers from the U.S. Klans, and was replaced by his old predecessor, Alvin Horn.

In March, the National States Rights Party had rallied in Ohio, nominating Arkansas governor Orval Faubus as its presidential candidate, with crazy ex-admiral John Crommelin as his running mate—simultaneously running for the U.S. Senate in the Democratic primary. In June, soon after incumbent John Sparkman crushed Crommelin's dreams, lapsed chiropractor and NSRP chief of staff Edward Fields moved party headquarters from Indiana to Birmingham, settling in a house on Bessemer Road, in the Central Park district.

Rallies aside, the spreading Klan revival wasn't limited to cross-burnings and racist slurs. The Dixie Klans, part of the new alliance, were prime suspects in the May bombing that killed a Negro mother, Mattie Greene, in Ringgold, Georgia. Her husband and their six kids all survived the blast, police reporting none of them involved in civil rights work, hinting that a mentally defective terrorist had dropped his parcel at the wrong address.

There'd been no accidents in Ouachita Parish two months later, though, when Original Knights member Robert "Zennie" Fuller gunned down five Negro employees with a shotgun, claiming they'd assaulted him *en masse* and he was forced to fire in self-defense. Three of his victims died immediately, a fourth expired after reaching a hospital, while the fifth was slowly battling back to something like recovery. Fuller summoned police, who claimed they'd found knives scattered at the scene, one still clutched in a lifeless victim's hand. Black witnesses, refusing to be quoted publicly, said Fuller had been arguing with the employees over tardy wages, striking one with a shovel before he picked up his shotgun. Needless to say, there would be no indictment for the massacre.

Bombing, however, was another matter. A new Civil Rights Act, passed by Congress in May, specifically addressed that problem in Title II, with federal bans on bombing "any building or structure," making false arson or bomb threats and fleeing across state lines to avoid prosecution for same. The maximum penalty for one such offense was five years in prison and/or a $5,000 fine.

The Bureau hadn't solved a bombing case so far, however, and Nolan was more interested lately in how Klansmen viewed the possible election of America's first Catholic president. Governor Patterson, despite his Klan associations, had come out in favor of Jack Kennedy, even spilling the beans to JFK about his role in the coming Cuban invasion when they'd met up at July's Democratic National Convention in Los Angeles. Two months later, Florida Klan leader Bill Hendrix had pledged his support to the NSRP ticket, prompting rival William Griffin of the

U.S. Klans to endorse Republican candidate Richard Nixon.

Those announcements made news, but the real hilarity had only come last night, during the third televised presidential debate. Kennedy looked cool, calm and collected on TV, while Nixon came off looking haggard, sweaty, and needing a shave—all that before Roscoe Drummond of the *New York Herald Tribune* asked JFK about a recent quote from Harlem congressman Adam Clayton Powell Jr. that "all bigots will vote for Nixon and all right-thinking Christians and Jews will vote for Kennedy rather than be found in the ranks of the Klan-minded." Kennedy had paused before acknowledging Griffin's choice of candidates, then added, "I do not suggest in any way, nor have I ever, that that indicates that Mr. Nixon has the slightest sympathy, involvement, or in any way imply any inferences in regard to the Ku Klux Klan. That's absurd. I don't suggest that I don't support it. I would disagree with it."

Tricky Dick, cornered and obviously flustered, could only say, "I welcome this opportunity to join Senator Kennedy completely on that statement. And that means that we can't have any test of religion. We can't have any test of race. It must be a test of a man." Nolan had laughed aloud at that, startling his family while thinking, *That's too little and too late. You're sunk with Negro voters now.*

Meanwhile, despite its new authority to hunt down racial terrorists, the Bureau had been more concerned with pressing COMINFIL investigations of the groups pursuing equal rights for all. A new outfit, founded in April, was the Student Non-Violent Coordinating Committee, bankrolled by an $800 grant from the already-suspect SCLC. Founding members included 126 veterans of recent sit-ins, plus delegates from nineteen northern colleges, from CORE, the pacifistic Fellowship of Reconciliation, the National Student Association (secretly funded in part by CIA contributions), and "New Left" spokesmen from the Students for a Democratic Society. Leaders marked for future Bureau scrutiny included Trinidadian-born Stokely Carmichael from D.C.'s Howard University, activist Charles Drew from South Carolina State University, North Carolina sit-in leader Joseph Jones, and five of the Nashville Student Movement including Marion Barry, selected as SNCC's first chairman.

People to watch, in Edgar Hoover's view—but for all the wrong reasons.

The federal action of a sort had followed "Bloody Sunday" in Biloxi, Mississippi when Dr. Gilbert Mason's April wade-in at a public beach sparked a weekend of violence that the *New York Times* called "the worst racial riot in Mississippi history." Police stood by and watched as armed whites attacked the protesters, leaving ten persons wounded by gunfire, many more injured by flying stones and beatings. Dr. Mason was the only person held for trial, convicted of disturbing the peace, and while the DOJ sued Biloxi in May, for segregating nationally funded beaches, the sand and surf remained all-white for now.

And was there any end in sight for Jim Crow's grim indignities? Not yet. O'Hara reckoned there'd be more blood flowing soon, as crazy people stood against committed abolitionists. He only hoped that somewhere, somehow, he could get involved on the right side.

———

FBI Manhattan Field Office: November 9, 1960

THE HOLLYWOOD BLACKLIST had finally expired, with ex-Red Dalton Trumbo publicly identified as the sole screenwriter for *Spartacus*, although he'd been omitted from the movie's list of a half-dozen Oscar nominations, four of them winners. Devon Gantt took passing note of that, but he was focused more on Mob matters these days, much of the action breaking in Nevada.

Out there, gaming authorities had published a "Black Book" in June, officially titled the List of Excluded Persons, whose mere presence on casino premises—including an attached hotel or restaurant—provided grounds for revocation of the owners' licenses. Gantt wasn't sure a short list of eleven names rated consideration as a "book," but there it was, after a year of soul-searching debate.

Nine of the final eleven were *mafiosi*: Chicago's Sam Giancana and Marshal Caifano, his man in Vegas; brothers Nicholas and Carl "Cork" Civella from Kansas City; "Trigger Mike" Coppola from Gotham; and from Los Angeles, the grim quartet of Louis Dragna, Joe "Wild Cowboy" Sica, "Johnny Bats" Battaglia, and Robert Garcia. Another Chicagoan, Murray Humphreys, was the list's only Welshman. Its sole Jew was Motel Grzebienacy from K.C., alias "Max Jaben."

That short list's omissions, notably among the "Kosher Nostra" crowd, allowed the Dalitz gang to work and play in peace, along with Meyer Lansky, Doc Stacher, Frank "Lefty" Rosenthal, and three recent Miami transplants who paid $10.5 million for the Fabulous Flamingo: Samuel Cohen, Morris Lansburgh, and Daniel Lifter. Lansburgh also owned the Eden Roc Hotel, a favorite stop for Jimmy Hoffa and his fellow Teamsters in Miami Beach.

Away northwest of Vegas, 435 miles distant on the California border, Stateline, Nevada, hosted the Cal Neva Resort & Casino, founded by former San Francisco gambler Elmer "Bones" Remmer, a self-described "big gun" and good friend of Dallas mobster Jack Ruby. Cal Neva customers could stroll across the Celebrity Room from the California side, crossing a painted line en route, and wind up in a legal Nevada casino. In July, Frank Sinatra and Dean Martin had acquired the property, failing to mention that their silent partner was Sam Giancana. Jack Ruby, meanwhile, kept visiting Cuba, palling with Lewis McWillie, who'd left jail and moved from the Tropicana to Lansky's Hotel Capri de Havana until Raul Castro gave up and shut the joint down.

One of the hottest *mafiosi* on the Bureau's present watch list was Johnny Rosselli, marked for his friendship with Sam Giancana and Judith Exner, Jack Kennedy's latest mistress since March. Giancana was also pumping Exner, often asking her for details of her pillow talk with JFK, while Exner also spilled details to kindly "Uncle Johnny" in L.A. Between April and August, Bureau agents spotted Exner visiting Kennedy eight times: twice at his Georgetown home, three times in Manhattan, once at the Fontainebleau Miami Beach, and twice in L.A.—at her apartment, and again at the Democratic convention.

G-men had Rosselli covered in Los Angeles, for the most part, but they kept losing track of him elsewhere around the country. Devon had the edge over his fellow agents there, learning from brother Colby that Rosselli, Giancana, and Santo Trafficante had signed on with the

CIA's plan to murder Fidel in Cuba. Between September 15 and November 14 they'd lost track of Johnny entirely, but Devon could've told them where he'd been: meeting Agency handler James O'Connell and Robert Maheu—a retired FBI agent, now a P.I. for billionaire Howard Hughes; hosting the same duo in Miami, where he'd introduced them to Giancana and Trafficante, using pseudonyms; escorting O'Connell to a Florida haberdashery, then off to Trafficante's secret hideaway; and helping the Outfit swing Chicago's votes to Kennedy on Election Day. A friend of Papa Joe since the 1930s, when Kennedy Sr. considered breaking into Hollywood but only wound up screwing starlets, Rosselli had also persuaded Frank Sinatra—another Exner ex-lover—to put her at candidate Jack's disposal.

Wheels within wheels, Devon thought. And somebody caught in their path was damned sure to be crushed.

———

LITTLE ITALY, *Manhattan: November 29, 1960*

DOM GIORDANO HAD BEEN SWEATING bullets for eleven months now since a jury had convicted twenty Apalachin delegates on conspiracy charges. What if someone in the prosecutor's office managed to identify more *mafiosi* who'd been present, filing charges against Dom, his father, and his brother?

Well, he could quit fretting over that. Just yesterday, three judges from the Second Circuit Court of Appeals had overturned all those convictions, sank the case for good, and gave the feds a scolding in the bargain. Dom still had the *Times* story in front of him and thought he might clip it, to carry in his pocket, just in case.

He'd never been much of a reader, dropping out of high school when they'd talked about him having to repeat ninth grade, but he'd remember this story and keep it close. Rereading it, he had to smile at Chief Judge Joseph Lumbard's choice of words. He said the twenty made men were convicted "without a showing that the gathering was in fact concerned with the commission of some unlawful act," and called relying on indictments "a boot-strap argument which is wholly unwarranted." The government's so-called evidence was insufficient—"flimsy," in fact—and proved only "the danger of a shotgun conspiracy charge aimed at everyone who gave an explanation inconsistent with the government's suspicion of the purpose of the gathering."

Too much talk, the way so many college boys expressed themselves. What mattered was the reversal of the verdicts with an order to dismiss all the indictments.

Smiling, he dialed Angelo's number, got him on the second ring, and said, "Hey, *fratellino*, did you hear the news?"

"What news?" Ange answered back.

"What are you, livin' underneath a rock? Get dressed. I'm swingin' by your place in ten. We're gonna fuckin' celebrate."

———

ATLANTA, Georgia: December 5, 1960

PAYTON SAWYER WAS 900 miles from home and feeling

badly out of place. He'd never ventured into Jim Crow
land before, now here he was in a mostly-Negro suburb,
sharing space with other members of the Nation and a
bunch of twitchy crackers who seemed like they couldn't
wait for something to go wrong.

Not only crackers, mind you; they were members of
the Ku Klux Klan, welcomed on this occasion to the home
of Jeremiah X, minister of Atlanta's Mosque No. 15. Seated
at the dining table with a fat "grand dragon" and a scrawny
"titan," neither one of them in robes, Jeremiah was
conducting delicate negotiations with occasional input
from his invited guest: none less than Malcolm X himself.

The trip, as Payton understood it, had been Elijah
Muhammad's idea. The Nation wanted Klan assurances
that they wouldn't attack its temples, in return for which
the Nation promised to abstain from joining civil rights
protests or speaking out in favor of armed self-defense
against white terrorists.

That must be tough on Malcolm, Payton thought,
given what he'd been through the past few months:
meeting briefly with Fidel Castro at Harlem's Hotel
Theresa in September; returning to the same venue a
month later for a rally in honor of Ghanaian Prime
Minister Kwame Nkrumah; visiting the UN for talks with
Egyptian President Nasser, Ahmed Sékou Touré of
Guinea, and Kenneth Kaunda of the Zambian African
National Congress; predicting that America's next revolution had begun in Harlem, anticipating that blacks would
be freed with aid from Russia's Red Army. Payton knew
the FBI was tracking every move he made, each word he
spoke, one of its August memos saying Malcolm was
collecting followers to run the NOI after Elijah's death,
whenever that might be.

Now, here he was—leaving his wife at home, expecting their first child by Christmas—listening while yahoos spelled out all their reasons for despising integration.

That wasn't a problem, in itself, since members of the Nation favored total separation of the races, but it had to stick in Malcolm's craw, just being close to people who would kill him in a second if they figured they could get away with it.

And in Georgia, they likely could—which was the reason Sawyer had a .38 revolver tucked under his belt, around in back, together with a six-inch switchblade in his pocket.

That aside, the Klan had offered an incentive for cooperation from the NOI. They'd volunteered to free up land in Dixie, with approval from "substantial individuals," and Malcolm had his orders to report the offer to Elijah in Chicago when his work was done. Malcolm would be flying from Atlanta to Chicago with one of his aides, while Sawyer and two other Temple No. 7 members caught a flight to Idlewild Airport in Queens.

For Payton's part, they couldn't end their southern sojourn soon enough, before he had to shoot some dipshit "knight" and wound up in the state's electric chair.

———

HARLEM: December 6, 1960

IKE SAWYER COULDN'T HELP it. Sometimes he still kept up with the latest narco news and tracked developments at

FBN headquarters, even though they no longer affected him.

This summer, a Bureau agent in Beirut had uncovered a network smuggling heroin through Paris to the States. Working with the Sûreté, they'd identified ringleader Étienne Tarditi's close friend to be one Mauricio Rosal, Guatemala's *chargé d'affaires* to Belgium and the Netherlands, who smuggled drugs and stolen diamonds in a diplomatic pouch. Lately, Rosal had been caught in Gotham with 100 pounds of smack, the largest U.S. seizure to date, while French authorities scooped up another 120 pounds.

On that note, albeit reluctantly, Director Anslinger had resigned after thirty years in harness, retiring to Hollidaysburg, Pennsylvania, where his ailing wife was virtually housebound. He was rumored to be working with novelist and former wartime correspondent William Oursler on a book about narcotics gangs, titled *The Murderers*. Ike reckoned he would buy a copy if he ever got the chance, and maybe read a bit about the cases he'd worked on.

Otherwise, his reading and most of his TV time focused on the continuing upheavals in Dixie. Tuskegee University called 1960 yet another lynch-free year, but they'd ignored the August case of Fred Robinson, washed ashore on South Carolina's Edisto Island with his skull crushed, eyes gouged out.

Sit-ins had spread to Greensboro and Oklahoma City, Nashville and Atlanta, where Martin Luther King Jr. took time to occupy a lunch counter stool briefly. When Negro students from Houston's Texas Southern University tried the same thing in March, Klansmen kidnapped demonstrator Felton Turner, hung him by his heels from a tree limb, beat him with chains, and carved "KKK" into his torso. In Jacksonville, where last year officials had named a new high school after Reconstruction-era Klan leader Nathan Bedford Forrest, sit-ins began in August. Days later, 200 Kluxers had beaten demonstrators on the street and cops killed a Negro driver fleeing for his life. Newspapers dubbed the melee "Axe Handle Saturday," after the Klan's preferred choice of weapons.

And then, just yesterday, another fleeting ray of hope from Washington: for the second time since 1946, the Supreme Court had ruled segregation of interstate bus depots unconstitutional in the case of *Boynton v. Virginia*. Ike fully expected southern cops and courts to keep right on ignoring the legalities, but this time CORE was making noise about testing the federal government's resolve with integrated "freedom rides," perhaps as early as next spring.

And wouldn't that be something, if they pulled it off.

More likely, Sawyer thought, a passel of them would be maimed or killed.

———

MANHATTAN: December 15, 1960

GREG JORDAN'S BROTHER, Carlo, was still celebrating the acquittals of all twenty Apalachin delegates from three years back, but in Greg's view, the *Cosa Nostra* had more problems on its plate than rousing victories.

In April, Johnny Dioguardi had another four years added to his prison time upon conviction in a federal court for income tax evasion. Senator McClellan's racket-busting panel had dissolved at last, after 270 days of hearings, grilling more than 1,500 witnesses and compiling 150,000 pages of testimony, issuing two interim reports and one final volume condemning Mafia corruption of various unions. Bobby Kennedy had resigned to lead his brother's presidential campaign, after publishing a book about the Mob titled *The Enemy Within.* As a parting shot, the feds had indicted Teamster president Jimmy Hoffa and Detroit banker Robert McCarthy Jr. for mail fraud, allegedly embezzling $500,000 in union pension funds from a land development project in Sun Valley, Florida, with trial impending at some undetermined future date.

From Italy, there came disturbing rumors that the *Cosa Nostra*'s living icon, Charley Luciano, was negotiating with a Hollywood producer, Martin Gosch, to serve as a "historical consultant" on a film about the Mafia. Greg wasn't overly concerned by that, having researched Gosch's background and discovered that he'd only had a hand in two movies so far: writing a first draft for 1945's *Bud Abbott and Lou Costello in Hollywood*, then flitting off to Spain in '57, to script a melodrama titled *Day of Fear* that never made it to the States. Aside from that, he had produced eight episodes of a 1948 TV talk show, *Tonight on Broadway*, and a single March 1951 episode of a dead-end sitcom, *The College Bowl,* starring Chico Marx as the owner of a malt shop.

Still, if Lucky started talking...

Closer to home and much more troublesome was Cuba, where Mike McLaney had lost $7 million on the Nacional, spent three months in jail, and failed to recoup his losses with a $102,000 bribe to Castro's short-term Minister of Gambling, Frank Sturgis. McLaney had since been deported, presently in Port-au-Prince and laying groundwork for a Royal Haitian Hotel, while Sturgis, based on stories from the grapevine, was now in the CIA's pocket.

The big Mob news this year, however, was the presidential race. By the time Jack Kennedy announced his candidacy on January 2, Papa Joe was already schmoozing with Sam Giancana, their meetings arranged by avid JFK fan Frank Sinatra. Giancana quickly pimped out Judith Exner to the would-be president, whose taste in women was eclectic, bordering on ravenous. Jack's father was a friend of countless mobsters from his Prohibition days. Sinatra, clearly star-struck, climbed aboard the bandwagon and hung on for dear life.

Dick Nixon, meanwhile, had his own gangland connections, dating from Mickey Cohen in the 1940s to more recent Cuban gambling junkets, where he'd bounced at least two hefty checks at the Sans Souci after losing heavily. A friendly California banker squared that up with Roughhouse Rothman, and Dick's superficial anticommunism pleased the recent tide of Cuban exiles who had landed in Miami and environs over the past year. Sworn enemies of all things Kennedy included Jimmy Hoffa and the Dixie Mafia's top man, Carlos Marcello of New Orleans, who had anted up $500,000 for the GOP while Hoffa rallied Teamster votes.

Against them stood Sinatra's "Rat Pack," busy filming *Ocean's Eleven* in Vegas and packing crowds into the Copa Room between sessions in front of the cameras, hosting a "Summit at the Sands" in February, wowing JFK with a mob of Hollywood royalty. Word of the gathering brought 18,000 reservation requests for the joint's 200 hotel rooms.

As the campaign gained momentum, Sinatra renamed his Rat Pack the "Jack Pack" and rewrote "High Hopes," his

Oscar-winning song from last year's movie, *A Hole in the Head*, including lyrics that ran:

K-E-double N-E-D-Y
   Jack's the nation's favorite guy.
   Everyone wants to back, Jack.
   Jack is on the right track.

IN WEST VIRGINIA'S critical primary, rife with anti-Catholic propaganda from the Klan and similar sources, Sinatra pulled Syndicate strings to stock jukeboxes with his latest tune, while Paul "Skinny" D'Amato and other mobsters ran around the Mountain State dispensing well-placed bribes and rival Hubert Humphrey—once the crime-fighting mayor of Minneapolis, now less naïve—quit the race, complaining that he couldn't afford to outspend Papa Joe or Sam Giancana.

Good for Frank and friends, but Jack Pack member Peter Lawford had the edge over Sinatra, married since 1954 to JFK's sister, Patricia. Sammy Davis Jr. was the odd man out, a one-eyed Negro song-and-dance man, lately engaged to Swedish actress May Britt, whose fifteen movies to date included a role in this year's *Murder, Inc.*, with Peter Falk starring as Abe Reles.

Life imitating art?

In July, Kennedy had clinched the nomination, despite a slam from Harry Truman, saying that he lacked sufficient maturity for the White House. Southern delegates also booed Sammy Davis offstage before he could sing the National Anthem, even though Davis had postponed his interracial wedding until after the election. Kennedy saved the day by choosing Lyndon Johnson as his quasi-southern running mate, and so the deed was done.

Dick Nixon's nomination on Chicago, ten days later, was a foregone conclusion, causing a rift in the Mob between those whose hatred of the Kennedys trumped everything, and those—like Giancana—who accepted Papa Joe's word that his son wouldn't pursue them once he occupied the Oval Office.

Which side would turn out to be the fools?

Moving into the fall campaign, married stars Tony Curtis and Janet Leigh opened their home to 2,000 "Key Women for Kennedy," arranged by JFK's youngest brother, Teddy, with Frank Sinatra present to charm the ladies. In Texas, confronting die-hard anti-Catholicism, Jack declared, "I am not the Catholic candidate for President. I am the Democratic Party candidate for President who also happens to be a Catholic. I do not speak for my Church on public matters, and the Church does not speak for me."

Four TV debates between the candidates made JFK a star, dazzling some 70 million viewers, while Nixon looked worn-out and seedy, prompting a call from his mother after the first show, asking if he was ill. A thirty-two-page advertising supplement in major Sunday newspapers didn't help, nor did a half-hour plea for votes on election eve, preempting *General Electric Theater* on CBS. On November 8, Kennedy won the closest presidential election since 1916, squeaking by with a victory margin of only 0.17 percent. He edged Nixon by 303 votes to 219 in the Electoral College, thanks in part to unpledged electors from Alabama, Mississippi and Oklahoma choosing Virginia Senator Harry Byrd.

Once it was over and Nixon conceded, many observers agreed that Jack owed his win chiefly to Illinois—via

Democratic boss Richard Daley and Sam Giancana—and to Texas, where certain registered voters maintained a time-honored tradition of casting ballots long after they'd died. Mobsters who'd supported Kennedy felt buoyant, certain that their help would be repaid by JFK's attorney general, whoever that might be, leaving the Syndicate alone. Joe Kennedy had promised them no less, in fact, urging his old Mob cronies not to worry. Giancana, riding high, told Judith Exner, "Hey, I put your boyfriend in the White House."

But, Greg wondered, *what will he do once he gets there?* FDR had lavished phony promises on *Cosa Nostra* leaders when he needed their support in 1932, then turned around and screwed them all.

Would history repeat itself again?

————

MIAMI INTERNATIONAL AIRPORT: December 22, 1960

COLBY GANTT WAS HEADING home for Christmas, briefly, knowing that he'd miss Florida's sun when he got back to Washington. The Cuban situation had compelled his presence here, and momentarily edged out the other issues that had kept the CIA in turmoil all year long.

This presidential campaign year had started with Jack Kennedy scaring Americans over what he claimed was a "missile gap" between the States and the USSR. He claimed that Russia had "the technical and industrial capability" to build 100 intercontinental ballistic missiles during 1960, "perhaps" increasing to 500 ICBMs " sometime in 1961, or at the latest in 1962." Columnist Joseph

Alsop took the bait, citing "classified intelligence" as proof Moscow could have 1,500 by 1963, while the U.S. lagged with only 130. All that was crap, as Colby knew from hard intelligence. U-2 and satellite surveillance—the Navy's "GRAB" system and the Agency's "CORONA" project—proved America had fifty-seven ICBMs already, compared to Russia's ten.

The Russians *did* have nifty air-to-ground missiles, however, one of which had downed a U-2 flight on May Day. Confident that pilot Francis Gary Powers must've died while plummeting to Earth, Washington had denied complicity until May 7, when Nikita Khrushchev publicly confessed, "I must tell you a secret. When I made my first report, I deliberately did not say that the pilot was alive and well. And now just look how many silly things the Americans have said."

Such embarrassment, with Eisenhower under fire from Congress and the press, unable to do anything but grudgingly admit he'd lied.

In the steamy Caribbean, Duvalier was frantic at the thought of Cuba sheltering and arming Haitian refugees —a documented fact—so Papa Doc cast Haiti's vote against Havana, supporting a trade embargo imposed by the Organization of American States. By then, Castro had welcomed Russian aid, and Eisenhower had allocated $13.1 million for the CIA's conspiracy to overthrow Fidel. Some of that cash went to train exile Brigade 2506 in Guatemala, more to Syndicate leaders who wanted to murder The Beard. Ike didn't ask questions, just doled out the loot.

Castro had forsaken his plan to resuscitate Mob-run casinos. His next step was seizing Cuban oil refineries— built by Anglo-Dutch Shell and two American companies,

Esso and Standard Oil—using the captured plants to refine Russian crude oil. Washington struck back by canceling sugar imports, whereupon Fidel nationalized American-owned sugar mills and sold the product to Moscow instead. By October, 550 other blocks of private property were nationalized, including pricey facilities owned by Coca-Cola and Sears Roebuck. When a French freighter, *La Coubre*, exploded in Havana Harbor, Fidel blamed American saboteurs. Castro seemed to enjoy the conflict: after Washington condemned his human rights standards, he'd lampooned the "super-free, super-democratic, super-humane, and supercivilized" treatment of Harlem's Negroes, trapped "in the bowels of the imperialist monster."

CIA Director Dulles, for his part, preferred action to words. In August he'd begun negotiating with the Mafia to kill the Castros and their buddy, Che Guevara simultaneously. When the goombahs seemed to drag their feet, the Agency pursued its own ideas, including exile snipers who were picked off one by one, then an exploding seashell and contaminated wetsuit, both to sink Fidel while he was scuba diving.

None of those attempts panned out, so Dulles hatched a plan for an armed invasion of Cuba, approved in turn by the National Security Council and the president. Eisenhower ponied up another $13 million from unwitting U.S. taxpayers, Dulles and Deputy Director for Plans Richard Bissell planning a full-scale invasion with some 1,500 troops. After Election Day, they'd briefed president-elect Kennedy on the scheme and assured him there should be no problem. JFK had signed off on the work in progress.

The Mafia's efforts, meanwhile, proceeded along a parallel track, helmed by Sam Giancana and Santo Trafficante, Johnny Rosselli acting as liaison with Bob Maheu and Howard Hughes. Dallas small-timer Jack Ruby surfaced from time to time, while *Don* Carlos Marcello permitted construction of training camps in Louisiana's bayou country, staffed by his hired muscle from the Ku Klux Klan.

And what could possibly go wrong?

In Southeast Asia, an Indonesian court had sentenced captive U.S. pilot Allen Pope to death, but frantic back-channel negotiations were keeping him alive, at least for now. August brought a full-scale Red revolt to Laos, Pathet Lao guerrillas capturing Vientiane, accepting Soviet aid, while U.S. bombers pounded the city. By year's end, that struggle between titans smacked of Spain's ordeal during the 1930s.

Divided Vietnam, as always, was a powder keg with a sizzling fuse. In the north, Hô Chí Minh imposed universal military conscription for indefinite terms. Below the 17th parallel, President Diệm continued his rampant nepotism, ignored a petition signed by eighteen prominent reformers, closed more opposition newspapers, and crushed a November coup attempt by three disgruntled paratroop regiments of his own army. The resultant crackdown sent 50,000 persons to prison, while thousands more fled northward, many subsequently returning with orders from Hô to subvert Diệm's regime. Reds founded a new National Front for the Liberation of Vietnam in the south, killing or kidnapping an estimated 3,000 government officials so far.

Africa was another roiling cauldron of trouble, starting with the Congo crisis, wherein nationalist Patrice Lumumba led the Congolese National Movement to oust the region's longtime Belgian masters. He claimed 58,000 members, while rival groups--Joseph Kasa-Vubu's Alliance of Bakongo and Moïse Tshombe's Confederation of Tribal Associations of Katanga—both wanted their slice of the pie. From riots that claimed some 500 lives, native Africans battling against Belgian troops and "European Volunteer Corps" vigilantes, Lumumba seemed to be the winner. By June he held office as first prime minister for the Republic of the Congo. Kasa-Vubu became the new nation's first president.

But not so fast.

In July, with Belgian paratroopers still ravaging the countryside, Tshombe declared the Congo's mineral-rich southern province of Katanga an independent state, with Élisabethville as its capital and himself as President. Two months later, President Kasa-Vubu fired Lumumba, branding him a communist. Lumumba's deputy, Antoine Gizenga, then proclaimed himself the leader of a new breakaway nation, the Free Republic of the Congo, distinguished as Congo-Stanleyville for its choice of a capital city. Moïse Tshombe soon renamed his State of Katanga the Republic of the Congo-Léopoldville.

Where did that leave Lumumba? Imprisoned under successor Joseph Iléo, while African National Congress guerrillas backed by Moscow waded into the melee, battling Belgians and fellow native Africans alike. Colby didn't like Lumumba's chances for survival, particularly after Moscow called for his release and Dr. Gottlieb from MKULTRA flew in like the Angel of Death bearing well-tested poisons.

Did the Congolese *really* believe that Washington would ever let them have a leftist government they'd picked out on their own?

Speaking of MKULTRA, the Agency had recently

formed a new front group, the Society for the Investigation of Human Ecology, led by Harold Wolff at Cornell University's Psychiatry Department, funneling cash to social scientists and medical researchers whose work might somehow benefit the CIA. The tab had already surpassed $600,000, with no end in sight.

In San Francisco, George White's current base of sex-and-drugs research, tattletale Liz Evans described White slipping LSD to unwitting victim Ruth Kelly, after she refused his offer to partake of MIDNIGHT CLIMAX orgies. One trip had sent her to the hospital, but since she couldn't finger White, George was still dispensing all manner of drugs to his human guinea pigs. As one Technical Services Staff member in Washington had told Gantt, "If we're scared enough of a drug not to try it out on ourselves, we send it to San Francisco."

Screw the civilians, anyway, Gantt thought. *Don't they know we pull this shit to keep them safe?*

CHAPTER 6

Declan O'Hara sipped a shot of Jameson, then slipped the flask into the glove compartment of his private vehicle, and munched two Altoids as he entered Bureau turf. The breath mints might not mask the whiskey's smell entirely, but at sixty-six and stalled below command rank as an SSA—supervisory special agent—what did he have to lose?

Alan Belmont hadn't joined the Bureau until 1944, but he now served as Assistant Director, third in line behind Hoover and Tolson, theoretically overseeing all investigative work. Bill Sullivan had graduated to command the Domestic Intelligence Division, presently conducting a new COINTELPRO campaign against the Socialist Workers Party, doubling as Hoover's go-to guy on the U.S. Intelligence Board, getting chummy with leaders of the CIA, DIA and NSA behind the Boss's back.

Another COINTELPRO project, though without a

formal designation, sprang from Speed's directive to investigate twelve Puerto Rican independence movement leaders—six of them in New York City—building up a dossier of dirt "concerning their weaknesses, morals, criminal records, spouses, children, family life, educational qualifications and personal activities other than independence activities." Hoover's dictum ordered "efforts to disrupt their activities and compromise their effectiveness," emasculating any bid for statehood, much less full emancipation from America.

The Smith Act, although still in force, had basically gone belly-up in June, when the Supreme Court reversed John Noto's 1956 conviction. Granted, on the same day, a majority of justices upheld the prison sentence handed down to Junius Scales in '58, but only on the grounds that he'd instructed fellow Reds in martial arts. Two weeks after those rulings, New Jersey's Supreme Court finally reversed Abraham Isserman's 1952 disbarment for defending CPUSA leaders at trial in '49.

Progress, O'Hara thought. But how much, really, in regard to John Q. Public's attitude?

And to Declan himself, it all meant next to nothing. Abigail was on his case, urging retirement, and their children—kids no longer—were established in their own careers. What kept him hanging on?

Perhaps to finally dig up the truth on Aloysius Gantt, his trip to Cuba back when FDR was still the president-elect, and Gantt's connection to the death of Thomas Walsh?

Could be. Or maybe he was just too stubborn for his own damned good.

———

FREDERICK DOUGLAS SAWYER PACED HIMSELF, the third lap around the track and entering the home stretch for a mile, a small voice in his head asking, *What am I doing here?*

It was a short story, only the latter part of it involving Fred. From what he understood, Bob Kennedy—the president's brother and now Attorney General—had barged into Director Hoover's office shortly after JFK's inauguration, asking why the Bureau had no Negro agents on its rolls. The Chief claimed it had several, but pressed for names, the only ones he could identify were half a dozen faux "G-men"—including Sam Noisette, his office boy, and five others assigned to the upkeep of the Old Man's limousines at the Gotham, L.A., and Miami field offices. During the last World War, Hoover had made them all "agents" to spare them from the draft, but when interviewed by Simeon Booker for *Ebony*, he'd claimed the Bureau "kept no records" of its agents' races.

Laying it on, he'd said, "I've always resented the fact that some groups say the FBI uses no Negro agents. We've paid no attention to race, creed or color. That has been my strict FBI policy."

Like when you fired my dad, Fred thought, his face deadpan. *Like when you cleaned house back in 1924.*

Bitter? Not overly, Fred thought. Why had he given in to the Bureau recruiter who'd come sniffing at his graduation from UCLA?

Okay, he'd pulled a hamstring in his final game on New Year's Day, against the Minnesota Golden Gophers, where the Bruins lost by nineteen points, and while that injury had long since healed, it had dissuaded scouts from signing Sawyer to a rookie pro contract. Rather than wait around in the hope of something breaking later on, he'd spoken to his dad long-distance, grabbed the Bureau's offer, and was midway through his fourteen weeks' training at Quantico.

The physical requirements weren't a problem, and he'd taken easily enough to guns, although he'd only gone out shooting with his father once, at a Manhattan range for law enforcement officers. As for the academics, he was doing well enough, although so-called police "science" had never much intrigued him.

Finishing his mile, Fred wondered—not for the first time—if he would be assigned to tracking Negro "radicals," the way his old man had before Hoover dismissed him more than thirty years ago.

And if he was, so what? The Bureau meant career stability, and even if his race stalled personal advancement through the ranks, how much longer could Hoover stay in charge.

Hell, how much longer could he even live?

———

FBI Headquarters: October 5, 1961

Tremors had been shaking up the DOJ since January, felt by prosecutors and G-men from coast to coast, and Aloysius Gantt was staying out of it as much as possible while watching history take shape before his very eyes.

According to the grapevine, when Jack Kennedy had named his brother Bobby as Attorney General, he'd defied their father's strident opposition for the first time in his life—as Bobby had in 1957 when he overruled their dad to serve as counsel for the McClelland Committee. New Vice President Lyndon Johnson had prevailed on southern Senate buddy Richard Russell to grant a simple voice vote on RFK's nomination. If they'd held a roll-call vote, said Johnson crony Bobby Baker, Jack's brother "would have been lucky to get forty votes."

Arriving at Justice, Bobby discovered that the Racketeering Section only had seventeen lawyers on staff. He'd bumped that to sixty and distributed a list of 1,100 mobsters marked for prosecution. When his staff asked for a definition of organized crime, he'd snapped back, "Don't define it. Do something about it!"

And so far, that seemed to be working. Under Attorney General William Rogers, Eisenhower's DOJ had indicted forty-nine mobsters in 1960 and convicted forty-five. So far this year, Justice had charged 121 gangsters, convicting seventy-three. Jimmy Hoffa was still at large—his Florida indictment with Robert McCarthy Jr. quashed in July by Judge Joseph Lieb, citing defects in the grand jury—but smart money said he'd likely be convicted soon, with a special "get-Hoffa squad" on his case.

Aside from new indictments for familiar crimes, the Kennedy administration also secured passage of the Interstate Crime Acts in September 1961, including a Travel Act (banning interstate or international travel in aid of certain specified crimes or to disburse criminal proceeds), an Interstate Wire Act (outlawing transmission of betting or gambling information), and the Interstate Transportation of Wagering Paraphernalia Act (forbidding delivery of gaming equipment to states where gambling was illegal). Those laws forced the Bureau's hand where its reluctant chief might otherwise have argued that he had no jurisdiction to proceed.

The year's big loser so far was Sam Giancana, fresh from claiming credit for the president's election. Gantt knew Judith Exner had transported unmarked envelopes from JFK to Giancana several times, the president telling his backdoor girl, "Don't worry, Sam works for us." You'd never guess that, though, from how the FBI was hounding Mooney with illegal wiretaps, break-ins, bugging, even fitting agents out with cleats and clubs to follow him when Giancana played a round of golf. Sinatra took the heat for that betrayal, working off his debt by playing Giancana's Villa Venice club in Chi-Town eight nights in a row, no charge, with Dean Martin and Sammy Davis Jr.

At the same time, while the K brothers were cracking down on all things Syndicate, the CIA was using their whole motley crew—mobsters, Klansmen, self-styled Minutemen and neo-Nazis—to train Cuban exiles for the reclamation of their homeland in April.

And what a god-awful fiasco that had been. Gantt didn't even want to think about his son's involvement in that epic failure, though his thoughts kept turning back to it regardless.

There'd be no liberation of Havana from "The Beard" and company this year. As for the future, who could say? So far, he knew one thing about the Kennedys: trusting them could be hazardous to his career and to his health.

———

BIONDI'S SOCIAL CLUB, Manhattan: October 8, 1961

"You watchin' what this Bobby prick's been doin' to the bosses, Dom?"

"It's pretty fuckin' hard to miss," Dominic Giordano answered brother Angelo.

"I mean, it's goddamn pitiful."

"You're preachin' to the chorus, *fratellino*."

"Shouldn't that be 'choir'?"

"Whatever. Fuck it. What I'm sayin' is you're right, okay?"

"Somebody oughta do somethin' about it."

Dom finished off his beer and flagged the barmaid for a refill as he nodded, saying, "Maybe someone will."

The way this little Bobby bastard treated wise guys was a crying shame, especially considering that he'd be out of work today but for their help around election time.

No one had done more for the Kennedys than Momo Giancana in Chicago, pouring money into the campaign and helping square away the votes, old Joe Sr. promising that *Cosa Nostra* could expect a fair shake under JFK. That, after Bobby tried humiliating him at the McClellan hearings, back in '59, insulting Sam for how he read his Fifth Amendment rights off of an index card.

Dom still recalled that TV broadcast, damned near word for word. Kennedy asking, "Would you tell us if you have opposition from anybody that you dispose of them by having them stuffed in a trunk? Is that what you do, Mr. Giancana?"

Mooney had declined to answer, maybe smiling just a little bit, and Bobby jumped all over him: "Would you tell us anything about your operations or will you just giggle every time I ask you a question? I thought only little girls giggled, Mr. Giancana."

Don Raymond Patriarca of New England had a rough

time with the hearings, too, questioned by Jack and Bobby Kennedy in tandem, but he'd let his temper show. Leaning into his microphone, the *mafioso* said, "Your sister has more brains than the two of you together."

Dominic had asked his father what that meant and heard the story. Back in 1941, Rose Marie Kennedy, just twenty-three years old, had been a party girl, rebelling against Papa Joe until he sent her to a special hospital without consulting Rose, his wife and the girl's mother. So-called doctors there had dug into her brain—the girl still wide-awake—until she couldn't answer questions anymore, leaving her in a kind of vegetative state. Since then, she'd spent her life in institutions built for "backward youth," her brothers seething inwardly but too afraid of their old man to speak their minds.

After *Don* Raymond mentioned Rose Marie in front of the committee, Bobby told a friend that someday he would nail "that pig on the hill"—referring to Patriarca's mansion on Federal Hill in Providence, Rhode Island. Ray was definitely on their shit list, but they hadn't nailed him yet.

"At least Carlos got back from down there in the fuckin' jungle," Angelo observed.

Dom didn't have to ask which Carlos that was. Everybody in Mob knew the Kennedys were out to nail Carlos Marcello, the southern *capo crimine* whose territory stretched from New Orleans to Dallas and Memphis. Aside from his criminal pursuits, Marcello was a friend of Jimmy Hoffa and the pair of them had shoveled cash to Richard Nixon during the election, hoping to keep Kennedy out of the White House.

That hadn't worked out, and once Bobby became Attorney General, he'd learned that Carlos had been under threat of deportation for the past nine years, based on a 1938 marijuana conviction. That was taking forever till Bobby dug up a phony passport claiming Carlos was born in Guatemala, rather than Tunis. He still reported monthly to his local District Immigration Office, but in March he'd been arrested on arrival, hustled to an airplane, and dropped off in Guatemala City without so much as a change of socks.

Of course, the Guatemalan government wanted no part of him. In May, a flying squad of cops had dragged Marcello out of his hotel and drove him to the border of El Salvador, where more police had dropped him on a jungle mountaintop near the Honduran border. Badly out of shape and dressed all wrong for trailblazing, Carlos had hiked some twenty miles before he reached a village, falling down along the way and fracturing three ribs. He'd only just returned to the U.S., sneaking into Louisiana at Vermillion Bayou, and had filed a case against that Bobby bastard for deporting him illegally.

A lot they cared, rich fuckers used to getting anything they wanted just by grabbing it. Dom couldn't picture three more years under the Kennedys, and what in hell would happen to the Syndicate if JFK won re-election to a second term? Was that even a possibility, after a fuck-up like the Bay of Pigs?

Marone, he thought, scowling. Like Frank Sinatra sang a couple years ago, something would have to give.

———

LUTÈCE, East 50th Street, Manhattan: October 10, 1961

THE FRENCH RESTAURANT WAS QUASI-NEW, opened in February by a pair of Andres. Owner Andre Surmain had come across from the old country, bringing along chef André Soltner—who would be quick to tell you that an accent on that "e" made all the difference. Lutèce seated a maximum of sixty patrons, but in style, and while its name apparently meant nothing special, its cuisine that was already the talk of the Gotham.

Wags would tell you that Lutèce meant romance—and wasn't that a rotten place to say goodbye?

Dave Jordan and his date, Fiona O'Hara, were parting company, she quitting Brooklyn Legal Aid and heading back to Washington, D.C., her birthplace, while Jordan stayed in the trenches, representing the impoverished, some of the city's low-rent criminals, and generally those shit out of luck.

They had agreed on playing hooky yesterday—Monday, Fiona off the clock already, Dave calling in sick—and flown to Cincinnati for the final game of the World Series, cheering as the Yankees wrapped it up in five, beating the hometown Reds at Crosley Field to make their triumph all the more embarrassing for Cincinnati coach Otis Douglas. It had been Dave's treat, over Fee's protests, and he'd also sprung for dinner—very possibly the last one they would ever share.

Dave didn't kid himself. Fiona told him there was nothing wrong at home, and he had no reason to disbelieve her, though they'd never done the meeting-parents thing. She wasn't really leaving Legal Aid, either, just transferring from one branch to another, out of state.

"You like the *coq au vin*?" he asked her, sticking to small talk.

"Chicken and wine," she said. "What's not to like? Your *bœuf bourguignonne*?"

"Beef stew with an accent, plus wine. It's delicious."

"We should talk some more, I guess," she ventured, sounding hesitant.

"I think we've pretty much been over it."

"You know, Washington's not that far away."

"Two hundred thirty miles," he said, nodding.

Call it four hours' driving time, about the same by train, maybe five hours on a bus with frequent stops.

To Dave, it might as well have been on Mars.

"You *will* come down and visit, right?"

"And you can come back here, sometime."

"We'll write and call."

All empty promises, to which he lied, "Sure thing." And changed the bitter subject, tossing out, "I hope you're saving room for *crème brûlée*."

———

THE LUBYANKA BUILDING: November 14, 1961

SOMETIMES—MORE recently of late—Colonel-General Leonid Babin felt that he had drawn close to the fabled End of Days. Time was surely against him now, at age seventy-two, with younger men inside the KGB undoubtedly imagining ways to remove him from their pathways to promotion.

Being younger didn't make them wiser or more cunning, it was true, but with his bastard son proceeding through his second year of high school in New Jersey, Babin had done virtually all that he could manage toward the advancement of his long-range plot against the hated FBI. Sometimes he wondered if it might be time to step back, possibly retire, but he hadn't worked up the nerve to do that yet.

The world kept changing, seldom for the better in his view, and that had been reflected at the KGB's top level in November. Alexander Shelepin had departed to become chairman of the powerful new People's Control Commission, overseeing all government, local administrations and enterprises. His replacement and protégé was Vladimir Semichastny, formerly First Secretary of the All-Union Komsomol and Second Secretary of the oil-rich, politically volatile Azerbaijan SSR. With only nine days on the job, Semichastny had created a "sabotage and terrorism" group—his words—within Nicaragua's four-month-old Sandinista National Liberation Front, plotting to depose dictator Anastasio Somoza Debayle. In like manner, Semichastny had announced support for other national liberation movements ranging from Southeast Asia to darkest Africa. New groups were bound to organize across the Middle East, and there were even murmurings from Canada, among the Frenchmen of Québec.

All that was fine and drew attention from Babin to foreign lands, but at the same time, Mother Russia faced conflicts closer to home. In May, a second Berlin Crisis had erupted, with construction started up in August on the construction of the Berlin Wall. In case America began rattling its sabers, Moscow had staged fifty-seven nuclear bomb tests at its Southern Test Site in Kazakhstan and the Northern Test Site at Novaya Zemlya. October's bomb, yielding fifty megatons, ranked as the most powerful thermonuclear weapon yet detonated on Earth.

And just as well, since October also widened the ideological rift between Moscow and Mao Zedong's China. Foreign Minister Andrei Gromyko severed diplomatic relations with Albania after First Secretary Enver Hoxha aligned himself with Mao in support of classic Stalinism.

And then, there was Cuba.

After America's failed effort to destroy Fidel Castro's regime in April, Premier Khrushchev—loath to admit that Russia lagged so far behind the USA in its production of ICBMs—conceived a plan to place strategic missiles in Cuba, just ninety miles from Florida. In Havana, Ambassador Alexandr Alexeyev opposed the scheme, claiming Fidel would not accept the gift, but Khrushchev was implacable, enamored by the concept of a "splendid first strike" capability to close the yawning missile gap. Speaking to highly placed officials, Khrushchev declared, "I know for certain that Kennedy doesn't have a strong background, nor, generally speaking, does he have the courage to stand up to a serious challenge." In a conversation which the premier wrongly thought was private, Khrushchev told his son, Sergei, "Kennedy will make a fuss, make more of a fuss, and then agree."

Perhaps, but Babin wasn't sure. In fact, after the Bay of Pigs, America had planted Jupiter ballistic missiles in Turkey and Italy. Scientists surmised that a nuclear war would wipe out one-third of humanity, but so far, Kennedy seemed willing to accept that risk.

To keep things interesting, sowing fresh dissension in the West, Major Anatoliy Golitsyn of the KGB's First Chief Directorate had defected from his post in Helsinki, sitting for interviews with both the CIA and Britain's SIS. One of the tidbits he delivered was a name: Kim Philby, a prized multi-lingual, widely-traveled British intelligence agent since 1940, groomed by the KGB's predecessor agencies for double agent status since 1934. Even now, fingered by Golitsyn as a traitor, Philby still retained his place with SIS, and likely would until hard evidence backed up Golitsyn's claim.

An enemy in turmoil was an enemy disarmed—but Babin wondered how much longer he could keep up with the game.

———

HARLEM: November 22, 1961

IN SERVICE to Inspector Patrick Flannery at BOSS, Payton Sawyer had filled his year with tracking Malcolm X specifically and filing what reports he could on NOI members across the country, fattening the Nation's NYPD dossier.

He'd been on hand in February, joining Malcolm's demonstration outside the United Nations complex in Manhattan's Turtle Bay neighborhood, protesting the murder of ex-Prime Minister Patrice Lumumba in the Congo. He'd turned up in March at Harvard Law School, watching Malcolm debate Walter Carrignan, founder of Harlem's NAACP chapter, over "The American Negro: Problems and Solutions." In April, he'd heard Elijah Muhammad himself at New York's Clark Hotel, dismissing claims of recent Negro "progress," vowing, "We never will believe in anything but the religion of Islam. Islam will give us absolute freedom, justice, equality and brotherly love."

In May Payton had traveled to Rhode Island's Brown University—no pun intended—where Malcolm had enthralled an 800-person audience. October found him at the Social Action Committee of the New York Community Church on East 35th Street, where Malcolm preached "The Truth About the Black Muslims" to the church's Social Action Committee, and he'd tuned in one week later to NBC's *Open Mind* program, when Malcolm discoursed on "Where is the American Negro Headed?"

One local setback had occurred three days after the NBC broadcast when Queens College banned Malcolm from speaking on campus, but just yesterday, CCNY Acting President Dr. Garry Rivilin had invited Malcolm to address the school's Eugene V. Debs Club.

All that, and even with those goings-on, the Nation's hottest news was mostly happening elsewhere. In June, George Lincoln Rockwell and ten members of his American Nazi Party had joined an NOI rally at Uline Arena in Washington, D.C., bringing extra swastika armbands for Muslim ushers to wear. Payton wasn't surprised, after December's Georgia meeting with the Klan, but it gave whites one more chance to denounce the Nation as a mindless hate group.

That was clearly LAPD's view, out west, where Mosque No. 27 had opened four years back, drawing complaints from white merchants that Muslims handed out flyers to patrons approaching their stores. On September 2, two white Safeway store detectives rousted temple members who were selling copies of *Muhammad Speaks,* at which point, if you could believe Norman Chandler's *Los Angeles Times,* the two dicks were "beaten and stomped" for their pains. Ironically, the Nation paper's headline that week had been "MUSLIMS SET FOR CHRISTIAN ATTACK," and they got it in spades when seventy-five L.A. cops rolled out to brutally suppress a "mini-riot"—aka, a peaceful barbecue—at Griffith Park.

Malcolm had flown out to help calm tempers in South Central L.A., while Mayor-elect Sam Yorty congratulated himself on Negro support at the polls. Now, ensconced at City Hall, Yorty tried to have it both ways with reporters, saying, "I stand all right with Chief Parker. I got him a double raise that he wouldn't have gotten otherwise. I'm planning on keeping him, but I want him to enforce the law and stop making remarks about the minority groups in this community because the police have had very poor public relations with the minority groups. This is not good for this community. We're not living in the South and I expect everybody to be treated equally and fairly and I expect police to enforce the law and I will expect they will do so."

Good luck with that thought Payton, *and in hoping L.A. would "act like a grownup city" with racist dinosaurs like Parker in charge of the streets.*

The only thing Payton could see, from where he stood, was a future of fire and blood.

————

Little Italy, Manhattan: November 24, 1961

THE ELECTION HAD GONE off as planned, but it closed out a year of upsets that, from near or far, were still felt from the largest *Cosa Nostra* families down to the smallest, with Greg Jordan's clan somewhere between the two extremes.

The year's good news: Frank Costello had been freed after a year in prison and retired—if you could ever use that term for living *mafiosi*, to his "honest" companies with gambling on the side. As for the rest...

A month before Frank hit the street, a federal grand jury blew the whistle on corrupt cops owned by Nick Civella's Kansas City family. To purge the scandal, Bobby Kennedy had recommended Clarence Kelly, a retired G-man, to replace the outgoing chief of police.

Last year, the Bureau of Narcotics had exposed the so-called "French Connection," smuggling huge quantities of heroin from Europe, through Canada into Gotham. Just yesterday, the FBN's informer—Albert Agueci, from Steve Maggadino's Buffalo family—had been found near Rochester, stripped naked and tortured to death, eyes burned out with a blowtorch.

Meanwhile, Frank Sinatra's gang had spent most of December last year planning a gala reception for the eve of Jack Kennedy's inauguration, calling on a host of stars to entertain the throng. Poor Sammy Davis Jr. had been disinvited at the last minute, for stealing time to wed May Britt. Soon-to-be First Lady Jacqueline had left the party early, still recovering from son John Jr.'s birth by caesarean section, but JFK had never bailed out on a swinging party in his life.

As the festivities wound down—attendees having anted $1.7 million for proximity to Jack—Kennedy stepped up to the microphone himself, in praise of good buddy Sinatra. "You cannot imagine the work he has done to make this show a success," JFK gushed, calling Frank "a great friend." Capping that salute, he'd said, "Long before he could sing, he used to poll a Democratic precinct back in New Jersey. That precinct has grown to cover a country, but long after he has ceased to sing, he's going to be standing up and speaking for the Democratic Party, and I thank him on behalf of all of you tonight."

But would he?

It wasn't long before Chief Hoover at the FBI dished up Sinatra's file for White House scrutiny. Attorney General Bobby didn't like the look of it, but he was mostly keeping quiet...for the moment. The Rat Pack and cronies spent ten days at Joe Kennedy's French Riviera place in August and returned for a September thank-you party organized by Papa Joe at the family's Hyannis Port compound, but cracks were visible in the façade.

For starters, a paperback titled *Sinatra and His Rat Pack* had been selling reasonably well, followed by a "Rat Pack roundtable" discussion on David Susskind's *Open End* late-night talk show. The *New Yorker* even got into the act, with a cartoon of a psychiatrist asking his middle-aged male patient, "What makes you think Frank Sinatra, Dean Martin and all that bunch are so happy?"

What indeed? Greg asked himself. And how long could the honeymoon endure?

———

MIAMI CIA OFFICE: November 30, 1961

So FAR, this year had been a pisser for the Agency, and Colby Gantt worried about what still might crop up in its final month.

It had begun with President Eisenhower's farewell address to the nation in January, warning America against the rise of a "military-industrial complex" Ike himself had done so much to build and nurture in the past eight years. He cautioned, "This conjunction of an immense military establishment and a large arms industry is new in the American experience. The total influence—economic, political, even spiritual—is felt in every city, every state-house, every office of the federal government. We recognize the imperative need for this development. Yet we must not fail to comprehend its grave implications."

Colby had watched the speech alone and asked his TV screen, "So what can anybody do about it now, dipshit?" And he'd answered himself: *Not one damned thing.*

Jack Kennedy was sworn in three days later—two days after the CIA opened its new National Photographic Interpretation Center under Director Arthur Lundahl. JFK proposed a sweeping "Alliance for Progress" in Latin America, but what he got was WHINSEC—formerly known as the School of the Americas when it first started teaching South American secret police special torture techniques. In May, naval pilot Alan Shephard rode an Atlas rocket into outer space, the world's first astronaut. Kennedy established a new Defense Intelligence Agency in August, followed by September's CIA collaboration with the Air Force, creating a National Reconnaissance Office under Director Joseph Charyk. Two weeks later, the Agency's new Langley headquarters finally opened for business.

But before most of that, the Caribbean had boiled over. In Haiti, Papa Doc breached the country's 1957 constitution, illegally staging a rigged election wherein he ran unopposed as president for life. After claiming 1.3 million votes, the ever-humble dictator told journalists, "I accept the people's will. As a revolutionary, I have no right to disregard the will of the people."

But Haiti was a fart in a whirlwind compared to the damned *Playa Girón* (Bay of Pigs) invasion. Ike had severed diplomatic relations with Cuba before leaving office, his invasion plan nearly completed and dropped on his successor like a foundling on the White House doorstep. The half-assed amphibious assault occurred on April 17, but not strictly as planned, with JFK withholding U.S. troops and air support from the CIA's exile Brigade 2506. The result: a classic cluster-fuck, with an estimated 4,000 persons killed or wounded, including one dead U.S. paratrooper and three airmen. Castro imprisoned 1,202 surviving invaders—nine "accidentally asphyxiated" in a closed transport vehicle—plus 687 alleged accomplices, mostly businessmen and ex-Batista soldiers.

The PR fallout had been hideous for JFK, not helped by Eisenhower's phone call stating, "The failure of the Bay of Pigs will embolden the Soviets to do something that they would otherwise not do." An echo of that sentiment came from Che Guevara, in a note to Kennedy that read: "Thanks for Playa Girón. Before the invasion, the revolution was weak. Now it's stronger than ever." An Agency mole in Moscow reported Nikita Khrushchev's observation that JFK was "too young, intellectual, not prepared well for decision making in crisis situations, too intelligent and too weak."

That was too much for Kennedy's ego to bear. Five days after the bungled invasion, he'd told brother Bobby, Allen Dulles, General Maxwell Taylor and Admiral Arleigh Burke to form a Cuba Study Group. That panel's June report, and the CIA's own internal assessment five months later, agreed that the Agency had exceeded its guerrilla warfare capabilities, failed to assess risks realistically, employed poor quality staffers, and omitted recruitment of internal Cuban resistance. In fact, the whole plan came off looking...well, irrational.

On November 28, Kennedy presented Allen Dulles with a National Security Medal, then fired him one day later, along with Deputy Director Charles Cabell and Deputy Director for Plans Richard Bissell Jr. Replacing Dulles at Langley was John McCone, a California-born industrialist who'd spent two years as chairman of the Atomic Energy Commission. Henceforth, said Kennedy, the Agency would be more closely supervised.

And three days after that housecleaning, Fidel Castro broke the long-expected news: he was a Marxist-Leninist and was converting Cuba's government to all-out communism.

As part of his new CIA control program, the president dismantled "Operation JMMOVE"—the covert training of Cuban exile guerrillas in Louisiana's swampland—but continued "Operation MONGOOSE," his predecessor's parallel scheme to assassinate Castro. Directed chiefly from the Agency's Miami "JMWAVE" station, MONGOOSE fielded 200 agents, its own fleet of 100 ships, and some 2,200 Cuban collaborators. Johnny Rosselli, in the thick of plotting Castro's death, toured the JMWAVE office, while a CIA spokesman assured G-men that Pittsburgh *mafioso* Joe Merola wasn't an Agency employee, merely an informant "in occasional contact with our Miami office."

So here was Colby, in Miami, supervising JMWAVE while the rest of the world seemed hell-bent on self-destruction. In Africa, four rival leftist factions strove to topple Portugal's colonial government based in Luanda. They included Holden Roberto's Union of the Peoples of Northern Angola and its fighting wing, the National Front for the Liberation of Angola; Viriato da Cruz's People's Movement of Liberation of Angola, with 4,500 men under arms in its People's Army of Liberation of Angola; Jonas Savimbi's Union for the Total Independence of Angola and its Armed Forces of the Liberation of Angola; plus the separatist Front for the Liberation of the Enclave of Cabinda, demanding independence both from Portugal *and* from Angola.

Who would win out in the end? Colby was betting on the arms merchants.

Meanwhile, from the Congo, news of Patrice Lumumba's death was making waves worldwide. MKULTRA's Dr. Gottlieb had cooked up a special potion for him last year, but the Agency's Congo Station Chief had scotched that plan, leaving Katangese troops to shoot him the old-fashioned way, along with seven of Lumumba's aides.

So much for human rights under the "new African freedom."

Southeast Asia was the same familiar steaming pot of glop. In Laos, the new administration had renamed Ike's "Operation Hotfoot" as "Operation White Star," doubling down on military aid to the Vientiane government while the CIA mounted its own "secret war," funded by opium exports carried abroad by Air America. Even so, the Royal Lao Army wasn't doing well, driven by Red troops from the Plain of Jars, on the northern Xiangkhoang Plateau. Moscow kept supplying the opposition with small arms and heavy weapons, extending the unwelcome parallel to 1930s Spain.

In Vietnam, 400 Green Beret "special advisors" had boots on the ground by May, preparing President Diệm's army to face an estimate 26,000 Việt Cộng guerrillas. In October, JFK wrote to Diệm, pledging that America "is determined to help Vietnam preserve its independence." From Hanoi, Hồ Chí Minh vowed to "fight on whatever the sacrifices, however long the struggle, until Vietnam is fully independent and reunified." The CIA had already mounted "Operation Plan 34-Alpha," waging covert actions against North Vietnam, trying to rival and offset Red slayings of 4,000 government officials in the south.

This time around, arms dealers had to share their profits with drug smugglers and Diệm's people, who'd never seen a dollar that they didn't want to steal.

At home—specifically, in San Francisco—Dr. Gottlieb and CIA psychologist John Gittinger flew in from Langley often, taking stock at George White's MIDNIGHT CLIMAX pad, where the hookers kept whipping johns on camera and White kept slipping acid to an ever-changing cast of hapless characters, sending them off on trips from which few would return with minds intact. Dr. Gittinger knew White as "Morgan Hall" and never missed an opportunity to interview him on his strange relationships with prostitutes.

All in the name of "national security," of course, and what true patriots could bitch about the CIA's use of their tax money?

————

M*ANHATTAN* FBI F*IELD* O*FFICE*: *December 12, 1961*

A*LTHOUGH HE DIDN'T CARE* for either of them personally, Devon Gantt had to admit the Kennedys were kicking ass and taking names in their pursuit of mobsters nationwide. One who'd felt the sting was L.A.'s Mickey Cohen, convicted on his second income tax evasion charge and shipped back to Alcatraz in late July. An appeal bond freed him in October, but in Devon's view, he didn't have a prayer of wriggling through the net. Once he was back inside, he wouldn't make parole until the early 1970s.

Two ranking *mafiosi* in the Bureau's crosshairs were Sam Giancana and his underling, Johnny Rosselli. G-men had Rosselli's California pad wired seven ways from Sunday, but they'd lost most of that coverage when he moved to Las Vegas, lodging at the Cleveland syndicate's palatial Desert Inn. Another complicating factor was the pair's tie-in with Judith Exner, still entrancing JFK whenever Jack could spare the time.

In April, said informers, Giancana sat down with the president in Exner's Chi-Town hotel room, no bug in place to relay what they'd talked about. Judith had visited the White House twice in May, cavorting undercover to the theme music from Broadway's *Camelot*. She was back twice more in August and most recently had rendezvoused with JFK at Papa Joe's retreat in Palm Beach, Florida.

Surveillance on Rosselli and his boss was complicated by their deepening involvement with the CIA on schemes against Fidel Castro. Devon knew more of that from his twin brother, Colby than from Bureau files, since Rosselli often dropped off of the FBI's radar.

What G-men *did* know was that Rosselli met with Giancana, Bob Maheu and the Agency's "Big Jim" O'Connell in March, in Miami, receiving cash and poison pills, the latter handed off to Cuban exile Rafael "Macho" Gener, who in turn gave the pills to Juan Orta, Director General of the Prime Minister's Office in Havana. When Orta failed the U.S. cause, Rosselli returned for more money and poison in April, this time entrusting the pills to Tony Varona, a Cuban lawyer, politician, and member of the anti-Castro Cuban Revolutionary Council.

The Bay of Pigs had frustrated Varona's murder plot, so Rosselli was back in Miami at month's end, dining with Exner, Giancana, and Frank Sinatra's friend "Skinny" D'Amato. In autumn, based on reports from informers, Rosselli personally met with JFK and Bobby at Mike McLaney's Palm Beach home, their words lost to posterity.

Gambler Lewis McWillie, meanwhile, was back in the States. He lingered in Miami long enough to assault a stranger wearing a "FAIR PLAY FOR CUBA" button, then flew to Dallas and renewed acquaintanceship with Jack Ruby before moving on again, to his new job at Lake Tahoe's Cal Neva Lodge.

Earlier this month, Bureau informant "CG T-51" described the efforts of John Drew—né Jacob Stein, a disbarred Gotham lawyer and former Lansky partner in bootlegging ventures, now a big wheel at the Stardust in Vegas—to intercede with Bobby Kennedy and halt Bureau surveillance on Giancana, but Momo was not at all satisfied with the results.

No shit, Gantt mused. By then, RFK was hounding Edgar Hoover to use any means at his disposal, legal or otherwise, to dig up more dirt on the Mob. To that end, Hoover launched a new Top Echelon Criminal Informant Program to, in his words, "develop particularly qualified, live sources within the upper echelon of the organized hoodlum element who will be capable of furnishing quality information." As Devon understood it, that boiled down to virtual free passes for the first Mafia honchos who signed on and started ratting out competitors.

So they'd be fighting fire with fire, and what was wrong with that?

———

FBI FIELD OFFICE, Birmingham: December 15, 1961

PEOPLE HAD ALREADY BEGUN to call the Kennedy administration "Camelot," but from where he stood, Nolan O'Hara
saw no royalty in shining armor, only heroes tottering on
feet of clay. He didn't doubt the president and Bobby had
their hearts in the right place—well, mostly—but as far as
great results in Dixie, Nolan didn't see it.

Take politics right here in Bombingham. Ace Carter
had renounced the Klan, he claimed and gone to work as
a lead speechwriter for George Wallace, still determined
not to be "out-niggered" when he ran for governor next
year. Meanwhile, a former Bureau special agent, Arthur
Hanes Sr., had been elected president of the Birmingham
City Commission and the next best thing to mayor. A
crony of Bull Connor who had left the FBI to serve
Hughes Aircraft and was thus embroiled in JFK's disas-
trous Cuban invasion, Hanes had been assigned to notify
the families of four Americans whose planes went down
in April. To win his present job, he had opposed rival Tom
King, screwing his rival with a photo frame-up that caught
King shaking hands with a Negro he'd never met before.
Dubbed "Washington's candidate" in smear flyers, King
had gone down to defeat. The victor celebrated with a
round of speeches to the White Citizens' Council and
John Birch Society.

And while that all went on, the Klans and their affili-
ates were growing stronger by the day.

Alabama's top man at the moment was Robert Shelton, a good friend of Governor Patterson. He'd merged his
Alabama Knights with Georgia remnants of the U.S. Klans
to form the United Klans of America in July, shifting

headquarters from Atlanta to Tuscaloosa, where he held court at a gin joint called the Anglo-Saxon Club. Montgomery's chapter of the UKA met weekly at the Little Kitchen in Ward Five, six blocks from the state capitol.

Around the same time, Georgia spawned an outfit they called Nacirema Inc.—"American" spelled backward, fittingly enough—and was providing demolition classes for a motley crew of "knights" from sundry factions if they weren't already skilled in using dynamite. On Labor Day, the NSRP held its annual convention in New Orleans, close to the bayous were certain party members had been training Cuban exiles for the shitstorm now known as the Bay of Pigs invasion.

And then came Mother's Day.

CORE had been waiting for a chance to test the Warren Court's ruling in *Boynton v. Virginia*, and they'd finally decided to launch integrated "freedom rides" aboard Greyhound and Trailways buses, leaving Washington, D.C., on May 4, hopefully arriving in New Orleans two weeks later. But the South, as volunteers for the excursion should've known, was not a hopeful place these days.

They'd hit the first snag on day one, when twenty Klansmen in Rock Hill, South Carolina, beat and bloodied team leader John Lewis. It should've been an omen, but the demonstrators were idealists and couldn't see what lay ahead of them when they reached Alabama.

In Birmingham, Bull Connor passed his orders to the Klan through Sergeant Tom Cook, known as a supporter of the KKK, if not an actual member. The brief was simple. Connor would allow the Klan free rein when integrated buses pulled into the Magic City, granting fifteen minutes of unfettered mayhem before officers swept in to make arrests. Cook pulled no punches: "We don't care if you burn, bomb, kill, maim, I don't give a goddamn what you do." Bull did have one request: if feasible, while mobbing riders at the city's two bus depots, Klansmen should attempt to strip them naked, giving Connor's men a chance to jail them for indecent exposure.

The first attack on May 14 occurred in Anniston, where Ken Adams let the local Klan unit. His men attacked the Greyhound first, slashing its tires, then trailing it a few miles out of town before they firebombed it. Only a lone highway patrolman—sent by Governor Patterson to eavesdrop on the riders' plans—rescued the demonstrators from a fiery death inside their bus or being clubbed to death at the roadside. When the lagging Trailways bus reached Anniston an hour later, eight Klansmen boarded and beat some of the riders, while demanding that their driver push on sixty-four more miles to Birmingham.

Unaware of the Greyhound torching, Shelton's men were at the wrong depot when the Trailways bus hit down. They had to rush but made it in time for the day's next riot, adding journalists and Negro passersby to their list of targets. One of the Bureau's paid informers, alcoholic Gary Rowe, was in the thick of it and loving every minute, too distracted or too drunk to care when a *Birmingham Post* photographer caught him on camera. Next up, a replacement Greyhound rolled in, and the whole bloody scene repeated itself. Police who finally showed up had all they could do to disperse giddy Klansmen, and still, mayhem continued past sundown. Informer Rowe, trolling for any Negro he could find, met one who'd fought back with a knife, inflicting a near-fatal wound on Rowe's neck.

The Kennedys were furious and frightened by their second major scandal, coming one month after the Bay of Pigs. Bobby sent DOJ assistant John Seigenthaler to sort things out, but Alabama proved too much for him. Five days after the first riots, a single bus rolled toward Montgomery, where Governor Patterson had threatened to fire any state troopers caught aiding G-men in civil rights inquiries. Now, taking heat from Bobby Kennedy, the governor agreed to guarantee safe passage for the freedom riders, but the troopers he assigned to guard the bus bailed out as they approached the capital. Riots resumed.

The cops, again, did nothing to curtail mob violence. Police Commissioner Lester Sullivan told reporters, "We have no intention of standing police guard for a bunch of troublemakers coming into our city." He was on the scene when Klansmen clubbed John Seigenthaler with a pipe and knocked him out. He lay unconscious in the street, and when a journalist asked why there was no ambulance on hand, Sullivan sneered, "He hasn't asked for one." The mob besieged a frightened crowd—including Martin Luther King Jr.—inside the black First Baptist Church till dawn, when Patterson belatedly sent National Guardsmen to disperse the mob.

And so the freedom rides passed on, escorted to the Mississippi border, where most of them were arrested, Negro demonstrators sentenced to a brutal stretch at Parchman's prison farm. One of those caged was Stokeley Carmichael. Smart and charismatic, Carmichael went into O'Hara's last report about the freedom rides and would, no doubt, soon have a dossier at Bureau headquarters.

Freedom rides were only part of Mississippi's action for this troubled year. Negroes who tried to vote or register their neighbors ran a risk of being beaten, knifed or jailed for violating Jim Crow laws.

The first fatality so far was Herbert Lee, an NAACP member and SNCC collaborator in Amite County. White state legislator E. H. Hurst shot Lee in front of several witnesses in broad daylight, one month after Hurst's son-in-law—Billy Jack Caston, cousin of Sheriff Dan Jones—assaulted SNCC worker Bob Moses. White jurors had acquitted Caston and Moses left town, but Lee remained to meet his fate. After the slaying, Hurst claimed self-defense and coerced Negro witness Louis Allen to support that lie in court. Still, Allen wavered, and an FBI memo reported rumors that "Allen is to be killed and the local sheriff is involved in the plot to kill him."

That hadn't happened yet, but Eli Brumfield was October's sacrifice to segregation. Stopped for speeding in McComb, he'd supposedly leapt from his car with a knife before he was shot. Another homicide by cop went on the books as "justified," and Nolan knew he couldn't do a goddamned thing about it...yet.

Away eastward, in Georgia, Klansmen and white students rioted against integration of the state university at Athens in January. Governor Ernest Vandiver had campaigned on a segregationist platform of "No, not one," and while he first threatened to close the school, he'd finally settled for the brief suspension of two Negro enrollees.

Nine months later, SNCC began making waves in Albany, the seat of Dougherty County in southwestern Georgia. Led by youngsters Charles Sherrod, Cordell Reagon and Charles Jones, the group began its rallies in October, seeking to desegregate public facilities, register black voters, and expose endemic rapes of young women by white assailants at all-black Albany State College. The *Albany Herald* slanted coverage of the "nigra" movement, while Police Chief Laurie Pritchett held the color line in conjunction with Mayor Asa Kelley. In nearby Baker County, relatives of Charles Ware had a lawsuit pending against Sheriff Warren Johnson for beating, arresting, then shooting Ware execution-style in custody. The field hand's crime: "flirting" with a female coworker who doubled as their white overseer's concubine.

In late November, SNCC and NAACP members, joined by officers of Albany's African-American Ministerial Alliance and Federated Women's Clubs, tried in vain to integrate the local Trailways terminal. December brought Reverend King and the SCLC to Albany, shadowed by G-men. Some SNCC activists gave King a derisive nickname—"De Lawd"—based on his avoidance of direct conflict, but King submitted to arrest, refusing to post bail until the city granted basic concessions. Leaving town, he woefully told journalists, "Those agreements were dishonored and violated by the city."

Huge surprise, thought Nolan, wondering whose neck would be the next one on the chopping block.

———

*H*ARLEM: *December 15, 1961*

I*KE* S*AWYER* DREADED SEEING this month's long-distance phone bill, but what else could he do with idle time except check out the year's only acknowledge lynching?

The victim, David Jackson, had been found by two boys in McDuffie County, Georgia, hanging from a tree in woodland near Augusta. The boys summoned police, who'd called the Georgia Bureau of Investigation, known for being infiltrated by the Klan. A lone investigator took one photo of the dangling corpse and ruled it suicide, but Sawyer learned the boys who found Jackson were saying he'd been handcuffed when they spotted him. The GBI's photo showed no cuffs on the victim's dangling arms, and Ike was trying to discern if racist cops had tidied up the scene to sell the suicide scenario.

It wouldn't be the first time or even the hundredth, Sawyer knew, wherein redneck police had covered up a racist crime. In Arkansas, the governor himself was helping perpetrators of the Little Rock bombings from 1959. All five had been convicted, their sentences affirmed by Arkansas's Supreme Court, but Orval Faubus wouldn't let it go. Calling their violence a side-effect Washington's effort to integrate Central High School, he'd personally paid fines and commuted sentences for all but one of the five terrorists. The one left out of clemency was J. D. Sims, who'd turned state's evidence and testified against the other four.

In Monroe, North Carolina, NAACP leader, and Black Guard organizer Robert Williams had invited SNCC's Jim Forman in June, to lead pickets around the Union County courthouse in support of Negro suffrage. Two months later, when freedom riders hit town, some 3,000 racists had mobbed courthouse protesters, sending several to the hospital while cops arrested twenty Negroes for "inciting a riot." By night, when Klansmen rampaged through the city's Newtown ghetto, Williams and friends sent them packing at gunpoint, briefly sheltering two stranded white motorists in a private home. Prosecutors slapped Williams, his wife Mabel, and four associates with trumped-up "kidnapping" charges, whereupon Robert and Mabel fled to Cuba, beaming messages back home via Radio Havana.

Ike wasn't keeping up with narco news so much lately, but he'd noted the passage of the UN's Single Convention on Narcotic Drugs. The new rule overhauled 1931's treaty by tacking on synthetic opioids such as methadone, pethidine, fentanyl, and others. In theory, the rule required signatory nations to punish unlicensed production, purchase, sale, distribution or transportation of said drugs, but it was still each UN member nation's job to see the law enforced.

Not my problem, Ike thought and turned back to his telephone.

CHAPTER 7

CLEVELAND, OHIO: MAY 7, 1962

FRED SAWYER HAD RECEIVED his first assignment for the FBI. He'd worried that be might be sent back home to Harlem, shadowing Black Muslims and tripping over brother Payton every time he turned around, so it had come as a relief when he was shipped off to the Cleveland field office, assigned to infiltrate and file reports on RAM: the Revolutionary Action Movement.

As he'd learned in training about various historical extremist groups, RAM was a spin-off from older, less radical organizations. Last year, at all-black Central State University in Wilberforce, Ohio, members of CORE, SNCC and the SDS had formed Challenge, a clique inspired by Professor Harold Cruse's essay titled "Revolutionary Nationalism and the Afro-American." Challenge soon expanded and morphed into the Reform Action Movement, led by Donald Freeman, a student at Cleveland's Case Western Reserve University, then took another leap early this year and changed "Reform" to "Revolutionary" on its letterhead. Today, as far as Fred could tell, it was the first group to merge Marxism–Leninism, Maoism, and Malcolm X's teachings in a call to rise up and destroy the "universal slavemaster."

By now, RAM had chapters across country, but only Philadelphia's unit used the true name, leaving members in Cleveland, Detroit, New York City and Oakland to hide behind front groups, employing a system of "rotating chairmen" to bring youngsters up through the ranks that had grown to three levels: full-time field organizers, a main "cadre" of dues-paying members, and a broader group of covert members who bankrolled RAM on the sly. RAM's structure was also split three ways, into "area units," "work units" dubbed the League of Black Workers, and "political units" tasked with infiltrating more moderate civil rights groups.

Joining the movement posed no problem for a young black man, but it took time for Fred to chart the group's structure for Bureau headquarters. He knew that RAM's far-left philosophy and calls for a "colonial war at home," patterned on the Việt Cộng, would get Director Hoover in a dither. He'd be champing at the bit to crush RAM's Black Guard, founded—in Philadelphia RAM leader Max Stanford's words—"to stop our youth from fighting amongst themselves, teach them knowledge of history, and prepare them to protect our community from racist attacks."

That would mean Negro revolt in Hoover's eyes, and what would come of that? Fred saw himself moving along the same path that his dad had followed, that his elder brother still was traveling with BOSS in Gotham, and he wondered how long he could stay the course.

———

DAVE JORDAN HAD another case of homicide on hand for Legal Aid, and this one—unlike most juvey delinquent matters—had been making headlines coast to coast. He wondered if Fiona, down in Washington, had noticed it, or if she even gave a damn.

The case had started two days earlier when a pair of cut-rate gunmen tried to rob the Borough Park Tobacco Company. NYPD Detectives Luke Fallon and John Finnegan caught the call and died in a flurry of gunfire. The shooters—Tony Dellernia and Jerry Rosenberg—escaped but were arrested soon after the crime. Seeking to please the press, Detective Captain Albert Seedman took it on himself to put Dellernia in a bizarre "perp walk," clutching his head in both hands, posing him for photographs while Seedman chomped on his trademark cigar.

The whole thing stank and Rosenberg was already considering a federal lawsuit against Seedman for his grand-stand play, but first, both triggermen would have to stay alive, if that were possible. Brooklyn District Attorney Edward Silver had the bandits earmarked for electrocution at Sing Sing, assuming neither one of them was shot "while trying to escape" before they'd had their day in court. Rosenberg was pleading innocent to murder, fingering Dellernia for killing both detectives, but New York's felony murder rule made all participants in any fatal crime subject to execution—even if they hadn't pulled a trigger or, perversely, if police turned up and accidentally gunned down an innocent bystander.

Sometimes Jordan agreed with Mr. Bumble's comment in *Oliver Twist*, by Charles Dickens: "If the law supposes that, the law is an ass—an idiot."

Still, it was all he had to work with now, and Dave knew that it might not be nearly enough.

———

BIONDI'S SOCIAL CLUB, Manhattan: July 4, 1962

"YOU GONNA CHECK the fireworks out at Central Park tonight?" Angelo Giordano asked his brother, talking with his mouth full from a fat Italian sandwich stuffed with mortadella, provolone and tomato, doused with olive oil.

"You want fireworks," said Dominic, working his way through a plate heaped with lobster ravioli, "wait till you see what *Don* Vito's got in store for Joe Cago."

"That fucker?" Ange took another bite but kept on talking. "You ask me, whatever Vito's got in mind for him, he has it coming."

Joe Cago—né Valachi, stuck with the Italian nickname meaning "shit"—was one of those who'd been locked up with Vito Genovese three years ago, for smuggling heroin. While they were doing time together in Atlanta, two months after April's hit on *capo* Tony Bender, Vito had begun suspecting that Valachi was a rat. He'd given Joe a classic "kiss of death," and Cago picked up rumors that another *mafioso* on the inside, Joseph DiPalermo, held the contract on his life. In June, Valachi found a pipe lying around somewhere and went after his would-be killer, but he'd fucked that up and brained a convict named John Saupp, having no ties to *Cosa Nostra*. Facing with execution for killing a fellow convict or waiting around till some wise guy nailed him, Cago had made *Don* Vito's fear come true by turning rat.

Right now he was holed up in FBI protective custody, spilling his guts, and who knew what would happen once that shithead Bobby Kennedy got hold of him?

Dom thanked his lucky stars that he'd had no connection to the Genovese *famiglia*, but would that be enough to save him when an insider was telling everything he knew, and making up more shit along the way?

———

MANHATTAN: *August 6, 1962*

SO FAR, Greg Jordan would've said the year had been a rocky one for mobsters in America and elsewhere, but at least one nagging threat had been removed in January when Charley Luciano died from a heart attack at Naples International Airport. He'd turned out to meet sometime filmmaker Martin Gosch but never got to see him this time, and rumors were flying that someone had slipped Lucky a poison pill to silence him. Whatever, he was back in Gotham now, at last, admitted to the U.S. as a corpse and planted at St. John's Cemetery in Queens, sharing his dirt nap with Salvatore Maranzano, Dasher Abbandando, and Happy Maione.

Six months later, Joe Profaci joined him at St. John's,

killed by cancer in the midst of fighting the rebellious Gallo brothers. Profaci's death had shaken *La Commissione*, and now another conflict labeled the "Banana War," was looming between Joe Bonanno and two rival bosses, Carlo Gambino and Tommy Lucchese. Meanwhile, Genovese *capo* Tony Bender had dropped out of sight in April, and no one expected him to surface before Judgment Day.

Court-wise, in May a Nashville federal grand jury had indicted Jimmy Hoffa for accepting a $1 million bribe, his trial provisionally slated for October. A squealer in the Teamsters union, Edward Partin, had flipped for the feds to shrink the sentence he was serving for murder, kidnapping, rape, and robbery. July had seen Carmine Galante slapped with twenty years on a narcotics rap.

The year's other big losers were both Hollywood celebrities who got their kicks from dabbling in the murky world of power politics. Frank Sinatra was still flying high on his Kennedy crush, installing a new helipad for JFK's Marine One, plus extra cottages and slick communications gear, ahead of Jack's Palm Beach visit in March. At the last minute, though, Director Hoover of the FBI had briefed the Kennedys on Frank's connections to the Mob, so JFK decided to stay with Bing Crosby instead. Humiliated and enraged, Sinatra took a sledgehammer to the new helipad, stripped presidential brother-in-law Peter Lawford of his Rat Pack privileges, and switched his party registration to the GOP.

An unexpected benefit for JFK from sleeping over at the Crosby ranch was Marilyn Monroe, who'd caused a bitter rift between Sinatra and Columbia's Harry Cohn back in the day when Frank was angling for a role in *From Here to Eternity*. Marilyn hit it off with Kennedy big-time, and two months later, for his gala forty-fifth birthday bash at Madison Square Garden, she'd wowed an audience of 15,000 with her steamy rendition of "Happy Birthday." By then, insiders knew they were an item, adding that the blonde bombshell also enjoyed a fling with the Attorney General when he was available.

In late July, during a weekend at Sam Giancana's Cal-Neva Lodge, Monroe was looking frazzled, popping pills and threatening to "tell all" about Jack and Bobby if they didn't shot her more respect. Peter Lawford and his wife half-carried Marilyn to catch a private plane, the ex-Rat Packer warning her to can the threats and cut off all connection to the Kennedys. Eight days later, Marilyn was dead, L.A.'s medical examiner ruling the cause of "probable suicide" via barbiturates. No one had yet explained why she was picked up by an ambulance, then brought back home to die within the hour, or why neighbors swore they'd spotted Bobby Kennedy hanging around the scene. Marilyn's last film—its ironic title *Something's Got to Give* —remained unfinished.

All in all, Greg mused, he'd take the *Cosa Nostra* over politics and movie-making any goddamned day.

———

FBI HEADQUARTERS: September 2, 1962

ALOYSIUS GANTT WAS FEELING RUNDOWN and depressed of late—no great surprise as he turned sixty-five when other men were settling for retirement in their so-called golden years. He hadn't dug much gold so far, but when it came to dropping Bureau secrets down a deep, dark mineshaft, he was in there digging with the best of them.

A daily dose or whisky helped with that, plus keeping busy at the job he'd been performing now for over forty years. These days, he had the SDS covered, reporting its "Port Huron Statement" written by staffer Tom Hayden, preaching the need for a radical overhaul of America's two-party system. The group's latest convention had squabbled over welcoming delegates from the CPUSA's Progressive Youth Organizing Committee but finally admitted them, all the while denying that the SDS was a communist front. That have-it-both-ways line would never fly with Edgar Hoover, and Gantt's notes should get a New Left COINTELPRO off the ground in short order.

While Speed and Clyde were mulling over that, Gantt did his best to keep an eye on updated reports concerning Santo Trafficante, John Rosselli, and assorted other mobsters whom he knew—thanks in large part to his son, Colby—were embroiled in CIA conspiracies to kill Fidel Castro. It wasn't all that hard to track the goombahs if you knew what they were up to, where to look.

In February, a wiretap caught Rosselli and Reno gambler Bill Graham discussing "The Professor"—Lansky cohort Doc Stacher—and the "inquisition" Stacher had been facing from a federal grand jury in L.A. One day later, Charles "Babe" Baron—a Chicago bookie and brigadier general in the Illinois National Guard—was overheard telling Rosselli that he had "taken care of that thing" and, sure enough, the grand jury had gone away.

Nothing suspicious there, of course.

In May, a Walter Winchell column told America, "Judy Campbell of Palm Springs and Bev hills is topic number one in romantic political circles." Campbell was the name of Judith Exner's former husband, whom she'd dumped in 1958, two years before she spread her legs for presidential candidate Jack Kennedy. Judith's affair with Kennedy was over by the time Winchell reported it, but he'd bounced back in August with a piece claiming that "Gov. Nelson Rockefeller's best-kept secret is a famous New York model who has made headlines."

Around the same time, a bug in Rosselli's apartment caught him chatting with a shady L.A. realtor, noting that Rosselli "related his impression concerning some unknown venture. He said that this guy is a pretty lively outfit, that they want to build it in Las Vegas too and they are going down to San Juan. Rosselli said that they are out of their minds if they go down to San Juan. He said Rockefeller didn't want anything like that down there and tried it for five or six years and now he finds out that he has to have it, so he is going for it, that they feel that they need it for the hotel."

As clear as fucking mud, Gantt thought, and filed the memo, hoping it would make more sense when he'd absorbed a shot or three of Bushmills Black Bush to promote his thought process.

And hell, it couldn't hurt.

———

HARLEM: *October 2, 1962*

IKE SAWYER HAD SAT up most of last night, watching the Klan and redneck students at the University of Mississippi try their best to close the school against one black man placed on campus under court order. They hadn't managed that, but they had killed a French reporter and a white bystander who'd come out to watch the show—no Negro victims this time, thankfully—and they had wounded better than 100 U.S. marshals sent to guard James Meredith, the target of intended lynching by the mob.

Ike had to wonder why the marshals hadn't opened fire with everything they had, instead of taking a defensive posture, being shot and stoned, having a stolen fire truck nearly crashed into their mini-fortress at the campus lyceum.

The local cops and state police, of course, did nothing to restrain the rioters. Governor Ross Barnett—the same dumb shit who'd thought the Chinese islands Kinmen and Matsu were Mississippi state employees—had been calling out for "help" from other parts of Dixie for a week before Ole Miss was scheduled to be integrated. The armed response included busloads of rednecks from Alabama, Georgia, and surrounding states, while Ku Klux "Wizard" Robert Shelton circled overhead in his own plane.

Why hadn't someone taken time to shoot it down?

The mob's chief ringleader, aside from Governor Barnett—who'd carefully avoided being at the scene—was former Major General Edwin Walker, who'd led the troops *supporting* integration five years earlier, in Little Rock, but then decided, as he put it now, that he'd been "on the wrong side" of that brouhaha. Fired by President Eisenhower in 1959, for making his troops read John Birch literature calling Walker's commander-in-chief a Red stooge, today Walker flew Rhodesia's racist flag outside his Texas home and vowed to go on fighting Negroes to the bitter end.

Well, not *today* exactly. Walker was among the rioters arrested at Ole Miss, treated by Bobby Kennedy to a vacation in the bughouse, where psychiatrists were trying to decide what made the loony tick. That wouldn't hold him long, but when he got out, there was still the possibility of jail time for his role in stirring up the riot.

And if that failed...well, Sawyer had added Walker's name already to his ever-growing bucket list. He likely couldn't get to Ross Barnett, but some crackpot living in Dallas was another story altogether.

Walker, in Ike's view, already owed for two men killed at Oxford. U.S. marshals and National Guardsmen wounded repelling the mob from its mission, but none of the rampaging rednecks were killed or injured.

Too damn bad, Sawyer thought.

At least the latest mêlée had distracted Sawyer from the narco news that dribbled in from time to time. In Washington, Senator Kefauver had switched from stalking mobsters to offending crooked businessmen. His latest statute—what he called his "finest achievement" in Congress—was the Kefauver-Harris Drug Control Act, requiring pharmaceutical firms to inform physicians of their drugs' side effects and limiting their patent rights to let generic versions hit the marketplace after a few years of blood-sucking corporate monopoly.

Before that piece of legislation passed, Kefauver's Antitrust and Monopoly Subcommittee had made company CEOs, and lawyers squirm for two long years, also highlighting corruption at the American Medical Association, whose journal banked millions per year from drug ads. Its articles might be peer-reviewed, but before Kefauver-Harris, advertisements for new drugs were on par with a con artist peddling used cars to idiots.

A prime example was thalidomide, produced in Germany—no huge surprise—and heavily prescribed for pregnant women worldwide as a cure for morning sickness. What they got instead were deformed infants with stunted limbs and other weird mutations no one in the drug business had ever dreamed of. Sometimes, looking at their photos in *Life* magazine or on TV, Sawyer felt mad enough to kill somebody for it, but he knew damned well he couldn't fly around the world to drop the hammer on rich assholes.

He would have to pace himself, to watch and bide his time, remembering that old men have their limitations when it came to settling scores.

———

CIA HEADQUARTERS: October 28, 1962

IT WAS NO PICNIC, Colby Gantt had found, retreating from the brink of World War Three. The planet had been *that close* to annihilation, just one button-push away, but now it looked as if the human race would live to scheme and fight another day.

Well, most of them.

And Colby, for the moment, was still clinging to his job.

The year had started off smoothly enough for Agency employees, launching the first A-12 supersonic reconnaissance aircraft in April, organizing and Office of Public Safety four months later, as part of JFK's U.S. Agency for International Development. Multilingual CIA "advisors" had been sent around the world, from South America to

Greece, Iran, Taiwan and South Vietnam, teaching secret police the fine points of interrogation and subversion against Reds in any form. LAPD was also part of it, sending some of its brutes to Venezuela as aides to President Rómulo Betancourt's "dirty war" against the Armed Forces of National Liberation.

Cuba, of course, was still the fly in the Western Hemisphere's ointment. In March, Castro had charged 1,179 Bay of Pigs participants with treason, seeing all of them convicted and sentenced to thirty years each. Eight days later, in the act of "generosity," he had released sixty wounded and sick prisoners to America, where they'd consume U.S. taxpayers' money rather than Fidel's.

The Kennedy administration hadn't let up on its plans to kill Castro, meanwhile, still using *mafiosi* and right-wing exiles from Cuba as their cannon fodder, getting little in return. JMWAVE kept busy in Miami and financed an exile military training camp outside Lacombe, Louisiana, set up by defector Frank Sturgis and his Free Cuba Committee. Jack Ruby from Dallas helped out when his strip clubs could spare him, and Johnny Rosselli had toured the camp once, to see where the Mafia's money was going.

And then, there was the Missile Crisis.

Two weeks ago, reconnaissance flights had revealed a Soviet missile site under construction near San Cristobal in Artemisa Province, ninety-eight miles southwest of Havana. JFK studied the photos, then announced that any attack on the States would bring full-scale retaliation against Russia and the Eastern Bloc. He'd also established a naval "quarantine" around Cuba, demanding the withdrawal of the missiles already in place. Overnight, "survival stores" sprang up across America, peddling canned food and bottled water, guns and ammo, prepping everyone for the apocalypse.

But it was not to be. Not yet.

This very morning, Khrushchev had "blinked" and ended the stare-down, ordering the removal of the missiles forthwith. The world relaxed, heaved a collective sigh of relief, and went back to ignoring troubles elsewhere.

Africa hadn't improved while Washington and Moscow were distracted by their pissing contest. The Mozambican Liberation Front was still battling to oust Portuguese colonial forces, and the Congo seemed to be imploding. Troops from Stanleyville had occupied part of Katanga Province, while a "traditional court" executed seven more Lumumba partisans for their "crimes against the Baluba people." One of the dead was Orientale Provincial President Joseph Finant, sparking retaliation by the Free Republic of the Congo. Where it all would end nobody knew, but Gantt was betting on native dictators to pick up with the mass murder and corruption where unwelcome Belgian overlords left off.

As far as Southeast Asia, the forecast predicted endless death and suffering.

An Indonesian court had sentenced Agency pilot Allen Pope to death in 1960, but back-channel negotiations had freed him this year, welcomed to Langley and assigned to flying covert missions for the Agency in other theaters of operation.

Laos had turned into a bottomless money pit for American taxpayers, though few of them knew where their money was going. "Project 404" had succeeded "Hotfoot" and "White Star," planting army and air attachés at Vientiane's U.S. embassy. The war-torn country was also a great testing ground for Green Berets and Pilatus Porter Short Takeoff and Landing fighter planes. There was a catch, of course, as usual. When Washington disbanded and withdrew its Military Assistance Advisory Group, only forty of the outfit's 2,000 native technicians were granted the U.S. asylum they'd been promised on day one. If the Reds triumphed, those left behind would get the chop, but life was cheap in Asia.

In JFK's State of the Union address, he'd told America, "Few generations in all of history have been granted the role of being the great defender of freedom in its maximum hour of danger. This is our good fortune." Two days later he'd lied through his teeth, denying that any U.S. troops were engaged in combat abroad. In February, two renegade South Vietnamese pilots bombed President Diệm's palace, but the dictator emerged unscathed with younger brother Ngô Đình Nhu, commander of the nation's Special Forces. By March, "Operation Sunrise" had premiered a new "strategic hamlet resettlement program," uprooting thousands of Vietnamese from their ancestral homes, cramming them into fortified villages that looked a lot like concentration camps.

In May, Secretary of Defense Robert McNamara had returned from touring South Vietnam, telling journalists, "We are winning the war." Presumably, he'd missed the Việt Cộng's battalion-sized cadres running virtually free around the country. Units of the North Vietnamese Army also strayed south from time to time, prompting the establishment of a Green Beret camp at Khe Sanh in Quảng Trị Province, watching out for infiltrators. "Mike Force" mercenaries, mostly Nùng tribesmen, helped out where they could, but Washington was learning that you only got what you paid for, and prices kept rising.

Starting this summer, U.S. Navy ships began conducting electronic surveillance off the coast of North Vietnam, daring Hồ Chí Minh to do something about it, but there had been no response at sea so far. Meanwhile, the National Liberation Front issued a surprisingly moderate manifesto, basically telling the U.S. to abide by terms of the 1954 Geneva Accords, but Washington was playing deaf and dumb, as Harry Truman had when Hồ requested aid against his country's French oppressors in the wake of World War Two.

Colby had heard insanity defined as repeating the same mistakes endlessly, hoping their outcome would change. Now he saw that played out in Asia, but no one at Langley valued boat-rockers. It was the same thing Gantt's father had told son Devon when he'd joined the FBI in 1942: to get along, you go along.

Stateside, where Agency spooks were still legally forbidden from working their mischief, "Operation GOLIATH" was thriving on U.S. soil, with some peculiar results. In January, after an anonymous phone tip, L.A. County sheriff's deputies found a Colt .45 in an abandoned car. They were still booking it into evidence when CIA contract employee Gerald Hemmings turned up to claim it, saying he'd lost the gun somehow in a nearby barbershop. Before the cops could book Hemmings for illegal possession, an agent from the army's CID arrived, persuading L.A.'s law to "keep it off the books" and out of newspapers. Always happy to help—and maybe knowing certain rival LAPD officers spent their vacations working for the Agency—deputies swept it all under the rug.

George White, meanwhile, seemed to be going off the rails big-time, if, in fact, he'd ever been *on* them. In August, with two MKULTRA cohorts, he'd tried to test the "musth" condition seen in bull elephants, evoking periodic rogue behavior. To that end, they'd gone to Oklahoma City's Lincoln Park Zoo and injected Tusko, a prized African specimen, with LSD. The pachyderm dropped dead eleven minutes later, to the consternation of its keepers, but White persevered, trying acid-dosed water on two more elephants in lieu of direct injections. White's notes reported that "neither elephant expired or exhibited any great distress, although both behaved strangely for a number of hours."

As a result, MKULTRA's overlords scaled back their hopes for LSD but had concocted several new "super hallucinogens" including a drug dubbed "BZ," which showed more promise as a cloak-and-dagger potion.

And if nothing else, it meant more money for the Agency's chemists, more hours on the clock as they started the sideshow all over again.

Some days, Gantt wondered what he'd gotten into with the CIA, but then he cashed his next paycheck and understood the philosophy of gap-toothed Alfred E. Neuman in *Mad* magazine: What, me worry?

Not on your life.

———

SERPUKHOV, Moscow Oblast: December 5, 1962

LEONID BABIN WAS NOT a religious man—he'd never been, and working at the upper level of the KGB certainly ruled it out—but he was wise enough to recognize the End of Days.

At least *his* End of Days.

He'd studied Latin as a youth, there being no way to avoid it till he quit school and left Russia on his first trip to America. One phrase Babin remembered was *praemonitus, praemunitus*: forewarned is forearmed. He'd been forewarned this time, and he was certainly forearmed, but Babin reckoned nothing he could do would save him now.

The word had come to him from one of his informers: Director Vladimir Semichastny had something against him, no specific details, but Babin had lost the trust of his immediate superior somehow, and Semichastny planned a move against him "soon." Babin had instantly collected certain files from secret storage, gathered weapons from the Lubyanka's arsenal, and hurried to Serpukhov in his GAZ M13 Chaika sedan without his normal driver.

Spare his life, at least, Babin had thought, *whoever else must die.*

December's snow delayed his passage slightly, but he'd made it through. There was a shredder at his dacha and he used it first, turning his secret files into thin strips of paper, which he fed into the roaring fireplace.

Might as well stay warm, while it's still possible.

To help himself survive a little longer, Babin had procured one of the newish AKMS rifles, basically a classic AK47 with a metal folding stock, plus twenty extra magazines of 7.62-mm ammunition. Babin doubted that he would live long enough to use it all, but just in case, he'd also brought along his standard-issue Makarov PM pistol, packing eight 9-mm rounds in each of the Babin's dozen magazines. For the finale, when it came, he'd also picked up half a dozen F1 fragmentation grenades, nicknames *limonka* ("lemon") for their shaped and the bitterness felt by targets on the receiving end.

Now, all he had to do was sip vodka while waiting for the party's late-arriving guests to show themselves.

The year—his seventy-third and *last* year—had gone sour early on. In June, there'd been the Novocherkassk massacre with 112 striking workers gunned down by Red troops, twenty-five of them killed. Two months later, Moscow had severed diplomatic relations with China, after Mao's People's Liberation Army crossed India's Himalayan border, touching off the thirty-day Sino-Indian War.

But the worst bit—the "capper," as Americans might say, had been the Cuban Missile Crisis in October. That brought sheer humiliation to Nikita Khrushchev, and it stood to reason that somebody else must pay for the Premier's mistake. How Babin had become that someone still remained a mystery, but he was past caring.

The only choice remaining to him now was death without disclosing the existence of his bastard son Stefan —now known, at age sixteen, as Stephen Barnes, a nearly straight-A high school student and star athlete in Trenton, New Jersey. Stefan would possess no memory of meeting Babin as an infant, but his strong adoptive parents, Russian sleeper agents in America, could probably be trusted to facilitate his growth and higher education, leading to enlistment with the FBI.

And if they failed somehow...well, Babin wouldn't know it, would he?

One thing he remembered from his childhood Bible classes was Ecclesiastes 9:5: "For the living know that they shall die: but the dead know not any thing, neither have they any more a reward; for the memory of them is forgotten."

Incredible, he thought, *even hilarious.* The very book

that Christians used to stoke their dreams of glory in the afterlife assured them there would be none.

Babin heard the three-car caravan before he saw it from his dacha's frosty window. The new ZIL-III limousines were black, sporting massive chrome grilles borrowed without permission from the Cadillac Fleetwood so popular with Yankee capitalist pigs. They might be armored, but he didn't care since Babin meant to let their occupants approach his hideaway on foot before he opened fire.

Three cars could seat nine passengers in reasonable comfort, maybe twelve if they were packed in for the two-hour drive south from Moscow. "The more, the merrier," said Babin to his empty living room. If they were crowded on the ride, his would-be slayers might be stiff and tired.

Of course, he couldn't win the fight, but as he lifted his Kalashnikov and cocked it, Babin reckoned he could give it one hell of a try.

———

HARLEM: December 13, 1962

PAYTON SAWYER FINISHED TYPING out his latest BOSS report on Malcolm X, briefly recapping last night's lecture to the crowd at Mosque No. 7, titled "The Black Man's History." It summarized Malcolm's tension with what the white man's media called "mainstream Negro leaders," which was swiftly coming to a head.

More interesting to NYPD, Payton surmised, would be the gossip presently surrounding NOI "prophet," Elijah Muhammad. Word had it that Elijah was screwing some of his Chicago secretaries aside from wife Clara, and members of Mosque No. 2 were deserting in light of that news. Malcolm himself had visited Chicago last week, questioning three women who had bastard children by Muhammad and had come home fuming that he'd placed his faith in an idol with feet of clay.

Even before that news broke, Malcolm had been living on the edge: addressing an audience from the War Resisters League; joining a panel of "Angry Negroes" on Gotham's black-owned radio station WWRL; debating ex-communist Bayard Rustin in Chicago, on the topic "Integration or Separation for the Black Man?"; learning from newspaper headlines that Negro activists James Farmer and Whitney Young dismissed him as a serious influence on Negroes; appearing at Park Manor Auditorium to declare that Negro communists, liberals, and socialists had closed ranks "to get rid of the common enemy with white skin"; seeking to debate with Martin Luther King, rebuffed by King's secretary with the observation that King "has always considered his work in a positive action framework rather than engaging in consistent negative debate."

The worst news of the Nation's year, generating the most heat, had come out of Los Angeles. In late April, scores of policemen had ransacked Mosque No. 27, shooting seven Muslims in the process, killing temple member Ronald X Stokes and leaving William X Rogers paralyzed. A police training manual, leaked to the press, described the Fruit of Islam's temple guards as "psychotic in their dedication and hatred of Caucasians, comparable to the Mau Mau or Kamikaze in their dedication and fanaticism." Never mind that Robert Stokes had died unarmed; the *Los Angeles Times* still attributed his death to "a blazing gunfight."

Outraged, Malcolm had flown to L.A., officiating at Stokes's funeral, telling 2,000 mourners and the white press corps that his death was "murder in cold blood." Elijah, meanwhile, vacillated on condemning the police and ordered son Herbert to minimize future mentions of Malcolm in *Muhammad Speaks*. Payton saw matters coming to a head before much longer, and President Kennedy hadn't helped much with November's Executive Order 11063, banning racial discrimination on federally-funded housing.

Payton, even though a cop and spy himself, saw Malcolm's point: how did it benefit Negroes to live in slightly better digs, when the police could break in anytime they chose and beat or kill the occupants with virtual impunity?

Sometimes, after a drink or two, Payton believed the war was coming between black and white. On those nights, brooding by himself, he wondered which side he'd be on.

———

EASTVIEW KLAVERN NO. 13, Birmingham: December 14, 1962

RYAN O'HARA SAT behind the wheel of his 1959 Chevy Impala, parked in shadow on Appalachee Street, in East Birmingham. Across the way, he watched a shabby building where the city's largest and most active klavern held its weekly meetings, waiting for his target to emerge and head for home.

Whether the bastard made it there alive or not depended more or less on him—and on O'Hara's mood when they were face to face.

He wasn't waiting for the Bureau's stoolie in the klavern, Gary Rowe, who'd wormed himself into the role of "Klokan Chief," or lead investigator for the chapter. No, the bastard Nolan wanted was the local group's top man, "Exalted Cyclops" Rudy Taylor, and he wasn't there on business.

It was strictly personal.

The Klan had been feeling its oats this year, cheering the City Commission when it retaliated for a Negro boycott of white stores downtown by cutting off its contribution to a county food bank mostly benefiting blacks. As Art Hanes put it, if the NAACP directed "nigger boycotts," it could damn well feed the city's colored poor itself. Despite his campaign promise to "sit down and talk to any group," Hanes had his own boycott in progress, shunning invitations to address all-black or integrated gatherings.

Bombings continued as they always had, with Bethel Baptist blasted twice, two other Negro churches also hit, along with two apartment houses still under construction. Alvin Horn had come out of semi-retirement, entering May's Democratic primary election for lieutenant governor. He'd run dead last among the contest's eight contenders but still walked away with nearly 13,000 votes despite his scandals in the past.

More recently, the Sunday prior to Labor Day, Klansmen had joined brown-shirted Nazis in Montgomery for the National States Rights Party's national convention, applauding speakers who included Jew-hating ex-Admiral Crommelin; Georgia radio announcer Wally Butterworth, publisher of the UKA's *Fiery Cross* and co-founder with Klan lawyer James Venable of the so-called Defensive Legion of Registered Americans; and Missouri's Robert DePugh, owner of a veterinary drug firm and leader of his own crackpot militia, dubbed the Minutemen.

Striving to match their Alabama colleagues, Georgia Klansmen had been busy in the counties around Albany, responding to civil rights protests by torching Negro churches at Dawson, Leesburg, Macon, and Sasser. Another "wrecking crew" from Sasser's Klan had also tried to raid a Negro home, but wound up getting shot themselves, then jailed by one of the rare cops inclined to do his job. Reverend King had made another pass through Albany, sentenced to seven weeks in jail when he refused to pay a fine for "disturbing the peace," then was evicted from his cell when preacher Billy Graham fronted bail against King's wishes.

Mississippi cops were killing colored men as usual: Corporal Roman Ducksworth Jr., going home on leave to see his folks, gunned down when he declined to take a "black" seat on the bus; and Otis Nash, a twenty-something epileptic who'd been threatened previously by Neshoba County Sheriff Ethel "Hop" Barnett, who'd told acquaintances, "If I ever get that nigger in my car again I'm gonna kill him." So it was in May, but it took two lawmen to murder Nash, Barnett and Deputy Lawrence Rainey, both firing at point-blank range.

That made two black men dead by Rainey's hand since 1959, and Nolan had him pegged as one to watch, although he doubted that the FBI would move against the fat, tobacco-chewing bigot. These days, Rainey and his boss were both Klansmen and proud of it, spreading terror through their county's black community.

Another Klansman-sheriff, Daniel Jones of Amite County, was still busily harassing Louis Alan, witness to the 1961 murder of Herbert Lee, who'd changed his story after lying under pressure to a grand jury that cleared the triggerman. So far this year, Jones—son of Amite County's Klan "Cyclops"—had beaten Allen with a flashlight, shattering his jaw, and gossip still placed Jones behind an ongoing conspiracy to murder Allen when the opportunity arose.

All that had been on Nolan's mind when he'd come home from work tonight and found Keely in tears, college sophomore Ryan and his sister, high school freshman Erin, both red-faced and furious over their mother's plight. They'd told the story while Nolan was holding Keely in his arms: a series of anonymous phone calls from heavy-breathing assholes who'd predicted that a funeral would soon be in the offing for "your nigger-loving FBI husband."

When they were finished talking, Nolan got his Browning Double Automatic Shotgun from the closet, handed it to Ryan with instructions to protect the house, then told his huddled family, "I'll be back in a little while, and this will be all right."

Now here came Rudy Taylor, last to leave the klavern clubhouse, strolling to his two-year-old Ford pickup truck as if he didn't have a worry in the world. That changed when Nolan loomed beside him at the driver's door and pushed the Klansman over with the muzzle of his Bureau-issued .38 revolver, asking him, "Do you know who I am, shithead?"

"No, sir!" Taylor replied.

O'Hara cocked his pistol, flashed his badge, and said, "Try that again."

"Well, um, I maybe heard about you somewhere."

"Close enough." O'Hara raised his piece, pressing the muzzle under Taylor's flabby chin. "Now listen up and make believe your life depends on it because it does."

"Yessir! I'm listenin'."

"The next time one of your assholes, one of their scrawny wives, or any of their bastard brats they got fucking their sisters thinks to call my wife and frighten her, the *very* next time, I'll be coming straight to you, Rudy. I'll blow the shit you use for brains out of your pointy little head. You understand?"

"Yessir! But I don't—"

"Shut your fucking mouth!" O'Hara snapped. "On second thought, maybe I ought to kill you now and do the world a favor."

"No! No, *please!*"

O'Hara waited till the "Cyclops" pissed his pants, then slid out of the Ford. Backing away, he told Taylor, "Remember this, dipshit. Don't ever let it leave your tiny, worthless mind."

And driving home, he stopped off at a state-run liquor store, to get Keely a bottle of the best red wine they had in stock.

———

MANHATTAN FBI FIELD OFFICE: December 20, 1962

THESE WERE great days to be a G-man, Devon Gantt believed. The Bureau was involved at last in hunting mobsters, though Director Hoover still remained obsessed with Reds and Negroes. The gloves were off, full-bore illegal tactics being used against the Mafia as they'd been used for decades against labor unions and political dissenters, and the stats were paying off: 350 mob indictments for the year, with 153 convictions.

There had been losses too, of course. Carlos Marcello of Louisiana was still fighting his peculiar deportation from last year, and the federal courts were leaning his way, even as Bobby Kennedy moved to deport Joe Civello, the Marcello family's front man in Dallas. Meanwhile, the DOJ's "hit list" of mobsters kept growing, lately including some 2,300 targets.

All that heat was bound to cause pushback from *Cosa Nostra*. A wiretap overheard Chicago's Murray Humphreys telling a caller, "Attorney General Tom Clark was always one hundred percent for doing favors." The Kennedys, by contrast, had proved treacherous, back-stabbers, taking help and cash for Jack's election, then slamming the door in their donors' faces. Making matters worse, old Papa Joe had suffered a stroke last December, paralyzed and unable to speak beyond a slurred, "No, no, no!"

Maybe he saw the trouble coming for his sons, knowing the people he'd made deals with and unable to repair the damage Bobby was intent on causing.

Bureau taps and bugs were busily recording threats against the Kennedys. Some passed along by Edgar Hoover—who despised both brothers—while headquarters sat on others, leaving them to fester. Meeting with his lawyer and another thug, Carlos Marcello had been caught reverting to Italian when he spoke of Bobby K: "*Livarsi na petra di la scarpa!*" That translated as "Take the stone out of my shoe," but when his goombah asked what they should do, Marcello calmed a bit, replying, "Don't worry about that little Bobby son of a bitch. He's going to be taken care of."

Other *mafiosi* were thinking the same thing. Take Philadelphia's Angelo Bruno, discussing Bobby with Jewish cohort Willie Weisberg while the Bureau eavesdropped on their chat:

WEISBERG: See what Kennedy done. With Kennedy, a guy should take a knife, like all them other guys, and stab and kill the fucker where he is now. I hope I get a week's notice. I'll kill him, right in the White House. Somebody's got to get rid of this fucker. He ain't gonna leave nobody alone.

Bruno: I know he ain't. But you see, everybody in there was bad. Brownell came. He was no good. He was worse than the guy before.

Weisberg: Not like this one.

Bruno: Not like this one. This one's worse, right? If something happens to him.

AND THEY'D TRAILED off laughing like they shared a joke nobody else was privy to. "The guy before," of course, was James McGranery, Tom Clark's replacement after Harry Truman had promoted Clark to a lifetime Supreme Court job. McGranery, as Devon knew, had been too busy hunting "pinks" like actor Charlie Chaplin to waste time on prosecuting gangsters.

All that fuss and fury from the Mob, and part of it was bound to be confusion over how the Kennedys could whip them with one hand while beckoning them with the other to assassinate Fidel Castro. Gantt's twin brother,

Colby, briefed him from time to time on what was happening in Florida and elsewhere, everybody hot to kill The Beard for JFK, even as Bobby spent his days trying to put the whole damned Syndicate in jail.

Maybe the title of poor Marilyn Monroe's last film had been prophetic, after all.

Something *did* have to give, on one side or the other. And when that happened, Gantt mused, God help them all.

———

FBI HEADQUARTERS: December 24, 1962

DECLAN O'HARA TAPPED his flask of Jameson as usual, before he went to work, and chewed his usual Altoids to hide the fact. It took a jolt these days, to keep him showing up, despite the media's endorsement of the Bureau's newfound zeal for chasing mobsters.

Sure, convictions of known *mafiosi* and their cronies had increased by 350 percent from last year, which had shown a 300-percent over 1960, but Edgar Hoover had only unleashed his agents to keep his own job. Speed's proudest moment of the year was *A Study of Communism,* his second book on Reds ghostwritten by Bill Sullivan, released just days ago by Holt, Rinehart & Winston. As with *Masters of Deceit,* Speed claimed the royalties would all go to the Society of Former Special Agents of the FBI, cheering the Chief since it was formed in 1937—and as usual, the cash would somehow find its way instead to Hoover's bank account.

If Jack and Bobby Kennedy gave Hoover daily fits, the

Boss was on a more amicable footing with Vice President Johnson, a neighbor of Hoover's on 30th Place Northwest in D.C. since 1938. Word had it that LBJ might be upgrading soon, befitting his new status, but he and the Chief had lived within eyesight of one another for nearly a quarter-century, and Hoover had used Deke DeLoach as Johnson's backdoor contact with the Bureau for nearly as long.

One byproduct of that relationship had helped Hoover in April of this year, when Arizona's Carl Hayden, chairman of the Senate Appropriations Committee, challenged Hoover's $60 million projected budget for a new FBI building. Hayden staffer and protégé Roy Elsen had run the numbers, but he reconsidered overnight after DeLoach turned in a report on Elsen's philandering sex life.

Did that count as blackmail, or was it just Washington business as usual?

Aside from naming brother Bobby as Attorney General, JFK had given Hoover another poke in the eye this very morning, commuting the sentence of former CPUSA karate teacher Junius Scales. The last Smith Act defendant to be freed from prison, Scales was already at work on a tell-all memoir, bound to put Bureau tactics under the microscope.

But if he couldn't hound Reds as he had in years gone by—simply because their ranks had withered to a shadow of the Party's former strength—Hoover still had Negroes like Martin Luther King and Malcolm X to spy on and harass. Reluctantly, the new Attorney General had approved "limited" taps and bugs on King, no doubt fearing that their exposure might destroy his brother's reputation as a civil rights crusader. Every bit of dirt turned up on King was grist for Hoover's mill, and that was what he lived for. *That* was how Washington worked when all was said and done.

Time to retire, O'Hara thought. *Maybe past time.*

But if he left the Bureau, what else would he do?

CHAPTER 8

"A FERTILIZER SALESMAN? SERIOUSLY?" Nolan asked the Bureau special agent who was piloting their nondescript Rambler American four-door sedan along U.S. Highway 49 northbound. They were roughly halfway through the 100-mile drive up from Jackson to the seat of Leflore County, watching out for redneck cops along the way.

"Dead serious," replied Agent Brett Nicholson. "He dropped the rifle at the scene, you know, an Enfield .303. We traced it back to the point of sale after it left the factory and ran the buyer down. He claims he let our fellow have it in a trade, a few years back."

The crime in question was responsible for Nolan being shipped from Birmingham to Jackson, helping with the hunt for a presumed white sniper who had murdered NAACP official Medgar Evers at his Jackson home, nine days ago. The shooting came just hours after JFK was on TV from Washington, telling America, "Today, we are committed to a worldwide struggle to promote and protect the rights of all who wish to be free." A little after midnight on June 12, Evers had parked in his driveway, stepped from his car, and took a bullet in the back. For some reason, the shooter left the rifle in the bushes where he'd hidden out, and here they were, en route to making an arrest.

The murder didn't really fall within the Bureau's jurisdiction, barring a conspiracy to rob the victim of his civil rights, but these days, when the president said, "Jump," Director Hoover clenched his teeth and asked, "How high?"

"A fertilizer salesman." Nolan couldn't seem to get it through his head.

"Not only that," said Nicholson. "Also a member of the White Citizens' Council and likely the Klan. Two Jackson cabbies say he asked them for directions to the Evers home, and then, there's a letter he wrote to the National Rifle Association. Want to hear about it?"

"Thrill me."

"This guy writes, 'We here in Mississippi are going to have to do a great deal of shooting to protect our wives and children from bad niggers.'"

"Sounds delightful. What's his name again?"

"Byron De La Beckwith."

Nolan frowned, wondering why that name sounded familiar. There was something, but he couldn't put his finger on it yet.

He wasn't thrilled about the temporary transfer out of Birmingham, leaving his wife and kids alone, but if today panned out, he could be back at home by Sunday, give or take.

And things were popping in Alabama. In January,

George Wallace had delivered an inauguration speech penned by Ace Carter, promising his voters "Segregation now, segregation tomorrow, segregation forever." The first convicts whose prison sentences he canceled out were four of Carter's former Klansmen who had mutilated Edward Aaron six years early, now back on the street after serving barely one-third of their time.

In Birmingham, meanwhile, Art Hanes and Bull Connor were standing fast against the SCLC's spring campaign against Jim Crow, fielding cops, attack dogs, and high-pressure hoses against demonstrators, many of them children. Racists didn't seem to mind the bad PR, but it alarmed enough voters to force a change in city government, scrapping the old City Commission for a revamped mayor and city council system. Hanes and Connor were both fighting that in court, backed by Klansmen bent on perpetuating "Bombingham's" reputation. So far this year, they'd blown up two Negro homes—one occupied by Martin Luther King's younger brother—and a black-owned motel that served as King's headquarters.

In April, fifty-eight miles to the northeast, a white mail carrier named William Moore had been gunned down while on a one-man "freedom march," wearing a sandwich sign denouncing segregation. Police traced the gun to Floyd Simpson, a "klokan" for Bob Shelton's United Klans, but he was free on bond, claiming an unknown "stranger" stole his piece to murder Moore. So far, Etowah County's grand jury seemed to believe him.

And while Alabama simmered, Mississippi seemed intent on boiling over. Governor-elect Paul Johnson had pulled a 62-percent majority by telling white voters, "Either you believe in states' rights, home rule, or you believe in turning over this state to a black minority." For emphasis, he advised them that the NAACP was a combination of "niggers, alligators, apes, coons and possums."

That passed for wit in the Magnolia State, where Negroes made up 45 percent of the population but only 5 percent of all registered voters. According to the last census, Mississippi's populace had suffered a net loss of 773 souls since 1950, while 86 percent of nonwhite families dwelt below the poverty line, and poor whites—the Klan's shaky base—weren't doing much better. Johnson's domain ranked forty-ninth among the fifty states in literacy, dead last in health care and economics.

Nothing to make anybody proud, as far as O'Hara could see, but Mississippi whites could still claim pride of place in béating, bombing, and burning out Negroes who demanded such "outrageous special rights" as suffrage and equal access to toilets.

Pulling into Greenwood, Agent Nicholson seemed to know where he was going, a benefit of serving as Jackson's resident agent. Most Mississippi cases were handled from Memphis or New Orleans since the Jackson field office shut down in 1946, but if things kept heating up, O'Hara guessed there'd have to be a second coming pretty soon.

"The asshole's lair," said Nicholson, as they pulled up outside one of the carbon-copy houses on a tree-lined street. "You ready?"

"As I'll ever be," Nolan replied.

They ambled up the concrete walk and tried the doorbell, Nolan rapping with his knuckles when it didn't seem to work. After a minute and a half, a slender man answered, his white shirt open at the collar, dark hair combed back from his oval face.

"Hep you?" he asked.

They badged him, Nicholson inquiring, "Are you Byron De La Beckwith?"

"In the flesh. What brings ya here?"

"We have a warrant to arrest you on a charge of homicide," Nolan replied.

"Do I know you?" asked Beckwith, peering closely at him. "Can't say I recall your name, but I *never* forget a face."

It all came back to Nolan then: two young Marines on Tarawa in 1943, one having just survived diving on top of a grenade that failed to detonate, the other bleeding badly from a wound near his waistline. Nolan could hear Beckwith informing him, before O'Hara helped him to the beach, about a quartermaster who'd been unable to fit his full name on the breast pocket of his fatigues.

"We *did* meet once," Nolan acknowledged, "twenty years ago."

"Funny old world," said Beckwith. "First, we're killin' Japs together; now I guess we's enemies." He cracked an eerie smile, saying, "Just lemme grab my hat, and we'll be on our way."

———

National Mall, Washington, D.C.: August 28, 1963

It was Ike Sawyer's second visit to the Lincoln Memorial. The first, in 1932, had been a whim provoked by curiosity. This time, he thought it must mean something more. Ike stood amidst the seething crowd—some of its members praying, others singing—and was suitably amazed.

D.C. wasn't his first road trip this year. That had

occurred in April when he'd driven from Gotham to Dallas in his three-year-old Chevy Corsair, which he expected was the last car he would ever own.

As the crow flies, Dallas lay 1,550 miles southwest of Gotham, but that route would've led Sawyer through a smidgen of Virginia, plus much greater distances through Georgia, Tennessee and Arkansas, all rabid Jim Crow states. He couldn't swing that with his New York license tags and what he would be carrying for ballast, so he'd gone the long way, from New York City on across the Midwest till he got to Wichita, Kansas, then south on I-135, through Oklahoma, into Texas.

It cost more and landed him in four flea-bag motels along the way, his driving stamina reduced a bit at seventy, but he'd arrived all right and set about stalking his target.

Edwin Walker had been flying high in racist circles since the nuthouse kicked him loose by court order last year, after the Ole Miss riot. He'd joined right-wing preacher Billy Hargis on a tour of the country they called "Operation Midnight Ride," stopping along the way to call upon America's military to "liquidate the scourge that has descended upon the island of Cuba." He was back in Dallas by April—Ike knew his travel schedule from the newspapers—and Sawyer had no problem locating his home on Turtle Creek Boulevard, in the Highland Park district.

There, on the night of April 10, Ike had unwrapped his vintage Mauser 35M bolt-action rifle with a Leupold telescopic sight attached and spotted Walker sitting at his desk, framed by a handy window. He had aimed, squeezed off—and missed the goddamned shot, no time to stick around and try again, as Walker hit the floor and wriggled out of sight.

Sawyer had spent a long week on the road, returning to New York. The good news: there had been no witnesses, and his 8.6-mm bullet had been too mangled on impact for ballistic tests. Not that anyone was looking for him, mind you. Who'd suspect an aged Negro and a former fed who lived halfway across the country from a demagogue so many other people hated?

In the papers, afterward, a Dallas cop had said, "Whoever shot at the general was playing for keeps. The sniper wasn't trying to scare him. He was shooting to kill."

Damned straight, but Ike had been too bleary-eyed to pull it off.

Now, here he was in Washington, anonymous and thankfully unrecognized by some 250,000 protesters who'd come to challenge the White House and Congress for a stronger stand on civil rights, most of the horde pledged to the creed of civil disobedience passed down from Gandhi via Martin Luther King.

Ike wasn't sure their tactics would succeed, given the TV news assaulting him each night from Dixie, but he knew this moment would go down in history. And he was part of it.

Nearly two years in the making, the protest was first announced as an "October Emancipation March on Washington for Jobs." By June, when spokesmen for the movement's "Big Six" groups had formed a Council for United Civil Rights Leadership, the date was moved forward; its focus shifted to the passage of a new Civil Rights Act surpassing all others to date, making discrimination in public facilities a federal crime.

Now here they were, all races drawn from points across America, arriving in the capital by car, by train, and buses by the hundreds—450 of them from Harlem alone, traffic wardens counting 100 per hour rolling through the Baltimore Harbor Tunnel. Under the sharp eyes of the police, marchers arrived with picnic baskets, water jugs, Bibles, and more hope in their hearts than any of them could contain.

Security was tight as a tick: 5,900 cops, 2,000 National Guardsmen and 4,000 regular soldiers, with liquor sales banned in D.C. for the first time since Repeal, hospitals stockpiling blood and canceling elective surgeries, but so far all was calm and peaceful. Even the placards being waved around were civil, the most strident Ike had seen so far reading, "There is No Halfway House on the Way to Freedom."

Speakers whose voices boomed over a pricey sound system included march director A. Philip Randolph, Walter Reuther from the United Auto Workers, the NAACP's Roy Wilkins, John Lewis from SNCC, plus various ministers, a rabbi, even onetime actress and cabaret star Josephine Hill—but everyone was waiting to hear Martin Luther King, the TV star of movement battles in Alabama and Georgia over the past eight years.

King took the podium at 1:30 p.m. by Ike's watch, and he'd launched into a speech that held the multitudes spellbound. His voice, reduced to human tones by radio and television, now rolled out across the Mall like that of God Himself, loving but frustrated by all the roadblocks people had erected in His path.

As he wound down, King summarized his dreams for an America reborn, eliciting heartfelt "Amens!" from thousands of voices together. King dreamed a classless society without racial barriers, from coast to coast and border to border, taking his rapt audience on a tour of the nation, focusing on mountaintops.

"So let freedom ring from the prodigious hilltops of New Hampshire," he declaimed. Let freedom ring from the mighty mountains of New York. Let freedom ring from the heightening Alleghenies of Pennsylvania! Let freedom ring from the snowcapped Rockies of Colorado! Let freedom ring from the curvaceous slopes of California! But not only that; let freedom ring from Stone Mountain of Georgia! Let freedom ring from Lookout Mountain of Tennessee! Let freedom ring from every hill and molehill of Mississippi. From every mountainside, let freedom ring."

Ike felt a tightness in his chest as if his heart—so long without true hope—might literally burst with yearning now, as King drove home his dream.

"And when this happens, when we allow freedom to ring, when we let it ring from every village and every hamlet, from every state and every city, we will be able to speed up that day when all of God's children, black men, and white men, Jews and Gentiles, Protestants and Catholics, will be able to join hands and sing in the words of the old Negro spiritual, 'Free at last! Free at last! Thank God Almighty, we are free at last!' "

Applause rose up to meet King like the rumbling of an earthquake, and the ground beneath Ike's feet seemed to be heaving, rolling with the sound. Ike only realized that he was falling backward in the final seconds of his life, cushioned by grass as he collapsed, eyes open, staring at the blue sky and whatever lay beyond.

———

MANHATTAN: *September 2, 1963*

FRED SAWYER STOOD between his brother Payton and his sister Keisha, clinging to the hand of six-year-old daughter Luvenia, while their father's casket lowered out of sight, into the open grave. His portion of the marble headstone shared with their mother Talitha, gone these seven years, still waited for a stonemason to etch Ike's name, his dates of birth and death, together with the platitude "Loving Husband and Father."

It had been a hassle getting Dad's corpse home from Washington after the march, twenty-one chartered trains packed with weary demonstrators upsetting the railroad timetables, but now the deed was done, nothing remaining on the to-do list except for filling in a hole.

Aside from Ike's children and granddaughter, the only graveside mourner was a white-haired Harlem barber who had known the kids since they were sprouts and who'd looked after Ike as male friends sometimes do, in the years since Talitha's passing. He was weeping softly now, dabbing at moist eyes with a paisley handkerchief, lips moving in what Fred supposed must be a prayer.

Or maybe it was just senility.

After the minister who'd barely known their father finished reading from his Bible, he shook hands with each of Ike's descendants in the order of their ages, with Luvenia coming last, then muttered his condolences and strode off through the boneyard toward some other chore awaiting him. When he was gone, nothing remained but for Ike's children to indulge in fleeting hugs and go their separate ways.

There was another hole in Fred's life now, and he was trying his damnedest to fill it with work. The Bureau kept him busy watching over RAM, lately supporting demonstrations in the black Philadelphia districts of Frankford,

Oberbrook, and Southwest Central City. There had been no violence yet, despite RAM's revolutionary message, only protests of the kind favored by Martin Luther King. Still, Washington demanded all the details, dates and names.

Fred sometimes wondered if he'd picked a dead-end job, wasting his life, but he kept such doubts to himself. He'd never shared them with his father, nor could he depend on Payton, doing much the same thing for NYPD to keep a roof over his head.

Hang on for now, he told himself again, not for the first time. *Wait and see what happens next.*

But why did that wise counsel put his nerves on edge?

————

FBI HEADQUARTERS: October 4, 1963

ALOYSIUS GANTT HAD FELT a brief pang of nostalgia back in March when Alcatraz was shut down as a federal prison. He recalled his escort duty on a boat carrying "public enemies" bound for The Rock. Some of them had died there—Dock Barker trying to escape in 1939, Al Bates from heart failure nine years later—but they were all just fading memories today.

Like me, Gantt thought and almost laughed aloud.

These days he kept his hand in by investigating COMINFIL targets and marking time until he got up nerve enough to finally retire. One of those targets was the growing SDS, drawing more than 200 delegates from thirty-two colleges to its latest convention at Pine Hill, New York. The group had chosen Todd Gitlin of Harvard as its new president, with Lee Webb from Boston University as national secretary, and while the SDS was drifting steadily leftward, it hadn't undertaken any actions yet.

The same could not be said for Martin Luther King, marked for intensified surveillance since the March on Washington. Bill Sullivan had lit that fuse with a memo to Hoover, saying, "In the light of King's powerful demagogic speech, we must mark him now, if we have not done so before, as the most dangerous Negro of the future in this nation from the standpoint of communism, the Negro, and national security."

Of course, the Bureau *had* "marked" King before, in 1955, as Sullivan knew well. His memo was a cover for the new campaign of planting microphones in King's home and in hotel rooms he used while traveling across the country. Bobby Kennedy's "short-term" permission for the bugging had long since expired, but once given an inch; Hoover was always known to take ten miles. His answer to Sullivan's memo ordered all field offices to "explore how best to carry on our investigation to produce the desired results without embarrassment to the Bureau," including "a complete analysis of the avenues of approach aimed at neutralizing King as an effective Negro leader."

Most of that paperwork now found its way to Gantt's desk, where he perused it, ticked off initials on the list of qualified recipients, and passed it on. Where the campaign was going, he couldn't have said, but he almost felt sorry for the preacher standing tall in Edgar Hoover's crosshairs.

Almost, but not quite.

———

LITTLE ITALY, *Manhattan: October 10, 1963.*

THE KENNEDY JUGGERNAUT against organized crime showed no sign of losing steam, which left Greg Jordan in a quandary about his family's future. Even Angelina—his wife of forty years, with their ruby anniversary impending —had been slipping from her longtime see-no-evil attitude, making occasional and seemingly off-hand inquiries as to whether they were safe.

In times like these, the worst since Kefauver's committee roamed the land, what answer could Greg offer her?

Speaking of Estes Kefauver, a lifetime of heavy smoking and drinking had finally caught up with him, producing an August heart attack that left the old gangbuster gasping out his final hours at Bethesda Naval Hospital in Maryland. Unfortunately, there'd been no such news regarding Senator McClellan, who had struck a mother lode of sorts with Joe Valachi, captivating TV viewers by the millions who reveled in seamy tales of *Cosa Nostra*.

Jordan blamed *Don* Vito Genovese for the September hearings where Valachi spilled his guts about the Mafia, its history, and how the "father" of his family had set him on his present course last year, trying to kill Valachi as the stoolpigeon he'd now become in fact. Call it a self-fulfilling prophecy, but while Valachi started out angry at Genovese, he seemed intent on bringing down the whole damned House of Mafia.

Granted, Valachi had been smalltime all the way, a button man and courier of drugs primarily, but now he was a star on television, walking the McClellan panel through the *Cosa Nostra*'s recruitment process, spilling everything he'd seen or heard over the past thirty-odd years in Gotham's underworld. He had the goods on several high-profile hits, and if his knowledge of gangland outside New York was vague at best, nobody seemed to care. As one Justice Department spokesman phrased it, Joe Cago had "showed us the enemy's face."

Or some of it, at least.

Aside from talking to the Senate, he had rambled on to various grand juries, state and federal prosecutors, and the FBI—which recently, impelled by Bobby Kennedy, had finally decided that a Syndicate existed in America. To save face, the Bureau's director had decreed that future memos on the Mafia—which he'd derided as a myth for over thirty years—should now call it "La Cosa Nostra," usually trimmed to "LCN," while countless non-Italian mobsters were downgraded to "associates."

Greg had to laugh at Hoover's passion for semantics, seeking absolution for his long-term negligence. Did he not realize that adding *la* to *Cosa Nostra* translated as "the our thing," a garbled tag that even an illiterate street soldier wouldn't recognize?

Revenge, as always, had its price. A headline story out of Washington claimed *mafiosi* had an open contract out on Joe Valachi, offering $100,000 to whoever killed him first. Some law enforcement agencies were rounding up Italian racketeers they hadn't booked since Apalachin, grilling them in hopes of turning up more stoolies, but NYPD remained contrary, denouncing Valachi's revelations as stale, threadbare rumors, pegging Valachi as "a small, publicity-loving bum" or no significance.

Love him or hate him, Joe Cago had no insights to share on Jimmy Hoffa, but the Teamsters' president was in hot water anyway. In March, he'd been indicted for jury tampering at his last mistrial, witness Walter Sheridan from the Kennedy "get-Hoffa squad" detailing a plot against himself and other investigators, wherein Hoffa planned to trap feds in an alley "and have a bunch of 'business agents' waiting for them."

Whether that was true or not—and Jordan thought it sounded quite a bit like Hoffa—Jimmy and seven code-fendants would be facing trial in Tennessee next April, charged with using fraudulent loan applications to loot the union's pension fund. Hoffa dismissed the latest case as "just another one of Bobby Kennedy's shenanigans," but insiders admitted he was worried and discussing plots to murder Kennedy.

Closer to home, the Mafia's ruling Commission faced a challenge that some journalists had started calling "the Banana Split." It stemmed from Joe Bonanno—hence the nickname—scheming with Joe Magliocco from the Profaci family to wipe out rival godfathers Carlo Gambino, Tommy Lucchese and Stefano Magaddino, along with Frank DeSimone in Los Angeles. Magliocco had assigned triggerman Joe Colombo to whack Gambino and Lucchese, but Colombo ran tattling to the marked men instead. The Commission summoned Bonanno and Magliocco to a sit-down, but Joe Bananas didn't show, leaving Magliocco to crack under pressure, forced into retirement with a $50,000 fine on top of that, the traitorous Colombo rising to replace him as boss of the former Profaci *famigila*.

The problem now: Bonanno still remained at large, ignoring calls from the Commission, brooding silently while the ruling panel replaced him with *caporegime* Gaspar DiGregorio. Where Bonanno might surface and what he might do were topics of media speculation, some wags upgrading the dispute from a "Banana Split" to a "Banana War." All the Giordano family could do was watch and wait, hoping that when the next shoe dropped, it wouldn't fall on them.

As for the Kennedys, Greg knew that plans were in the works to rid America of them by one means or another. Pundits reckoned JFK would be a reelection shoo-in next year, but at least one *mafioso* had other ideas. As Jordan heard it from the Sunshine State, Santo Trafficante had been talking of extreme measures to Cuban exile allies in Miami. One of those, ex-Minister of Education and ardent Castro-hater José Aleman, had expressed fears of a second term for Kennedy, in a meeting at Miami's Scott Bryan Hotel. Santo had tried to calm him, saying, "No, José, he is going to be hit."

Bluster or prophecy?

Whichever, Jordan didn't feel like placing any bets on Camelot's longevity.

————

SAIGON: November 3, 1963

OUTSIDE THE DẦU Khỉ Club in Chợ Lớn, Saigon's China-town, rain poured from a slate-colored sky but failed to drop the temperature below eighty degrees. The bar's name translated as "Monkey's Head" in English, but there were no simians in evidence, headless or otherwise, as Colby Gantt worked on his third bottle of Tiger beer.

The panic that had gripped Saigon over the past two days was spent now, Colby hoping that by morning he could catch a flight from Tân Sơn Nhứt Airbase to Tokyo, and onward from there to the States. Call it 8,200 miles overall, some nineteen hours by air, not counting stopovers, but he could drink and sleep en route until his feet were back on friendly soil.

The only question nagging at him now was where the Agency would send him next.

It clearly wouldn't be to Russia, where a firing squad had executed Colonel Oleg Penkovsky, a high-ranking member of Soviet Military Intelligence, in May. It also likely wouldn't be to Germany, where JFK had delivered his now-famous "*Ich bin ein Berliner*" speech in June. Sipping his beer, Gantt wondered whether anyone had tipped the president to his faux pas as yet—in essence saying, "I'm a jelly donut"—but he doubted it.

Who'd want to drop that news on the Commander-in-Chief so soon after he'd established a hotline between the White House and the Kremlin, followed in July by a partial nuclear test ban treaty with the Soviet Union and Britain? Henceforth, after seventeen years of radioactive blasts ranging from ground level to the stratosphere, detonations would be limited to underground facilities such as the Nevada Test Site, northwest of Las Vegas.

A week after that, keeping pace, the CIA had created a new Directorate of Science & Technology helmed by Deputy Director Albert Wheelon, a pioneer of space-based surveillance programs.

On Earth, of course, setbacks seemed inescapable. The worst so far this year, in January, had occurred when British SIS agent Kim Philby vanished from Beirut, leaving his wife befuddled at the home of Glencairn Paul, First Secretary of the British Embassy. Another seven months elapsed before Philby surfaced in Moscow, claiming sanctuary and Soviet citizenship after sixteen years of undercover service to the MGB, MVD and KGB. The wife he'd left behind was number two, her alcoholic predecessor having been poisoned at the Philby home in Crowborough, East Sussex, six years earlier.

Aside from feeding reams of bullshit to the Gehlen Org in Germany, Philby had looted SIS files for secrets on Moscow's behalf since 1947. Suspected of treason in 1954, Philby had tried his hand at journalism, then was "cleared" and welcomed back to cloak-and-dagger work by Foreign Secretary Harold Macmillan in October 1955, resuming his double agent's role throughout the Middle East. KGB defector Anatoliy Golitsyn had named Philby as Moscow's man in 1961, yet still he remained on the Queen's payroll for another two years, until simmering tension convinced him to flee, leaving the SIS and CIA with egg-smeared faces.

Things were running more smoothly in Latin America, where the Agency's Special Activities Division had opened its International Police Academy this year, training foreign officers in the fine arts of interrogation and subversion. Colby had a copy of the IPA's first manual, titled *Counterintelligence Interrogation*, focused chiefly on "coercive interrogation of resistant sources." That sounded better than "torture," but it amounted to the same thing, suggesting that suspects should be kidnapped in the predawn hours, stripped and blindfolded, held incommunicado at secret locations, deprived of sleep and food, kept in small rooms windowless and soundproof, dark and without toilets.

All in a day's work, defending "national security."

In Haiti, Papa Doc Duvalier's *Tonton Macoute* needed no such instruction, though secret policemen must have shaken their heads at some of their dictator's antics. Seized by uncommon generosity in April, Duvalier had freed rebel Clément Barbot from prison, then quickly regretted it. During the manhunt to retrieve him, Duvalier heard rumors that Barbot had magically changed himself into a black dog, inciting slaughter of all such canines on the island by presidential command. It was July before searchers tracked down Barbot in human form and murdered him at last, by which time Haitian exiles had prepared for an invasion from the neighboring Dominican Republic. Their attack in August failed, inciting new rounds of arrests and torture by Duvalier's regime.

Cuba, naturally, still remained a major focus of the CIA's attention, lately embodied by "AMLASH," latest phase of the attempt to kill Fidel. AMLASH was, in fact, a single operative: Dr. Rolando Cubela, founder of Cuba's Student Revolutionary Directorate and a Castro loyalist until 1962, when he soured on Marxism and offered his services to the Agency. Overseeing branches of his student movement in Miami and New Orleans, Dr. Cubela had accepted money and a poison pen, the latter meant to kill Castro, but nothing had yet come of it.

While Cubela stalled, other groups proved more active, including the Movement for Revolutionary Recovery and a spin-off, the Catholic Democratic Movement, which had received a green light for construction of a paramilitary training base outside Lacombe, Louisiana. One of those involved in that training was William Guy Banister, a twenty-year FBI veteran and former head of the Chicago field office, later Assistant Superintendent of the New Orleans Police Department, now a private eye, radical Minutemen supporter, and arms supplier for multiple anti-Castro exile groups. Unstable at the best of times, Banister operated from an office at 544 Camp Street, which oddly hosted both the anti-Castro Cuban Revolutionary Council *and* the ostensibly pro-Castro Fair Play for Cuba Committee.

Smoke and mirrors, Colby thought, *designed to keep the FBI and public mystified.*

Circling back to Southeast Asia, the forecast called for more chaos, destruction, and bloodshed. In Laos, Air America inserted and extracted U.S. personnel and weapons, conducting a lucrative sideline in opium and heroin supplied by Hmong tribal leader Vang Pao. In September, hostile ground fire downed a C-46 near Xépôn in Savannakhét Province, killing three Americans and one Chinese crewman.

Next-door in South Vietnam, the Việt Cộng had been scoring victories all year, starting with January's Battle of Ấp Bắc, which made front-page news in the States. President Diệm chose military leaders not for skill, but their Catholicism and personal fealty to him, meaning they weren't the sharpest knives in the drawer but could be counted on to bully Diệm's enemies. In May, Buddhist protesters marched against Diệm's ban on religious flags celebrating Buddha's mythical birthday, prompting government troops in Hue to mow down an unruly crowd, killing a woman and eight children.

On July 4, symbolically, a Buddhist South Vietnamese General, Tran Van Don, approached the CIA with his idea to overthrow Diệm. A new U.S. ambassador, Henry Cabot Lodge, reached Saigon in August, tasked by the State Department to evaluate Diệm's regime. Three days later, Lodge reported back, saying, "There is no possibility, in my view, that the war can be won under a Diệm administration." Jack Kennedy approved the pending coup, granting an interview to Walter Cronkite in September, calling Diệm "out of touch with the people" of South Vietnam, adding his hope that confidence in government might be restored "with changes in policy and perhaps in personnel."

And yesterday, exactly that had happened. Rebel military officers led by General Dương Văn Minh, armed with assurances of American support, had seized Diệm and brother Ngô Đình Nhu, *de facto* warlord of the nation's southernmost quadrant, executing both with point-blank gunfire in the rear compartment of an army truck.

So much for Eisenhower's fabled "miracle man."

Colby had viewed the corpses, snapped a photo to embellish his report, and couldn't wait to put the whole damned country in his rearview mirror. Staying on to fight were 16,300 U.S. military "advisors," bankrolled by $500,000 to keep the latest threatened domino from toppling.

The news at home was bad for MIDNIGHT CLIMAX mastermind George White. CIA Inspector General John Earman had dropped by the "pleasure" pad on San Francisco's Chestnut Street and was so appalled by what he'd found that he had recommended closure. White was clinging to the fragile raft so far, but whether he would sink or swim remained an open question.

Compensating for the pending shutdown of that MKULTRA sideshow, Langley continued its Quixotic search for a "truth drug" in the guise of an academic study, through the Society for the Investigation of Human Ecology. John Earman's report panned further LSD experiments as "too unpredictable and uncontrollable for any tactical use," but hope sprang eternal at Langley, convincing Gantt that dabbling in mad science would continue.

If he ever met George White again, Colby would make damned sure the nitwit hadn't slipped something into his drink.

———

MANHATTAN: November 25, 1963

"I STILL CAN'T BELIEVE it. Can you?" Fiona's voice on the long-distance line sounded tense, almost frightened. Dave Jordan could tell that she'd been crying before calling him.

"I'm starting to," he said. No point in telling her that he believed or that a part of him expected nothing less than sudden death for President John Kennedy.

"It's such a tragedy," Fiona said. "I mean, not only for the country but the family itself. You know they lost a child less than four months ago?"

"I did know that," Dave answered.

Patrick Kennedy, the third child of Jack and Jackie, had arrived prematurely in August and died less than two days later, from respiratory complications. Now, Dave realized, John Jr.—three years old this very day, as TV journalists kept harping on—would be the martyred president's last child.

Before the past weekend's events in Dallas, David and Fiona hadn't spoken in four weeks. Make that four weeks plus two days, but who in hell was counting? She had phoned him from her Legal Aid office in Washington when news of the shooting first broke, and then came all that followed. Both of them were home today, Monday, by order of the newly minted president, who had decreed a day of mourning save for essential emergency workers.

And a lot of good that did the Kennedys, aside from putting their grief on display.

Dave was vaguely aware of JFK's trip to Texas on Friday, cheered by hundreds at Love Field in Dallas, rolling on from there toward the Dallas Trade Mart in a motorcade that carried him through Dealey Plaza at the city's heart. Days earlier, someone had plastered Dallas with 5,000 flyers branding Kennedy as "WANTED FOR TREASON," accusing him of being "lax" on communism and "appointing anti-Christians to Federal office," But on Friday, as 200,000 cheering Texans lined the motorcade's routes, Nellie Connally—the state's First Lady, riding with her governor-husband in Kennedy's open limousine, remarked, "Mr. President, you can't say Dallas doesn't love you."

Ironically, those were the last words JFK would ever hear.

Shots struck the limousine at half-past noon, mortally wounding the president, gravely injuring Governor Connally. A mad dash to Parkland Hospital ensued, where Kennedy was pronounced dead at 1:00 p.m. The first news broke on CBS-TV, interrupting a live broadcast of *As the World Turns*, and Kennedy's corpse was back in Air Force One, winging toward Washington by 2:38, when new president Lyndon Johnson took his oath of office, flanked by his wife and his predecessor's blood-spattered widow.

From there, the news kept coming, washing over Jordan in one stunning wave after another while he spoke at intervals with Fee, doing his utmost to console her and make sense of what had happened.

At 1:50, Dallas cops had busted Lee Harvey Oswald at a local theater, ostensibly for gunning down a uniformed patrolman an hour earlier. Oswald had tried to shoot them, the detectives claimed, but his cheap pistol had misfired.

By 6:00 p.m., Air Force One was back at Andrews Air Force Base in Maryland, met by Bobby Kennedy and other dignitaries, all in shock. Pathologists at Bethesda Naval Hospital began JFK's four-hour autopsy ten minutes before Oswald was formally charged with the beat cop's murder. By 11:26 p.m., new charges had been laid against Oswald, accusing him of the president's assassination.

From Saturday morning till now, Dave and Fiona had been on the phone as much as possible, and screw the bills. He'd offered to come join her in D.C. and wait the awful weekend out, but she had hemmed, hawed, and declined.

So be it.

The weekend's events were now indelibly imprinted on Dave's brain. The presidential corpse had come home in a casket before dawn on Saturday, lying in what they called "repose" till Sunday. A Requiem Mass was performed in the East Room on Saturday morning, the prince of Camelot oblivious inside his box. On Sunday afternoon, some 300,000 persons had lined Pennsylvania Avenue, watching Kennedy's flag-draped coffin roll toward the Capitol Building on the same caisson that carried FDR's remains nineteen years earlier.

In the rotunda, Jackie and her children knelt to pray before their lost husband and father. Senate Majority Leader Mike Mansfield, Speaker of the House John McCormack, and Chief Justice Earl Warren delivered brief eulogies, then ordinary people were admitted, 250,000 of them shuffling past the coffin and its watchful guards. So many came that dignitaries scrapped their plan to close the building overnight and let the grim procession last for eighteen hours straight.

And on that same Sunday, a Dallas nightclub owner named Jack Ruby had appeared as if from nowhere in the precinct basement, at half-past 11:00 a.m. Central Time, while officers were walking Oswald to a car for transfer to the county jail. Ruby had fired once, into Oswald's abdomen, and doctors at now-famous Parkland Hospital pronounced the possible assassin dead at 1:07.

Now, at long last, it was nearly over, JFK Junior's grim birthday party winding down. Dave and Fiona talked nonstop, only her fits of weeping interrupting them, while an estimated million mourners watched the funeral procession move from the Capitol back to the White House, then to St. Matthew's Cathedral, and finally to Arlington National Cemetery. TV reporters claimed the last such assembly of foreign leaders and royalty had been in 1910, at the funeral of Britain's King Edward VII. It was past 3:30 when the casket was interred and Mrs. Kennedy lit an "eternal flame" designed to burn natural gas forever—or until some madman pushed a button and the whole damned world was fried.

Coincidentally, Chet Huntley told the world, presumed assassin Lee Oswald had gone into the ground at the same time, 1,360 miles away, at Fort Worth's Rose Hill Cemetery. Seven reporters served as pallbearers, laying him to rest beneath a plain flat stone that Dave assumed would probably be vandalized within a day or two.

"Sorry," he said, aware that he'd missed some remark from Fee. "Could you repeat that, please?"

"I need to see you, Dave. I can come up there if you like, or—"

"No, I'll come to you. Just let me check on when the next train's headed south."

"Okay. I'm looking forward to it."

He already had Fiona's address but had never used it till now. "Should I bring anything?"

She didn't seem to hear him that time, coming back with, "Who would do something like this? One man? I can't believe it."

"Christ, I wish I knew."

But in his heart, Dave reckoned he might have a fair idea.

————

LITTLE ITALY, Manhattan: November 25, 1963

"LOOK AT THAT," Angelo Giordano said, sneering. "You think she wants to blow him one more time before they put him under?"

Dominic glanced over at his brother, frowning. "Jesus Christ," he answered back. "That's sacrilegious shit you're talkin' now."

"Fuck 'im," Ange said. "And fuck her, too. You'd like a piece a that, I bet."

"Gimme a break."

In front of them, in living color on Dom's Westinghouse TV set, Jackie Kennedy was kneeling at her husband's coffin, dressed in black, head bowed in prayer.

The set had cost Dom $1,300, brother Ange cracking wise about the waste of money, but Dom didn't care, even though most programs still aired in black-and-white.

"So, who you figger took him out?"

"That Oswald character," Dom said.

"Yeah, yeah." Ange fanned the air with one hand. "But I mean, who put 'im up to it?"

"You don't believe the newspapers? They're sayin' the commie drilled Kennedy and Ruby didn't want the widow comin' back for Oswald's trial."

"Hey, fuck the papers. When's the last time you remember that they got a story straight?"

"I heard that."

"So? Who, then?"

"Some things," Dom reminded him, "it's better not to know." Of course, he had a few ideas but wasn't sharing them just yet, not even with his *fratellino*.

"Awright. Can you just put some football on?"

"Forget it. This shit's all they're showin', all day long."

"So, let's go out and get a beer, eh?"

"What's that in your hand, *finnochio*?"

Ange drained his bottle in a single swallow. "See? All gone."

"Awright, then," Dom said. "But you're buyin' the first round."

––––––

FBI Headquarters: November 27, 1963

Declan O'Hara wondered if the grim events in Dallas were inevitable. Certainly, they had been presaged by the current DOJ's progress against mobsters. Indictments and convictions had gone up again this year—615 and 288, respectively, while IRS man-hours spent on Mob cases had increased more than tenfold since 1960, up from 8,836 to 96,182, resulting in 288 cases of tax evasion being filed.

So far, the only win on record for the Syndicate belonged to Carlos Marcello, acquitted of fraud charges in New Orleans on the same day JFK was shot. Seated with Marcello were defense attorney George Gill and an oddball whom Gill sometimes used as an investigator, David Ferrie—who, in turn, sometimes moonlighted as Marcello's private pilot, as when Carlos had returned from Guatemala two years earlier. Strangely, Ferrie had skipped Marcello's victory party, taking off with two cronies to Galveston and Houston on the afternoon of the assassination. They claimed they'd wanted to go ice skating or hunting, but they took along no skates or shotguns.

What in hell was up with that?

One thing O'Hara knew was that the FBI's reaction to the president's murder had been consistent with Director Hoover's style and well-known loathing of the Kennedys. He'd phoned Attorney General Bobby at RFK's home in Hickory Hill, Virginia, interrupting a meeting on organized crime to say, "The president's been shot."

Just that, and *click,* dead air. Hoover hadn't called back when Bobby's brother was pronounced dead. That news came Captain Tazewell Shepard, a naval aide to the late president. Afterward, discussing Hoover's phone call with his staff, Attorney General Kennedy remarked, "I think he told me with pleasure."

The president had been dead less than thirty minutes when Hoover fired off a memo to field offices across the country, calling for the investigation of a possible conspiracy with focus on the Ku Klux Klan. By 4:00 p.m. Hoover had changed his tune, branding Lee Oswald a pro-Castro Red who'd defected to Russia in 1959, renounced his U.S. citizenship, then married a KGB officer's niece and returned stateside seventeen months before Kennedy's murder.

The Bureau knew all that because one of its men in Texas had interrogated Oswald twice, at least, since his return. Hoover painted the triggerman—if such he was, in fact—as a demented loner acting on his own. Jack Ruby's murder of the suspect helped with that, allowing Speed to turn his back on any evidence of a conspiracy. A memo from November 25 declared, "There is nothing further on the Oswald case except that he is dead. The public must be satisfied that Oswald was the assassin; that he did not have confederates who are still at large; and that evidence was such that he would have been convicted at trial."

"Bullshit," O'Hara muttered to himself.

He'd been through Oswald's background with a fine-toothed comb. Sired by his mother's second husband in New Orleans, back in 1934, Oswald had never known his father, who had died two months before his birth. An uncle he loved was on Carlos Marcello's payroll. Mother Marguerite dumped two of her sons at an orphanage, but the place rejected Lee as too young, so she'd left him with a neighbor, finally getting Lee in with his brothers the day after Christmas 1942.

His life had gone downhill from there: a move with Marguerite to Dallas and her prospective third husband in January 1944; threatening his landlord with a knife in August 1952; slapped with truancy charges in April 1953; back to New Orleans with his newly divorced mom in

January 1954; joining the Civil Air Patrol and meeting Captain David Ferrie eighteen months later; dropping out of one high school in October 1955, then from another in September 1956.

The Marine Corps might've saved him, when he'd joined up in October 1956. Its brochures promised to "build men," but that didn't work out for Lee. He'd barely qualified as a "sharpshooter"—the equivalent of a C+ or so —and was accepted into Jacksonville's Naval Air Technical Training Center, emerging as an aviation electronics operator with a "Confidential" security clearance. Still, discipline eluded him. Stationed in Japan, Oswald accidentally shot himself with a contraband pistol and was court-martialed twice, for the gun and for assaulting a superior. Released from the brig in August 1958, he'd bounced around various posts, scoring "poor" on a Russian language test. Discharged to help his injured mother one year later, he'd left the States for Russia a month after that, and thereby hung a very different tale.

In Moscow, he played tourist for a bit, then attempted suicide when his visa expired, landing in a psychiatric ward. Upon release, he'd requested Soviet citizenship, moving to Minsk while the U.S. State Department stalled him. A month before his twenty-first birthday, the Marine Corps changed his discharge status to "undesirable," but Lee didn't care. He'd proposed to one girlfriend and she turned him down, two days before rejecting Russian citizenship but seeking an extension of his residence permit. In February 1961 he'd approached the U.S. embassy, seeking to return stateside, but staffers dragged their feet with "preliminary inquiries."

And then, Oswald found love or something like it at a trade union dance, the closest thing in Moscow to a nightclub. Marina Prusakova hailed from Arkhangelsk, residing with her uncle Ilya Prusakov, a KGB colonel. She'd accepted Lee's proposal three days after the Bay of Pigs debacle and they were hitched ten days later. Oswald reapplied for entry to the States, this time bringing his wife. The embassy wasted more time, then caved and granted his request in June, along with a loan of $435.71. Lee and Marina reached Fort Worth on June 14, and G-men questioned Oswald for the first time twelve days later. By July 14 the newlyweds were sharing digs with nagging Marguerite, making their life a little slice of hell on Earth.

Oswald's remaining months were muddled and mysterious. He'd socialized with anti-communist Russian exiles led by George De Mohrenschildt, a petroleum geologist and possible CIA contract agent, separated from Marina and infant daughter June, and ordered a .38 revolver by mail, followed by a cheap Italian Mannlicher-Carcano rifle. Both weapons arrived in March 1963. In April he'd moved to New Orleans, renting an apartment and finding work at the William B. Reily Coffee Company. One of his coworkers was Jean-Pierre Lafitte, a Corsican drug smuggler positively known to be involved with CIA shenanigans.

In May, Oswald had requested a charter from the pro-Castro Fair Play for Cuba Committee, listing his office address as 544 Camp Street on the application and on 1,000 cheaply printed pamphlets. In a bizarre "coincidence," that building also housed ex-G-man Guy Banister's private eye firm and his *anti*-Castro Free Cuba Committee. Reilly Coffee fired Oswald on July 19, roughly two weeks before he'd approached Cuban exile activist Carlos Bringuier with an offer to help his campaign against Castro. They'd duked it out on Canal Street four days later, when Bringuier caught Lee handing out FPCC literature, prompting Oswald's guilty plea to a charge of disturbing the peace. Between those events, Carlos Marcello mobster Nofio Pecora posted Oswald's bail. The controversy got Lee several TV spots, including a debate against Bringuier that was the talk of New Orleans.

All for what, exactly? To make folks remember his name and suspicious Red ties?

In Late September, Oswald rode a bus to Laredo, Texas, and crossed into Mexico. Another bus took him to Mexico City, where he'd booked a hotel room before visiting the Cuban and Soviet embassies. Or *had* he? CIA men had the Russian embassy staked out and photographed all comers, but the visitor they'd pegged as "Lee Oswald" bore no resemblance to the slender, nervous-looking proper owner of that name.

Denied a Russian visa, "Oswald" caught another bus, this one to Dallas, where the real Lee disembarked on October 3 and checked in at the YMCA, then filed an unemployment claim. He worked briefly for a printing company, then signed on at the Texas School Book Depository, from which he'd allegedly shot JFK and Governor Connally seven weeks later. In his free time, he attended ACLU meetings and a rally addressed by crackpot racist Edwin Walker. FBI agent James Hosty questioned Marina twice in early November, whereupon Lee left a note at the Dallas field office, warning Hosty to stay away from his family.

On November 16, a man who resembled Oswald made a royal pain of himself at the Sports Dome rifle range in Dallas, firing randomly at targets other customers were using. When chastised, he made a scene, loudly announced his name, then stormed out of the place.

Laying a false trail? Declan wondered.

Kennedy's Texas trip had been announced on September 26, causing some folks to suspect that lone-gunman Oswald took the Book Depository job specifically to stage an ambush, but how could that be true when he started work there on October 16 and JFK's parade route wasn't finalized for another month, withheld from the press until assassination day?

The Bureau had Lee's movements on that final day under a microscope, from rolling out of bed at 6:30 a.m. to arriving at work with a "long paper bag," which the two best witnesses claimed was too small to contain a disman-tled rifle. Some other witnesses had glimpsed "a man" on the depository's sixth floor—the alleged source of the shots—but they couldn't agree upon which window he'd occupied, and a cop had found Oswald using a vending machine two floors down, moments after the shooting.

Beyond that, Oswald *had* left work within three minutes of the murder, along with most other depository employees. He'd ridden a bus and taxi back to his Beckley Avenue rooming house, arriving at 1:00 and leaving three minutes later—after his landlady said a police car had sounded its horn from the curb. By 1:16, someone had shot Patrolman J. D. Tippit in the Oak Cliff district, one mile southwest of Lee's rooming house. The last pro runner's record for a mile, in 1962, had been three minutes and fifty-four seconds, but he'd been running flat-out on a track, with no pedestrians, traffic, or stoplights to impede him.

At the latest murder scene, one witness swore *two* men shot Tippit, while another described a lone killer totally unlike Oswald: "short and somewhat on the heavy side, with slightly bushy hair." From there, the real Lee Oswald reached the Texas Theatre, just over half a mile distant, arriving twenty-four minutes after Tippit fell. Why was he slowing down after a slaying in broad daylight? Never mind. He'd made a point of entering the theater without buying a ticket, and its manager had called the cops. Detectives rolled, based on erroneous descriptions from the Tippit incident, and caught Oswald alive when his .38 —allegedly in great condition less than half an hour earlier—refused to fire.

The rest was history: Oswald booked into custody, three lineups, grilling, and a press conference just after midnight, where Lee declared himself a "patsy" and requested legal aid. During that photo op, District Attorney Henry Wade announced that Oswald was connected to the anti-Castro Free Cuba Committee, whereupon Jack Ruby called out from the back row to correct him, saying "Fair Play for Cuba."

And how had Jack known *that* when Lee's involvement with the FPCC was a New Orleans hiccup that last made news in the Big Easy three months earlier? Perhaps they'd never know, since Ruby—a Chicago hood gone native, grieving for the Kennedy's by his bizarre account—had silenced Oswald, sacrificing his own freedom, some thirty hours later.

From informers, Declan knew one man was still pursuing the New Orleans leads. Orleans Parish D.A. Jim Garrison had smelled a rat on November 22, when ex-G-man and right-wing agitator Guy Banister quarreled with employee Jack Martin in a saloon, pistol-whipping him after Martin shouted, "What are you going to do, kill me like you all did Kennedy?" Police questioned Martin at

Charity Hospital, recording his tale that Banister knew local whack-job David Ferrie, who Martin called a "getaway pilot" for JFK's assassins. When G-men questioned Ferrie, he'd denied it all. Martin, in turn, suggested Ferrie might have "hypnotized" Lee Oswald into shooting Kennedy.

The Garrison investigation didn't seem to be progressing, but a newsman out of Baton Rouge, one Amos Guidry, was already sniffing avidly around the fringes, seemingly convinced that any talk of a conspiracy was "crazy" and "delusional."

Says who? O'Hara asked himself. And who was pulling Guidry's strings?

———

HARLEM: December 5, 1963

THE SHOCK of JFK's murder was wearing off—or maybe Payton Sawyer was becoming more accustomed to assassinations after Medgar Evers fell in June, early November's slaughter of the Ngô brothers in Vietnam, then Dallas and Jack Ruby gunning Oswald down on live TV. His father's death in August had been bad enough, slight consolation found in hanging out with brother Fred and learning he was tied up at the Bureau with the same shit Payton kept pursuing on behalf of BOSS.

Small fucking world, he thought, beginning with their father during World War I, and neither of them had escaped that dreary cycle yet. Payton couldn't decide if he should laugh, cry, or just tie one on and let the riptide carry him along.

Malcolm X and the Nation of Islam were still making waves across white America, beginning when the far-right California Senate Fact-finding Committee on Un-American Activities claimed "an interesting parallel between the Negro Muslim movement and the Communist Party, which is the advocacy of the overthrow of a hated regime by force, violence or any other means." Neither group pursued that line, in fact, but if it kept white voters nervous, it was bound to help so-called conservatives in office.

Malcolm *did* assail the FBI in two successive February speeches, blaming the Bureau for "religious suppression" of Muslims and saying, "The FBI spends twenty-four hours a day infiltrating or trying to infiltrate Muslims." He'd flown to Phoenix in April, for a contentious meeting with Elijah Muhammad at Elijah's winter home, and found himself reassigned as interim minister of Mosque No. 4 in the nation's capital. From there, in May, he'd condemned JFK's handling of the Birmingham crisis, then later dumped on L.A.'s Mayor Yorty for running "a Ku Klux Klan police force."

Back in Harlem by June, Malcolm had spoken on "The Black Revolution" at Abyssinian Baptist Church and led multiple rallies, straying back to D.C. long enough to criticize August's March on Washington as a sham. After President Kennedy's slaying, Elijah Muhammad had ordered his ministers to keep silent on that subject, but Malcolm popped up nine days later, telling his audience, "Being an old farm boy myself, chickens coming home to roost never did make me sad; they always made me glad." Elijah hit the roof at that, suspending Malcolm for ninety days under strict order of silence.

Meanwhile, student minister Clarence 13X Smith had

founded an NOI offshoot he called the "Five Percent Nation," changing his name to "Allah the Father." That claim of personal divinity reflected Smith's belief that all of his followers had God somewhere inside, and they could tap that power by adhering to his proposed system of "Supreme Mathematics" and a "Supreme Alphabet." Females, on the other hand, were "earths" designed to complement and nurture men through their submissiveness. His sect was named for Allah's claim that only 5 percent of black humanity truly obeyed the righteous will of God.

And if that sounded like a load of crap, it was—but BOSS still craved intelligence on Allah and his flock, something for Payton to pursue while Malcolm held his tongue and privately considered any future that remained for him inside the NOI.

In Dixie, Payton granted, recent news was grim enough to make most Negroes lean toward picking up a gun. Bombings continued apace, four adolescent girls killed and twenty-one other victims injured when Klansmen blew up Birmingham's Sixteenth Street Baptist Church on the second Sunday in September. A riot had ensued, claiming two more black lives: one shot by neo-Nazi assholes on a motorbike, the other by police. Colonel Al Lingo of the State Police—introduced at Klan rallies as "a good friend of ours"—brought in his trigger-happy troopers, while Sheriff Jim Clark drove 100 miles north from Selma to join in the fun with his "posse" of deputized Klansmen.

After all that, three bombs rocked the state university campus at Tuscaloosa, "Wizard" Robert Shelton's head-quarters and G-men had charged a state National Guardsman with setting the charges. In Florida, outside

St. Augustine, Klansmen had beaten four Negroes and doused them with gasoline prior to immolation, when the county sheriff arrived and charged the victims with assaulting their would-be killers.

Payton knew his dad was right: nothing ever changed, at least not for the better, where his people were concerned. And in his darker moments, Sawyer wondered what his role was in preserving that unwholesome status quo.

———

FBI MANHATTAN FIELD OFFICE: December 11, 1963

IT WAS all about the Mob these days, since Dallas, and for all his former interest in that subject, Devon Gantt was feeling overworked of late.

The good news: he only had two mobsters to track, but both turned out to be whoppers. John Rosselli, as Gantt knew from Bureau files and private conversations with his brother Colby, had been neck-deep in the CIA's conspiracies against Fidel Castro since August 1960. During this year, while G-men lost track of him repeatedly, the cocksure *mafioso* spoke to columnist Jack Anderson in March, reporting that he'd just dispatched a three-man hit team into Cuba. A month later, Rosselli and the Agency's William Harvey chartered a boat from Miami to "go fishing." Between furtive meetings with Sam Giancana, he'd also flown to Bimini in May, for a sit-down with CIA spooks, ex-president of Cuba Carlos Prio, and former head of Cuban State Security Fabian Escalante. June brought Rosselli to D.C., prompting Hoover's order that agents "follow closely," then the DOJ had unaccountably terminated surveillance on November 5, two weeks and change before President Kennedy's murder.

Devon wasn't sure exactly what to make of that, but there was no denying his other subject's link to the events in Dallas. Jack Ruby was a central player in the fatal weekend's grim events and closed it out by bringing down the final curtain.

Ruby's file was fat, jam-packed with leads that might mean anything or nothing. Born Jacob Rubenstein in 1911, the Chicago native had been raised by a violent alcoholic father and a crazy mom who racked up multiple vacations in the loony bin. Jacob had quit school in third grade and was removed from his parents' "care" at age twelve, by court order. By 1933 he was in California, peddling horse racing tip sheets for mobsters in Frisco. Four years later he'd returned to Chicago, helping Al Capone's successors infiltrate labor unions. Cops suspected him of killing a union reformer, but they never made it stick.

The army drafted Jack in 1943 and cut him loose in early '46 when he'd returned to working for the Mob and was among Chicago's delegation sent to Dallas, where a clumsy bid to bribe the county sheriff blew up on their faces. Somehow, Jacob—who'd changed his surname to "Jack Ruby" by then—avoided prosecution and remained in town to run a string of bars and strip clubs, doubling as a bagman for city police who never met a bribe they didn't like. In 1950 he'd returned briefly to Chi-Town, offering his services to Estes Kefauver as an informant, but the senator was smart enough to turn him down.

So it was back to Dallas, and he'd been there ever since, aside from countless visits to New Orleans and Havana during and immediately after Castro's revolution.

FBI surveillance placed him in the company of John Rosselli, and he'd visited *Don* Santo Trafficante Jr. after Castro jailed the Tampa *mafioso* for a while in 1959. He'd also bragged of arms deals carried out with Israel, but the evidence was vague at best. The only people Ruby knew better than gangsters were Dallas policemen, who swilled free booze at his various clubs and snagged "dates" with his strippers whenever they pleased.

All that was normal in "Big D," but then Jack Kennedy decided that his reelection might depend on winning Texas, and a sinister new pattern started to emerge.

A month before the Dallas hit went down, Mob talk placed Ruby in New Orleans, huddling with Rosselli, Frank Caracci from Carlos Marcello's family, and Lee Oswald. Other rumbles said that Ruby was supposed to give Oswald a passport, money, and a ride to Mexico after the hit on Kennedy, and there had been at least one sighting of Oswald with Ruby and Officer Tippit at Jack's sleazy Carousel Club. Beyond that, it was evident that Ruby was involved in something big from the moment that JFK took his bullets: first appearing at Parkland Hospital; next turning up at police headquarters for the supposed assassin's press conference, correcting the D.A.'s mix-up of pro- and anti-Castro groups; and finally silencing Oswald forever, ensuring himself life imprisonment or worse.

If nothing else proved Ruby's link to a conspiracy in Dallas, there was still his high volume of long-distance phone calls during the months preceding Kennedy's assassination. Normally content with three or four toll calls per month, Jack had gone off the rails from summer 1963 until his final date with Oswald in the precinct basement. Some of his contacts were mobster Harry Tannenbaum at a New Orleans bar owned by Carlos Marcello's brother, Peter; gambler Lewis McWillie, who also received a pistol from Jack via airmail; Sam Giancana's Dream Lounge in Cicero, Illinois; the Old French Opera House in New Orleans; Genovese family soldier Joe "The Wop" Cataldo in New York; Hoffa-Trafficante associate Irwin Weiner in Chicago; Marcello mobster Nofio Pecora in New Orleans; Outfit member Barney Baker in Chicago; Teamsters official Murray "Dusty" Miller in Miami; on and on it went.

And at the same time, Jack was traveling. Six days before Kennedy's slaying, he flew to Las Vegas and checked into the Tropicana Hotel, a joint closely linked to Rosselli and now-retired Frank Costello. On November 19, street talk had him meeting with Officer Tippit, who in turn dined with Oswald at a Dallas café the next day. On November 20 he visited the Dallas office of Lamar Hunt, son of far-right oilman H. L. Hunt and sponsor of the flyers that branded JFK "WANTED FOR TREASON." later that day, he met with mobster Sam Campisi at Campisi's Egyptian Lounge. Next morning, an hour before the assassination, Jack popped into the *Dallas Morning News* building, overlooking Dealey Plaza, and hung out at ad salesman Don Campbell's office until 12:25 p.m., still lingering when shots rang out from Elm Street. Two hours later, Ruby phoned an associate of imprisoned mobster Mickey Cohen, asking his contact to line up a lawyer in case Ruby needed one soon.

In jail after shooting Oswald, Ruby first claimed insanity, blaming it on antidepressants he'd been taking, then switched to his fable of loving the Kennedys so much that he couldn't bear watching Jackie sit through the media circus surrounding a trial. Anyone dumb enough to buy that, Devon thought, would likely believe the Tooth Fairy had loaded Jack's gun.

And while Ruby sat in jail awaiting trial, other people with links to the case had been dying.

First up was Karyn Kupcinet, occasional actress, daughter of a *Chicago Sun-Times* columnist and TV talk-show host. She'd spoken to a California phone operator on November 22, twenty minutes before the assassination, warning that JFK would be murdered in Dallas. Six days later, she was found dead in her Los Angeles apartment, a coroner ruling that she'd been strangled. Sheriff's detectives suspected a boyfriend, but none of their several leads had panned out.

The next victim was Jack Zangretty, a mobbed-up Chicagoan who'd run a motel and seafood restaurant at Oklahoma's Lake Altus-Lugert. On November 23, Zangretti had told friends, "Three other men, not Oswald, killed the President. A man named Ruby will kill Oswald tomorrow and in a few days a member of the Frank Sinatra family will be kidnapped, just to take some of the attention away from the assassination."

Sure as shit, Ruby shot Oswald the following day, and Frank Sinatra Jr. had been snatched from his room Harrah's Lake Tahoe on December 8—the same day Zangetty's corpse was found floating in Lake Altus-Lugert, shot in the chest by persons unknown. Frank Sinatra had retrieved his son on December 10, after paying a $240,000 ransom. G-men were now tracking a trio of suspects in that case, led by "mastermind" Barry Keenan, youngest-ever member of the L.A. Stock Exchange.

If there was no conspiracy behind the Kennedy assassination, as Chief Hoover now insisted, what should Devon make of Kupcinet and Zangretty? Were they modern prophets tuned in to a psychic true-crime network? Or was something seriously rotten in Denmark?

Whatever, he'd keep digging—at least long enough to satisfy his private curiosity, unless it put his own head on the chopping block.

CHAPTER 9

Princeton University, New Jersey: September 8, 1964

Stephen Barnes surveyed the dorm room he'd be sharing with another freshman student whom he'd never met. It was about the size he guessed a standard prison cell must be, although more comfortably furnished. On the wall above one single bed, a poster with a photograph of Arizona's Barry Goldwater told Stephen, "IN YOUR HEART YOU KNOW HE'S RIGHT." Beside it hung a pinup photo of Ann-Margaret wearing little but a smile.

A fascist and a slut from Hollywood, Barnes thought, smiling as if such icons were as natural as breathing in his world.

No one he met at Princeton would have guessed his world lay 4,700 miles away, I Moscow, where the hero-father he could not recall had lived and died, but still financially supported him and his adoptive parents. How else could Stephen have afforded Princeton, even with his parents' salaries combined? Despite his top-ranked grades in high school and his stellar SAT performance, he'd have been excluded without monthly payments to his college fund from overseas, during the past ten years.

One of the many things he'd learned while growing up in Trenton: capitalist higher education, save for state schools with the lowest academic standards, were simply cogs in the American money machine, absorbing cash and spitting out compliant workers.

True, there'd been some changes lately, at schools ranging from UC Berkeley to Columbia, but Stephen knew those stirrings—feeble still, and far from revolutionary—were nothing compared to the upheavals suffered by his Mother Russia in her day.

But here he was, a freshman at the country's fourth oldest university, founded in 1746 and christened with its present name 150 years later. It was one of eight schools in the so-called "Ivy League," a name dreamed up ten years ago by the National Collegiate Athletic Association, now assumed to represent selective admission, academic excellence, and social elitism. It lacked the ghoulish charm of Yale, with its "secret" Skull and Bones society alleged to hold the bony cranium of Apache war chief Geronimo, but Stephen didn't need those trappings.

He already had a path to follow: pre-law studies with an emphasis on history, three years at Princeton Law, and then an application to the FBI by 1971 or '72. He wasn't sure Director Hoover could survive that long—he was already sixty-nine and out of shape, if not obese—but his true father had allowed for that.

One man's embarrassment was less important than destroying his established cult of personality from the inside.

The door opened behind him and a smaller young

man entered, short hair parted on the left, his sport shirt buttoned at the neck without a tie, his brown wingtips gleaming.

"Hey, there!" the new arrival said. "I hope you're Barnes."

"That's me."

They shook hands, almost gravely, as the other said, "Edmonds. But you can call me Jack, roomie." He nodded toward the Goldwater poster, asking, "You've heard of the senator?"

"He's hard to miss," Barnes said.

"If only we could vote, eh?"

Smiling, Stephen told him, "I'm with you."

———

FBI HEADQUARTERS: October 5, 1964

Aloysius Gantt sat at his desk, reviewing files—same old, same old—and felt his standard morning pang of bitterness. No matter how the Bureau and society might change, it didn't seem to do him any good.

Clyde Tolson's stroke, for instance. Gantt had hated him with righteous envy for the past thirty-six years, but even now, in frail condition, he was still the Chief's best friend on Earth and number two in charge. Gantt, four years older, knew damned well he'd rise no higher on the ladder of command.

Another symbol of pathetic change was happening right now on Alcatraz. The prison had shut down last year, reverting to the National Park Service, but in March a smallish mob of Indians had occupied The Rock. Calling themselves IOTA—Indians of All Tribes—they seemed intent on staying put until somebody granted their demand to cede the property at its projected worth of forty-seven cents per acre, something under ten bucks for the whole damned thing.

While that charade played out, the New Left was evolving nationwide and drawing greater Bureau scrutiny. Out west, at Berkeley, the "Free Speech Movement" seemed to be focused chiefly on the right to curse in public, mouthpiece Mario Savo vowing to crush the "odious machine" that ran American society for profit. On other campuses, the SDS was on the verge of splitting from its parent group, the Student League for Industrial Democracy. Its leadership was drifting closer to a new "Black Power" movement, led by malcontents like Stokeley Carmichael and Hubert Brown—called "Rap" by his admirers, out of Baton Rouge. Although affiliated with the Student Nonviolent Coordinating Committee, both men were moving toward rejection of nonviolence as preached by Martin Luther King and others whom they branded "Uncle Toms."

And where did Gantt fit into such a world?

Increasingly, these days, he thought it might be sitting on his ass at home.

————

CIA Headquarters: October 17, 1964

COLBY GANTT PREFERRED FIELD WORK, but at his age, with forty in the rearview mirror, it was nice to visit home from time to time, get reacquainted with his wife and son, the latter starting on his senior year of high school now.

And if he hadn't been at Langley, he'd have likely been

stuck on Taiwan, promising ancient Chiang Kai-shek increased support now that the Red Chinese had detonated their first A-bomb yesterday, an atmospheric test defying Western treaties at the Lop Nur test site in Mongolia.

Another plus: he wasn't stuck in West Berlin, coordinating with their Federal Intelligence Service to figure out what was happening in Moscow. Three days earlier, Premier Khrushchev had been deposed at a Central Committee meeting, replaced by Alexei Kosygin, with Leonid Brezhnev as First Secretary. Behind all that, Gantt sensed the guiding hand of KGB Director Alexander Shelepin, himself elevated to Deputy Prime Minister by the shakeup.

That likely meant more Cold War tension for the future, but of late, Colby had been in Texas, working with Uruguayan police at a training facility run by the Office of Public Safety at Los Fresnos, in southernmost Cameron County. Their education included the usual torture techniques, surveillance, and practice with weapons their country could purchase with Washington loans.

In Haiti, 1,600 miles from Los Fresnos, Papa Doc was mopping up the remnants of another peasant coup, this one led by Catholic priest Jean-Baptiste Theovges, heightening tension between Port-au-Prince and the hostile Dominican Republic. Nearby Cuba was still a target for subversion by Laureano Batista's Christian Democratic Movement. Operating from the De La Barre Estate in Lacombe, Louisiana, bankrolled by the Agency, Batista was always happy to receive donations from private groups such as the crackpot John Birch Society.

Southeast Asia was, as usual, a smoking tinderbox. In Laos, the CIA's "secret war" was fielding Hmong guerrillas in a so-far futile effort to retake the Plain of Jars, with covert support—and drug smuggling—carried out by Air America from its new headquarters in Washington's World Center Building at 1600 K Street Northwest. The U.S. Air Force handled most of "Project Waterpump," training Laotian military pilots at Udorn Royal Thai Air Force Base. In their spare time, USAF "advisors" flew surveillance flights and mid-to-low-level combat missions under the codenames "Butterfly" and "Yankee Team."

No boots on the ground, right, if they were all airborne.

Vietnam's big news from August was the Gulf of Tonkin incident, provoked by U.S.-funded naval surveillance and amphibious raids against North Vietnam. It didn't read that way in headlines, naturally, when a group of Hồ Chí Minh's torpedo boats allegedly attacked a couple of American destroyers sailing in international waters, riling Congress enough to hand LBJ a blank check for military escalation. The Pentagon was claiming three Red boats destroyed, four crewmen killed, our side unscathed but for a single bullet hole in the USS *Maddox*, not a scratch for its sister *Turner Joy*.

President Johnson seized his new power without believing in the provocation. When Secretary of Defense Robert McNamara claimed another Red attack in September, LBJ snapped, "You just came in a few weeks ago and said they're launching an attack on us, they're firing at us, and we concluded maybe they hadn't fired at all. For all I know, our Navy was shooting at whales out there."

In Saigon, a bloodless January coup replaced General "Big" Minh with General Nguyen Khanh as South Vietnam's new leader. Secretary McNamara told the world that Khanh "has our admiration, our respect and our complete support," adding, "We'll stay for as long as it takes. We shall provide whatever help is required to win the battle against the Communist insurgents." Translation: ten years past the Geneva Accords and counting, there would never be an election to unify the bisected nation if Washington had its way.

In March, the National Security Council recommended bombing North Vietnam, and LBJ jumped on that like the proverbial duck on a June bug, launching the first of innumerable air raids. Summer found 56,000 Việt Cộng guerrillas active in the countryside, reinforced by North Vietnamese Army regulars pouring south along the Hồ Chí Minh Trail. Johnson fought back by escalating CIA "Operation Plan 34-Alpha," incorporating seaborne raids against North Vietnam's coastal radar stations. GOP hopeful Barry Goldwater, having vowed that "extremism in defense of liberty is no vice," suggested he might nuke Hanoi if he should be elected president.

Colby doubted that wishful thinking would become a reality, but further U.S. escalation in the region was a lead pipe cinch. At home, meanwhile, MKULTRA was reborn on paper as MKSEARCH in June, pursuing and expanding Agency experiments with drugs in quest of mind control. The mad science had spread to Canada under British psychiatrist Donald Ewen Cameron, father of the "psychic driving" concept spawned from his attempts to cure schizophrenia by erasing existing memories and reprogramming the patient's psyche. Suddenly awash in CIA black money, Cameron commuted weekly from his home in Albany to Québec's Allan Memorial Institute at McGill University, working his magic and reporting back to Langley. In the UK, psychiatrist William

Sargant pursued similar studies at London's St. Thomas Hospital and Belmont Hospital in Surrey, experimenting on patients without their consent and risking similar long-term damage. Stateside, the Defense Department "volunteered" numerous soldiers who their folks at home might not entirely recognize in years to come.

What troubled Colby most of late was the Warren Commission's investigation of Dallas and JFK's murder. It helped that Edgar Hoover had his own man on the panel, Congressman Gerald Ford from Michigan, filing reports to supplement the Bureau's bugs and taps on other key commission members. Better still was Allen Dulles, fired by the late president and still resenting it, who steered the commission firmly toward a "lone nut" verdict both on Oswald and Jack Ruby. As for any worries about publishing commission evidence, Dulles laid them to rest, assuring fellow panelists, "Americans don't read." The commission's final report criticized certain Secret Service procedures but gave the FBI a free pass for failing to deal with Oswald, while finding "no significant link between Ruby and organized crime."

And ignore that funny man behind the curtain, while you're at it.

It doesn't get much better than that, Colby thought, with a satisfied smile.

———

LITTLE ITALY, Manhattan: October 23, 1964

GREG JORDAN DIDN'T like the news that came to him these days, through television and the press. Bobby Kennedy was no longer Attorney General, replaced by Nicholas Katzenbach, but the Camelot crusade against the *Cosa Nostra* hadn't faltered yet, with over 900 indictments this year and 480 convictions.

The year's big fish was Jimmy Hoffa, first convicted of bribery and jury tampering, then fraud, facing eight years in prison if his appeals fell through. Edgar Hoover had leaked dirt on Bobby Kennedy from Bureau files to defense attorney Roy Cohn but in vain. Oddly, while Hoffa had reportedly joined in the plot to murder JFK, he'd balked at slinging mud against his prosecutor out of "principle," which made no sense at all to Greg.

Worse news by far was the "Banana War" now hanging over Gotham. Following last year's conspiracy by Joe Bonanno to assassinate two fellow godfathers from *La Commissione,* Bonanno had been summoned to a last-chance sit-down late last week. Instead of showing up, he'd disappeared, supposedly kidnapped by gunmen outside his lawyer's apartment building on East 37th Street. If the abduction was legit, the other lords of *Cosa Nostra* didn't seem to know about it. They'd replaced Bonanno as boss, against the wishes of Bonanno brother-in-law Frank Labruzzo and son Salvatore Bonanno, known to one and all as "Bill." The battle lines were drawn, and when—not *if*—the shooting started, it might not be confined to Manhattan.

Already, in Rochester—340 miles northeast of Gotham on Lake Ontario—local *capo crimine* Jake Russo had vanished the same as Bonanno. A Russo aide, Albert Alberti *had* been found, blasted with shotguns in the Bronx, and while rumors were blaming Russo successor Frank Valenti, no one really knew which end was up these days.

Time to retire, Greg thought, sick of the life and then some at age sixty-eight, but who would watch over the Giordano family if he withdrew? His brother Carlo, five years older, still seemed fit enough, all things considered, but he wasn't much with numbers, much less keeping double sets of books for every enterprise the family controlled.

As far as nephew Dominic, forget about it. He was pushing forty, but still acted like a teenage hothead when his blood was up—and that seemed to be more common of late than when he was a callow youth. Dom's brother Angelo was marginally smarter than a bag of hammers, but Greg didn't like to think about what might befall the family with him in charge.

Inevitably, his thoughts strayed to Dave, tied up with Legal Aid, but Greg would rather die himself than draw his son into the Mob's grim underworld.

As if in answer to that thought, he felt what had to be a pistol prodding his left side, held by a goon whose carbon copy gripped Jordan's right arm. "You needta come with us," the shooter said and steered him toward a jet-black Lincoln Continental idling at the curb.

You're too damned old for this, Greg told himself, *if you don't see it coming.*

He climbed into the backseat without struggling, sat between his escorts, two more soldiers up in front, one at the wheel, the other turning toward him with a silencer-equipped pistol.

"What's this about?" he asked the gunman in the front seat.

"Time to take a little ride," the triggerman replied. "Don't getcher hopes up about comin' back."

―――――

Biondi's Social Club, Mulberry Street: October 30, 1964

"No word yet?"

"Not a fuckin' peep," Angelo Giordano told his brother as Dominic slid into the booth across from him. "You know I woulda called you, right?"

"Just hopin',"

"Shit. We woulda heard somethin' by now. I tell ya it's the *lupara bianca*."

"Maybe," Dom admitted, grudgingly.

Lupara bianca translated to English literally as "white shotgun," but made men took it to mean "white death"—a job where the intended victim disappeared without a trace and never popped back up again. Aside from hiding evidence from cops, it could mean spreading punishment around a dead man's family, denying them the closure of a Mass and proper burial, wondering day and night if there would be a phone call or a postcard to resolve the mystery.

"It's like the Hawk," said Angelo. "They only found his ass by pure dumb luck."

Ernie Ruppolo that would be, supposedly knocked off by Vito Genovese, for the testimony Ruppolo had given at *Don* Vito's murder trial some twenty years ago. The jury had acquitted Genovese, and Ruppolo claimed squealing was "a favor," since the state couldn't try Vito twice, but Genovese had a long memory.

The one-eyed Hawk has surfaced in Jamaica Bay, despite two concrete blocks tied to his feet that were supposed to keep him underwater permanently. Cops had managed to ID him from stomach mesh put in after a long-forgotten operation, while an autopsy revealed Ernie was shot five times, by two pistols, and bore eighteen stab wounds to let the methane gas leak out of him while he was decomposing.

Even so, he didn't want to stay submerged.

"You figure Uncle Greg went out that way?" asked Angelo.

"Fuck if I know," Dom said. "I'm worried more about Pop now. He's in the dumps and doesn't give a lotta thought to home security."

"We need payback," Ange said.

"You're goddamn right, but who's behind it? Tell me that, and we can make a move."

"No word yet, but I'm workin' on it."

"So, work harder," Dom ordered. "And why'n hell are you still sittin' here?"

————

FBI HEADQUARTERS: November 9, 1964

IT WAS A FINE MONDAY, Declan O'Hara thought, for handing in his resignation from the FBI.

He had been working up to it for months—hell, *years*—and now, approaching sixty-nine years old, he'd finally, inevitably had enough. There ought to be a few years left, he thought, for spending time with family and drinking to forget.

Okay, so he might never know what Aloysius Gantt was doing in Havana more than thirty years ago when Burton Wheeler died en route to being appointed as

Attorney General and rid the DOJ of Edgar Hoover, but so what?

Some things were just too big, too terrible to know.

Such as the Warren Commission's predetermined verdict on Dallas, for instance. LBJ had received the group's final report on September 24, and it was published for America at large to read three days later. It had overlooked the strange events surrounding Lee Oswald and, even more bizarre, had cleared Jack Ruby of any but the most casual, coincidental links to gangland. Never mind Jack's plea to testify in Washington, telling Earl Warren from jail, "My life is in danger here. I want to tell the truth, but I can't tell it here." In the testimony Warren had recorded, Ruby lied, wept, and acted like a lunatic. Already facing the electric chair for Oswald's murder, he deserved an Oscar for the nutcase role he'd played for the commission.

Even so, the final judgment hadn't gone without a hitch. On August 28, a month before the report was printed, Assistant Director Alan Belmont received a memo about commission General Counsel James Lee Rankin, warning that "Rankin advised because of the circumstances that now exist there was a serious question in the minds of the Commission as to whether or not the palm print impression that has been obtained from the Dallas Police Department is a legitimate latent print impression removed from the rifle barrel or whether it was obtained from some other source."

Planted, for instance?

Belmont had convinced the panel to accept the palm print, but he'd sweated bullets doing it, and Declan personally had his doubts.

Ditto the panel's magic-bullet theory, in which one

slug from Oswald's cheap-ass rifle had inflicted had inflicted six wounds on JFK and Governor Connally, imbedding itself in Connally's thigh, then dropping on a random Parkland Hospital stretcher with barely a scratch on the bullet's surface. It defied the laws of science and ignored a dead-end back wound found on Kennedy at his first autopsy, but it was better than nothing. A lame "delayed reaction whiplash" theory tried to cover why the president's skull had exploded, driving his body *backward* from an obvious frontal impact, but by September 1964 many Americans were happy to mimic the fabled Queen of Hearts by believing impossible things.

And the Kennedy death list kept growing. In January, Tippit slaying witness Warren Reynolds—who'd described a shooter clearly not Oswald—survived a violent assault in Dallas. Ex-Ruby stripper Betty MacDonald alibied alleged attacker Darrell Garner, then "hanged herself" in jail while locked up for fighting with a roommate. In February, someone shot Eddy Benavides, look-alike brother of another Tippit murder witness. March claimed Hank Killam, husband of a Ruby employee and acquaintance of Oswald, found with his throat cut, while a heart attack silenced Bill Chesher, said to have info linking Oswald to Ruby. April saw Bill Hunter, a reporter who'd penetrated Ruby's apartment on the day Oswald died, "accidentally" shot by a Dallas policeman supposedly dropping his gun.

May was a busy month for the Grim Reaper. Gary Underhill, a CIA agent who claimed his bosses were behind the JFK assassination, allegedly shot himself in New York. Soon afterward, private investigator Hugh Ward, formerly employed with David Ferrie by Guy

Banister, died with New Orleans Mayor deLesseps Morrison in a Mexican plane crash.

Skip to June, when a heart attack killed Guy Banister, his widow telling journalists she'd found Fair Play for Cuba pamphlets at his Camp Street office. In August, persons unknown shot Teresa Norton, another of Ruby's former employees. Jim Keith, another newsie who'd scoured Ruby's apartment last November 24, died from a karate chop to the neck. Finally, October saw Mary Pinchot, one of JFK's ex-lovers, gunned down while strolling along the towpath of Washington's Chesapeake and Ohio Canal. Police detained suspect Raymond Crump Jr., based on eyewitness descriptions, but the case fell through in court.

Last week's election had been one more straw straining the camel's back for Declan. A worried LBJ had tasked the Bureau to investigate various critics and the staff employed by rival Barry Goldwater. Edgar Hoover dished up some dirt on his own, leaving the smaller stuff to Deke DeLoach, ensuring that Johnson would waive Hoover's retirement on account of age. One unexpected morsel was the news that Johnson aide and confidant Walter Jenkins had been nabbed by police in a men's room, charged with "disorderly conduct" a month before the election. That euphemism for homosexual activity still stung, a decade after the McCarthy-era "Lavender Scare," and other journalists soon learned that Jenkins had taken a similar fall in 1959. LBJ lawyer Abe Fortas tried to soft-pedal the charge, but Goldwater's staff still ran with it, printing bumper stickers that read, "LBJ— LIGHT BULB JENKINS: NO WONDER HE TURNED THE LIGHTS OUT" and "ALL THE WAY WITH LBJ, BUT DON'T GO NEAR THE YMCA."

It hadn't mattered in the end. Johnson buried Goldwater in a landslide of 43 million votes versus 27 million. Barry only carried his home state and five more in the Deep South where white voters loathed the latest Civil Rights Act. In the crucial Electoral College, Johnson had claimed every one of its 538 votes.

But finally, it had been Edgar Hoover's mania for stalking Martin Luther King that pushed Declan over the edge toward quitting. Ever since last August's March on Washington, surveillance had been escalating steadily. Four months ago, en route to claim an unexpected Nobel Peace Prize, King had criticized the Bureau for assigning mostly-southern agents to the heart of Dixie, where they never seemed much interested in pursuing civil rights cases. O'Hara knew that much was true: not *all* of them were southern boys, but Hoover leaned toward posting them near home once they'd completed rookie rounds of other offices. The Chief, of course, had called his own press conference, spewing a new version of the crap he'd thrown at *Ebony* two years ago, about his "many Negro agents," this time calling King "the most notorious liar in the country."

If he'd let it go at that, another of his all too common temper tantrums, Declan might've let it pass. But no, he'd tasked Bill Sullivan to write a letter, posting it to King along with edited recordings lifted from his various hotel rooms on the road, caught literally with his pants down in the presence of assorted women, some white, none of them his wife.

The letter was unsigned, but how could anybody listen to the tape without knowing exactly where it came from?

Before that mailing on November 21, Sullivan had

dispatched a memo to the Boss, smooching Speed's back-side as he wrote: "It should be clear to all of us that Martin Luther King must, at some propitious point in the future, be revealed to the people of this country and to his Negro followers as being what he actually is—a fraud, demagogue and scoundrel. When the true facts concerning his activities are presented, such should be enough, if handled properly, to take him off his pedestal and to reduce him completely in influence. When this is done, and it can be and will be done, obviously much confusion will reign, particularly among the Negro people. The Negroes will be left without a national leader of sufficiently compelling personality to steer them in the proper direction. This is what could happen, but need not happen if the right kind of a national Negro leader could at this time be gradually developed so as to overshadow Dr. King and be in the position to assume the role of the leadership of the Negro people when King has been completely discredited."

Sullivan's choice as a replacement for De Lawd was Samuel Pierce Jr.: conservative to a fault, first Negro partner in a major New York law firm, first black member of a Fortune 500 board, and one of the first Negroes to argue a case before the U.S. Supreme Court.

O'Hara had a bootleg copy of the King letter on file, had nearly memorized it, and had thought of turning it in with his resignation, but decided that would be too much. It read:

KING,

In view of your low grade, abnormal personal behavior I will not dignify your name with either a Mr. or a Reverend or a Dr. And, your last name calls to mind only the type of King such as King Henry the VIII and his countless acts of adultery and immoral conduct lower than that of a beast.

King, look into your heart. You know you are a complete fraud and a great liability to all of us Negroes. White people in this country have enough frauds of their own, but I am sure they don't have one at this time that is anywhere near your equal. You are no clergyman, and you know it. I repeat you are a colossal fraud and an evil, vicious one at that. You could not believe in God and act as you do. Clearly, you don't believe in any personal moral principles.

King, like all frauds your end is approaching. You could have been our greatest leader. You, even at an early age have turned out to be not a leader but a dissolute, abnormal moral imbecile. We will now have to depend on our older leaders like Wilkins, a man of character, and thank God we have others like him. But you are done. Your "honorary" degrees, your Nobel Prize (what a grim farce) and other awards will not save you. King, I repeat you are done.

No person can overcome facts, not even a fraud like yourself. Lend your sexually psychotic ear to the enclosure. You will find yourself and in all your dirt, filth, evil and moronic talk exposed on the record for all time. I repeat—no person can argue successfully against facts. You are finished. You will find on the record for all time your filthy, dirty, evil companions, male and females giving expression with you to your hideous abnormalities. And some of them pretend to be ministers of the Gospel. Satan could not do more. What incredible evilness. It is all there on the record, your sexual orgies. Listen to yourself you filthy, abnormal animal. You are on the record. You have been on the record—all your adulterous acts, your sexual orgies extending far into the past. This one is but a tiny sample. You will understand this. Yes, from your various evil playmates on the east coast to others on the west coast and outside the country you are on the record. King you are done.

The American public, the church organizations that have been helping—Protestant, Catholic and Jews will know you for what you are—an evil, abnormal beast. So will others who have backed you. You are done.

King, there is only one thing left for you to do. You know what it is. You have just 34 days in which to do it (this exact number has been selected for a specific reason, it has definite practical significance). You are done. There is but one way out for you. You better take it before your filthy, abnormal fraudulent self is bared to the nation.

O'HARA HADN'T FIGURED out the thirty-four days gibberish, which fell on Christmas Eve, two weeks *after* King claimed the Nobel Prize, and Declan frankly didn't give a shit. He'd had enough, and he was getting out—maybe too late to save his soul, but with a little time, at least, left on the clock.

He'd drop the letter on Miss Gandy's desk this afternoon, and that would be the last they saw of him at headquarters.

———

MANHATTAN: November 23, 1964

JOHN KENNEDY HAD SLEPT beneath his pale eternal flame for one year and a day when Dave Jordan answered his phone at home, smiling as Fee launched straight into her thought without the benefit of salutations.

"So, I got them," she said. "I was the first one in the bookstore when they opened up this morning. That's a hundred bucks I'll never see again, but I'm determined to read every freaking word of it before I'm done."

Freaking was just about as close as Dave had ever heard Fee come to swearing, not counting some of the times they'd been in bed, and she forgot herself. He didn't want to go there in his mind right now, and smiled instead, while telling her, "Hello, yourself."

He didn't have to ask which "them" she had in mind. Fiona had already pored over the Warren Commission's 889-page report, and now she'd bought the twenty-six companion volumes of hearings and evidence said to support the panel's findings.

"Sorry," she was saying now. "I just got—"

"Bowled over? Carried away?"

"Smart aleck."

"I'm well known for it."

She veered back onto course. "Can you believe it's all right here? They've got testimony or depositions from 552 witnesses, more than 3,100 exhibits. It's—"

"Massive. I hear you. Your free time's booked up for the next couple years."

That slowed her down. "You know I didn't mean—"

Dave cut her off again. "But what about the stuff they *didn't* publish, the material that's sealed till 2039? I personally don't expect to be around that long."

"You might surprise yourself," she teased.

"By living to be 115?"

"Who knows? By then, they'll likely have a pill to make you live forever."

"And the only ones who can afford it will be fat-cat millionaires."

"Who says you won't be one of them?"

"My bank book, for a start."

She changed directions, asking, "How's your family?"

"They're getting by," he answered vaguely. What else could he say? *My old man's missing, likely murdered by the Mafia, leaving my mom alone and nothing in the world that I can fucking do about it?*

Not today. Not *any* day.

"Okay then, if you're doing well..."

"I might be down your way next month if you have any time to spare from reading or whatever."

Did he hear a note of pleasure in her voice, behind the spoken words as she replied?

"Just call ahead. Give me a day or so to get things squared away."

"Will do. And in the meantime, try not to go blind with all the fine print."

"Such a kidder. Wait till you see all of this."

"Can't wait to get a look at it," Dave said and didn't mean a heap of dusty books.

———

Harlem: December 10, 1964

One thing Fred Sawyer had to say about his Bureau job after three years: it kept him on the move. It was unusual to land back on his old home turf, the first time since his father's funeral last year, and while he hadn't dropped a dime to brother Payton yet, Fred knew he'd better get around to it before they had a chance encounter on the street or in some neighborhood diner.

If nothing else, he longed to ask how Payton's job was going, and if he was having any second thoughts.

Have to be careful, though, Fred told himself. *Spill too much, and it might get back to BOSS, which meant the Bureau would find out about it soon enough.*

A shooting was the cause of his return to Harlem this time. Yesterday, someone had put two bullets into Clarence 13X—alias "Allah," prophet of the Fiver Percenters—but they hadn't killed him. He was on the mend and had already told his followers they should forget about revenge.

A hopeful sign, amidst the sound and fear of the year about to end?

The FBI was working overtime to drive a deeper wedge between Malcolm X and Elijah Muhammad via infiltration of the NOI and what headquarters memos called "sparking of acrimonious debates within the organization" via fabricated rumors. Malcolm, meanwhile, focused on the Bureau's failure to resolve a rash of terrorism in the South, referring to the murders of three civil rights workers in Mississippi, saying, "Hoover, admits that they know who did it, they've known ever since it happened, and they've done nothing about it. Civil rights bill down the drain."

How long, Fred wondered, *before it was Malcolm down the drain?*

He'd been in Cleveland during January when a Negro coalition called the United Freedom Movement planned demonstrations at all-white Murray Hill School in the city's Little Italy. Fearing a riot, city leaders talked the UFM's leaders out of holding their protest, but white racists gathered anyway, beating and stoning any Negroes they found on the street. White cops stood by and watched it happen, making no arrests.

In northern California, RAM district leader Ernie Allen had returned from a visit to Cuba, organizing several disparate groups into a "Soul Students' Advisory Council" that published a journal called *Soulbook: The Revolutionary Journal of the Black World*. So far, their revolution was confined to prose and poetry, but Sawyer had his eye on journal editors Bobby Seale and Huey Newton, marking them as radicals to watch in future.

RAM's Philadelphia chapter had seen some real action in August, taking a break from the publication of its bimonthly newspaper, *Black America*, and single-page newsletter *RAM Speaks*, to join in three days of rioting around Cleveland Street. A botched traffic arrest had set things rolling, and while Sawyer couldn't prove RAM activists were at the root of it, he had some feelers out to double-check.

But first, before he followed up on that, he had to track his brother down and maybe spring for drinks while he was picking Payton's brain. Fred wasn't trusting Payton to decide his future for him, but he should be able to provide some insight on their similar professions, and to when and what he viewed as their long-term outcome.

Personally, Fred had an uneasy feeling in his gut, afraid that it would only worsen over time.

———

CONCORDIA PARISH HOSPITAL, *Ferriday, Louisiana: December 11, 1964*

FRANK MORRIS WAS a dead man talking. He'd suffered third-degree burns over most of his body last night, when Ku Klux terrorists had torched his shoe repair shop on Ferriday's main street, forcing Morris at gunpoint to remain inside until his clothing had burned off, then fleeing toward Vidalia, the county seat, in a dark-colored sedan. There was no way on Earth that Morris would survive his injuries, but morphine gave him the ability to talk in fits and starts.

Devon Gantt and fellow G-man Clement Wade were standing at the victim's bedside now, trying to question him while Ferriday Police Chief Robert Warren and Fire Chief Noland Mouelle stood by, watching. Gantt had a shiny smear of Vicks across his upper lip, trying in vain mask the smell of roasted meat, and marveled that he couldn't tell Frank Morris had been black before the fire.

Interrogation of a man this close to death—collecting what the Bureau called a "dying declaration," normally admissible in court—was difficult at best. Scorched lips and lungs made speaking doubly difficult for Morris, while the morphine drip was mercifully clouding his mind. He'd managed to describe his murderers as "two white friends," but either couldn't or wouldn't give up their names.

Gantt tried again. "Do you remember when these men were last in your shoe shop? Are they customers? Did you ever repair their shoes?"

Morris released a smoky sigh, then murmured, "I don't know exactly who the men was. One had on khaki pants and he was pouring gas out and when I got up to see he hit the window. He hit the window and broke the window-pane out and while he was breaking windowpanes out I come out to catch this joker. He had a shotgun, told me, 'Get back in, nigger.'"

Agent Wade chimed in. "Have you ever seen them before?"

Of course he had, Gantt thought, *if he's calling them friends.*

"I can't say who it was," Morris replied. "I probably seen them before...jacket on, had a shotgun and I went back in the house. Sure had a time getting myself out cause man, it's....bout gone."

Devon had been transferred from the Manhattan field office to Baton Rouge five months ago, passing through Jackson, Mississippi, on his way and running into former friend Nolan O'Hara, son of another G-man Devon's father had known in college, decades earlier. They'd shared a cup of mediocre Bureau coffee, but there wasn't time for any catching up in depth. Devon hadn't seen O'Hara since the latter part of 1941 before Nolan went off to the Marine Corps and came home from the Pacific with a shitload of awards for valor.

Was it Gantt's imagination that his former almost friend was subtly looking down on him these days?

Fuck it.

The move from Gotham to Louisiana, leaving wife Camille and seventeen-year-old son Wyman in New York, had come about from LBJ goading the Chief to put more agents in the South, preferably some whom Dr. King couldn't dismiss as rednecks cozy with the KKK.

Wade tried another angle of attack, asking Morris, "Were they as big as you or were they smaller?"

"The one with the gun was bigger than me," Morris wheezed.

"The biggest one?"

"Yes. I was gonna get up to the door, see. I stood by the door. He told me to get back in there."

"Get back into your little room?"

They knew Morris lived in a backroom of his shop.

"No, sir," said Morris. "In the shop."

"He told you to get back inside the shop?"

"Yes."

"Where the fire was?"

"Yeah."

"You didn't go back to your bedroom?"

"I had to go back in the bedroom to get out."

"I see, and the place was on fire then?"

"No, sir. He struck the match."

"You saw him strike the match?"

A nurse entered and told them all, "He needs to get some rest now. Y'all can try again, later."

Gantt thought about protesting that there might not be a later, but he let it go, trailing the locals and his short-term partner back into the hallway, shaking hands with Chiefs Mouelle and Warren before walking back with Wade to where they'd left their Bureau-issue car.

Frank Morris was the second local murder victim Devon knew about so far. The first, back in July, was Joseph Edwards, nicknamed "Joe-Ed," who'd been working as a porter at Vidalia's Shamrock Hotel until he vanished, his car found abandoned outside Ferriday a week later. On the front seat, police had found a noose and bloodstains, but the parish sheriff, known to be a member of the Klan, refused to treat the disappearance as a likely murder.

Devon couldn't say exactly who'd abducted Edwards or incinerated Morris, but he knew the Ku Klux faction they belonged to. It was called the Silver Dollar Group because each member used a silver dollar minted in his birth year as I.D. among his fellow crackers. Drawn from the ranks of three larger Klans, disgusted with the "sissy" attitude of other so-called knights, the SDG's hard-core fanatics had pledged a "fight to the death" in defense of Jim Crow.

One member on the Bureau's radar, presently untouchable, was Concordia Parish Deputy Frank DeLaughter, who'd carried a grudge against Morris because the repairman expected payment for resoling DeLaughter's boots. Distressed at parting with the cash, a day or two before the fire DeLaughter told his fellow goons, "That nigger isn't acting right." The outfit's leaders, Raleigh Glover and Roger Fuller—who had gunned down five Negro employees back in 1960, killing four and skating on a phony plea of self-defense—apparently decided that the penalty for acting "wrong" was agonizing death by fire. In Joe-Ed's case, the victim had been marked because a lodger at the Shamrock saw a Negro vaguely matching his description slip into a white female guest's room.

So far, Gantt had the Silver Dollars pegged for four killings, at least, two each in Mississippi and Louisiana. He knew that Fuller, not afraid to steal or pimp out whores if he was short of cash, had left his former Klan— the Original Knights—after he was accused of skimming money from its treasury. Four other likely Silver Dollar victims, one of them a nosy journalist, had been kidnapped and whipped in Washington and East Feliciana Parishes, but both had crawled away from it alive.

A major problem when it came to coping with Louisiana's Klan was Governor John McKeithen, inaugurated in May, who'd struck a deal whereby the state paid Ku Klux leaders to restrain their psychopathic members from launching a wholesale reign of terror. McKeithen's goal, aside from outright bribery, was touching base with Klansmen "on a liaison basis" to keep them in line. But from the current death toll, plus the rising score of Negro homes and churches set afire, Gantt thought the weird alliance wasn't working out for shit.

Whether Gantt could produce hard evidence against the SDG was problematic. If he did, a greater problem would be getting Edgar Hoover's office and the DOJ to prosecute. As long as he was stuck in this backwater, though, he meant to do his best and maybe teach the bastards how to live in fear, the way their victims had for decades.

Hell, if nothing else, leaning on redneck trash might brighten up his days.

———

FBI FIELD OFFICE, Jackson, Mississippi: December 12, 1964

LATELY, Nolan O'Hara felt as if he'd been dropped in the middle of a brand-new Civil War. Dixie had been enraged these past ten years, beginning with the Warren Court's *Brown* ruling against segregated schools, followed by sit-ins, freedom rides and such, but now the armed camp that was Mississippi had its heels dug in, resisting an "invasion" by black and white volunteers from the North, pledged to register Negro voters for the Council of Federated Organizations.

Founded in 1962, the COFO lived up to its name, an umbrella alliance uniting members of CORE, SNCC and the NAACP to push this year's "Freedom Summer" in the Magnolia State. SNCC spokesman Bob Moses had announced the Mississippi Summer Project back in January, making sure that redneck cops and vigilantes had plenty of time to oil their guns, stock up on dynamite, and plan how best to stem the tide of "commie race-mixers" before it washed away Jim Crow for good.

One group that had been fighting for a decade to forestall social equality, the White Citizens' Council, had little to show for its efforts these days. It hadn't kept James Meredith out of Ole Miss, where he'd completed his degree last year, and since then two more Negroes had enrolled without a riot greeting them. Statewide, while most Negroes still couldn't vote, the registration numbers had been creeping slowly upward, and a few stores—gasp!—were even letting colored patrons use their restrooms on occasion.

To the minds of hard-core Mississippi racists, it was time to try another tack, reviving dormant chapters of the Ku Klux Klan, some masked as "Americans for Preservation of the White Race," and the National States Rights Party had planted roots around Meridian, two hours east of Jackson in Lauderdale County.

Mayhem had begun in January, with Klansmen shooting up eight black-owned stores and homes in McComb. At month's end, white terrorists had finally assassinated Louis Allen, blasting him with shotguns in his Amite County driveway only hours prior to his intended flight from Mississippi to the North. Sheriff

Daniel Jones, who'd threatened Allen's life repeatedly, couldn't be bothered to investigate.

In February, Nolan had attended Byron De La Beckwith's first trial for the sniper death of Medgar Evers, watching as the all-white jury failed to reach a verdict. Eight days later came the formal debut of an outfit called the White Knights of the KKK, led by Samuel Holloway Bowers, a certifiable lunatic who ran the quaintly-named Sambo Amusement Company in Laurel, sharing quarters with a male business partner on the premises. That didn't seem to bother Sambo's followers when he issued an "Imperial Executive Order" in June, declaring:

THIS SUMMER, within a very few days, the enemy will launch his final push for victory here in Mississippi. This offensive will consist of two basic salients:

One—Massive street demonstrations by blacks used by communists, designed to provoke whites into counter-demonstrations and open, pitched street battles to provide an excuse for:

Two—A decree from subversive authorities in charge of the national government declaring martial law.

When the first waves of blacks hit our streets this summer, we must avoid open daylight conflict with them. We must reveal their leaders as the immoral hypocrites they are.

As Christians, we are disposed to kindness, generosity, affection, and humility in our dealings with others. As militants, we are disposed to use physical force against our enemies. How can we reconcile these two apparently contradictory philosophies? The answer, of course, is to purge malice, bitterness, and vengeance from our hearts.

WHEN RATIONAL OBSERVERS finished laughing at that gross hypocrisy, they had to face the new Klan's four-step level of confrontation. Project 1 was a threatening phone call or visit. Project 2 was a cross-burning, preferably on the target's property. Project 3 was a beating, flogging, arson, shooting into buildings, or bombing. Project 4 called for "extermination."

One day before the White Knights had their public coming-out, they'd whipped three victims, rebounding one night later to flog two more, all around Natchez in Adams County. They'd also bombed the homes of a union leader and a Negro family whose son had entered classes at a formerly all-white school. Finally, on the twenty-eighth, they'd ambushed victim Clinton Walker outside Woodville, killing him with rifle fire and shotgun blasts.

In March, the raiders threatened Negro farmhand Richard Butler at Kingston, then doubled back in April, running his car off the highway and wounding him with birdshot. His crime: being "too friendly" with a white man and the latter's wife. To cap the month, Klansmen had fired on three homes occupied by COFO members in Greenwood.

A second trial for Byron De La Beckwith rolled around that month, enlivened when ex-Governor Ross Barnett—law partner of Beckwith's defense attorney—barged into court and shook Beckwith's hand in front of the jury. Another mistrial resulted, celebrated by fiery crosses blazing in sixty-one different towns statewide.

Two days after that show, Negroes had organized the Mississippi Freedom Democratic Party, vowing that they'd have a voice at July's Democratic National Convention or know the reason why.

In May, the Silver Dollar Group had kidnapped college students Henry Dee and Charles Moore from Meadville, allegedly interrogating them about deliveries of nonexistent weapons to a group of mythical Black Muslims in the neighborhood. Their corpses hadn't turned up till July, dredged from the Mississippi River, where they'd been chained to a Jeep motor and train rails, left to drown or bleed to death from their extensive injuries. Two Klansmen—James Seale and Charles Edwards—were held for that crime, both confessing to police, but a pinhead justice of the peace dismissed the Bureau's evidence and set them free.

Then came the case of Michael Schwerner, James Chaney, and Andrew Goodman, finally compelling a response from Washington. Schwerner, a COFO activist, was Jewish, dubbed "The Beard" by Klansmen who despised his facial hair nearly as much as his liberal politics. On Memorial Day, he'd traveled with Chaney—a Negro from Meridian—to speak at Neshoba County's Mt. Zion Methodist Church, urging its congregants to register as voters for the upcoming election.

Bowers and his bullies heard the news, which tipped the "Wizard" over to full-blown insanity, assuming that it wasn't his default position anyway. He'd ordered a "Project 4" on Schwerner, but still needed some means of snaring his victim, who'd gone north with Chaney to Oxford, Ohio, coaching youthful volunteers for Freedom Summer.

In the meantime, police found three Negroes—two men and a woman—dead in a car outside Woodville. The county corner blamed their deaths on carbon monoxide poisoning, surmising that they'd fallen asleep with the engine running, but a Negro mortician described all three as having suffered close-range "buckshot" wounds.

On June 16, White Knights raided a service at Mt. Zion Church, beating its parishioners, then returned one night later to burn the place down. On the same night, they'd whipped a Negro in Jackson and, three days later, set off five more bombs in McComb—rapidly replacing Birmingham in news reports as "Bomb Capital of the World."

Cops couldn't seem to catch the bombers, but they had no difficulty jailing Negroes—including two who'd cursed at anonymous hate-callers, thereby violating Mississippi's "phone harassment law." The goons who'd placed the calls, meanwhile, would never see the inside of a court unless they wandered in as spectators.

On June 20, Schwerner, Chaney and Goodman—another Jew from New York City—drove back to Meridian and heard the news about Mt. Zion Church. The three of them traveled to view its ashes the next day, commiserating with the church's battered congregants, but when they missed their 4:00 p.m. deadline for getting back to COFO headquarters, friends started had calling every law enforcement agency they knew of for assistance.

On the same night that the trio disappeared, terrorists firebombed Sweet Rest Church of Christ in Rankin County, running up their score.

The Bureau had begun its search for Schwerner and his friends on June 22, led by Agent Joseph Sullivan. Attorney General Robert Kennedy ordered 150 agents from New Orleans to join in, and Nolan was recalled from Birmingham, where he's been working on September's "BAPBOM" massacre of four young girls in church. Al Lingo's state police had blown that case by charging "Dynamite Bob" Chambliss and two other suspects with misdemeanor explosives possession, fined them each $100, then reconsidered and dropped the charges.

On June 24, two hikers found Mike Schwerner's burned-out station wagon in the Bogue Chitto swamp, and the manhunt shifted from a missing-person case into a full-fledged murder investigation. President Johnson sent 400 U.S. Navy seamen to join in the search, while state and local cops stood on the sidelines, cracking racist jokes. Bureau headquarters offered a $25,000 reward for information, acting on the theory that someone *always* talks.

Needless to say, white state officials took the manhunt badly. Neshoba County Sheriff Lawrence Rainey— the murderer of two black men before he won election to his present job—told reporters the three missing men were "just hiding and trying to cause a lot of bad publicity for this part of the state." Governor Paul Johnson speculated that the trio "could be in Cuba," while the State Sovereignty Commission kept local lawmen advised of the manhunt's progress. In Washington, Senator Eastland lied outright to LBJ, telling the president, "There's not a Ku Klux Klan in that area; there's not a Citizens' Council in that area; there's no organized white man in that area, so that's why I think it's a publicity stunt."

In fact, as time would prove, conspirator Edgar Ray Killen, a self-ordained preacher, was both Neshoba County's Klan recruiter and a self-proclaimed close friend of Eastland, often boasting of near-weekly visits to the Senator's Sunflower County plantation.

But that word reached the Bureau later.

While the manhunt dragged on through July, searchers found the corpses of Henry Dee and Charles Moore, along with another victim, fourteen-year-old

Hubert Orsby, still clad in the CORE t-shirt he'd worn on the afternoon he disappeared. More bombs exploded in Ruleville, the seat of Eastland's home county, plus in Longdale and McComb. Shaken by the near-anarchy in Dixie, Congress passed the Civil Rights Act of 1964 on June 29, banning all discrimination in government, hiring, and public accommodations. LBJ had signed it into law three days later.

The same day Congress passed that law, another Mississippi Negro, Jasper Greenwood, turned up dead, lying beside his car 100 yards from Vicksburg's Main Street. Relatives had reported him missing on June 21, and cops found $61 on him, ruling out robbery. A backwoods coroner claimed that he couldn't list a cause of death "due to the body's condition," but a Negro undertaker told the family that Greenwood's throat was slashed.

Ever irrational, the Klan expanded its pool of victims. At the onset of July, they'd terrorized a white McComb couple, husband a wealthy realtor, daughter the reigning "Miss Mississippi." Their apparent crime: denouncing random bombings that had turned their town into a national disgrace. More bombs struck at the home and business property of Natchez's white mayor after he condemned the violence.

On July 10, Edgar Hoover flew to Jackson under heavy guard, reopening the field office he'd shut down eighteen years ago. Governor Johnson feigned a welcome but left grumbling when the Chief gave him a list of state policemen known to serve the Klan and brutalize Negroes picked up on phony charges.

One day after Hoover's visit, Georgia Klansmen murdered Lemuel Penn, Assistant Superintendent of Washington, D.C.'s public schools and a lieutenant colonel in the U.S. Army Reserve, returning home from summer training with two other Negro officers who'd managed to survive the shotgun blasts. Martin Luther King showed up in Mississippi shortly after that, showing support for the Freedom Democratic Party, followed by more bombings and more churches going up in flames.

The DOJ's reward offer bore fruit on July 31, a turncoat Kluxer sketching a map of the burial site for vanished victims Schwerner, Chaney, and Goodman. Three days later, agents finally removed them from an earthen dam located on a Klansman's farm. Schwerner and Goodman had been shot once each; Chaney had taken three slugs after being beaten, likely with a heavy chain. Now that the "hiding out in Cuba" fable wouldn't fly, the bulk of Mississippi's leaders moaned and groaned, lamenting that their state was getting so much bad publicity.

Tough shit, O'Hara thought.

The MFDP held its state convention four days after the three murder victims were retrieved, choosing all-black electors for the Democratic National Convention in Atlantic City. Some of their stirring speeches made TV and worried Lyndon Johnson in the Oval Office. Overnight, Chief Hoover ordered twenty-seven G-men, two stenographers and a radio expert to mount round-the-clock surveillance on Mississippi's rude upstarts, reporting back to him directly, and from his lips to the president's big ears.

The final clash came two weeks later when white delegates from Mississippi fought acknowledging their Negro counterparts. Senator Hubert Humphrey—once a civic gangbuster in Minneapolis, today a senator and Johnson's designated running mate—advised "patience" and walked away, the leader of the MFDP delegation promising "to pray for you some more." The upshot: no black delegates would see the inside of Atlantic City's Boardwalk Hall, and Mississippi's all-white delegation vowed its loyalty to LBJ.

Back home, the mayhem continued. Bombings were rife in McComb, around Natchez, and elsewhere. Beatings, drive-by shootings, and nocturnal arsons multiplied. In Merigold, police killed Negro Nehemiah Montgomery, claiming he'd tried leaving a service station without paying for his gas.

Bright and early on September 2, Hoover's office sent another memo to all SACs from coast to coast, launching a new program dubbed COINTELPRO—WHITE HATE. All Klansmen, plus their allies in assorted neo-Nazi groups, were earmarked for the same mostly-illegal treatment long reserved for leftists and black militants. The goal, in broad strokes, was to spotlight racist groups, destroy their public image by fair means or foul, create dissension among members, and cut off funding from the "normal" public at all costs.

O'Hara recognized the latest COINTELPRO's methods from the Bureau's playbook for demolishing the CPUSA. G-men would dole out money to informers and ignore their private crimes as long as they were useful; mount all-out "psywar" against target groups with whispering campaigns and phony stories planted in the media; audit Klan leaders' tax returns and tie them up in court on charges, true or false; employ *agents provocateur* to foment crimes, which then produced arrests; and falsely branding loyal bigots as snitches through a method called "bad-jacketing." An empty Bureau car might sit outside a Klansman's home all night, and when it left near dawn, his neighbors would be slandering him as a fed.

The violence wasn't ebbing yet, much of it still involving bombs around McComb, but late September brought whispered threats of martial law in Pike County, while white officials begged the Bureau for a "second chance." As if by magic, nine Klansmen were jailed—ironically, no Silver Dollar thugs or White Knights, but all members of Bob Shelton's equally savage United Klans. That might've been the end, but even though the dynamiters all pled guilty to assorted felonies, they caught a break from Circuit Judge W. H. Watkins, appointed to office by Ross Barnett. Instead of prison time, the nine received probation and a thirty-minute lecture from the bench attempted murders brushed aside as Watkins cited their "youth" and "good families," opining that the terrorists had been "unduly provoked and undoubtedly ill advised."

And so, the war went on, combatants partially distracted by the year's presidential campaign. George Wallace entered three Democratic primaries, recorded strong showings in Wisconsin, Indiana, and Maryland, then bowed out, gloating that he'd made his point regarding northern "liberals." Bob Shelton publicly endorsed Goldwater, even though the candidate was Jewish and his running mate a Catholic, but Barry couldn't make the grade with only Arizona's votes and less than half of Dixie's.

Meanwhile, the National States Rights Party's campaign had been a farce compared to Goldwater's tragedy. A June delegation in Birmingham nominated racist has-been John Kasper for president, with Jesse Stoner as his running mate. Matt Murphy Jr., the national lawyer for the United Klans, was the convention's keynote speaker, but it didn't help. On Election Day, the NSRP reaped fewer than 7,000 votes nationwide and none where it mattered, in the Electoral College.

Now the bloody year was winding down, with few points on the Bureau's side of the scoreboard. Two White Knights *had* confessed to the Neshoba County lynching— one a lookout, the other an eyewitness to the slayings— and on December 4 the DOJ had charged nineteen alleged conspirators, including Sheriff Rainey and Deputy Cecil Price, "Preacher" Killen, and two triggermen, James Jordan and Alton Roberts. No one had fingered "Wizard" Bowers yet, but in the end, it hadn't mattered. Six days after the arrests, U.S. Commissioner Esther Carter of Meridian dismissed all the charges, ruling them based on "hearsay."

So we go back to work, thought Nolan. *Wear the bastards down, ruin their lives and families by any means available. And next time, maybe get it right.*

———

HARLEM: December 29, 1964

WALKING the ghetto streets four days past Christmas, Payton Sawyer couldn't miss the signs of Harlem's most recent upheaval, in July. He'd been fourteen when the last race riot rocked Harlem, but this one's aftermath was all too familiar, all too depressing.

It began as all such riots seemed to do, with the police. NYPD Lieutenant Thomas Gilligan had fired three shots at fifteen-year-old Jimmy Powell, striking him twice and killing Powell in front of twenty-odd eyewitnesses. Gilligan claimed he'd fired in self-defense, and as the crowd was gathering, another cop claimed that he'd found a knife lying nearby. Good news for Gilligan, bad news for New York City, as six nights of rioting ensued in Harlem and the Bed-Stuy neighborhood. Neighbors swore the knife was planted, CORE ramped up the volume with a demonstration at a nearby school, and *Life* magazine featured photos of helmeted cops beating an unarmed black man who lay supine, screaming on the sidewalk.

The final tab: two dead, including Powell, 500 persons injured, 465 locked up, with estimates of property damage ranging upward from $500,000. Passage of the Civil Rights Act two weeks earlier had been no help at all.

With Harlem and Bed-Stuy still raging, Rochester had exploded next. Summoned by calls from the "Mothers Improvement Association of the Eighth Ward," police responded with a K-9 unit to arrest a drunk at a block party. Images of Birmingham's attack dogs mauling children last year let the fuse, and it required National Guardsmen to suppress the rioting—the first such use of troops in any northern state since 1863. When the smoke cleared, four people were dead, 350 injured, and nearly 1,000 jailed, with 204 stores looted or burned.

As far as Payton's work for BOSS, he had no problem staying busy, filing loads of paperwork. In January, after Elijah Muhammad summoned Malcolm X to Phoenix, stories spread that Malcolm had been "isolated," loyal Black Muslims forbidden to speak with him. February brought a former aide at Mosque No. 7's confession that he'd been assigned to kill Malcolm with a car bomb. In March, Malcolm had split from the Nation of Islam, announcing the creation of his own Muslim Mosque Incorporated, while the *New York Times* claimed he sought to create a "black nationalist party." Three months later, he'd launched a new Organization of Afro-American Unity, Elijah responding with demands that Malcolm surrender his home and auto, both owned by the NOI. Malcolm replied through the pages of *Ebony* magazine, telling an interviewer that NOI leaders "have got to kill me. They can't afford to let me live. I know where the bodies are buried, and if they press me, I'll exhume some."

In April, Elijah served Malcolm with an eviction notice, the legal hearing pushed back to May, then to June. Malcolm used that time to your Africa and the Middle East, returning to address a crowd at Harlem's Audubon Ballroom on the topic of Elijah Muhammad's six illegitimate children. Police and private guards watched over Malcolm after multiple anonymous death threats, with Payton standing guard duty on several nights. Malcolm's eviction trial finally happened, the judge "reserving sentence" pending further inquiries. Days later, the *New York Post* published Malcolm's open letter to Elijah, calling for an end to mutual hostility.

No sale.

On July 3, two men assaulted Malcolm at his home in East Elmhurst, prompting increased police surveillance. Two days later, four Negroes with knives had menaced Malcolm as he left the house and started toward his car. Two days after that, NYPD logged another failed attempt on his life. Malcolm flew back to Egypt, seeking a respite from threats, but returned to find that Civil Court Judge Maurice Wahl had ordered his eviction by the end of January 1965. J. Walter Yeagley, Assistant Attorney General in charge of the Justice Department's Internal Security Division, ordered an investigation to decide if Malcolm was in violation of the 18th-century Logan Act, banning unauthorized negotiations with foreign governments deemed hostile to America.

Nothing had come of that investigation yet, as far as Payton knew, but Malcolm had geared up for war. September's *Ebony* published a photo of him with an M1 carbine, peering from a window of the home he'd been ordered to vacate. From Chicago, an FBI mole inside Mosque No. 2 filed a report saying, "Anyone who opposes the Honorable Elijah Muhammad puts their life in jeopardy." In December's issue of *Muhammad Speaks,* one Louis X opined that "such a man as Malcolm is worthy of death."

And where did Payton Sawyer stand in all of that?

Right now, he wished to God that he could answer that question himself.

EPILOGUE

BOGALUSA, LOUISIANA: DECEMBER 31, 1964

POLICE CHIEF CLAYTON DAWES was running late, but no one gathered in the cheap motel room south of town, on Highway 21, gave any thought to taking off before he showed. Dawes knew damned well they'd wait for him because he was the answer to their prayers. Assembled in the room when he arrived were Bogalusa's mayor, Jason Brooks, and Arvin Pendleton, Grand Giant of the Klan in Washington Parish. Their meeting would determine Bogalusa's fate, and maybe that of all Louisiana in the bargain.

Arvin's knights had not been idle in the past year, burning down five churches, a Masonic hall, and two homes that had sheltered so-called civil rights workers. Its Ku Klux membership was large enough to earn their small community the nickname "Klantown USA," and to provoke an armed reaction from its Negroes, organized and armed last month under the title Deacons for Defense and Justice.

If that wasn't one step shy of revolution, Dawes had asked himself, *then what in hell was it?*

From its foundation in 1906, Bogalusa had been a company town built and owned by Great Southern Lumber, the proprietor of homes, stores, schools, public utilities, even the town's rigidly segregated parks. Great Southern had maintained its own paramilitary force, the Self-Preservation and Loyalty League, to maintain strict "labor discipline" after World War One, when uppity blacks tried to start up a union, rubbing out four leaders of the half-assed movement when they wouldn't listen to reason. Alas, the SPLL was no more, but Pendleton's Original Knights had taken its place when CORE scouts Bill Yates and Steve Miller hit town, pushing the ridiculous idea that Negroes ought to vote and otherwise start thinking for themselves.

When he had downed half of a frosty Anheuser-Busch, Dawes went into his pitch. "We've got a hard year comin' up," he said. "Our way of life is ridin' on the line, and I, for one, don't plan on lettin' niggers snatch it all away from us."

"Hell, no," growled Pendleton. Mayor Brooks just nodded, scowling.

"So, first thing, you know I only got ten officers on salary. That means I'm gonna have to deputize a slew of volunteers for the duration, makin' sure our laws and customs are respected by the local niggers and whoever else they drag down here to help 'em out."

"I'll getcha all the men ya need," said Pendleton, stifling a burp behind one meaty fist.

"Part one of that is men in uniform," said Dawes,

"keepin' the peace by daylight, when goddamn reporters got their cameras out. Part B is what goes on at night, and that's the key to it, takin' these half-assed, puffed-up Deacons off the checkerboard before they get an army raised against us."

"Lotsa bayou country hereabouts," said Pendleton. "Gators and buzzards gotta eat, the same as you and me."

Again, the mayor nodded, not saying squat.

"I got together with these shits from CORE already," Dawes announced. "Told 'em they can forget about police protection if they stick around. My men have better things to do than nursemaid fuckin' commie race-mixers."

The mayor nodded more vigorously, seemed about to speak, but then apparently thought better of it.

"There's still the goddamn FBI to think about," said Pendleton. "You've seen what they been up to in Miss'ippi, 'Bama, and in Georgia."

"Fuck a buncha feebs," Dawes answered back. "I promise you one thing right now. Niggers ain't gonna rule this town."

A LOOK AT: CRIMES OF HONOR
(THE BUREAU BOOK 7)

Book No. 7 of *The Bureau, Crimes of Honor,* follows the surviving protagonists through the tumultuous years between 1965 and 1973. The civil rights movement expands and urban ghettos burn through "long hot summers," while the war in Southeast Asia escalates with corresponding protests in America. The FBI inaugurates new extralegal operations labeled COINTELPRO—BLACK HATE and COINTELPRO—NEW LEFT, attacking any groups and individuals who fail to meet Chief Hoover's definition of "true Americans." More high-profile assassinations rock the nation and Lyndon Johnson withdraws from the next presidential campaign, succeeded by Richard Nixon awash in Syndicate money. Once in office, Nixon heaps new fuel onto the fire in Vietnam and brings the war home, wielding lethal force against campus protesters. Black Panthers, Weathermen, and other radicals respond in kind. Ryan O'Hara joins the FBI, while his father is forced from the Bureau by Hoover. The director's death in 1972 permits Erin O'Hara to become one of the first female FBI recruits since 1924, entering the academy as burglars expose the Bureau's COINTELPRO operations and the Nixon White House lurches into Watergate. Dominic Giordano seeks to lead his Mafia family in new directions, at risk of his life. The era ends in scandal and dissension, verging on America's first resignation of a president.

ABOUT THE AUTHOR

A California native, Michael Newton has published 215 books under his own name and various pseudonyms since 1977. He began writing professionally as a "ghost" for author Don Pendleton on the best-selling Executioner series and continues his work on that series today. With 104 episodes published to date, Newton has nearly tripled the number of Mack Bolan novels completed by creator Pendleton himself.

Newton's first book under his own name was *Monsters, Mysteries and Man* (1979), a survey of unexplained phenomena for younger readers. While 156 of Newton's published books have been novels—including westerns, political thrillers and psychological suspense—he is best known for nonfiction, primarily true crime and reference books.